Carmen Reid is the bestselling author of the *Personal Shopper* series starring Annie Valentine.

as worked as a newspaper journalist and ınist, but now writes fiction full-time. Carmen vrites a series for teen readers, *Secrets at St Judes.*

ıugh deeply in love with NYC, she lives in ʒow, Scotland, with her husband and two ren. Her hobbies include gazing into vintage llery shop windows and daydreaming about ems' fabulous former owners.

Carmen online for all her latest news, compe- ıs and exclusive content, plus Anne Valentine's lous fashion blog!

www.carmenreid.com
www.facebook.com/carmenreidbooks

*Also by Carmen Reid*

THREE IN A BED
DID THE EARTH MOVE?
HOW WAS IT FOR YOU?
UP ALL NIGHT

*Starring Annie Valentine*

THE PERSONAL SHOPPER
LATE NIGHT SHOPPING
HOW NOT TO SHOP
CELEBRITY SHOPPER
NEW YORK VALENTINE

*And for teenage readers*

SECRETS AT ST JUDE'S: NEW GIRL
SECRETS AT ST JUDE'S: JEALOUS GIRL
SECRETS AT ST JUDE'S: DRAMA GIRL
SECRETS AT ST JUDE'S: REBEL GIRL
SECRETS AT ST JUDE'S: SUNSHINE GIRL
SECRETS AT ST JUDE'S: PARTY GIRL

# The Jewels of Manhattan

CARMEN REID

TRANSWORLD PUBLISHERS
61–63 Uxbridge Road, London W5 5SA
A Random House Group Company
www.transworldbooks.co.uk

**THE JEWELS OF MANHATTAN**
**A CORGI BOOK: 9780552163187**

First publication in Great Britain
Corgi edition published 2011



A CIP catalogue record for this book is available from the British Library.



Addresses for Random House Group Ltd companies outside the UK can be found at: www.randomhouse.co.uk
The Random House Group Ltd Reg. No. 954009

The Random House Group Limited supports The Forest Stewardship Council (FSC®), the leading international forest certification organization. Our books carrying the FSC label are printed on FSC® certified paper. FSC is the only forest certification scheme endorsed by the leading environmental organizations, including Greenpeace. Our paper procurement policy can be found at www.randomhouse.co.uk/environment.

Typeset in 11½/15pt Palatino by
Kestrel Data, Exeter, Devon.
Printed and bound by
CPI Group (UK) Ltd, Croydon, CR0 4YY.

2 4 6 8 10 9 7 5 3 1

*For Claudie and Sam*

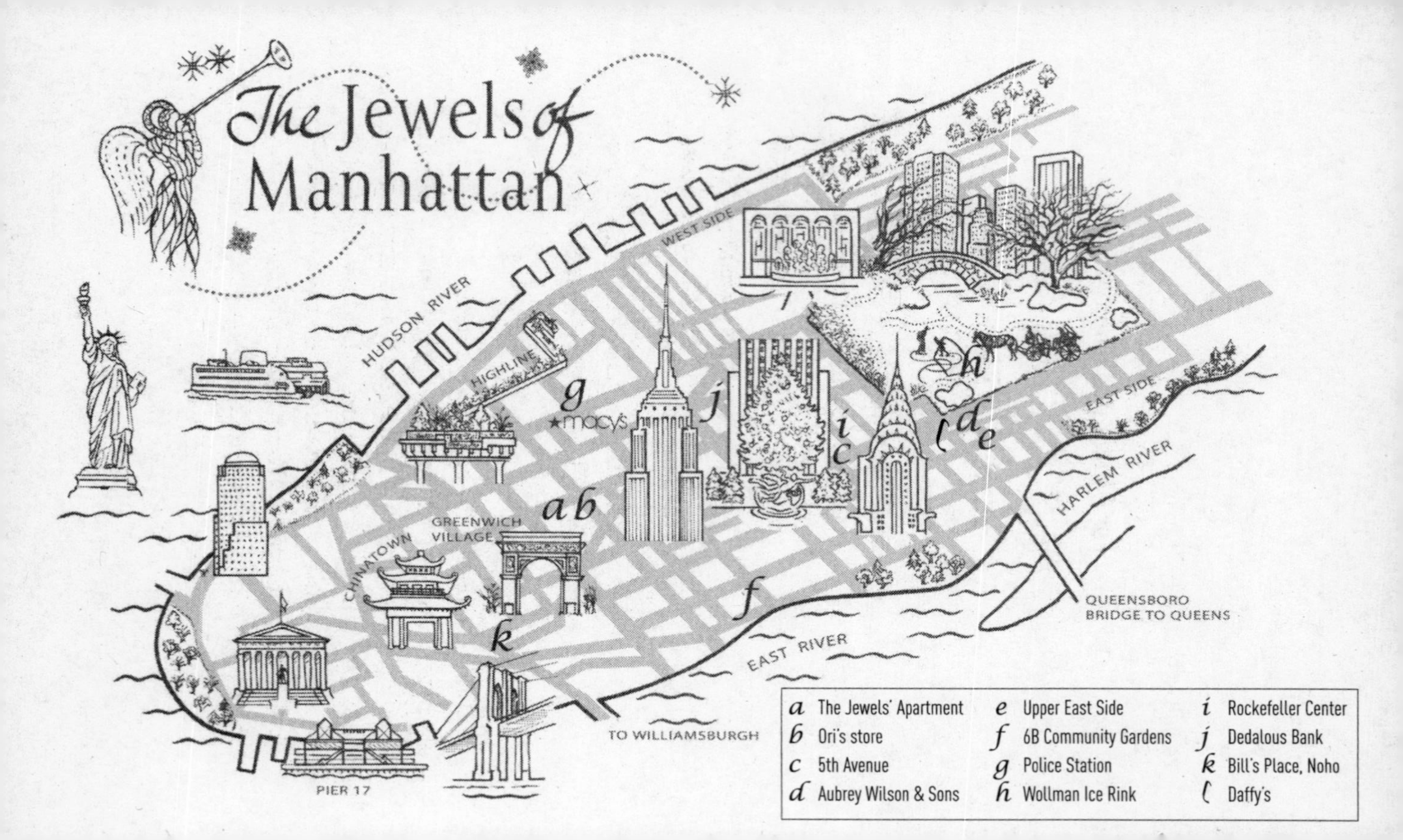
The Jewels of Manhattan
HUDSON RIVER
WEST SIDE
HIGHLINE
macy's
GREENWICH VILLAGE
CHINATOWN
PIER 17
TO WILLIAMSBURGH
EAST RIVER
EAST SIDE
HARLEM RIVER
QUEENSBORO BRIDGE TO QUEENS
a The Jewels' Apartment
b Ori's store
c 5th Avenue
d Aubrey Wilson & Sons
e Upper East Side
f 6B Community Gardens
g Police Station
h Wollman Ice Rink
i Rockefeller Center
j Dedalous Bank
k Bill's Place, Noho
l Daffy's

# Chapter One

*'So I'm in the park, jogging, when this guy pulls out a gun and asks for my watch.'*

*'Betty, how terrible! Were you scared?'*

*'No, Lauren, I was humiliated. I'd left my Cartier at home.'*

Mrs Henry St Claire-Trevellian and Mrs Emery Hewitt III at lunch on the Upper East Side

'Oh look at this window, it's too cute!'

Amber, full of Christmas spirit and chicken noodles, was walking home with her sister along West 17th Street. Every store window here and across the whole of Manhattan was dressed up with sparkling lights, canned snow and angels.

She pulled to a stop outside Bijoux Rox to admire

the beautiful new display. Tiny masked marionette burglars in striped sweaters, with sacks on their backs, looked as if they were abseiling down onto the diamond-studded treasures, fat pearl necklaces and jewelled watches below. The velvet backdrop had been dusted with a light coating of fake snow and everything winked and twinkled enticingly under the fairy lights.

'Oh that is so pretty!' Sapphire exclaimed, stopping beside her big sister. 'We have to go in, c'mon, just to take a look. It's so Christmassy in there.'

Amber shook her head.

'No. We're almost home and I bet everything in there costs like 1,000 bucks. I'm not exactly in a jewellery buying place right now, and anyhow, I thought you preferred vintage.'

'I do, but I just want to have a little look,' Sapphire pleaded, giving her best melt-the-heart smile.

Amber began to soften.

'Oh boy . . . you're not dreaming about engagements and diamonds and weddings all over again, are you?'

'No!' Sapphire insisted, but Amber didn't quite believe her.

Sapphire took her arm and pulled her in through the door.

* * *

'Hi there and welcome to my store, I am Ori.' The owner greeted them with a smile and a small bow. 'Always at your service.'

He was a round, cheerful-looking man, almost completely bald, in a striped shirt and smart grey pants both of which looked strained at the buttons.

'Take your time, have a look around. If you see something you'd like to try on, no problem!'

'Hi there, that's very kind,' Amber replied.

'Be my guests, take all the time you need. I'm guessing you are sisters – and you know why? You're both tall and lovely and your bracelet matches her earrings. Clever, ha?'

'You're right,' Sapphire said with a smile.

Amber saw Ori shoot a glance at the clock, then at the package on top of the counter. It smelled like a hot knish from the deli on the corner of the street, and already it was staining its paper bag with oil.

It was just two minutes till 9 p.m. and closing time, but he obviously wanted to be a good salesman.

'If you like something, please, just ask and try it on. Christmas is coming,' Ori insisted. 'But I'm just going to close the shutters for the night, OK?'

At the touch of a button, metal shutters began to roll down over the front window.

'Oh, look at that wonderful pendant—' Sapphire began, but her words were drowned out by the roar of a motorcycle. The sisters swung round to see the bike drive right up onto the sidewalk in front of the jeweller's. The biker got off and marched in, slamming the door shut.

'Hey,' Ori growled. 'That door cost $4,000. You're in the wrong place – the attorney's office is next door, one up.'

But then a second motorcycle reared up over the kerb and in burst another man also in top-to-toe leather with a black helmet. His tinted visor was pulled down. Amber stepped protectively towards her younger sister. She knew almost at once that these were not two messengers at the wrong address. These guys wanted something.

The first biker pulled out a black handgun.

Amber gasped and felt her knees buckle.

'Take it easy,' Ori managed to say as he raised his hands and backed away from the guy.

'Get down!' The biker waved his gun at the sisters.

Amber and Sapphire dropped to the floor like stones.

Biker number two drew a claw hammer from his jacket and walked straight up to Ori, who cowered back against the wall.

With a violent smash, the biker brought the hammer down on the glass case in front Ori. The first blow only cracked the toughened surface, but the second strike broke through. Golden bangles, bracelets and diamond rings were scooped up and thrown into a black backpack.

The biker moved straight on to the next case as the second man worked the other side of the shop.

Amber's cheek pressed hard against the limestone tiling on the floor as broken glass, dropped rings, bracelets and jewels fell all around her.

She'd seen the gun, she knew this was an armed robbery, now all she could think about was whether she and Sapphire were going to be shot. She heard a low groan of fear and realized, in an out-of-body way, that it was coming from her. She pressed her lips shut, but didn't close her eyes.

She looked over at Ori standing slumped against the wall watching the ransack of his beautiful store.

She saw the back of Sapphire's precious blonde head right in front of her. Sapphire's shoulders were moving rapidly up and down; maybe she was panting, or sobbing silently.

Amber reached out her hand to touch her sister comfortingly on the back. Then she focused on the biker with the gun. The thought of him using the gun on any one of them petrified her.

All of the cases lining the walls had been smashed and emptied, and now the man with the gun turned to face Ori as the other guy moved towards the door.

'No, no,' Ori pleaded as the gun was raised, 'you have what you want. Just go.'

A cellphone began to trill. It took a moment for Amber to recognize the ringtone as Sapphire's.

The man swivelled, bent down and pressed the nose of the gun to Sapphire's cheek.

'No!' Amber cried out. She even dared to lift her head and move her arm around her sister's waist.

'We're not going to make any trouble,' she promised.

The gun stayed right against her sister's head.

'Don't shoot her,' Amber pleaded, 'please don't shoot my sister.'

Now Sapphire began to talk, in a terrified whimper: 'Please sir, don't kill us. We're nice people. We're good people. We're not from New York, we're from Texas.'

Amber knew she had to grab the nozzle of the gun, so that if it went off it wouldn't be pointing at Sapphire's head.

There was no other option.

'Barton! Forget it. Let's go!' the biker at the door called urgently.

Ori leaned against his countertop for support.

'My heart . . . too many fatty snacks . . .' he warned.

But the biker raised his gun.

# Chapter Two

*'Did you see what Michael has done to her hair, Betty? It's criminal!'*

*'Oh Lauren, Michael is one angry, angry stylist. I don't think being gay is working out for him.'*

When the terrible thud sounded, Amber instinctively threw her head to the floor and tightened her grip round her sister's waist.

Sapphire's scream and Ori's shout made a terrifying sound which reverberated around the little store. Amber looked frantically over at the gunman, more frightened than she thought she could bear.

He was at the door . . . he was leaving . . . he was going to go. But still he turned once again and brandished the gun.

This time Amber managed to scream. Low, hoarse and utterly panicked.

The second bullet exploded into the wall clock, sending glass and metal showering across the store. The door slammed and they heard the second motorcycle roar into life and speed away.

Ori gasped and clutched at his chest, Sapphire lay moaning on the floor while Amber sat up, shaking all over, her eyes glued to the wreckage of the clock. She couldn't move or speak until the silence finally told her that it was over. The men had gone.

'Sapphire? Sapphire, are you OK?' she asked urgently, getting to her feet, the tiles beneath her crackling and slippery with shards of glass.

'I'm fine,' Sapphire replied, sitting up carefully, sending more splinters to the floor, 'j-just fine,' she stammered and reached out shakily for her big sister.

'You're sure?' Amber wrapped her arms around her.

'Yes. Oh! My . . . Oh, my . . . that was so scary. That was the scariest thing ever. I don't . . .'

'Girls, girls!' Ori wheezed. 'I hate to interrupt,' he called out, 'but can one of ya call 911?'

'Are you OK?' Amber asked.

His breath rasped in and out of his chest as he said, 'He missed me. He hit the wall, then the clock. But I . . . I don't feel so good . . . chest pains. I have high blood pressure, high cholesterol. I think this could be it. This could be the big one . . .'

As Sapphire hurried over to help him, Amber took out her cell, fingers shaking so hard that it took several attempts to hit the numbers.

'Any pain in your left arm?' Sapphire asked Ori.

'No . . . no . . .' he gasped.

'I think you could be having a panic attack,' she told him, her voice soothing and calm.

'Oh my . . . oh my goodness. If I make it through this,' he gasped, 'I'm never eating another knish ever again. They don't call them heartbombs for nothing, you know. My doctor, she's been warning me . . . for years. Lose the weight, Ori, or you won't see your girls graduate from college.'

'Shhh . . .' Sapphire told him. 'Deep breaths, calm down.'

'Should I look in the back for a chair?' Amber asked.

'Sure.'

Within moments, a blue and white NYPD squad car was pulling to a stop outside, lights flashing, siren blaring. Two police officers, a man and a woman, stepped out and took charge.

Then the ambulance showed up and the store filled with people. The police officers asked Amber and Sapphire all the most urgent questions as paramedics put Ori on a stretcher and hooked him up with an oxygen mask.

He wouldn't lie down, kept pushing the mask

aside to give instructions to the police as the paramedics tried to calm him.

'Fourteen years in the business, never had a break-in before!' he told them. 'Big guys on big motorcycles, BMW I think. Tinted visors so we couldn't look into their eyes, officer. And one of them was wearing a gold ID bracelet with a diamond stud. But that's all I saw. Big guys,' he repeated, 'especially the one with the gun.'

The officers radioed alerts, rolled out yellow tape and directed pedestrians to the other side of the street.

'Any witnesses? Any more witnesses see anything?' a substantial black woman, who had introduced herself as Officer Dayell, gun and baton swaying with her hips, called out across the street. As she strode back into the store, she looked reassuring and capable.

'Don't be touching anything now,' she told the sisters. 'Is there an office in the back where you can wait to see the detective?'

Ori, on his way out of the store on the stretcher, pulled his mask off again: 'Sure, use my office, make yourselves at home . . . drink my coffee! Have some friends round! What do I care? The stock's gone anyway – the whole three mill.'

'Sir!' the paramedic said and pushed the mask back in place.

'I think he's going to be just fine,' Officer Dayell told them.

The sisters walked to the windowless room at the back of the store where they found a desk, chairs and neat piles of paperwork.

They pulled up two of the plastic chairs and collapsed into them.

'Oh my gosh!' Sapphire whispered and laid her head on her sister's shoulder for comfort.

'It's OK,' Amber said, hugging her, 'we're safe. We're going to be fine.'

'Three million dollars?' Sapphire repeated Ori's words. 'I'd never have stepped in here if I'd known.'

'Yeah, well, some of his diamonds are *rocks*.'

Amber realized her bag of groceries was still in her hand, a little crushed from her time on the floor.

'Some salad?' she offered Sapphire, jokingly.

Sapphire shook her head.

'Iced tea?'

Sapphire nodded, so Amber brought out the bottle, with hands which still shook uncontrollably. 'That was scary,' she whispered.

'Yeah,' Sapphire agreed, taking a drink from the bottle of tea.

They heard the storefront door opening and a male voice call out: 'Hey, Noreen, what have we got here?'

Officer Dayell replied: 'Hey, Jack, we got ourselves a $3 million smash 'n' grab. You on nights this week?'

'Uhuh,' came the reply and footsteps crunched over the broken glass.

'Witnesses through the back,' Officer Dayell said.

'Uhuh. I'll just take a look-see first.'

More crunching footsteps.

'Panic button not activated?'

'No. The guy got shot at, twice. Guess he wasn't in the mood for panic buttons.'

'What have we here? One oily bag . . . and one spinach knish – untouched! The evening just got a whole lot better.'

'You ain't gonna eat that?'

'This ain't evidence, Noreen. This is the jeweller's chow-bag. There's no blood on it, or nothing.'

'Jackie, you are grossing me out.'

The office doorway filled up with a tall, muscular white guy. His hair was dark, curled and close-cut and his broad face looked around thirty. He was wearing a long, heavy-duty raincoat, his collar and tie had been loosened. His face looked a little sweaty, as if he'd run over here.

In one hand he held a beaker of coffee, in the other, Ori's knish. He'd already taken a bite.

'Hey, I'm Jack Desmoine, your detective for tonight.'

He smiled at the sisters, put the coffee cup down, then pulled a notebook and pencil from the pocket of his crumpled pants: 'Sorry to meet ya in such distressing circumstances. We have a lot to do, but I'll try and make it as painless as possible. Forensics are on their way.'

Officer Dayell appeared in the doorway. 'You watch out for him,' she said, pointing at Desmoine and shooting a wink in Amber and Sapphire's direction.

'Thank you, Noreen. OK.' Detective Desmoine pulled up a chair, took a slug of coffee and another bite. 'So it's Miss Jewel and Miss Jewel? Sisters?' he said, through a full mouth.

Both nodded.

'From what I heard from the officer outside, you were both very brave. D'you wanna get started with names, addresses, employers, then we'll go through exactly what happened here tonight?'

He wiped his mouth with the back of his hand and took another bite.

'I'm Sapphire Jewel, 6P 566, 17th Street . . .' Sapphire began.

'I'm the same address. Our apartment's just four doors along,' Amber chipped in.

'You don't look very alike,' Detective Desmoine said.

The sisters glanced at each other. They'd heard

this often enough. On first glance, they looked like family: both tall, with long limbs and straight hair, but Amber's eyes and hair were brown, her skin a sallow tan and her features pretty in an interesting, unusual kind of way.

On a good day, Amber would describe herself as 'kinda' pretty. Her intense brown eyes and wide lips were her best features; her nose was a little too solid looking, her eyebrows too straight and too bushy. Whatever work she did with the tweezers, the brows always caught up then got ahead.

Whereas Sapphire, sister-in-the-middle, with her creamy complexion, high cheekbones, little button nose and bright-blue eyes, was the acknowledged family beauty. She had the kind of blonde hair and finely honed face that made people stop and stare, but she was almost embarrassed by the attention she caused, and always wore her beauty lightly. Their youngest sister, Em, was the one who worked every gift she had been given in every possible way.

*'No point in being a rose if you ain't gonna bloom,'* was one of Em's favourite expressions.

'Well, I guess we're sisters – not identical twins,' Amber said.

The detective just shrugged, asked some more questions and wrote down answers.

'Your employer?' he asked Amber.

'Dedalous Bank,' she told him and gave the address.

'Sounds fancy. Are you one of those lucky girls who gets a $200,000 bonus after Christmas while the rest of us just get our credit card bills?'

'No. Not at all. I'm still quite new.'

'How long have you been with the bank?'

'Seven months. Ever since I moved to New York.'

'And you, Miss Jewel?' he asked Sapphire. 'Maybe I should call you Miss Sapphire and Miss Amber, just to make things easier?'

'I'm at Aubrey Wilson & Sons, the auctioneers. In the antique jewellery department. I've been there for just over five months. Ever since I came to New York, along with Em,' she answered.

'Em?' the detective asked.

'She's our youngest sister,' Amber explained, 'and in case you're wondering, she doesn't look like either of us.'

'Right.' The detective glanced up at Amber.

'The three sisters, ha? Isn't that a play?' he asked.

'Chekhov,' Amber replied and found herself looking into brown eyes underneath surprised eyebrows.

'Pretty fancy. Where ya girls all from originally?' Desmoine asked, taking a swig of coffee.

'Texas,' Sapphire answered.

'Oh my.' Desmoine gave a smile at this.

'What?' Amber asked.

'Nothin',' he said, but he was still smiling.

As he lowered his chin his eyes remained on hers and held her gaze a little too long.

Amber smoothed her corporate-smart skirt over her legs and saw his look travel down with her hands. It stayed on her legs too long as well.

'So you were coming home from work, Miss Amber? And, Miss Sapphire, I'm guessing from your outfit you were at the gym?'

'Yeah,' Sapphire replied, 'we met up to do a little Christmas shopping.'

'In a jewellery store?'

'We were just looking,' Amber replied.

'Ha. That'll teach ya. I guess you're not real New York till you've been caught up in some kind of gun fun,' the detective said, turning to his notebook again.

He had clumsy handwriting, many of the letters printed. Obviously not a college boy, Amber thought.

'OK, girls, my first very serious question,' he began. 'Any previous convictions? Any prior felonies, indictments, court papers or criminal history? Because this is $3 million worth of armed robbery here. You're the only ones we've got so far, so we have to check you out good.'

Sapphire and Amber looked at each other in astonishment.

'You don't think *we*—'

'We were just . . .'

Detective Desmoine began to laugh: 'Just routine. Relax, it's just routine. If you're not guilty you have nothing to worry about.'

## Chapter Three

*'So she said: "I love your building.*
*How do you get an apartment here?"'*

*'And did you tell her: "You've got to be someone,*
*marry someone or kill someone"?'*

Later that night, the sound of keys jangling against the door let Sapphire and Amber know that Em was home.

'Goddammit!' Em yelled from the other side of the door.

'I'll get it.' Amber jumped up from the saggy green couch.

'That freakin' lock's going to kill me!' Em said, bursting into the room, keys and bulging plastic bags in her hands.

Em was shorter, darker and curvier than her sisters. But she played it all up. She elongated her legs with high-heeled boots, she wore short skirts and dresses tightly cinched at the waist and let her generous curves spill up and over in low-cut tops.

Her hair, currently a blackcurrant shade of purple, had deep bangs then fell in a loose tumble to her shoulders. In contrast to Amber's bare-faced look and Sapphire's discreet touches of make-up, Em went for bold eyeliner, today black and a peacock shimmer of green-blue eye shadow.

Em liked to be noticed. In fact, make that, Em *loved* to be noticed.

Dropping her bags on the floor, she rushed to hug first Amber and then Sapphire: 'OMG, I could not believe your message! I got out as soon as I could . . . Are you OK? I mean, are you really OK? You could both have been killed!'

Amber clicked off the television.

'It's on the news,' she said. 'But we told the police no names.'

'So what happened?' Em perched her miniskirted butt on the back of the couch. 'Tell me everything.'

'We were in the jeweller's . . . we just went in to have a look around and then the robbers came in,' Amber explained. 'They made us lie down, they ransacked the place, they shot at the owner, but missed and they held a gun to Sapphire's head.'

'No way!'

'Yeah,' Sapphire confirmed, 'but Amber saved me. She told the guy with the gun to leave us alone.'

'You did not?!' Em said, amazed. 'Girls, you must have been sweating like turkeys before Thanksgiving.'

'Yeah. Sapphire spoke to him too, told him not to shoot us because we were good people from Texas!' Amber laughed. Now that it was all over she felt weirdly light-hearted and light-headed, happier than she'd felt in weeks.

Em asked questions and they went over every little detail until her curiosity had been satisfied.

'I cannot believe you guys!' she exclaimed, finally.

'You're not real New York until you've been involved in some kind of gun fun,' Amber said. 'That's what the detective told us.'

'Is he the guy down there? In the white shirt, with the black hair?' Em asked.

'Yeah, I guess,' Amber answered. 'Did he have spinach from a knish all over his teeth?'

'Oh please! He was totally freakin' gorgeous,' Em said, 'and he was checking me out too.'

'Yeah, that'll be him.'

'You think he's gorgeous?' Sapphire asked, pulling a face in disagreement.

'Oh yeah: cute as a sackful of puppies and *haaaht*,' was Em's verdict. 'Hot as the food in my bags. I hope y'all very hungry,' she added, making her accent totally Southern belle. Em loved to do accents, just as much as she loved to dress up, transform her look and get into character.

'Jeeez, Em, it's after eleven. You're not expecting us to eat?' Amber was trying to sound horrified. But Em worked at Bill's Place, currently NoHo's hippest, and the dishes she brought back were impossible to resist.

'Mmmmm . . .' Sapphire inhaled the scent coming from the plastic bags, 'it's been a very stressful evening. Maybe just a little late night snackette. You know, now that it's over – I feel great!' she grinned.

Em handed out boxes of pasta and steaming ragout.

'How much food are you allowed to take out of that place? Do they know?' Amber asked. 'I mean, can't they use some of those leftovers?'

'Of course they know . . . kinda . . . you know me, I can always, always get away with more,' Em winked.

Amber raised her eyebrows. 'Em, that is stealing.'

'C'mon, get stuck in, I know y'all been chewing on salad and granola bars all day.' This came with a wicked smile. 'Anyway, it's not stealing. It's redistributing. There are too many people in New York who have too much. Do you know who came in tonight?' Em added. 'Don Paulozzi, the musicals producer. So guess what I did?'

'No! You didn't!' Amber groaned, already guessing. 'You're going to get fired!'

'I sang him the entire cocktail menu. He loved it. He has my number now, I've friended him and he may call. I could be hours, even minutes away from my Broadway break!'

Em went over to the window and looked down into the street.

'Can you believe the police are still there?' she asked. 'Like two hours later.'

'They have to dust for fingerprints,' Amber answered, 'swab for DNA and—'

'Make sure the owner didn't do it for the insurance, right?' Em broke in.

'He thought he was having a heart attack,' Sapphire protested.

'I can't see him,' Em said. 'Sergeant Cute.'

'Detective Cute,' Amber corrected her, 'I mean, Detective Desmoine. We have his card.'

'No! Are you gonna call him?'

'Huh? It's in case we remember anything else urgent. We also have to go to the station to sign our statements or something. Sapph gave such great descriptions,' Amber added. 'I mean, you noticed their heights, their exact clothing, even the make of their boots – the detective was really impressed. They'll probably catch those guys because of you.'

Sapphire shuddered at the thought.

'I didn't get a good look at them,' she said. 'They had helmets on and the whole thing was over in like three minutes.'

'Wow . . .' Em sounded almost impressed, 'three minutes?!'

'The detective wasn't real hopeful about DNA. They had gloves, boots, everything,' Sapphire said.

'But one of them was called Houghton, right?' Amber added. 'That's what you told the detective.

'*Houghton?*' Em repeated in surprise.

'Yeah . . . I'm not going to forget that name, am I?' Sapphire added.

'It just sounded like Houghton,' Amber offered. 'I thought it was more like Barton.'

'But the owner's insured, right?' Em asked, then gulped down another mouthful of ragout, sending flecks of tomato sauce across her chin.

'I guess . . .' Amber replied.

'So he'll get his money back. He probably didn't have a heart attack. And those guys got away with . . . ?' Em asked.

'About *three million dollars*' worth of stock.'

Em almost choked. 'You have got to be kidding me! Three million?! In that little store down there? Jeeez. They made one million per minute! Is it a mess?'

'The place is wrecked,' Sapphire replied. 'All the cases are smashed, there's broken glass everywhere, jewellery is scattered all over the floor.'

'Were you in your gym clothes?' Em asked. 'Your sneakers?'

'Yeah,' Sapphire confirmed. Since coming back to the flat she had showered, rinsed the glass splinters from her hair, and changed.

'So have you looked at your sneakers?'

'Huh? What d'you mean?'

Em pointed to the gym shoes.

'Well you never know, something could have got stuck in the treads.'

'No way!'

But still, Sapphire reached for the shoe, turned it over and examined the rubber grooves.

'Oh my gosh . . .'

With her fingernail, she prised out the item lodged in the sole.

Amber and Em crowded forward to see as Sapphire held out a diamond stud earring.

'I have to go down and give this back,' Sapphire said anxiously.

'I don't think so!' Em insisted. 'Keep it as a reward. Well, how do you like that, huh?' She looked at them both in turn, green eyes glittering. 'Assuming the owner's insured and OK: someone's made *Three. Million. Dollars* in a victimless crime.'

# Chapter Four

*'Her beautiful daughter has lost her job . . .'*

*'But that's perfect, Lauren, now that girl can really concentrate on finding a husband.'*

'I have the recent accounts for your charitable foundation, Mrs De La Hoz,' Amber began nervously, 'and there are some . . . well, there are some concerns.'

Amber reached across the shiny boardroom table and handed over a page of figures to the lavishly dressed and bejewelled middle-aged lady sitting opposite.

The woman, Mrs Eugenie De La Hoz, glanced over the page and her puffed-up, made-up, surgically enhanced face registered no expression whatsoever.

'What seems to be the problem?' she asked haughtily, directing the question at Amber's boss, who was also seated at the table.

Calmly, Robert folded his hands together and said, 'Amber, would you mind explaining?'

The rat. He didn't even have the decency to face Mrs De La Hoz with this himself. He was going to let her deliver all the bad news.

'Well, over the past four years, it would seem . . . and I may have misunderstood,' Amber went on, choosing her words carefully, 'but it looks as if the only payments this charitable foundation has made are to its own administrators and every one of them is a relative of yours, Mrs De La Hoz.'

Mrs De La Hoz's face flickered. If she was feeling an emotion, the lifts, tucks and quarterly Botox top-ups would make it impossible to read.

'And just what seems to be the problem?' she repeated, voice icy now, steely eyes fixed on Amber.

Amber swallowed. She clocked the woman's weighty gold necklace, studded with diamonds, the genuine reptile bag in her lap and the egg-sized ruby winking on her finger. Wasn't Mrs De La Hoz rich enough? Did she have to defraud the Internal Revenue Service with some phoney charity which quietly siphoned off hundreds of thousands of dollars to her nieces and nephews?

'Well, I'm not sure that the IRS will view this as appropriate behaviour for a foundation.'

'Doesn't charity begin at home?' Mrs De La Hoz snapped.

There was an uncomfortable silence.

Then the dragon lady took a breath, and in an angry voice, she began: 'Do you have any idea how little interest the IRS has in private charities? It takes them years to notice any tiny little hitch and even then, you're just given a slap on the wrist. So don't worry about it. Don't even look into it. I certainly didn't ask for any investigation here. Rules are made to be broken. As my ex-husband, the Provider, always says: rules are for the little people. You're a young girl; you need to learn these valuable lessons. And Thank You.'

There was no mistaking the dismissive tone of voice.

Mrs De La Hoz had clearly had enough of Amber pointing out the little irregularities in her vast and complex financial affairs and she wanted to talk to her much more senior investment advisor alone.

'Thanks very much for your input Amber, I think I can take it from here,' Robert said, then with a fake smile and curt nod of his head, he added, 'Why don't you shoot off now and get into costume? It's Wacky Wednesday for the rest of the day.'

'What on earth is that?' Mrs De La Hoz asked, disapprovingly.

'It's all about dressing up,' Amber replied, 'and raising money – for charity.'

* * *

Two hours later Amber was walking into a stark white waiting room. She took a seat and turned to smile at the hot dog sitting next to her.

'You too?' the hot dog asked.

She nodded and took off her Stetson.

'It doesn't look good,' the hot dog added. 'Everyone who's come out of that office so far has either been crying or cursing.' He stuck out his padded hot-dog hand. 'I'm Wayne by the way. Wayne from New Client Accounts.'

'Amber Jewel,' she replied, making the hand shake, 'from Asset Management, though not for much longer, I guess. I can't believe this. I nearly get shot in a robbery last night and now it's surprise lay-offs day!'

'You nearly got shot? That is rough. Hey, you could be getting a transfer to a different department rather than downsized.'

'Yeah, you too,' she said, trying to be reassuring. But the situation looked bleak.

The waiting room was entirely white without a single window, picture or magazine for distraction, so their eyes kept returning to the dark wooden door with the silver plaque which read: PAUL GLAZER – DIRECTOR OF PERSONNEL.

Glazer the eraser, as he was known all around the Dedalous Bank. Lately, a trip to Glazer's office had rarely meant anything good. All month long, from every one of the bank's departments, people had been sent to Glazer's office never to return.

Amber fidgeted with the fringing running down the side of her suede jeans and tried not to let her heart burst with anxiety. She'd only been in New York for seven months, she needed this job and she'd worked so hard to find it. Her sisters needed her to have this job, because she paid the biggest share of the apartment rent. Her mother needed her to have this job: the small end-of-year bonus Amber had expected was supposed to go towards the mortgage on the ranch back home.

'Nice costume,' Wayne told her, straining his face round the hole in the hot dog outfit to take a closer look. 'Jesse from *Toy Story*, right?'

'Yeah, *Toy Story* 2,' she smiled.

'Nice braids,' he added. 'You look at home in cowgirl clothes. Your boots look all beat up and authentic.'

'I guess,' she added. 'I grew up on a ranch.'

'Really?' The hot dog's eyebrows disappeared up into his costume. 'Where?'

Amber was from Bluff Dale, Parker County, Texas. But this was such a small place that she replied, as she usually did, 'In Texas, near Fort Worth.'

'Oh yeah, I've heard of Fort Worth. So what are you doing in New York?'

'I was kinda hoping banking would pay better

than cattle ranching,' she told him, 'but maybe it's not going to work out like that.'

'Right . . . and if they . . . if he . . . if you're . . .' Wayne began.

Amber nodded to show she understood. No one wanted to say the word 'fired' out loud right now.

'Will you go back home?' Wayne asked.

'Nope, I spent half a year looking for a job like this in Texas and I couldn't find one, so no, I'll have to get something else in New York.' Amber tried to make this sound less of a big deal than it really was.

'Do you know how many unemployed bankers there are in this city right now? Every second barista in Starbucks used to work for a bank.'

She felt her stomach knot into a ball.

'Why do you think he's calling people in on Wacky Wednesday?' Wayne asked. 'We're in costume, raising money for charity. I mean I'm sitting here dressed like a wiener – didn't even get time to change.'

'Maybe because he don't give a damn,' Amber replied.

The door flew open and a girl in a Cinderella ball gown ran out, giving a stifled sob before she disappeared out of the waiting room.

'She didn't even leave her slipper,' Wayne said mournfully.

There was a man in the doorway now: light-grey suit, black hair, clipboard in hand. Glazer the eraser.

'Wayne Albright,' he said, reading from his list.

Wayne gave a cheerful wave and stood up. 'That'll be me.'

Glazer took in the wiener suit with a look of derision, then said, 'You can go back to your department, there's been a rethink.'

Wayne looked from Glazer to Amber and back again, delighted relief all over his face.

'Thank you . . . thank you, sir. This is amazing. Thank you, so much.'

'Just go,' Glazer said, 'before I change my mind.'

Then the wiener was gone and Amber – standing now, because she felt it was only polite – was looking straight into the eraser's cool blue eyes.

'Miss Jewel?' he asked.

'Yessir.'

'Follow me.'

Amber sat down in the chair that was offered. If she'd not been so tense and focused on Glazer, she might have enjoyed the spectacular view from his window across uptown Manhattan, skyscraper windows flashing in the December sunshine.

Instead, she looked at his face and tried to take in everything he was saying.

He read out her name and her particulars from a

file lying on his desk: the date her employment had begun, her job description, her recent appraisals.

'All relatively good,' he declared, 'so why do we have to let you go? You are entitled to ask.'

There it was, just slipped in almost casually.

Let You Go.

The bank was going to let her go. Even though she didn't want to, hadn't asked . . . She was only 24 and about to be unemployed all over again.

'I'm sorry, Miss Jewel, you're the newest member of your department, you're still on probation, we have to downscale the department for financial reasons and I'm afraid that means you must be the first to leave.'

'But I'm really good at my job,' she managed to say.

'Yes, I'm aware of that. There's only one strike against you: apparently you questioned a not-for-profit foundation set up by the De La Hoz family.'

Ah. She'd suspected that would come back to bite her on the butt. But already? Had Mrs De La Hoz arranged for her to be fired?

'I didn't want the foundation to be the subject of a tax investigation,' Amber said in her defence.

Glazer raised an eyebrow.

'The De La Hoz family are very, *very* important clients of the bank. We try to accommodate them in every way we can. But that doesn't matter now.

What you need to know are the terms and conditions of your . . . *severance.*'

He enjoyed saying that word: he said it with relish.

From the blur of detail that followed, Amber took in the main points. She was leaving now, right after this meeting. A security guard would watch her as she cleared her desk and her locker. She would get one month's salary. There would be nothing else and, above all, no share in the end-of-year bonus.

So nothing to give Mother for the ranch mortgage.

As Glazer ushered her from his office, he held out his hand for her to shake.

'I'm sorry your time at the bank has ended so soon,' he told her, trying and failing to sound sincere.

Feeling dazed, Amber raised her hand and the briefest of handshakes passed between them.

'I'm sure you'll quickly find yourself choosing between many exciting new opportunities,' he added.

'Yeah. Right,' she dared to reply.

# Chapter Five

*'There are so many crazy people in this city, that's why I trust Fifi's opinion so much.'*

*'Fifi can't give you an opinion, Betty. She's a chihuahua.'*

Everybody comes to New York for a reason.

To find success; to find love; to find a more exciting life than the one on offer back home.

No one comes to New York to be fired; to spend months writing applications, searching for opportunities, flunking interviews, worrying about making the rent and eking out the remains of their money.

This was at the forefront of Amber's mind as she marched down street after street away from the job she no longer had at the bank. At least she'd been allowed to change clothes. Her cowgirl costume was in a bag in one hand, her briefcase – a gift from

Mother when she'd moved to the city – in the other.

Last year, she'd spent *months* searching for bank jobs, first in Texas, then in New York. It would be terrible to go back to the hunt again. All the applications. All the rejections. All the searching for inspiration in books like: *Fire Up Your Career, The Will to Win* and *Strive for Success.*

She did not want to go back to wearing sweatpants, eating Cheetos and searching the internet for divine intervention because surely nothing less was going to land her a new job, pay the rent on the apartment, and buy the presents for Christmas.

No. She would not go back there. Something would come up. This was New York City! Something *would* come up.

She pushed her long hair over her shoulders and marched on in her grey office pantsuit, thick coat and the sensible flats required for negotiating New York pavements, kerbs and subway stairs. For comfort, she ran her fingers over the turquoise and silver bracelet given to her by her beloved rancher Daddy.

Amber had texted both her sisters as soon as she'd left the bank for the last time and they'd ordered her to head uptown and meet them for an emergency team-talk lunch.

Although it was early December golden winter sunshine lit up the hundreds of windows soaring into the clear blue sky.

New York roared, as always. Cars were revving at the stoplights, desperate to move on, people were striding along the sidewalk. It was impossible to join the throng and not share their sense of uplifted purpose. Rubbing shoulders with this busy world almost made her feel better. This was New York City, she reminded herself. She would be OK.

Soon, Amber was on Fifth Avenue. Seven months in the city and still she couldn't walk along here without stopping to gaze at the view. The soaring skyscrapers parting like a sea for the mighty, wide-laned, traffic-jammed Avenue which ran all the way from north Manhattan to south.

Her phone bleeped with a message and what she read brought a smile: *Calling all volunteers. Tree planters wanted. Urgent. Hey, you can even hug the trees too if you want. Fitch.*

Amber, who'd lived on a ranch all her life, before New York, volunteered at least once a week at a community-run park and gardens. Digging in the earth, getting her hands dirty and helping the plants to grow was her downtime. It helped her to relax and reminded her of back home.

*Be there as soon as.* she replied. *Amber x*

A half-hour later and she was at Aubrey Wilson & Sons, auctioneers, Sapphire's swanky workplace in the heart of Park Avenue Princessland. Wilson's had been auctioning jewels, paintings, silver and every kind of *objet* since the doors had opened in 1854.

The wide windows displayed a selection of treasures and dates of forthcoming sales. Amber knew that the revolving doors led into a hushed and luxurious world of marble tiling, doormen in livery and viewing rooms filled with jewels, antiques and the kind of Upper East Side gazillionairess who wears golden Chanel shades indoors, along with layers of caramel-coloured cashmere.

But Amber no longer had to go in the front door; she'd been to meet Sapphire so often that she was now allowed to use the staff entrance. So she turned down the narrow alleyway at the side of the building and tapped the 10-digit code into the keypad.

The door unlocked and Amber stepped in.

Cataloguing One was Sapphire's office, on the second floor, right next door to the boss, Mr Wilson's office. He had an adjoining door, so he could come in and check on his quite possibly favourite recruit whenever he needed to.

Amber knocked and heard Sapphire reply, 'Come on in.'

Her sister's blonde head bobbed up from behind the computer screen.

'Oh hi there!' she said with a big smile and stood up to hug Amber. 'Are you OK? It's so terrible. I am so, so sorry for you.'

Amber couldn't help smiling because it was always nice to see Sapphire. She was Southern charm personified, sweet and pretty as a fresh peach pie. She always dressed nice, she always talked nice; she minded her manners and cared passionately about the details in life.

When anyone asked Sapphire why she'd moved from Texas to New York, Amber had heard her give a string of reasons.

'For the art – aren't the galleries so amazing? Better than anywhere else in the States.'

'For the culture: the exhibitions, the theatre, the art shows . . . to die for.'

'I moved for my job. I work for the auctioneers, Aubrey Wilson & Sons. They've been in the same building on the Upper East Side since 1854, isn't that *amazing*! I'm training to be an antique jewellery expert. I just completely *adore* antique jewellery, it's so romantic!'

Really, Amber knew, Sapphire had come to New York to find a husband. A good one. A truly wonderful husband.

She'd also come here to try to forget about Forde Houghton, oldest son of the Annetta North Houghtons, whom she had been engaged to marry until that terrible, terrible thing had happened . . . just *eleven* days before the wedding.

Sapphire still avoided, if she could, anything to do with the number 11.

'I feel completely weird,' Amber told her. 'Maybe I'm in shock. But I don't want to get depressed.'

'No,' Sapphire agreed.

'This is New York, there must be hundreds – *thousands* – of jobs I could do.'

'You're so right.'

'But we'll talk about it over lunch.'

'You're a little early, I can't get away for another fifteen minutes.'

'Can I look through the sales brochures?'

'Sure. I know how you like to follow the money,' Sapphire smiled.

It was true; the catalogues fascinated Amber. She liked to see who was selling, who was buying and where all these treasures had come from in the first place.

'There's a seismic shift going on in global economics and these brochures give a lot of clues.'

'Aha . . .' Sapphire didn't sound convinced.

'The English gave up their best jewels almost a hundred years ago. They sold to the Americans.'

'Except for the Royal Family,' Sapphire reminded her, 'the Royals sell nothing. They don't exactly need to.'

'But now the Americans are selling treasures to

the Russians, the Chinese and the Brazilians. It's the way the world works. Follow the money. Follow the jewellery. I wonder who the Brazilians will be selling to in fifty years' time?'

'Jewellery is all about romance, Amber, not money.'

Amber snorted and opened the first catalogue in the pile.

'Oh, Sapphire, dear?'

Mr McAndrew Wilson, one of the great-grandsons of the original Aubrey Wilson, stuck his head round the connecting door.

'Yes, Mr Wilson?' Sapphire replied, tucking her copy of *A Touch of Grace* into her desk drawer, Amber noticed.

Sapphire adored Grace Kelly. For Sapphire, the beautiful Princess Grace – although dead for nearly thirty years – remained the ideal American woman in every way.

And yes, there was no doubt that with her cool blue eyes, pale skin and dark blonde hair, Sapphire was something of a Grace Kelly lookalike herself. She dressed in an elegant, simple, Grace Kelly way too, and Amber knew that Sapphire would like her life to be much more like a black and white movie.

'Did you finish cataloguing the bracelet collection?' Mr Wilson asked.

'Yes sir, Mr Wilson, everything's back under lock and key.'

'Excellent, thank you. Some interesting items, didn't you think?'

Mr Wilson, in his usual outfit of brightly striped shirt, yellow vest, bow tie and monogrammed slippers shuffled over to Sapphire's desk, his wiry grey hair up on end.

'The Victorian emerald and diamond with the—'

'The cat?' Sapphire asked. 'The catch in the shape of a cat's head?'

'Yes.' A grin spread across Mr Wilson's craggy cheeks. 'I rather liked that. Didn't you?'

He cast a glance at Amber.

'You remember my sister, Mr Wilson, she's waiting to take me to lunch,' Sapphire explained.

'Yes of course. Hello, Amber.'

'I hope you don't mind her coming up here. She loves our brochures.'

'Not at all. Every brochure reader is a potential customer.'

'Here's hoping,' Amber replied, with a grin.

'Now . . .' Mr Wilson turned back to Sapphire, 'I've asked Fergus to come up and take a look at your lovely cataloguing work.'

At the mention of Fergus's name, Amber could see a blush spread from the collar of Sapphire's snowy blouse past her turquoise earrings and up to her hairline.

Amber had already heard a whole lot about the

Honourable Fergus de Mordaunt who'd joined Aubrey Wilson & Sons just three weeks ago all the way from Edinburgh, Scotland, where he'd worked for Sotheby's, the famous auctioneers.

Sapphire talked about him with the confused mixture of excited and trying not to be excited, which Amber read as the beginnings of a Major Crush.

There was a knock on Sapphire's door and when it opened, Mr Wilson exclaimed: 'And here he is!'

Fergus, the Honourable one, walked into the room.

'Hello, Mr Wilson – and Sapphire,' Fergus replied with a charming smile.

Amber looked him over. He was an appealing, wholesome combination of tall, broad-shouldered and blond, but with a boyish, freckled face. She even checked out his teeth and saw that they weren't too wonky or typically British at all.

He was in chinos and a multi-striped shirt with an even brighter tie. Maybe this was why Mr Wilson had chosen him for the job. Maybe they had bonded in some especially zany gentlemen's outfitters.

'Fergus, come and talk to Sapphire here about the Victorian bracelets.'

Sapphire looked up shyly.

'Hello,' Fergus said.

'This is Sapphire's sister, Amber,' Mr Wilson added. 'I'll leave you all to it.' With a glance at his antique pocket watch, he slipped back through the adjoining door.

'Hello there.'

Fergus flashed a charming smile at Amber then walked round Sapphire's desk to stand beside her. Sapphire seemed to go slightly to pieces and looked up at him in blushing confusion.

'Aren't the pictures of the bracelets up on your screen?' he asked.

'Oh . . . yes!' She turned to her computer, grateful to have something to look at.

But when she pressed a key, Fergus asked gently: 'Have you been googling me?'

Amber saw a look of horror pass across Sapphire's face before she clicked the file shut and stammered: 'No . . . not . . . no . . .'

'Oh,' he said, sounding almost disappointed. 'It's an old name, been around for a few hundred years.'

'What – Fergus?' she asked.

'Mordaunt,' he replied, 'not many de Mordaunts around. Fergus is nothing. If you go to Scotland, you'll find yourself tripping over Ferguses – the place is knee deep in them. Have you ever been to Scotland?'

'No,' Sapphire said; then, summoning true Grace Kelly charm, she added, 'But I would love to go. Apparently it's beautiful.'

'In places,' he agreed.

Fergus spent several long minutes looking appreciatively through her photographs of English Victorian and Edwardian gem bracelets.

Then he asked Amber if she'd like to take a look.

'No, I'm good. I was hoping I'd be allowed to take Sapphire for lunch some time soon.'

'Yes, of course. Sorry. I'll walk down with you. If you want to pop into the viewing room on your way out, I'll show you the latest display.'

'Pop?' Amber asked.

'Pop in? Is that one of those expressions that just doesn't work over here?'

'Maybe not.'

Sapphire had another cute little meltdown. She was trying to get her bag and her coat together, but put her arm in the wrong sleeve, then turned and knocked a pile of papers off her desk.

'Jeepers,' she said and bent down to pick everything up.

'Jeepers?' Fergus repeated. 'That's sweet.'

'Cute. It's a whole other language,' Amber told him.

They rode the elevator down, Amber making small talk and asking how Fergus was settling into New York while Sapphire blushed and fiddled with her hair. Amber could tell Fergus and Sapphire were totally interested in each other; the elevator space was thick with it. Fergus kept glancing at Sapphire when he thought she wasn't looking, then glancing away when she did.

Amber was trying to decide if she should do anything to bring these two closer together. It was six months since Forde Houghton and Sapphire hadn't been on one single date since – despite offers. But was Fergus the right guy for Sapphire to date after the Forde fiasco? Was Fergus nice enough, good enough, for her sister?

The elevator doors pinged open and the sisters followed him into the opulent hush of the main viewing room. This was where all the valuables next up for auction were available for the public to gaze at. Thick glass cases, twinkling lights and sumptuous velvet cushions made every single piece of jewellery displayed here look like an irreplaceable treasure.

Amber branched off, noticing that whenever Sapphire stopped to look at a case, Fergus stood close beside her and explained something about the necklace or ring on display.

'A seventeenth-century emerald . . . isn't that amazing?' Fergus was telling Sapphire. 'Look at the way they used to cut the stones. They didn't like sparkle, the way we do, they wanted colour, richness and depth. And look at these, so sweet . . .'

He steered Sapphire with a light touch on the shoulder towards a case of seven rings punctuating a green velvet cushion.

'Celtic love rings or Claddagh rings. Back then, everyone married for money, but very poor people were allowed to marry for love.'

As Amber approached the case, Sapphire bent close to study rings shaped into hands clasping a golden heart.

'The heart represents love, the hands are friendship and the crown above is for loyalty.'

'Oh,' she exclaimed, 'they're beautiful.'

'In this one,' Fergus pointed to a ring with five stones in a flower cluster, 'there's an amethyst, a diamond, onyx, ruby and emerald. So it spells: "adore".'

'Oh!' Sapphire gasped once again. 'I thought romance was a modern thing.'

'Never!' Fergus said, 'it's been going strong since the thirteenth century at least.' He turned to face her. 'Sapphire?'

There was a pause.

'Mmm?' she asked, not lifting her eyes from the glass case.

'I just wondered would you – and you, Amber – would you both like to have dinner with me and my flatmate? Roomie. I think I'm supposed to call him my roomie. One night . . . you know . . . if you're not too busy. I mean . . .'

And there it was. The offer of a first date.

Sapphire looked too astonished to speak, so Amber

replied: 'That's real nice of you. We could think about doing that, couldn't we, Sapphire?'

Face almost ablaze, Sapphire managed: 'Yes . . . how about tonight?'

Blushing some more, she corrected herself, obviously determined not to play it too keen. 'I mean – tomorrow? How about tomorrow night?'

# Chapter Six

*'Lauren, I just love what you've done to your face. You'll have to give me his number.'*

*'Botox is the best. Now I don't have to worry about whether I should smile or not, because I can't!'*

'Tomorrow's Thursday,' Amber told her sister once they'd exited Aubrey Wilson & Sons.

'Thursday's the new Friday,' Sapphire said. 'Anyway, he was fine with it. Just has to check with his *flatmate* . . . come on, you're fine with it too. What else would you be doing? Community gardening?'

'A whole lot of new applications and résumés, I guess.'

'Oh, Amber, I'm sorry. But come out with us. OK? What if his *flatmate* works in a bank and has some amazing new lead for you?'

'What if his *flatmate* is some kinky weirdo who just

wants to get me back to their apartment for creepy stuff involving his grandmother's underwear?'

'Euwwwww. *Grandmother's underwear?!* But nobody's ever tried to make you wear . . .'

'Let's not go there.'

Amber gave a shudder: 'On my last date I had to get the hell out of Dodge, as they say back home.'

Three streets later and the sisters were at the chichi designer boutique where Em worked as an assistant five days a week.

New York being as expensive as New York is, Em also held down her nightclub waitress job three or four nights a week and she had secured a part in a so-far-off-Broadway it was in fact in Williamsburg theatre production which took up all the rest of her time.

Despite all this effort, Em could only afford to share the tiny two-bed apartment which Amber and Sapphire were already renting when she had arrived in town, fresh from drama college. So everyone took turns for their month on the couch.

Em had come to New York to Get Famous. Back home she already was famous. She'd been on the cover of *Parker County Magazine* three times: once when she played the lead in the high school's big deal, end-of-year production, again when she made prom queen, and just lately when she moved to New York to try for the Big Time.

Of course, when Sapphire had called off her wedding to Forde Houghton – well, then they'd all been featured in a gossipy inside-page article, but that didn't really count.

Amber and Sapphire stood at the store window and waved at Em behind the counter.

She gestured for them to come in.

'I'm gonna be ready in like five seconds,' Em told them, 'but shut the door, c'mon in, get outta the cold. Cold enough out there to freeze hell over.'

'You're gonna have to wear more than that if you're coming out with us,' Sapphire warned, pointing to the skimpy miniskirt and vest combo Em had going on today.

'Amber, I'm real sorry about the bank, it's a total bitch. But I can only come out for like thirty minutes,' Em said. 'I have to leave early to get to a rehearsal tonight and . . .' she dropped her voice, 'Marlese is not exactly going to be cheerleading me out the door.'

'That's fine,' Amber said.

Just then the boutique's front door opened and a skinny, bright blonde woman walked in dripping with jewels, labels and an up-to-the nanosecond handbag.

She looked Sapphire and Amber up and down and decided she could demand attention without having to wait for them to finish.

'Hi, I am returning this,' she said and dumped a plastic bag on the counter.

Em's green eyes met those of the rail-thin, lovely blonde.

'Hello, *ma'am,*' Em said, making sure the woman knew Em was much, much younger than her. 'How may I help you?'

The blonde pulled a beautiful dress, which even Amber could recognize as Some Important Label, out of the bag.

'I want to return this.'

'Do you have your receipt? And did you purchase this dress no more than fourteen days ago?' Em asked. 'This looks like Fall Missoni. The last of it sold out weeks and weeks ago. We're all stocked up now with Winter and the first of Spring.'

'I don't need a receipt or a return-by date,' the blonde hissed. Her eyes narrowed. 'Look at this dress. It's falling apart, it's totally ruined.' She pointed to the burst stitching on the side seams and complained that the colour had faded in the dry cleaning.

Amber wanted to laugh. The lady truly thought she was entitled to her money back. She clocked the platinum wedding band and ginormous three-carat diamond ring on the woman's fourth finger.

Now she realized Em was probably dealing with a special class of Upper East Side Princess. One of the LWDW.

Ladies Who Don't Work.

Ladies who *did* work understood how stores had to operate and how people made their living.

But the Upper East Side Ladies Who Didn't Work were a breed apart. Daughters of the super-rich, married to the super-rich, they were under the delusion that the whole of the Upper East Side existed just to fulfil their every demand.

'I think I'm going to have to call my boss to deal with this,' Em said and quickly punched the number into the desk phone before the blonde could intervene.

'Marlese? Could you come down please, I have a customer who wants a refund. On a *Fall* Missoni.'

Within moments, the blonde and Marlese were engaged in the verbal equivalent of bull meets matador.

'. . . I have never been so insulted in all my life . . .'

'. . . Ma'am, this dress has been worn, all season long to every party in town by the looks of it. We do not refund worn clothing.'

'It's ruined!'

'Ma'am, you ruined it!'

'I will never, ever set foot in this shop again.'

'You know what, ma'am? I wouldn't want you to.'

Amber and Sapphire retreated to the far side of the store and Em tidied up as the argument raged. She straightened hangers, picked up fallen items, refolded tops and rolled up the very expensive velvet devoré scarves set out in a basket close to the cash desk.

At the peak of the argument, just as Marlese looked ready to frogmarch the blonde from the store, Amber saw Em slip one of the rolled-up scarves into her large canvas tote bag.

This wasn't by accident.

When the blonde had finally flounced out of the door, Missoni dress in hand, promising to call her lawyers, Em told her boss: 'I'm going out for something to eat, OK, just thirty minutes. Not one moment longer.'

'Twenty!' Marlese called after her.

Em picked up her tote bag and went out without giving any sign she'd heard this.

As soon as they'd rounded the corner from the boutique, Amber asked, 'Em, why are you risking your job by stealing from the store?'

'What?' Em said, snapping straight into the role of wide-eyed innocent.

'That scarf in your bag. I saw you take it. You haven't paid for it, have you?'

'Oh, Em . . . how many times do we have to warn you?' Sapphire asked.

'It's not stealing,' Em replied, pushing her arm down on top of the bag and marching ahead of them, 'it's borrowing. Sometimes I borrow stuff from the store and put it back later.'

'I don't think you do,' Amber replied.

'It's not stealing,' Em repeated. 'Marlese is allowed to write some losses off as theft and when I'm in the store I make damn sure no one else steals anything.'

'If it's not stealing,' Sapphire wanted to know, 'then what is it?'

'It's rebalancing,' Em began. 'I take things from very upmarket stores because in New York, people have way too much. More than they can ever appreciate. The blonde will phone her lawyer and she will get a refund, I can promise you. Trust me, in this town, everyone is stealing, from the top down. Plus the universe owes me something for all the negative karma I'm having to deal with right now. I mean, guys, I'm fifth down the bill in a bad play in Williamsburg. This was so not the plan.'

# Chapter Seven

*'The super in our building always knows just what's going on.'*

*'Oh, ours too. He is such a gossip. We call him Wikileaks.'*

After lunch, Amber rode the subway downtown to Union Square. She walked through the busy farmers' market, past the Christmas tree sellers, the jugglers and the hustlers and out onto 17$^{th}$ Street. Three blocks along was the cramped apartment she shared with her sisters.

Between 5$^{th}$ and 7$^{th}$, 17$^{th}$ Street was chic. Amber walked past cafes, the cutest children's toy store, an upmarket stationer's, bakeries with bespoke cakes, handmade muffins, artisanal bread – all dressed up with wreaths, lights and holly for Christmas.

Just as she approached the door to her apartment

block, Amber saw that the lights were back on in Ori's store, Bijoux Rox.

Through the window, she could see Ori, once again in a shirt and smart grey pants, sweeping the floor. She tried the door and found it was open.

'Hi, how are you?' she said, when he looked up from his sweeping. 'Do you remember me . . . from last night?'

'Oh my goodness! Of course I remember you. How are you?'

He placed the broom against a wall and walked over to her. For a big, round man, he was dainty on his feet.

'How are you?' he asked again. 'Are you Miss Amber or Miss Sapphire? No gunshot wounds, huh?'

She shook her head: 'No, I'm Amber. We were all lucky. How's your . . . chest?'

'Ha! Your sister was right: panic attack. Those bastards didn't kick off anything fatal, thank goodness. But what a thing, huh? And for you girls, boy you sure picked the wrong moment to window-shop. Thank you for giving statements and offering to be witnesses, a lot of people would have just walked out saying "no thanks". But you're really OK? Flashbacks?' he asked, looking concerned.

'Not yet. But maybe they'll come. I just got laid off from my job today.'

'What! You got laid off! They should be giving

you a raise, pinning a medal on your chest. Do they know about what happened here? Good grief. That is too bad. I'm real, real sorry.' He looked it too. 'And in this economy, huh? But a smart girl like you . . .'

'Who knows? I'll look hard,' Amber told him.

'I want to give you and your sister a reward. When the new stock comes in, come, bring your boyfriends and pick out a very special Christmas gift. Seventy per cent discount for you. Below cost.'

'Really? Are you sure?'

'My Christmas gift. You girls had an influence. I think he'd have shot at me again if you hadn't been here.'

'Well . . . thank you. No boyfriend, so am I allowed to buy myself something?'

'Of course!'

'You can't rely on anyone else to make you happy,' she added.

'Oh, a cynical one, huh?' Ori smiled at her. 'I've seen it all in this store, believe me. But there's someone for everyone. You've just gotta let them in.'

Amber shrugged.

'Now tell me about your beautiful bracelet. It's a piece of antique Navajo, isn't it?' Ori asked. 'Did you buy that for yourself too?'

'No . . . my daddy gave it to me,' Amber replied, her hand moving to the cleverly wrought burnished silver and turquoise.

'Aha!' Ori's smile widened. 'I know all about girls who love their daddy too much. I have two of them! The more you love your daddy, the harder it is to find a man who matches up to him. It's true. So what is Daddy going to give you for Christmas? If you want to bring him along to Ori, I'm sure we can find something very special.'

'Oh . . . no . . .' Amber tailed off and swallowed hard.

She was in the middle of the second year. People had warned her that the second year was the hardest and in so many ways they were right. It had taken almost a whole year for the loss of her daddy to truly sink in, to become real. Now, midway through the second year, it couldn't be ducked or denied. She had to face right up to it.

'My daddy passed the summer before last.'

Ori didn't seem to understand.

'He passed? You mean he *died*?'

All of a sudden Amber was enveloped in a bear hug.

'Oh, you poor baby. This is terrible! And you're so young and you obviously loved him so much. This is the saddest thing I've heard all day, all week, all year!' Ori exclaimed.

When he finally let go of her, he asked, 'How did this happen?'

Amber had thought she was getting better at

talking about it but now she felt her throat tighten up and the prickling begin behind her eyes.

'A coronary. No warning . . .' she managed, 'he just went out to the fields one morning and . . . didn't come back.'

Ori, maybe used to emotions of all kinds in his store, conjured up a Kleenex, put it into her hands and for a few moments, she had to hide her face.

'A heart attack,' Ori repeated in a whisper. 'Didn't I promise last night I'd give up the knishes, lose the weight? I gotta make a start.'

'I should go,' Amber told him.

'I am so sorry,' he said very sincerely.

Amber hurried up the flight of steps which led to the four-storey brownstone, subdivided into many apartments, one of which was their home.

She unlocked the front door and entered a shabby, old-fashioned hallway with a tumble of mail on the tiled floor.

Carefully she looked through the envelopes, magazines and leaflets, pulling out everything with her name on it and stacking the other letters on top of the wooden side table – dull and old-fashioned like everything else in this house. Then she went up the carpeted stairs to the attic rooms.

A cramped space formed the sitting room-meets-kitchen of the Jewel sisters' apartment. Most of the space was painted a dulled and dirty cream, the carpeting was brown, the kitchen was brown and most of the furniture was dark brown or dark green. Glamorous, it was not.

A used breakfast bowl, a scatter of cereal and splashes of milk decorated the kitchen countertop: which meant Em had eaten here. Sapphire's comforter was still spread over the couch and a jumble of laundry hung wherever space had been found: on top of the kitchen stools, from the window catch, even over a side lamp.

Amber dropped her keys, bags and the handful of mail onto the countertop. Now she spotted the scatter of brown droppings in amongst the cereal remains. Oh good grief, something else was living in this apartment. Something furry . . . she shuddered at the thought, then landed heavily on the couch as her eyes filled up with tears.

Daddy was still gone. They'd had to witness that horrible robbery . . . they had mice . . . or maybe worse . . . and now she'd lost her job.

'This is not my life,' she whispered to herself, 'this is *not* my life.'

# Chapter Eight

*'She looked stunning: her skirt was Versace, her top was Gucci and the shoes were definitely Manolo.'*

*'Where was she going?'*

*'She's 14 years old. She wasn't going anywhere. Besides, she was already in New York.'*

When Amber opened the apartment door on Thursday evening, she thought they'd been robbed. Then Sapphire stepped out of the bathroom looking amazing, and Amber realized that the scene of chaos was Sapphire Getting Ready for The Date.

'Wow,' Amber said, closing the door behind her, 'you look good as a chocolate cherry cupcake . . .'

'With a cherry on the top,' Sapphire finished their daddy's favourite compliment.

'Great outfit. Shame about the living room, obviously.'

The shabby green couch, the floor, the kitchenette stool, the rickety bookshelves – even the TV – were all draped in clothes.

Despite this effort, Sapphire was wearing just what Amber could have told her she would wear: her navy silk shift dress. The sleeveless one with the empire line and the two perfect darts which made it fit so well. Not too loose, not too tight, just perfectly ladylike and Sapphire-like. Her purple suede sling-backs were the same. Not too high, not too pointy, just perfectly elegant and tasteful.

'Do you like my necklace?' Sapphire asked, putting her hand up to the short string of oversized pearls. 'They're fake, obviously. I don't usually do fake, but even Jacqueline Kennedy Onassis wore fake pearls.'

'Well, I guess that's OK then,' Amber smiled.

'I'm a trainee jewellery expert, going out with another trainee jewellery expert. The jewellery is important. Is it the right thing?'

'Your earrings aren't fake,' Amber pointed out.

'Can you see them?'Sapphire asked, pulling her hair back from her face.

'Yeah, they look real pretty,' Amber said of the small, deep-blue sapphire studs her sister had been given for her twenty-first birthday.

'You're so pretty,' Amber added. 'I hope you can see that.'

Sapphire stood in front of the framed mirror beside the front door and looked herself over critically; she rubbed off some of her blusher then applied a second coat of lip stain.

'Bright-blue eyes – check,' Amber teased. 'Small straight nose, check. Rosy full lips, check, high cheekbones, peaches and cream complexion, check. Yup, you're good to go. As Mother always says: when looks were handed out, missy, you got more than your fair share.'

In a small voice, half not wanting to be heard, Sapphire whispered, 'I'd have made a beautiful bride.'

Amber put her hand soothingly on her sister's back and looked into the mirror with her. 'Shhh,' she said, 'you will be a beautiful bride. And there will be this wonderful man right beside you. Much more worthy than—'

'Don't say his name.'

'You look beautiful. We'll check the English guy out and have fun. If he's not worthy, you'll just keep looking. We'll help you.' Amber squeezed her sister's shoulder in encouragement.

'He's Scottish. Not English. Try to remember that. But what about you? You need to change, freshen up. Have you been out looking for a job all day?'

Amber nodded: 'Always a blast. Then I went to the gardens to help plant some stuff.'

'It's been like an age since you even tried to go on a date.'

'This so does not count as a date for me. I mean, I've never even met the guy.'

'Yeah, but you have to dress up!' Sapphire insisted. 'Get outta your jeans, get the dirt out from your nails.'

'I don't like dressing up,' Amber complained.

'Your black silky pants and the green top with the sparkles. OK? That way you're comfortable but not too showy.'

'OK,' Amber agreed, grudgingly. 'Where are we going?'

'We're meeting them at the Rockefeller Plaza beside the ice rink,' Sapphire said, smiling. 'So Christmassy . . . so romantic.'

'And when?' Amber asked, looking at her watch.

'Eight.'

Amber shook her head. 'Call and tell him right now we're gonna be late. The subway's shut between 23rd and 34th, there are people all over the sidewalk, every bus and cab is full.'

'Hurry up!' Sapphire exclaimed. 'We've got to go.'

'Plus it smells like rain,' Amber said, heading to her room for a quick change.

'No one can smell rain. Not even in Texas. I don't believe you.'

*   *   *

They were on Fifth Avenue, gazing in dismay at the jam-packed sidewalks, watching cabs crawl past bumper to bumper and trying to decide how they could get uptown in twenty-two minutes when the first cloudburst hit, lashing fierce, icy rain down onto the streets.

Sapphire screamed and scampered under the glass walkway of the nearest store, attracting the glare of the security guy. Despite Amber's warning, she was still wearing the suede shoes and carrying a beautiful lime-green suede clutch. Just one drop of rain and they would be ruined for ever.

'Told you,' Amber said and opened the small umbrella she'd brought; too small to shelter both of them and the clutch, but they tried anyway.

There was no subway until 34th Street, no chance of an empty cab, and now sheets of rain were splashing off the sidewalk and onto Sapphire's precious shoes.

In some countries, sudden showers of rain cause the flowers and fungi to pop up miraculously out of nowhere. On Manhattan Island, umbrella sellers appeared as if out of the cracks in the sidewalk.

'Please, sir!' Sapphire called to the man in the soaking-wet batik shirt who had materialized right in front of her with an armful of black umbrellas. 'Can I buy one?'

He hurried towards her, choosing one from his collection. 'Fifteen dollars,' he informed her.

'Really?!'

Once she was under the umbrella, she took out her cell to message Fergus again.

'Shall we just walk?' Amber said, looking at the packed avenue ahead of them.

'It's too far!' Sapphire wailed. 'We have to find a bus. Look at my shoes!'

When they finally managed to jam-pack-squash themselves into the third bus that came along they had to listen to wet, harassed New Yorkers complain.

'Do you mind, lady?'

'I need this seat more than you!'

'I rang the bell, you shoudda pulled over.'

Amber saw the pained expression on Sapphire's face. Her sister had lived in New York for nearly half a year but she still couldn't get used to the bad manners.

'Wouldn't this city get along a whole lot better if people could just be polite and respectful to one another?' she asked Amber.

'It's not Parker County,' Amber replied. 'No one's gonna tell your mamma if you misbehave.'

'Thank you, sir, you just try have a nice day now,' Sapphire told the driver with a generous smile when it was her turn to exit the bus. He rolled his eyes at the crazy Southern girl.

'She just got here,' Amber explained.

'We're a stop too far north!' Sapphire shrieked, opening her little umbrella against the heavy rain and dashing under the nearest awning. Her wet clutch began to ring.

It was obvious from the immediate softening of Sapphire's face who was on the other end of the line.

'We're on . . .' Sapphire glanced up at the street sign and told him the cross. 'You'll come and get us? OK. We'll wait right here.'

She and Amber tucked in under the awning and grew colder and wetter.

'My stockings are soaked,' Sapphire complained, starting to shiver. 'Is my make-up running?'

'You look perfect,' Amber told her.

'You too.'

Both girls looked down the sidewalk, hoping to spot Fergus.

'There he is,' Sapphire exclaimed.

Amber looked through the rain. Certainly some-one tall and blond was striding up the sidewalk, parting the sea of people with a golfing umbrella the size of a small planet. As he got closer, Amber could see it was Fergus, in a thick green tweed overcoat, some kind of paisley scarf slung about his shoulders – perfect auctioneering hero wear. He waved as he caught sight of them.

'Hello! Terrible night,' he called out, somehow looking shy, sheepish and terribly happy all at the same time. 'Sapphire . . . you look like a princess.' After a moment or two, he gallantly added, 'Amber – you too, of course.'

But Amber could see he and Sapphire were dazzled by each other and she didn't mind just coasting along in the slipstream.

'Oh. That's very sweet,' Sapphire replied slipping her hand around the arm he offered her and stepping under his umbrella.

'My flatmate is guarding our table,' Fergus explained. 'Follow me.'

Through the rain, through the crush on the sidewalk, they made their way towards the Rockefeller Plaza.

'Why is it so busy?' Sapphire wondered.

'Christmas shopping,' Amber reminded her.

'Plus they've put up the tree,' Fergus said.

'Oh the tree!' Sapphire exclaimed. 'How exciting!'

They turned into the square flanked by skyscrapers, and because none of them had ever been in New York for Christmas before, despite the rain, despite the dense mob of people, they had to wow at the scene.

A vast tree, smothered with lights, had been set up at the foot of the skyscrapers and in front of it sparkled a bright white ice rink. Skaters whizzed and pirouetted, gliding through the small puddles the rain was leaving on the surface.

'Oh how amazing!' Sapphire declared.

'Sure beats the hell out of the Bluff Dale high street decorations,' Amber joked.

'It's beautiful – as if a magic spell's been cast over the city,' Fergus said. 'I love all the shop windows. They are so over the top,' he said, pointing to a window where adult-sized angels were batting feathery wings in time to the flashing light display.

'Follow me,' he instructed. 'Phillip will be chewing the flowers on the table by now.'

In the restaurant, a smart, business-dinner kind of place, they followed Fergus to the table.

As soon as Amber set eyes on Phillip, she suspected her date would not go as well as Sapphire's.

Phillip looked too like her former boss, Robert. Same kind of pinstriped suit, same gold signet ring on his little finger, same critical I'm-not-really-enjoying-this look on his face. He shook her hand then once they'd all sat down, looked through the menu and placed their orders with the waiter, he fired so many questions at her, she began to think she was at a job interview

Her replies seemed to make his eyebrows shoot higher and higher.

'You grew up in *Texas*?' he asked, his expression close to horrified.

'You've *lost your job*? Uh-oh. Loser territory.' He actually backed away from her as he said it, as if unemployment might be as catchy as a virus.

'It's not like I tried to lose my job, I was good at it. I thought I was learning real fast . . .'

'Well, you must have been doing something wrong. If you're working twice as hard as everyone else in your department, you will not get downsized, I can promise you.'

'That . . . that is just . . .'

Amber could feel her face flush. She was starting to get angry with him now. What did he know about it?

She felt the stab of Sapphire's pointy shoe against her ankle, warning her to calm down.

'So . . . ahem . . . what brought you to New York, Sapphire?' Phillip decided to turn from Amber to her sister.

Sapphire leaned back in her chair. She seemed to be studying Fergus's face very closely, very carefully. Suddenly Amber had a premonition of what she was about to do and gave Sapphire a little kick to try and stop her.

Sapphire jumped. 'Well,' she said, then paused and dabbed at her lips with a napkin, 'I was just about to explain to Fergus. It's not a happy reason.'

'Sapphire had a bad break-up, that's all,' Amber put in. She saw a look of concern flash across Fergus's face.

'More than that,' Sapphire added.

Why was Sapphire about to do this? She obviously liked this guy and he seemed really OK, but did she need to admit to the whole wedding disaster on their first date?

'It was much more than a bad break-up,' Sapphire admitted. 'It's a biggie. I have to get it out there and clear the air.'

Fergus leaned over to touch her arm, looking concerned.

'So I'm just going to come right out and say it. OK?'

'Are you sure, Sapph?' Amber asked.

'Sapphire, don't feel you need to tell me anything you don't want to,' Fergus said quickly, looking nervous.

'I was engaged,' Sapphire blurted out. 'I was supposed to be married in June. Last summer. I was supposed to be a June bride.'

Fergus, Phillip and possibly even the nearby tables were all leaning over to listen now.

'Oh my goodness!' Fergus gasped. 'How lucky . . .'

'Lucky?' Sapphire repeated.

'Well . . . for me, I mean.' He blushed and Amber couldn't help smiling. Sapphire seemed to have found the nicest guy on the planet.

'I called the wedding off eleven days before the date.'

'What happened?' Fergus asked.

'Forde turned out to be seeing someone else.'

Fergus reached over the table again and put his hands over Sapphire's. 'I can't believe it,' he said.

'I caught them . . .' Sapphire hesitated, 'which is really all I want to say about that. It was horrible. And when he saw me, he said he still wanted to marry me, he was just . . . just . . . *getting things out of his system*.'

'Oh, Sapphire, how terrible. Horrible.'

'It was a big, big deal. A scandal. Wasn't it, Amber?'

Amber nodded, although really she'd never liked Forde. She and Em had secretly been relieved when the whole thing was blown out of the water.

'It was a big Texan wedding,' Sapphire went on. 'The Bluff Dale Jewels and the Annetta North Houghtons. I mean, that's the cream of Parker County, near Fort Worth, society.'

'I love the way you say that.'

'What?'

'*Fhot Wuthh*.'

'All the guests had to be told,' Amber carried on at a nod from Sapphire. 'Mother was the one who decided on the wording.' In best Southern belle accent, she added, '"*Because Forde Houghton has so deeply disappointed her, Sapphire Jewel has no choice but to call off their wedding. All gifts will be returned*." She had it printed on pale-blue cards that were sent in pale-blue envelopes to all of the guests. Sapphire gave her engagement ring back, obviously.'

'What a nightmare,' Fergus tried to sympathize, but looked increasingly relieved. Maybe he'd thought Sapphire was going to tell him something worse, or maybe he was just glad she was still available.

'Returning the gifts,' Sapphire began, 'was like watching the home I thought I was going to have being taken apart before I'd even moved into it. All the flatware, the stemware, the silverware in the pattern I'd chosen when I was eight.'

Although Sapphire's bottom lip was now close to trembling, Fergus looked confused.

'Flatware?' he asked.

'All the china. It was Italian Spode, blue and white. Not so fancy you couldn't use it every day, but still smart enough for dinner.'

'I know that pattern,' Fergus added, 'my grandmother's china is Spode, it's the one with the people in the Italian countryside and Roman ruins.'

'Yes, created in 1816 when the Romantic poets were alive and travelling from England to Italy was—'

'The height of sophistication! An Imari Oriental border, designed by Joshua Spode himself.'

Amber realized that Sapphire had quite possibly found her soulmate and she wondered if she would ever find someone with as much in-depth knowledge of detective fiction, or ranching, or growing stuff, or finance and figures . . .

'The stemware was Royal Brierly: Mayfair, and the silverware . . .'

Sapphire's face clouded over.

'Oh, what's the matter?' Fergus asked, voice full of sympathy.

'It's just so sad . . .' A tiny tear slid from the corner of Sapphire's eye. 'I was taken to the department store when I was eight to go and pick my silverware pattern. It's like first communion for a Southern belle. You look through the catalogues and you choose your pattern. The one that all your relatives are going to buy you a piece of for every birthday and Christmas until you're married. And wedding gifts complete the set. So it was all ready. It was all laid out. Now, it's all back in boxes again waiting for my life to begin.' She brushed the tear from her cheek.

Amber tried hard not to roll her eyes. Yes, she and Em had silverware in their chosen patterns too, but Amber's was boxed up in the attic at home and she'd be more likely to sell it than to ever set out a fancy table with it. The whole tradition was just so old-fashioned.

'And my silverware is Old English Fiddle, made by Arthur Price of Sheffield. One of the oldest—'

'Cutlery patterns. Perfectly balanced, created in the 1600s,' Fergus finished her sentence. 'What an amazingly sophisticated choice for an eight-year-old.'

Sapphire sniffed.

'This happened in June?' Fergus asked.

She nodded.

'But you're so young.'

'Twenty-two now,' Sapphire said with a resigned sigh.

'You have all the time in the world, Sapphire, to find the man who is going to be eating from Italian Spode with Old English Fiddle with you for the rest of your life.'

'That's *just* what I keep telling her,' Amber said, shooting Fergus a smile.

'Why, you are so very kind,' Sapphire told him, 'but being engaged to Forde, then having to break it off, it makes me feel so . . . so second-hand!' she blurted out in distress. 'That's why I had to move up here, I couldn't take all the sympathetic looks and gossip behind my back.'

'So wise.'

Sapphire reached into her clutch bag, found a Kleenex and dried her eyes, then blew her nose very gently and politely.

With a bright smile in place, she looked across the table at the astonished Phillip and said in her best hostess voice, 'That's really quite enough about me. Now why don't you tell me why you moved to New York?'

Fergus had to laugh at this.

'You're wonderful,' he said. Then he got up from his seat, walked round the table, bent down until he was level with Sapphire's face and said, 'Can I kiss you?'

# Chapter Nine

*'Oh no, Lauren, I don't think he's a suitable man for her at all.'*

*'You're right, of course. He has to* rent *in the Hamptons and he buys* Italian *shoes.'*

'You do know why *you* were let go, right?'

It was 9.35 a.m. and Amber was sitting at a cafe table opposite Robert, her boss in the life she'd had . . . up until Wednesday.

This was where she'd most often eaten lunch when she'd had her job – no, make that her blossoming career. The cafe was right across the road from Dedalous and every now and then, when she glanced over to the entrance, she could see people come and go. Sometimes members of staff that she recognized, and sometimes super-affluent Mrs De La Hoz-type client, hurrying in with their worries about how to invest that spare $4 million. Or how to keep their latest $1.6 million profit out of 'the clutches' of the IRS.

Sitting here opposite Robert, watching the entrance, knowing she had no job and exactly one month's salary left, she was getting a pain in the stomach.

'Well . . .' Amber began, 'was it Mrs De La Hoz? Did she complain?'

Robert nodded. 'She did, and that didn't exactly help your case. But it was a downsize. We had to let some people go.'

'So the bank didn't have enough money left and lots of people had to leave and it was last in, first out, right?'

'Yeah, but why were *you* chosen, Amber? Why are *you* out of a job and why are so many others still here? That's the kind of question you need to be asking yourself.'

'Gosh, well . . . there could be a ton of reasons for that. I'd only been there seven months . . . other people had seniority, I went to A&M, not Harvard . . . I'm Texan, not New York . . . any kind of reason you like.'

'You're too good at closing loopholes instead of opening them, and you're not a team player, Amber,' Robert said.

Amber looked up at him, trying to keep the hurt

she felt from showing on her face. But this was hard to hear.

'I really appreciate your bravery in asking to see me like this,' Robert added, 'it takes a lot of courage. And you have a lot of courage. But if you really, really want to know why I picked you for the downsize and not, someone else, then listen and learn.'

Robert was making annoying gestures. When he said 'listen' he pointed at his ear, when he said 'learn' he pointed at her, his gold signet ring glinting in the light. Now, all of a sudden, she realized what a pain he had been to work with. She remembered how her disappointment at being fired had been mixed with a spritz of relief that she would no longer have to deal with Robert every day.

'You are not a team player,' he said, pointing at her again. 'You are not a corporate girl. You think for yourself and you're too independent. These are amazing qualities, but not for my asset management team.'

'Oh.'

She felt winded. Would anyone else hire her if this was what her former boss thought? Plus, what kind of reference would he give her?

'Is there any corporation in New York that would like an independent-minded trainee asset manager?' he went on. 'I don't know. This may feel like a step down, but I have a friend . . .' Robert felt inside his suit jacket, brought out a card and handed it over to her.

'I don't know how much looking you've done yet, but it's tough to get hired right now. This guy, he's running a new cold call operation. Selling investments. Maybe you're tough enough to give that a try.'

She took the card.

Robert wanted her to be a cold caller: one of those people who sat in some warehouse in Hoboken and phoned Mr T.J. Penney in Nebraska to try and interest him in some crappy fund that would charge him 9.5 per cent a year and make him exactly 0.2 per cent if he was lucky.

Jeeeez. She'd hoped he'd be able to offer her a much better lead than this.

'Call him,' Robert urged, 'it's not what you think. He's a good guy and he's hiring smart people on excellent commission. You'll sail in there and it's just for now. Make some money to tide you over. Things will turn around, everyone will be hiring again soon.'

He glanced at his watch. Amber glanced at hers. He'd only been with her for seven minutes, but already he wanted to go.

'Well . . . thanks very much for your time,' Amber began. 'I guess I've gotta go. I'm meeting my sister and we have to show up at a police station. We were witnesses to an armed robbery.'

'Where was that?' Robert asked.

'On our street: West 17th.'

Robert stood up, brushed down his $2,000 bespoke suit and turned to go. Without one shred of sympathy he told her: 'Ouch, I guess that'll happen if you have to live downtown.'

# Chapter Ten

*'Don't they make a gorgeous couple?'*

*'Betty! He is way too old for her. Thirty-four years too old for her.'*

*'I mean her and the necklace: that is at least $100,000 worth.'*

'You're back to see us again?'

Fergus threw Amber a bright smile as he strode into Sapphire's office.

'Not exactly. I'm meeting Sapphire,' Amber explained, 'we're going to the police station together. We have to go see the detective on the case. But it shouldn't take long.'

'Oh yes, Sapphire told me all about the robbery. You were both so brave.'

Sapphire was at her desk, beaming at Fergus. Amber

couldn't help smiling too. See, that was Sapphire – so sweet, so trusting, always jumping straight into love.

'Do you have to go right now?' Fergus asked. 'Because I'd love to tell Sapphire about what might be coming up for auction unexpectedly at the next jewellery sale.'

'Oh yes!' Sapphire glanced at her watch. 'We've got a few minutes, don't we?'

Amber nodded.

'One of Mr Wilson's special clients, Mrs Eugenie De La Hoz.'

'I've never heard of her,' Sapphire said.

'Well I have . . . but long story,' Amber said.

'Mrs De La Hoz is apparently facing an unexpected tax bill and needs to sell some very important pieces quickly.'

'Really?' Amber was surprised. Mrs De La Hoz had maybe had to face up to one of her many tax avoidance schemes.

'So what's she selling?'

'Well . . . it's not confirmed yet, she's hasn't completely made up her mind, but . . .'

Amber drew closer. His excitement was infectious and she too wanted to hear what might be coming up for sale.

'She's told him she might like to sell one or two of the pieces she owns from the Duchess of Windsor's collection.'

'No!' Sapphire breathed, eyes alive with excitement.

'The Duchess of Windsor?' Amber repeated; even she'd heard of the Duchess of Windsor's legendary jewellery collection. 'Didn't her jewellery all get sold off years ago?'

'Yes, but now and then the people who bought, resell it. There's always a frenzy when the pieces come back on the market,' Fergus explained.

'These are some of the most wonderful jewels in the world,' Sapphire whispered, 'some of the most fabulous and extravagant. Plus, it's such a romantic story. I mean, she was a divorcee and the *King of England* gave up his *throne* to marry her!'

'Then they spent the rest of their lives living in Paris and commissioning very, very expensive jewels,' Fergus added. 'She famously said no woman could be too rich or too thin.'

'Then she'd have felt right at home in New York,' Amber said.

'Has Mrs De La Hoz got any of the Cartier pieces?' Sapphire wanted to know.

'Oh!' Fergus smiled, delighted that she had just as much interest in the subject as he did. 'Not just any old Cartier pieces. It seems she has a panther brooch.'

'No! One of the panthers made by Louis Cartier just for the Duchess?' Sapphire exclaimed.

'Yup. Solid gold, studded with diamonds, two brilliant rubies for its eyes. It sold the last time for half a million. Who can tell how much it will be worth now.'

'Half a million dollars for a brooch?' Amber asked, not quite able to take it in.

'It's iconic. Cartier still makes panther brooches,' Sapphire added.

'Not like Louis made them for the Duchess. There were lots of rumours that they were . . .' Fergus leaned over the desk and whispered the word: 'lovers.'

Sapphire gave the slightest of shivers.

'She cheated on the Duke?' Amber asked.

Sapphire made a face. 'But that's terrible.'

'Just rumours. If anyone knows for sure, they've never said.'

'But the King gave up the throne for her. He gave her everything she could ever have wanted. Why would she cheat?' Sapphire asked. 'And there are all those bracelets with secret romantic inscriptions. They were devoted to each other. I don't think she cheated. I think people are just being mean.'

'Isn't she lovely?' Fergus asked Amber, then reached down for Sapphire's hand, put it to his lips and kissed it. 'I'm so lucky to have you here. You could have been shot that night.'

Now it was Amber's turn to shiver: 'Please don't talk about it.'

'Shhh!' Sapphire insisted. 'Everyone round here thinks I'm like some amazing heroine who saved the owner of the store or something . . .'

'You are, Sapphire,' Fergus said. 'If you hadn't asked the robbers to leave you alone, maybe they wouldn't have.'

'Fergus?' Sapphire turned up her blue eyes towards him and in that moment, still holding her hand tightly, Fergus didn't look as if he could refuse her anything.

'Our mother is coming to town this week. Would you like to meet her?'

'Of course! Absolutely. I'd be honoured.'

'She's staying at the Astoria, of course, they have a special Junior League Floor,' Sapphire explained. 'She says it's the only place in Manhattan where she truly feels safe.'

Fergus's brow creased; he'd clearly only understood a little of this. 'What's a Junior League and why would you mother still be in one?'

'Oh, it's this whole Southern sorority thing, kind of a club,' Amber began. 'Once you're in, you're in for life, you have to be the right kind of person to be asked to join and . . . oh, you know, you probably have to be born south of the Mason–Dixon Line to understand it.'

'Right.'

'Mother is very, *very* Southern,' Sapphire warned.

'*Very* Southern,' Amber added, 'and that's a warning.'

# Chapter Eleven

*'So they had to call in the police, Lauren.*
*Imagine. To that address!'*

*'The police?! How will they ever live it down? And all*
*because she didn't hire the right kind of maid.'*

'Have you ever been in a police station before?' Amber asked Sapphire as they headed up the staircase towards the entrance.

Sapphire shook her head.

'No need to be nervous, I guess. He said it was just a formality; another interview going over the same questions.'

'I don't like this,' Sapphire said. 'What if he really does think we're in on it? Like he said—'

'He didn't say that! He just said he had to rule us out. It was routine. Anyway, it doesn't matter if he thinks we were the bikers pointing the guns. We weren't! So no one can ever find us guilty of it.'

'But you hear about this kind of thing all the time. Miscarriages of justice. Innocent people accused. It gives me the shivers.'

'Hush up, Sapphire,' Amber said as they approached the reception desk. 'Hi there, ma'am, we're here to see Detective Jack Desmoine.'

'Third floor. Room 318,' the stressed-out woman behind the grille barked at them.

'Thank you, ma'am,' Amber replied graciously.

'Thank you so much,' Sapphire added.

Seeing the queue for the elevator, they decided to take the stairs. On the third floor, the sign for rooms 300 to 320 took them through a series of grey, messy corridors stacked with filing cabinets, plastic chairs and water coolers.

'Guess this is it,' Amber said and tapped on the door.

'Who is it?' called a voice from the other side.

'The Jewel sisters,' Amber replied.

'Oh, right . . .'

There was a pause followed by clattering noises.

'Maybe he's clearing up for us,' Amber said to Sapphire with a smile.

Then the door was open and Jack Desmoine stood in front of them once again.

'Hi, girls,' he said with a smile and held out his hand for them to shake.

Such a big hand, such a tall man, Amber couldn't help thinking now that she was up close to him. He towered a good four inches or so above her and his chest and shoulders were so broad they seemed to fill the doorway.

'C'mon in. Can I getcha a coffee or something?'

'No, I'm fine thanks.'

'Me too,' Sapphire agreed.

'It's OK. It's not poisoned or anything. Unfortunately we don't lace it with the Truth Drug either. That would make my life so much easier.' He walked behind his desk, pulled up his chair and sat down, indicating that they should do the same.

'Today is just paperwork, Miss Amber and Miss Sapphire, unless you've remembered anything else or have something else to tell me.'

Amber and Sapphire looked at one another.

'No,' Sapphire said.

'No, we told you everything,' Amber added. 'Is there any update? Have you caught anyone?'

'Ha!' Detective Desmoine gave a little laugh at this: 'two motorbikes, possibly BMW, two tall black guys, one called something that sounded like "Houghton". No DNA. And a great big missing bag of jewels. That's all we gotta go on. Despite your excellent descriptions, miss,' he nodded in Sapphire's direction, 'it's not a lot. So no, we have not caught anyone. But it's early. Sometimes it takes a long time to catch people. We're definitely looking.'

A cellphone began to ring and the detective reached into the top pocket of his shirt.

'Desmoine,' he snapped. 'Right . . . aha . . . well, keep it short. I've got witnesses I need to deal with here . . . Texan witnesses. Yup, you don't get that every day . . . Aw man! *Fourteen?* You know I hate to bring in babies . . . is there anything we can do? Can't he help us with our inquiries and earn himself a reprieve?'

As he talked, Amber found herself studying him. She remembered the brown eyes . . . and such dark eyebrows. Then he glanced her way and with a start, she realized she'd been looking too long and quickly turned away.

This room, it was so bare; not tidy exactly, but not a mess. Paperwork lay in piles, there was an old computer, a phone, nothing on the walls at all and a view of the back of the next building.

There was also a mug on the table with a Giants logo.

Jack ended the call and clicked the cell off. As he put it back into his pocket, he followed Amber's gaze and asked her, 'Do you follow the Giants?'

'No. Hell, no. The Dallas Cowboys, of course.'

'Yeah, sure. I've seen them play, when they're in town.'

'OK, so what do you need us to do?' she asked. 'It's just that Sapphire has to get back to work.'

'Right. Yes, of course.'

Desmoine began to shuffle through the wire in-tray on his desk. 'Here are your statements. I want you to read right the way through them, then if you're happy with everything, sign at the bottom.'

As Sapphire and Amber read through the print-outs, Desmoine couldn't help asking, 'Have you found a new job yet, Miss Amber?'

Amber gave a gasp: 'How did you . . .'

'I called your employer. Part of checking your references, making sure you're all who you say you are. Very sorry to hear about that,' he added, 'but you'll get something quickly, I'm sure.'

'I have some good leads,' she told him.

'That's the spirit. And you volunteer at a community garden?' he asked.

She nodded.

'That's nice. I don't think I met a nice banker before.'

'Asset manager,' she corrected him.

'Is Ori going to get all his money back?' she asked, to change the subject.

'Ori? Oh, the store owner? He's enjoying protracted negotiations with his insurance company. I think it will work out. He'll get a good percentage of what he lost covered and then he'll be able to open his doors again.'

'Might take him a long time to get over it,' Sapphire said sympathetically.

'How are you girls?' Desmoine asked. 'Not too shaken up? Not too scared to ever go into a store again, I hope?' he asked, a little teasingly.

'No. We seem to be OK,' Amber told him.

'Well, it's a weird thing, post-traumatic stress, sometimes it makes people do strange stuff, sometimes it doesn't kick in till years later, or it might never bother you at all. We have a whole victim support network, so if you need help, please let us know.'

Amber signed her name on the statement, then Sapphire did the same. They handed the papers to Desmoine.

'I guess that's us, then,' Amber said, standing up. Desmoine was giving her an antsy feeling. She wanted to be out of the office and away from him, yet she couldn't stop looking at him. She kept moving her eyes to something else in the room, but they would swivel right back to him.

'Yeah . . .' Desmoine also stood up, 'Well, I have your numbers. Home and cell. If I need to call you about anything. If we catch the guys, you'll have to testify. So, I'll call with a progress report.'

'Thanks, detective,' Amber said.

'Jeez . . .' Amber said as soon as they were out in the corridor again. 'He's a strange guy.'

'I thought he was kinda sweet,' Sapphire protested. With a smile she added, 'You just think he's strange because he likes you.'

'He does not.'

'He does too!'

'Well if he does, then he's definitely a strange guy. We all know that's the only type I attract.'

# Chapter Twelve

*'Do you know what he told her? "New York isn't just a city. It's a feeling".'*

*'Yes and in his case that feeling is: "I've reached the limit on all my credit cards".'*

As the curtain closed on Em's production, the small audience clapped. Amber and Sapphire looked at each other uneasily.

It wasn't a good play. And Em had put in a terrible performance. She'd forgotten lines, she'd been uncomfortable on stage – and even worse, the girl starring opposite Em had been the only good thing about the whole show.

Whatever 'it' was, Angelina Waltham had it. When she stepped on stage, everyone had eyes only for her. She was as pale and insubstantial as a fairy, with a delicate halo of gingery-brown hair, and her little sweetheart face just drew you in.

'Angelina . . .' Amber began.

'I know,' Sapphire said.

'No one could get enough of her,' Amber added. 'Her voice . . .'

Angelina's voice had been thrilling in range and register. The audience had been tuned in and listening.

'Shhh!' Sapphire said. She didn't want to hear any more about how good Angelina was compared to their sister.

'Plus, she's so young, she looks like a teenager. Em is going to completely freak,' Amber warned.

'I know.'

Twenty minutes later Em stormed into the little bar close to the theatre where she'd arranged to meet them. Her face was as dark and thundery as Amber had expected.

She threw herself into the chair opposite her sisters. 'You don't need to tell me. Just don't even say anything. I stank. I totally stank. In fact, the entire play stank. The only good thing about the show was Angelina.'

'No, don't be crazy . . .'

'You delivered some wonderful lines . . .'

'I loved your part . . .'

'You're really good . . .'

Her sisters protested hard, but Em wasn't having any of it.

'I stank,' she repeated mournfully.

'Let me get you a cocktail,' Amber offered.

When she came back to the table with the drink, Em was telling Sapphire: 'She's only eighteen. Eighteen! There are girls like Angelina coming out of drama school every day, fighting for the parts I'm fighting for. All better than me. They can act, they can sing, they can dance. They look like movie stars! They're going to get all the parts before I can even get a look in. Plus they're younger than me. I'm twenty-one, guys, and I'm stuck in Williamsburg *stinking* in some *stinking* play!'

Sapphire put her arm around her sister. 'Please don't say that. Please. You're good. You've always wanted to act, you love acting, so please stop bumming out because this one little show hasn't worked out for you.'

'Maybe they're not bringing out the best in you,' Amber added, 'maybe these guys just aren't your crowd.'

'No,' Em agreed, 'when I'm with them, I feel about as welcome as a skunk at a lawn party.'

Amber laughed and thought of home. She wondered how long she would have to live somewhere else before she stopped thinking of the ranch as home. That thought brought her to Mother and the mortgage . . . there wasn't any risk, was there? There wasn't any fear that the ranch would have to be sold? She needed to talk to Mother, go through the details with her again. Mother wasn't as good with the figures as Daddy had always been.

Em took several gulps from her glass then looked at her sisters in turn. 'I am never going to be a star,' she declared sadly. 'I am *never* going to be a star. Maybe you both know that. Maybe you found out tonight, maybe you've known for a while . . .'

Both sisters made to protest, but Em shushed them.

'No, listen. I've been thinking about this for a few days and I'm only just tonight ready to admit it out loud. I always thought I had what it takes. But I don't. I don't have it. I'm not good enough. I'm not determined enough. I'm never gonna work hard enough at it. I am never going to be a star,' she repeated, then in a much quieter, sadder voice, she added, 'And I always thought I would . . .'

She broke off, looking lost, her eyes swimming.

'Please, Em,' Amber insisted, 'you're having a bad night, don't—'

'I quit the play,' Em added.

'No!' Sapphire cried. 'That will look terrible when—'

'I audition somewhere else? I'm not gonna,' Em said. 'It's over. It's really over.'

'For now,' Sapphire said. 'Maybe you just need a break for now.'

'You can say that if you want to. But I think it's really over.'

Em bent her head and quickly brushed a tear from the corner of her eye: 'So Plan A: have a wonderful career – well, that's completely blown,' she said, trying to sound upbeat. 'I guess I need to move on to Plan B.'

'Which is?' Sapphire wondered.

'Marry a millionaire, obviously,' Em joked.

'Oh, man, why don't we just skip that one and could you please let me know what Plan C is?' Amber asked.

'I have no idea. Let me go get fresh drinks while I try and figure it out.'

'Uh-oh,' Amber said to Sapphire. They had lived through many madcap-Em ideas before. 'Em's making a plan. Remember the fund-raiser nude barbecue?'

Sapphire snorted a little bit of cocktail from her nose: 'Eeek!' She grabbed for a tissue: 'We were all grounded just for sending out the invites and the only person who turned up was Creepy Guy from your year.'

'Oh, man, and never forget Em's rodeo video which got sent to Steven Spielberg.'

'Please, you're not allowed to remind me of *all* the crazy-Em ideas. But I have faith: one of these days, one of her ideas will come off. Big time.'

'I hope so. She's really down. She won't really quit acting, though?' Amber asked. 'It's what she's always, always wanted to do.'

'I hope not,' Sapphire said.

When Em came back to the table with another round of cocktails, she wanted a change of subject: 'Enough about me. Please tell me all about your day. What's going on with the fabulous Fergus? How was Detective Dreamy at the police station?'

Amber filled her in about their trip to the precinct station, then Sapphire began to tell Em all about the Royal treasures possibly coming up for auction.

'Mr Wilson is already having a meltdown and it's still not been confirmed,' Sapphire went on. 'But the Duchess of Windsor's jewels, they are so very, *very* special. These pieces only come up once every few years and the collectors go crazy. It's the closest you can get to buying Royal jewels. British Royal jewels never, ever come up for sale. They're all kept in the family and handed down.'

'Wow!' Em looked impressed. 'So the Duchess is the American who married the man who was going to be the King of England.'

'Yes, Wallis Simpson,' Sapphire explained. 'He gave

up his throne to marry her. It's just so unbelievably romantic. Then they lived in Paris . . .'

'And he bought her lots of expensive jewellery,' Em added, 'maybe to make up for the fact that she wasn't going to be Queen.'

'Remember, she's the one who said a woman could never be too rich or too thin,' Amber prompted.

'I guess she never knew about Victoria Beckham,' Em said. She arched an eyebrow. 'So what might get sold?'

'An original panther brooch, a platinum and emerald necklace, and maybe a third piece – it's not confirmed yet. The panther is *amazing*. Commissioned under Louis Cartier himself. I've already seen photos.'

'And how much is everything going to sell for?' Em asked, leaning across the table, eyes bright with interest.

'Who knows? When they were first auctioned twenty-four years ago, they cost hundreds of thousands of dollars.'

'Wow!' Em exclaimed. 'Some people can afford to have a lapel pin that costs more than most people's houses, huh?'

'And there are so many more jewellery collectors now, all over the world, who seem to have *millions* of dollars to spend,' Sapphire added.

'Is Wilson's taking on lots of extra security?' Em asked.

'I guess . . . gosh, I hadn't even thought of that.'

'It's just days since you had a *gun* held to your *head* in a jewellery store and you haven't even thought about security?' Em shook her head in despair.

Sapphire grimaced.

'Well they'll have to do something to keep those precious gems away from all the thieves in the world,' Em added, stirring at her cocktail thoughtfully.

'Em?' Amber asked. 'How come there's hair sticking out of your bag?'

'Oh do you like my new wigs?' Em said, pulling one long straight blonde and one curly dark wig from her tote.

Sapphire tutted.

Amber rolled her eyes: 'Don't tell . . . they've been "liberated" from the backstage dressing-up department.'

'Exactly,' Em confirmed with a wicked smile. 'Those people have given me nothing but bad vibes and negative karma. So I'm rebalancing.'

She pulled the blonde wig on her head and pouted her way perfectly through two lines from a Britney Spears song. Then broke off to ask:

'Talking about rebalancing . . . Amber, isn't Eugenie De La Hoz the multimillionairess *bitch* who got you fired from the bank?'

# Chapter Thirteen

*'She really liked him, Betty, but it was obviously never going to work.'*

*'Tell me about it. His apartment was in the Fifties, hers was in the Seventies. That's like a million miles in real money.'*

'Hello, is that Mrs Kirkton?'

'Is this a cold call?' snapped the woman's voice at the other end of the line.

'Good morning, Mrs Kirkton,' Amber persisted as cheerfully as she could, 'we've been given your name and telephone number because—'

Brrrrrrrrrrrr.

Another hang-up.

She crossed the name off the list on her desk. She had made hundreds of calls. Hundreds! But there were still scrolls of names to work through and hours left in her day. Unless she got just one person to sign up for something, she would have earned just $40.

'My soul is in the process of being destroyed,' she whispered to herself.

Worst of all, any moment now and Jed, her team manager, was going to come over and give her another pep talk. She would stab him in the eye with her sharpened pencil. Honest to God she would.

'Amber!'

The hand of Jed was on her shoulder. 'How is my best Texan girl getting along? Yee ha! Ring them numbers, make them sales.'

He was all jokey, touchy and feely. She *hated* him. She'd been at the warehouse office in Hoboken (how had she guessed?) for less than four hours and already she wanted to die.

Jed looked down at her list. When he saw all the crossed-off names and numbers, he frowned.

'Amber, Amber,' he shook his head, 'you came so highly recommended.'

'I'm very good at advising clients who want to be advised,' she said pointedly. 'I'm very good at selling excellent products to people who want to buy.'

'Let me show you how we go about things here . . . once again,' he said with an actorly 'I'm slightly disappointed' sigh and shake of his head.

Showily he set the timer running on his ugly gold

watch, then redialled the number Amber had just tried.

'Mrs Kirkton, hi!' Jed boomed down the phone.

Without a pause, he continued: 'You are on an exclusive list of high-worth individuals – did you know that? High-worth individuals deserve the very best. The most exclusive deals, the most personal attention. That's why we want to offer you a personalized financial advice service . . .'

And on and on it went, until Jed was handing Mrs Kirkton back over to Amber to take down the details of where to send the contracts, mouthing: 'Forty-one seconds' and tapping at his watch.

Amber wrote down Mrs Kirkton's details and wondered if Mrs Kirkton of Timpany, Connecticut had even the slightest idea of what she was signing up for. This service was going to cost her 6 per cent a year of her savings, before it even made her a penny.

And this totally legitimate *stealing* was going on all around her.

Suddenly she thought of Ori Kogon and the jewellery store. At least he'd been insured when the thieves got to him – better protected than poor Mrs Kirkton.

She wanted to leave. She wanted to walk right up to Jed, throw her laminated pass at him and tell him to carry right on ripping people off without her. But she'd looked at her bank account before she came to work this morning and it told her that she needed this job for now. Even if she only made $40 a day, that was $200 a week. It would keep her almost afloat for just a little bit longer.

'Hi there, Mrs Kirkton, my name is Amber Jewel . . .' she said into the phone just as cheerfully as she could manage.

'Amber, I *love* him. I totally, totally love him and I think he feels the same way about me. Honestly, I know I can tell you this because you won't laugh, but I think . . . well, who knows, but by Christmas we might even be engaged. Really!'

Amber held the phone to her head as, tired and demoralized, she clicked off the TV and pulled up the blanket she'd thrown over herself as she lay on the couch. Damn, it was cold inside and out now. Real cold. Like nothing she'd ever felt before at home in Texas.

*Engaged?!* It was a little difficult to take Sapphire seriously. She'd only met Fergus a couple of weeks ago, and already she was picking out her bouquet . . . again. She had been exactly the same – way-too-crazy-too-early – about Forde Houghton, and look how that had ended.

Amber felt guilty. She wished she'd made more effort to get to know Fergus that night she'd been out with them. Here was her little sister staying over with him, thinking engagement rings, happy-ever-after – and who was he? What was he like? Amber had no idea.

And she should, because after the Forde fiasco Sapphire needed help making decisions like this.

'You should see how he's fixed up his place,' Sapphire added. 'I'm there right now.'

'Where is he?' Amber wondered.

'He's gone out to get us something to eat. His room is just so cute. He has plaid rugs on his bed and photographs of his family dog. She's a golden retriever called Biscuit. Isn't that so nice? His wardrobe is full of all the kinds of things a real British gentleman has, Amber. He's like my very own Cary Grant.'

Amber thought of Fergus, big, blond and blushy, and tried to stifle a giggle.

'What kinds of things? Swords? Shields? The family crest?' she joked.

'Tweed jackets . . . bow ties . . . a tartan dressing gown . . . ooh, and gorgeous leather brogues.'

'What?'

'Shoes. Plus he's got one of those tortoiseshell hair-brushes without handles.' Sapphire's voice dropped to a whisper, 'He's the one, Amber, I just know that he's the one.'

'Based on his choice of hairbrush?!'

'He's British. I love the idea of marrying someone

British. Imagine what Edinburgh must be like. So beautiful. So old. So *historic.*'

'But engagements, baby. Marriage?! What's the rush? So soon after—'

'Don't mention that beast!' Sapphire hissed.

'You can go visit Edinburgh, you can even move there if you like. No one says you have to marry the guy first.'

Amber carried the phone over to the kitchenette. There was a carton of Chinese in the fridge that she could try and bring back to life in the microwave.

'I really hope for your sake he's as good as he seems to be,' she told Sapphire, making a mental note to check this guy out properly. The next time she met him, she would only drink coffee, he'd not be allowed to bring some preppy roomie and she'd interview him thoroughly.

As Amber crouched down to open the fridge door, something *scuttled* right there in front of her eyes.

She shrieked and dropped her cell. The animal scuttled some more.

She stood up quickly and there, running across the countertop, was a small brown rat. Oh, man! Definitely a rat. Small, yes. But with a long thick tail – much bigger than a mouse.

'Amber? What is it?!' Sapphire shouted down the line.

Amber picked up the cell again. 'Sapphire, we have a rat. A badass rat. No kidding. Absolutely straight as a fast trip to the outhouse.'

Sapphire gave a strangled sob. 'You need to leave the apartment. You can't stay there on your own with a rat! When is Em back?'

'Soon. Look, I'm sure I can manage. It's just one night. OK? We'll get some kinda rat catcher in tomorrow morning. First thing.'

'But you're at work.'

'I'll quit. It's terrible, by the way; I hate every moment of it. It's all about selling totally inappropriate financial products to patsies. It stinks.'

'But, Amb . . . if you don't have a job, how will we make the rent? Isn't it better to have a bad job than no job?'

Amber let out a sigh. 'I don't know,' she admitted, feeling close to tears. 'But I do know that I can't go out and do that all day and then come home to rats. Can things get any worse?'

'Yup,' Sapphire replied. 'Don't forget Mother's coming to town.'

Em came home from the nightclub an hour later with a bottle of pre-mixed Mai Tais and a bulging bag of food.

Even though it was late, she insisted on serving out big portions of the delicious Thai chicken dish and pouring the two of them generous glasses of cocktail mix.

'What is in this?' Amber asked after a sip.

'Rum and more rum and a whole load of other happy-making ingredients. Drink up!'

'We have rats,' Amber told her once they were settled on the couch, facing each other, plates of food in their laps, blanket over their legs.

'Who cares? We're about to get evicted.'

'Huh?'

What had Em done now?

'I've been carrying this around in my bag,' Em said, and tossed her a crumpled envelope. 'Didn't want to show you until you'd got a new job. Thought you might completely freak out on me . . . it's an eviction notice. Our landlord knows I'm still here, Amber, even though you told him it was just temporary.'

'You have got to be joking me,' Amber exclaimed. 'What does it say?'

'That you are subletting, in breach of contract, blah, blah, blah and we've all got to be out by December 24th.'

'Christmas Eve?! Well, that is a nice touch.'

For several minutes Amber chewed, thought, then took a hefty swig of Mai Tai.

'We're not going to be able to stay in Manhattan, you know that, don't you?' she told Em. 'We can't share another two-bed the size of a box of matches and there isn't anything with three beds this side of the Brooklyn Bridge that we can afford.'

Em shrugged, took a few more mouthfuls and said: 'I've been thinking and thinking. I've been doing so much thinking my brain hurts.'

'Yeah . . . what about?'

'About how terrible your clothes are for one, Miss Amber Jewel. I mean, good grief, if you're not wearing jeans and a plaid shirt, you're walking around in some saggy sack of a pantsuit looking like you should be answering the phone at the Parker County municipal offices. In fact, the girls who answer the phone there are waaaay more glamorous than you right now. I mean, no make-up, no nails . . .' Em pointed her fork in the direction of Amber's head. 'And when did you last get a haircut? You do not look like you was born and raised in Texas.'

'Yeah well, I've been busy . . . and . . . kinda depressed,' Amber said defensively.

'Yeah well – you need a scrub up and I might just get started on you tomorrow. I've been touring the shops, I have some new things. But I'm not telling you about that now. What I want to know is: how much money do you think a girl needs?'

'For what?'Amber asked.

'Needs to live on for the rest of her life. You must know – I mean, you worked with all those fancy clients who had so much money in the bank that they never needed to do another day's work. How much does that take?'

'Em, I thought you'd given up on your dream of a starring role,' Amber said gently. 'So you don't need to worry about never working again – it ain't gonna happen.'

'I know, but how much would it take?'

'Well . . . it depends. How much money would you like to have every year?'

'Say . . . $70,000 a year.'

Amber spluttered her drink. 'That's a lot.'

'Yeah, well, how much would I have to have in the bank to have $70,000 coming to me every year?' Em insisted.

'OK . . . well . . . if you wanted to have $70,000 a year just in interest you'd need to have a million dollars in the bank earning you 7 per cent a year. That way, you don't need to touch your million, you're just living off the money it makes. Seven per cent a year isn't exactly easy to make, by the way, but with a million in the bank you'd be able to make the right kind of investments. You'd want a spread between safe, guaranteed and slightly higher risk,' she added.

'Getting a little too technical for me there,' Em said, 'but basically, if I have one million dollars in the bank, I get to live off $70,000 a year without raising a finger.'

'Yeah.'

'A million dollars in the bank . . .' Em repeated. She drained her glass and reached over for the bottle. 'We're going to have one more, right?'

'I'm supposed to be back at my wonderful, fulfilling, totally inspiring new job tomorrow,' Amber said, putting her hand over the glass.

'C'mon,' Em urged, 'you said it was terrible and you were going to quit.'

'I know but . . . the apartment . . .'

Em nudged her hand aside and refilled her glass before she could protest.

Halfway down her third top-up of Mai Tai mix, Em exclaimed, 'So if we had *three* million dollars, we'd all be able to live on $70,000 a year without having to worry about making another dollar ever again!'

'Yeah,' Amber laughed, 'so if you could just sort that out for us, Em. Obviously, we'd have to pay taxes – unless you were planning to move us to a tax haven – and could that be somewhere sunny, please, because it's real cold out and I am not loving it.'

'Maybe . . .' Em took another sip of her drink, then her green eyes glittered at Amber just like a cat's.

'Maybe I'm planning something big, something real big . . . maybe I'm planning a way for all three of us to live happily ever after.'

'But *you* don't do planning,' Amber reminded her.

She felt warm and fuzzy with the alcohol now. 'I'm the planner. You're the crazy, reckless, impulsive one.'

'Exactly,' Em said, *'you're* the planner, Amber; Sapphire has the *in* and I am the reckless one who'll walk on the wild side to get what I want.'

'What the freak are you talking about now?' Amber asked with a sigh. It was late and Em was getting trashed.

'We have the whole set-up. The three sisters can all come together for this. We are all in position and you and Sapphire don't even know it yet.' Em was smiling at her, talking in a whisper, eyes still glittering in the low light. 'It's like a sign, Amber. The perfect trio. I think this was meant to be. This is our Plan C.'

'Em, you have lost the plot. What the freak are you talking about?' Amber repeated.

Em leaned right in close and in the lowest possible whisper, only just audible to Amber, she said, 'We're supposed to steal the jewels.'

'Huh?!'

'The Duchess of Windsor's jewels. We're *supposed* to steal them from the auction house, sell them to a collector and all live happily ever after.'

Amber burst out laughing.

'Bedtime,' she said in her best big sister voice. She stood up and helped Em from the couch. 'Brush your teeth and go to bed, baby girl. I'm sure you're gonna feel a whole lot more sober in the morning.'

# Chapter Fourteen

*'He said he would take her to the Bahamas for her birthday.'*

*'Oh dear!'*

*'I know, she was so hoping he'd take her to Cartier.'*

The next morning, when Amber opened her eyes, the clock showed she'd overslept by almost an hour. She sat up, felt her forehead throb and remembered the Mai Tai mix with a shudder.

Just like that, she knew that she wasn't going back to Jed's broiler house. There had to be other ways to make a living – there just had to be!

Right now she had to get up, swallow a Tylenol and figure out what to do with her life.

It was silent in the apartment. Sapphire hadn't come home and Em had already left for her boutique job.

Amber stepped out of her bedroom and saw a chair had been placed in front of her door. The note taped to it read: *'This is for you, Missy Amber. Slip it on and let it change your life. Em.'*

There, hanging on the back of the chair was a snow-white fur jacket. A *real* fur jacket? Could it be? Wasn't white fur *ermine*?

Amber couldn't resist running her hands over the soft-as-snow collar. It definitely felt real. Just how much could this piece have cost? Amber had no idea. Had Em bought it? Did she have that amount of room on her credit card?

Or had Em *stolen* it?

If Em had stolen a real fur jacket, possibly worth thousands of dollars, then Em was headed for trouble. Sooner rather than later.

Amber picked the jacket up and couldn't resist slipping her arms into the satin-lined sleeves.

Oh my gosh.

It fitted perfectly. She felt the soft whisper of fur stroke at her wrists and she pulled the collar tightly up at her neck. Glancing over at the mirror, she saw how glamorous she looked even with mussed hair and jammies.

She picked up her cell and texted Em: Did u steal this jckt?

A few moments later came the reply: Brrwed not stolen! Enjoy! Do not wear with jeans!

Back in her bedroom, Amber tried to pick out an outfit to go with the jacket. It had been a long time since she'd had to think about what to wear, because every weekday she wore her office clothes and every weekend she wore jeans and cycled over to her gardening volunteer work.

So now, when she looked in her wardrobe for something interesting to wear with an ermine jacket . . . nothing exactly leapt out.

There was a silky navy-blue blouse with frills way back there. Something Mother had given her last Christmas, but she'd still never worn it. Maybe it would go with an ermine jacket.

Nothing else in the wardrobe looked like an obvious fit. Should she go look in Em's cupboard? There might be a skirt – one that wasn't too tight or too short. Em would have the right kind of boots too. Em's feet were a whole size smaller than Amber's but the jacket didn't look like it wanted comfortable shoes.

In Em's tiny closet, Amber found a bright-blue wool pencil skirt which looked about knee length and some lace-up high-heeled black boots. As she considered the boots, Amber wondered what she was thinking. What was really different about today? The only different thing – and it wasn't good – was that she was going to quit a job and start looking again. Would it be easier to look for a job in a pencil skirt and fur jacket?

Skirt and boots in her hands, Amber was heading out of the room when she saw the computer print-outs on Em's untidy side table.

The top one was a copy of a small news item about how the Duchess's jewels might be coming up for sale again at an 'as yet unnamed New York auction house'.

Amber leafed through the other pages. Em had been doing research late last night and she'd found other news stories about the Royal jewels. Circled in bright-red pen was the headline COLLECTORS SPEND MILLIONS IN DUCHESS FRENZY. There was a grainy black and white picture of a brooch which was hard to make out.

Amber set the pages down again, feeling uneasy, but she reminded herself that Em was an impulsive, occasional shoplifter. She was not a real thief. She was not a criminal. Whatever she'd said about stealing the jewels last night was a joke. And if Em was obsessing slightly about the Duchess of Windsor and her jewellery, it was only because Em was going through a difficult time right now.

Back in her bedroom, Amber put on the silky blouse, the pencil skirt, breathing in to get the zipper done up, then the boots and finally the jacket.

She looked in the mirror and laughed. It was too much. She didn't look like herself at all. But maybe that was fun for today. In fact, the jacket still begged for more, so she took dangling gold earrings from her jewellery roll. Earrings she could remember wearing only once before. Then she brushed her hair, pulled it back in a tight ponytail and added a slick of berry-coloured lip gloss.

Amber gave her reflection a sophisticated smile. Now she looked much more Manhattan: Upper East Side, to be exact.

'Hi, I'm Amber Jewel,' she told the mirror.

'Hello there, my name is Philippa de Clavel,' she tried out – wondering why that name had leapt into her head. She giggled at herself.

Switching on her cell, she decided to get the difficult call of the day over with as soon as possible. 'Hi, could I speak with Jed, please?' She stroked at the jacket for comfort as she waited and felt her heart thud.

'Good morning,' Jed's voice came on the line.

'Hi, Jed, it's Amber Jewel . . .'

'Now, please don't be calling to tell me you're sick. I know I was a little rough on you yesterday, but the first few days are the toughest. You'll get there.'

'No, I'm not sick. I quit,' Amber said simply.

'You quit? You can't quit on my ass, I've spent hours training you.' Jed sounded angry now.

'I can. I quit.'

'We can't pay you for the time you've worked.'

'Of course you can, I'll send in an invoice,' she said in a voice so firm, she startled herself. Maybe this was the jacket talking

'Good luck with that!' Jed snapped and slammed down the phone.

Well, she hadn't expected it to be pleasant.

She stalked to the kitchenette and made herself a small instant coffee. Then she turned on her laptop, wrote out an invoice, emailed it to Jed's office and included the line, 'Payment within 30 days or legal action will be started.'

The big bully. Of course he had to pay her the lousy little amount for the work she'd done. It would just about cover her train fare to Hoboken and back.

Amber went through her email and searched all her top job-hunt websites; there were some new opportunities, new companies to write to – it didn't look so hopeless. It really did not. Then, not long after 9 a.m., she decided to go out and get something for breakfast.

On 17th Street, Amber suddenly felt very conscious of her new outfit. The boots were difficult to walk in, the skirt made her steps too short and as for the jacket – the jacket was so showy, it just about made her blush.

What if Em *had* stolen it? What if there were photos of this jacket on the news? Everyone she passed seemed to be looking at the jacket with way too much interest.

The lights were on in Ori's store and for the first time since the robbery, a small display of jewellery had been set up in the window, although the marionette burglars had gone.

Amber decided she had to go in.

Inside, she could see that the store had been tidied up and repainted. New cases were in place and a new clock was up on the wall.

'Hi, it looks great in here,' Amber told Ori who was standing behind his counter looking through a brochure. 'Looks as if nothing ever happened.'

'Hello, Miss Amber! Now you keep thinking like that. I'm going to keep thinking like that too. We cannot let those bastards take away our peace of mind, our inner serenity. Right?'

He gave a quick smile.

'So you've re-stocked?' she asked, taking a look round the store. There was much less jewellery on display than before. 'Have they found any of the jewellery that got stolen?'

'Nothing. Those jerks even took the specially commissioned puppets! The only thing I've had back is the diamond stud posted into my mailbox by your sister. She's a very sweet girl. Not many people would have done that.'

'No, but Sapphire is straighter than straight,' Amber agreed. 'How will you get back everything you lost?' she wondered. 'Is there some kind of register of lost jewels?'

'Yeah, I guess so. But I don't know if the kind of people those guys sell to will be checking it much. They'll probably offload my beautiful stuff for about one quarter of what it's worth. That's what the detective said. Breaks my heart. All my beautiful, responsibly sourced South African diamonds. Those creeps will turn three mill into $500,000. The guy with the gun will probably make $350,000, the young one maybe $150,000. They're probably giving the stuff away. Some Bronx babe is walking about right now with a $100,000 diamond round her neck and she don't even know it. Breaks my heart,' he repeated. 'Wanna low-fat cream-cheese bagel? There are two inside this bag.'

'No, I'm good, thanks. So you gave up the knishes?' she asked with a smile.

'I'm on the healthy heart programme. Following every one of the doctor's orders.'

'Good for you.'

'Are you and your sister OK?' Ori asked. 'You look OK. In fact you look good, by the way. Nice jacket.'

'Oh . . .' Amber was so unused to getting this kind of compliment that for a moment she didn't know what to say. 'Thanks,' she managed, 'we're fine. But it might be a while before we go shopping for jewellery again.'

Ori shook his head vigorously. 'No. You guys come in when I'm fully stocked up and I'm gonna do ya a once in a lifetime deal. You had an influence. Who knows how it might have gone if you two hadn't been here? I could be dead, instead of getting heart healthy.'

He patted his chest.

'That's real nice of you. I'll make sure Sapphire knows. Are you covered? I mean, are you going to get all your money back?'

'Almost. There's a big excess: $200,000. But the insurance is pretty much going to give me $1.3 mill.'

'I thought you lost $3 mill?'

'Retail. Three mill retail equals $1.5 million to me.'

'Right.'

'And what about you? Are you sure you're OK?'

'Totally fine. Sapphire seems good too.'

'Well, I want you both to come back and look again.'

'Thanks,' Amber smiled. 'We'll think about it.'

'You need some nice diamonds to go with that fancy jacket. Is that ermine?' he asked.

'Oh, I don't know . . .' she patted her arm, unsure. 'It was a . . . gift. From my mother.'

'Well, you must be one very special daughter. But I know that already.'

'I guess I should go now . . . you take care of yourself and I'll let Sapphire know what you said,' Amber added as she pulled open the door.

Walking away in the unfamiliar heels, she looked down to make sure she didn't trip over some bump in the sidewalk.

'Whoa! Take it easy . . . oh – Miss Amber?'

The person she'd nearly smacked right into was holding her at arm's length. She looked up and saw Detective Jack Desmoine. His face broke into an amused smile.

'Sorry,' she apologized. 'I wasn't looking.'

'No! You in a hurry? Going somewhere nice?'

'Just going to grab some coffee.'

'Well let me buy you that coffee, then.'

'Really?'

'Sure. Why not?'

'Aren't you on your way to see Ori?'

'Yeah, but I'm kinda early. And if I don't drink at least one coffee every hour, I turn into a werewolf – or is it a pumpkin? I don't know, I've never left it that long.'

Amber couldn't help breaking into a slight smile.

'C'mon. Never turn down a free coffee. What's this place like?' He gestured to the Dainty Cupcake Cafe across the road which was pink and white and all about beautifully decorated delicate lactose and wheat-free cupcakes which came in at around 85 calories each.

'No,' she shook her head, 'you look more like a Muffin Bakery kinda guy.'

'Ha . . .' he narrowed his eyes. 'Are you making assumptions about me, Miss Amber? That's my job. I'm the detective, remember. But yes, the Muffin Bakery sounds good.'

It took several minutes to walk there, during which Amber struggled with the heels and the skirt while she let Desmoine update her with the robbery news – not that there really was any.

Faced with the overwhelming array of treats in the bakery, the detective managed to narrow it down to three muffins for himself, then insisted Amber have white choc-chip with blueberry and not the breakfast bran she'd chosen.

He paid for everything, despite the obvious smart of pain on his face.

'Phew! Midtown prices. Almost as bad as uptown now,' he said, settling in a chair across the little table from her.

'Do you work all over Manhattan, Detective Desmoine?'

He smiled at this. 'It's OK, you can call me Jack. But I'm going to carry on calling you Miss Amber.

Cos I kinda like it. I think it suits you.'

'Jack . . .'

She liked that name. It suited him.

'Yeah . . . all over Manhattan,' he answered her question. 'Depends on the crime. I have some special areas of interest.'

'So nothing on the guys who did the jewellery store?'

'Not yet. But we got a bullet, which is always helpful, and we're keeping a close eye on several jewel stores in less dazzling neighbourhoods.'

'Ori, Mr Kogon, said those guys would only sell what they stole for one quarter of what it's worth.'

'Yeah, if they're lucky,' Jack said, taking a big bite of muffin. 'Mmmm. Fantastic.' After several chews, he added: 'Unless it's a real collector's item, you take a big, big loss on the value of stolen jewellery. Not that I'm advising it as a business plan,' he joked. 'How are you and your sister doing? Not too traumatized? Not planning on suing Ori's insurers for compensation? That happens these days.'

'Gosh no. No, we're fine.'

'How did your boyfriend take it? Was he comforting?'

'What? Oh – I don't have one.'

'Right . . .' He paused at this information, then asked, 'Any sign of a job yet?'

'Well, I had one, but it only lasted a day.'

Jack's eyebrows rose, thick caterpillar brows that stood out against his pale skin. The eyes beneath the brows were intelligent-looking and didn't leave her face. Amber's first impression of him had been that he wasn't the sharpest knife in the drawer, but now that she looked into his face more carefully, she knew she'd been wrong. She suspected the mind behind those eyes was rarely at rest. 'How come?' he asked, taking another big bite.

'How come what?'

Distracted, she'd forgotten what they'd been talking about.

'Your job only lasted a day,' he said, smiling at her.

'Oh, it was a terrible job, selling cheap shares to people who thought they had a clue. Making money for the bosses and ripping the clients off.'

'Ha.' Jack gave a shrug. 'Isn't that capitalism?'

'It isn't what I want to do.'

'What do you want to do?'

It was Amber's turn to shrug. 'Get back into asset management, I guess.'

'What is that? Looking after other people's money for them? The kind of people who have so much money they don't even know what to do with it? Sounds like a nice problem to have.'

'I guess. Life sure seems a lot easier when you have lots of money.'

Jack shook his head and tossed the remains

of muffin number one into his mouth. 'Nah. The suicide rate you would not believe. Then the wrangling, even the murders over the inheritance. The rich have just as many problems as us. Maybe even more.'

'Well, it doesn't look like that from where I'm standing.'

'You've lost your job. It's a tough time. But you seem like a smart girl, a determined girl.' Jack went on, 'Did they fire you because you spent way too much time thinking for yourself instead of thinking for them?'

'Ha! Something like that.'

Amber looked down at her blueberry muffin and broke off a small corner. She began to chew it thoughtfully.

'What is this jacket you're wearing? Are you off somewhere fancy? I'm not sure if I get you in this jacket. You look like a jeans, plaid shirt and Stetson kinda girl.'

'It didn't go well the last time I wore a Stetson,' she told him, smiling.

'I bet you look good in a Stetson. So what's with the jacket? Are you trying out the Park Avenue Princess look?'

He reached over and touched her sleeve. She started slightly. 'No. Em dared me to wear it for a day. She said it would change my life.'

Now it was Jack's turn to laugh. 'Is it working yet?'

Amber found herself laughing back.

He had cute little dimples at the side of his smile and one of those little scoop-outs on his chin. She hadn't noticed that before. Must be hell to shave. She realized with a burst of surprise that while she wasn't sure if she even liked Detective call-me-Jack Desmoine, she was definitely attracted to him.

An unexpected little crush. It was kind of exciting, she hadn't had a crush for a long time now. Did the cop have a crush on her? She was desperate to find out. Sapphire thought he liked her – but did he? *Really?*

'Has this jacket changed my life? I dunno,' she answered him with a smile, 'it's only 10.40.'

'It looks cute,' Jack offered, 'but I think you need to figure yourself out a little. I guess that's what being twenty-four is all about.'

'How do you know . . . ?'

'I have your date of birth on file, remember.'

'Right.' Amber felt a little too scrutinized. She leaned back in her chair.

'So you grew up on a ranch?' he asked. 'Now that's unusual, I don't come across many witnesses who grew up on a ranch.'

'In Manhattan, I guess not.'

'Is it one of those ranches that's been in the family

for generations? Did some young gun stake his claim back in the 1800s and Jewels have been there ever since?'

Amber shook her head. 'No. It's better than that. My daddy won the ranch in a card game.'

Jack rolled his eyes and laughed. 'Now that is good. That's real Wild West. When and how did this happen?'

Amber looked Jack in the eye. The story was well known amongst friends and family back home, but it wasn't something she'd ever told a stranger.

'Go on,' he said, voice teasing and low, 'I won't tell anyone.'

His friendly eyes were on hers, inspiring her trust.

'Well . . . I was two years old, Sapphire was on the way and my daddy was just another ranch hand, real good with cattle, smart on a horse, but with no land of his own,' she began.

'His boss was a gambler who loved to drink and one night, when my daddy stayed stone cold sober, the stakes grew higher and higher until the whole ranch was on the table. And my daddy won.'

Jack gave a low whistle.

'Poker?' he asked.

'Texas hold'em.'

Jack smiled at Amber, drained his coffee cup, then said, 'Now, that's the best story I'm going to hear all day. He won the ranch in a card game. Huh.'

He looked at his watch. 'I have to go,' he told her. 'Ori will be waiting for his progress report.'

Amber felt sorry that he couldn't stay, but, determined not to let her disappointment show, she pointed to the third, untouched muffin on his plate and said, 'They'll wrap that for you.'

'Right. I could give it to Ori as a peace offering since I don't have much to tell him.' He picked up the plate and for a moment seemed unsure what to say.

'Thanks for mine,' Amber said, pointing at her half-eaten muffin.

'Any time. So, Miss Amber – can I call ya?'

# Chapter Fifteen

*'I think we know just what kind of people we are dealing with, Lauren.'*

*'Oh yes. The kind that have to* buy *their furniture. There's not one dime of old money there.'*

'Blue Italian Spode!' Sapphire held the dainty little side plate in her hand and gazed down at the painted scene. 'They have *Spode*. This is the china I want to eat from for the rest of my life. I still can't believe I had to send it all back.'

The sisters were in Barneys department store right on Madison. It was open late and they were supposed to be Christmas shopping but no one had actually bought any gifts yet.

This was Em's idea. She and Amber had collected Sapphire from work and walked her from the Upper East Side to here, marvelling at every beautiful store window on the way.

They'd gazed at vintage diamond necklaces in the antique jewellery boutiques. Sapphire had stopped to admire oil paintings in the art galleries. And once they were on Fifth Avenue, every window was more tempting than the last. They window-shopped jewels, Louis Vuitton handbags and designer outfits worth thousands of dollars. Now Em was leading them through the luxurious homewares section of Barneys.

'Which ones were your crystal glasses?' Em asked, walking towards the wall of stemware.

'Oh!' Sapphire hurried over. 'There they are!' she exclaimed with a sigh of loss.

'Those are so, *so* beautiful,' Em said, lifting one of the delicate crystal wine glasses and holding it up.

Sapphire took it from her hand and gazed at it wistfully. 'I should be in my wonderful home, serving chilled white wine to my dinner guests . . . I'd even planned to be pregnant by now.'

'Jeeez, give it up, Sapphire,' Amber complained. 'You'd be married to that jerk who wouldn't be back at the beautiful home yet because he'd have a little business to attend to in a motel room on the way home from work.'

'Ouch!' Em said, giving Amber a dig in the ribs. 'You don't need a husband to have a beautiful life full of beautiful things, Sapph, you just need money.

Lots and lots of money. Let's go get something to eat here. My treat.'

'Your treat?' Amber asked. 'You quit your play and you can definitely not afford to buy us dinner here.'

'I have two jobs and I have plastic. I don't need the play – and anyhow, you bought most of the cocktails the other night. Now it's my turn.'

Em chose sparkling wine to go with the meal and when she'd made Sapphire and Amber drink a second glass, she began to talk about money again.

'So you, Sapphire, would like a beautiful house, full of beautiful things. If you were rich you could buy the crystal glasses, the Spode china, plus you could unpack all that silverware that's been accumulating since you were eight and start using it. Imagine! If you were rich, you could start living the way you wanted to live without having to wait for Mr Right.'

Em turned to Amber. 'Imagine being rich enough to solve all our problems – even Mother's. Imagine it, Amber. You could do anything you wanted to do. You could be exactly the kind of person you wanted to be, without a single self-help book, if you could just get your hands on the money. It's only money . . . but it could set us all free.'

There was an intensity to Em's look which was making Amber uneasy.

Sapphire giggled. 'Antique jewellery experts don't earn that much. And they never will earn that much.'

'But they could . . .' Em hinted.

'Oh man, Em, you're not going to start up with the crazy Plan C idea again, are you?' Amber asked.

'What do you mean?' Sapphire asked, looking up.

'Sapphire, you know which jewels are the most important and the most desirable,' Em began. 'You know the names of *all* the important collectors. Plus you're right there, you work at the auctioneers,' she went on, her voice low but perfectly clear. 'You're an *insider*.'

Sapphire just looked at Em blankly. 'What in the heck are you talking about?' she asked.

'Do you never feel tempted to *take* anything from Wilson's, Sapphire?'

Amber rolled her eyes. This was nuts. Em had always been pretty wacky and way out there, but this was *nuts*.

As Sapphire finally understood what Em was trying to tell her, her face flooded with astonishment.

'Stealing??!' she hissed. 'You want *me* to *steal* things from my work so that you can sell them?'

Em began to protest, 'Well, not exactly . . . in fact . . . not even you—'

'But what else can you mean, *exactly*?' Sapphire demanded.

'I've been thinking about it. I've been thinking about it a lot,' Em began, topping up Sapphire's glass. Her sister just glared at the wine. 'I'm the thief,' Em continued. 'I steal stuff all the time. I shoplift. I'm good at it. I've never been caught. Amber is the money girl. She knows all about "International Financial Transactions" otherwise known as: moving big sums of money about. You're the insider, Sapphire. You just need to tell me when to be where. That's all. That is all!'

Excitement flashed over Em's face as she added, 'We can do this, Sapphire, and you can have everything you've ever wanted. You will never have to work again. We'll solve Mother's mortgage problems – and we'll all live happily ever after.'

Then, trying not to sound too cynical, she added, 'Without having to find a handsome prince.'

Sapphire looked at Em, then at Amber.

'Em?' Amber decided it was time to get one thing clear. 'Are you on drugs?'

Em laughed. She threw her head back and gave a tinkly, slightly scary little laugh, which Amber found just as frightening as the thought that her sister might have chemically altered her mind.

'No,' Em said, her laugh stopping abruptly, her eyes now darting between her two sisters, 'I'm on fire.'

Sapphire's jaw dropped a little.

But if Em thought she was somehow softening, Em thought wrong.

Sapphire drew her mouth into a tight line, and

took in a breath. 'Never!' she exclaimed. 'I will never, ever be involved with stealing anything. Count me out. Forget about it. What are you thinking, Em? I mean, we watched a robbery, me and Amber. Someone held a gun to my head, shot at the owner and raided the whole place. That's what stealing is, Em. Now the police are after them.'

'I'm not talking about a robbery or guns!' Em protested. 'Just shoplifting. Very upscale shoplifting.'

Sapphire shook her head.

'What would Mother think?' she asked. 'Or Daddy? Bless his soul. Or Fergus?' Nostrils flaring, she added, 'Or Princess Grace?! Stealing is just not something Princess Grace would or could ever do.'

# Chapter Sixteen

*'If only your mother could be more like my mother, Lauren.'*

*'What? Dead?'*

*'Exactly.'*

'Why, hello there, mister. I am Mrs Howard Jewel from Bluff Dale Valley, Parker County, Texas, and we will be requiring another pitcher of margaritas.'

Amber looked over at Em and rolled her eyes. Their mother was in New York and still introducing herself as Mrs Howard Jewel of Bluff Dale, Parker County.

However, at the Astoria, with its Junior League floor, the staff must be used to this kind of Southern belle behaviour.

The first pitcher was already empty, making the

mother and daughters reunion much less spiky than it might otherwise have been. Although Amber didn't feel nearly as tanked up as she'd like to be for the inevitable career discussion to follow.

Mrs Howard Jewel – 'Mother' to her daughters, Ruby to anyone who'd either been to school with her, or known her for longer than twenty years – was enthroned on an over-upholstered hotel chair.

She was over-upholstered herself. A lifetime of Southern eating will do that to all but the most severely disciplined, but Mother wore her red silk kaftan-style dress with aplomb and a generous selection of impressive gold jewellery.

'So what was I saying? Oh yes . . . even Mrs David Wetherstone of the Creek Estate Wetherstones has not been able to save her beautiful house from the ravages of commercialism. She is going to have to open her doors from May through September to paying guests. Apparently the roof needs replacing and it's going to cost hundreds of thousands of dollars that the Wetherstones just don't have. But there's no question of selling the house, she told me. Wetherstones have lived there for five generations.'

'Is she going to dress up like Scarlett O'Hara and give the tourists the authentic *Gone With The Wind* experience?' Em asked with a smirk.

'Scarlett no, but there is talk of meeting the visitors in a ball gown and treating them to an old-fashioned

Southern afternoon tea,' Mother replied. 'So, do you know who I bumped into at the club just the other week?' she asked, as the waiter approached, took away her used glass and poured a large measure of margarita into a fresh new one.

'Thank you most kindly, sir. Well, it was Suzy. You know my old friend Suzy Tellman. She told me that Minty Clayton, you know, of the Paradise Golf Club Claytons, is going to marry—'

Here she broke off and patted Sapphire's arm sympathetically. Immediately all three sisters understood.

'Forde Houghton.'

'Minty?' Amber gasped.

'She's only eighteen!' Em squeaked.

'Is Forde getting married?' Sapphire asked, sounding a little bewildered. 'You think he might have tried to tell me. Himself.'

'Apparently Minty is twenty. So he's only eight years older. But after what happened to Sapphire, you'd think certain families might want to be a little more careful with their precious youngest daughters,' Mother sniffed. 'I mean there's tacky . . . and there's *tacky, tacky.*'

There it was, the ultimate insult: tacky, tacky.

Mother was still not done with that Forde Houghton. He had humiliated her daughter, and therefore her, in the most public way possible. She would never, ever forgive him. And she would certainly never let anyone who was anyone in Parker County society think that she had ever forgiven him.

'Well, good luck, Minty,' Em said, holding up her glass. 'I hope she's done something to deserve all the bad shit that's coming her way.'

Mother glared. She didn't need to give her swearing lecture, they'd heard it so many times before.

'Sorry, but this is New York,' Em said quickly.

'When you come home, you cannot use language like that,' Mother exclaimed, 'or you will be discussed.'

'That's all I want out of life, Mother,' Em replied, in deepest Texan drawl. 'To be discussed.'

'Oh you don't need to worry about that. All three of you are being deeply, deeply discussed already.'

'Fergus!' Sapphire said, jumping up from her seat in excitement as her brand-new boyfriend walked in through the door of the bar. 'Mother, Em – this is Fergus.'

After Fergus had given Sapphire a gentle kiss on the lips, he shook hands with her sisters and then, with much gracious attention, with her mother.

'Lovely to meet you, Mrs Jewel. Sapphire's told me so much about you.'

A glass was brought, filled to the brim and quickly refilled as he told them all about himself and his journey from University in Edinburgh, Scotland, to New York, via work stints in London and Hong Kong.

'I'm crazy about Sapphire,' he was telling Mother. 'She is the sweetest girl I've ever met.'

'Do you think he's for real?' Em whispered to Amber.

'If he is, then he's perfect for Sapphire,' Amber pointed out.

'I'm not sure he can keep up with Mother on the cocktail drinking front.'

'Who can?'

The sisters watched how happy Sapphire was in the presence of Fergus.

'He seems really, genuinely nice,' Amber whispered to Em.

'She deserves someone wonderful after what she's been through.'

'Hey, don't we all?' Amber joked, then added, 'If this guy does anything to hurt her, I'll kill him. We *should* have killed Forde.'

'Certain people,' Em reminded her with a dark look, 'decided to call off the revenge plan at the last moment.'

'I still think tarring, feathering and making someone walk down the high street naked is a little last century – maybe even a little century-before-that.'

Fergus and Mother were absorbed in a conversation about a Parker County family who had lived in Britain. Fergus listened at length but finally had to admit that no, he didn't think he knew them.

'I bet your mother wants you back in England,' Mother told him.

'Scotland,' he corrected her gently. 'My family lives in Edinburgh.'

'I want all my babies back in Texas,' Mother added, pulling a distraught face at her girls.

'Uh-oh,' Amber warned, 'here we go.'

'I could sort everything out just the way they want it. Amber could work at the Bank of America in Fort Worth . . .'

'I don't think so,' Amber protested. 'I did try for a long time to get a job in Texas, remember.'

'Em knows perfectly well she could star in every play she ever wanted to star in at the Fort Worth auditorium.'

'Oh, Lord!' Em exclaimed.

'Plus you'd make the cover of the *Parker County Magazine* at least once a quarter. I'd make sure of that. I know Verity Lane.'

'Oh please, Mother!' Em hissed.

'And Sapphire . . . well, for my lovely Sapphire,' Mother went on, patting Sapphire's hand fondly, 'I have any number of charming young men from proper, respectable families with bloodlines – but my Sapphire seems to be taking care of that side of things all by herself.' She smiled at Fergus approvingly.

'Simply wonderful,' Fergus replied, making an attempt to drain his second, or was it already third, glass of margarita, 'what a simply wonderful mother you have, Sapphire.'

'Are you OK?' Sapphire asked him with concern.

'Why? Do I not look OK?'

'No. You're pale,' Sapphire said.

'I've got a pounding headache. I'm not sure that whatever is in this glass is going down well.'

'For a British guy, you're not much of a drinker,' Em added.

'Honey, maybe it's time for him to take a cab home,' Amber suggested to Sapphire, wondering if Fergus had treated himself to a few glasses of Dutch courage before he got here.

'Fergus, would you like me to see you home?' Sapphire asked.

'No!' Fergus got up, but looked a little unsteady on his feet. 'I need to see *you* home, my lovely girl.'

'C'mon, let's get a cab,' she coaxed him and, after kissing Mother goodnight, she began to lead Fergus out of the hotel bar.

'Don't cross his threshold,' Mother called after her in a voice almost as slurred as Fergus's. 'Don't even cross the threshold and don't fall for that lie about a cup of coffee either. It's the oldest trick in the book.'

'Mother!' Amber scolded. 'We're in the Astoria bar. You will be discussed.'

'I do not want to be discussed,' Mother added much more quietly, 'but I think it still goes on. Even though we've had the ranch for over twenty years, in some places what your daddy did is still discussed.'

'What do you mean?' Amber asked.

'Well, you know all about the card game . . .'

'Of course,' Em said.

On the very rare occasions when Howard Jewel had retold the story to his daughters, he'd explained that he'd won the 600-hectare ranch with his friend Art Rigby because he was the only man not drinking, so his wits were sharp. He rarely touched a drop, plus he was good at maths, a card counter.

Just a few weeks after the game, Art had decided ranch-owning was not his plate of tacos and had made over his share to Howard. The Bluff Valley ranch had then been run by Howard until the day of his sudden death eighteen months ago.

'What happened to the owner? The man who lost the ranch to you?' Amber remembered asking her daddy.

'Drank himself to death,' had been the brief reply.

'Are people discussing the mortgage?' Amber asked her mother now. 'You know I won't be able to give you money for that this year. I'll go to the bank with you and we'll get it extended. I hope it won't be a problem.'

'I've known Wesley Crane at the bank since he was in diapers,' Mother said, as if that settled it. 'You will all still come home for Christmas, won't you? I booked those fares weeks ago for y'all.'

'Well, I guess so, but we have to find a new apartment first,' Amber said doubtfully.

'So what was being discussed? About Daddy?' Em asked to distract Mother from the Christmas line of questioning.

'I went to Art's funeral last week,' Mother began. 'I hadn't seen the Rigbys for years, but I heard Art had died and they came to your daddy's service so it seemed only right, and afterwards we were at the house, eating a beautiful chicken and green bean casserole . . .'

'The number one Southern funeral casserole dish,' Amber chipped in.

Mother flicked up her eyebrows and carried on.

'We were talking about the old days when . . . when . . . well, it all came up again.'

Amber and Em were startled when Mother suddenly gave a sob.

'What is it?' Amber said, reaching over to put a soothing hand on her mother's arm.

'Oh, it was all about the game – and how Howard and Art won the ranch between them. But then Art decided to give it all to Howard. There is still talk – all these years later – that Howard cheated and Art gave him the ranch because he didn't want any part in it.'

Amber slammed her drink down on the table. 'Who said that?' she stormed. 'When Daddy's not even here to defend himself!'

'Oh I don't know who started it, but somebody did and then everybody wanted to talk about it. *Is it true?* they were asking. *They're all dead now . . . the ranch is yours, you can tell us. Is it true that Howard cheated?*'

'And you told them *no*!' Amber exclaimed. She'd never heard anything about this before. She'd never known there was any kind of rumour about her daddy. It was so long ago. Her daddy had been running his ranch very successfully for twenty-two years when his good ol' heart had suddenly stopped beating.

'Of course I told them: no it wasn't true,' Mother said, her voice an agitated whisper now. She was in the bar of the Waldorf Astoria. This was not a place to make a scene.

Then she sat up, reached out her hand for her glass and took a steadying sip.

'But I need to share it with you,' she said, still whispering. 'I can't carry it on all alone. You see . . . Howard did cheat. He only ever told me once. But it's true. He cheated to win the ranch.'

# Chapter Seventeen

*'Oh, he was absolutely the perfect father.'*

*'He used to come to town twice a year, Christmas and her birthday, to take her shopping at Tiffany's.'*

Two hours later Amber was still crying, tucked up in her bedroom with her laptop on her knee as she read and reread her daddy's ranch blog online. Reading his thoughts, his observations on the cattle through the seasons, was the closest she would ever get now to a conversation with him.

Daddy had been a six foot three man-mountain, deeply tanned and so broad that when you put your arms around him, they barely made it round his back. His serious blue eyes were always scanning the horizon, the way a cattleman's do, constantly on the lookout for something.

But he *cheated*. He cheated to get his ranch!

It didn't matter what Mother had said to try and justify the crime: 'That ol boy who owned it, he was no good. He was drinking himself down and the ranch was going down with him. Your daddy had the sharp wits to win but only if he nudged the cards in the right direction.

'He never cheated at anything ever again in his life. He never played another card game. He was a straight man, Amber baby. He did the wrong thing, but for the right reason.'

Amber, lying in her bed, unemployed in New York, felt just as bereft and inconsolable tonight as on the day Em had called her at work with the news that Daddy had been found out in the fields, stone dead.

She remembered looking out of her office window, wondering why Em would pull such a sick joke on her. It had taken long, long minutes for the truth to settle down on her.

The worst days of Amber's entire life had followed and she just hoped she would never have to live through a death as shocking or devastating ever again.

Now, although it was well after midnight, there was a tap on her bedroom door.

She didn't answer.

'C'mon,' Em pleaded, 'I've made you a cup of coffee.'

'Decaf?'

'Yeah right, cos you're gonna be sleeping like a baby tonight.'

With this Em stepped into the room.

'Where's Sapphire?' Amber asked in a choked and tearful voice.

'She called. She's staying over. She thinks dream-boat is sick so she's watching him.'

'You didn't tell her though, did you?'

'No. But she should know. We can't keep it from her. It's part of the family story now.'

At this, Amber felt another sob well up in her throat. Em sat down on the edge of her bed and handed her a cup of milky coffee. Amber had to ask, 'How come you don't even seem upset?'

Em just smiled.

'Because I'm not upset,' she admitted, 'I'm re-lieved. I feel like this huge weight has been lifted off my shoulders.'

*'What?'*

'It's always so obvious what you and Sapphire got from Daddy. You're really smart and real good at maths, just like him. Sapphire, she's a sweet-natured, old-fashioned Texan, just like him. Me . . . I always wondered what it was about me that was like Daddy. Sometimes, I even wondered if we were related . . . or if Mother had strayed . . .'

'Em!'

'But it's true, I don't even look like you guys, I'm shorter and curvier and we're just . . . different.'

'Em,' Amber said, but with much more sympathy now, 'please don't think like that. Of course we're sisters.'

'But now . . . now I know that on those times when I'm prepared to walk on the wild side to get what I want, I'm just like my daddy.'

Amber might have protested, might have wanted to howl out her anger once again that Daddy had cheated, had based his whole success, his whole *life* on a lie. But when she looked at Em, she saw tears of happiness shining in her eyes and she couldn't bear to argue with her.

'I feel like this is the most important thing I've ever found out about Daddy,' Em said, 'or myself. He stole big, Amber. He cheated once and won himself a whole ranch. He always used to say, "Think big!"'

Amber nodded, 'But—'

'Now I see what he meant,' Em said and she had that excited, reckless look to her again, 'when I stole that jacket—'

'You said you borrowed it!'

'From the *universe*,' Em said with a shrug, as if that explained it. 'Do you know why I steal stuff? Because it's exciting, because it gives me a buzz. But until I took that jacket, I'd only stolen things that were small and unimportant – things that wouldn't get me in much trouble if I got caught. I took the jacket to test myself, to see if I could pull off something big.'

'Em, I feel a little scared for you. This is not thinking straight.'

'Don't be scared for me. I've found what I love to do! You know how I took that jacket? It was a rush . . . it was a blast! I went into the store and I played the part. I've seen enough of those Ladies Who Don't Work come in and act as if they own the place, so I turned myself into one of them. I went in, I looked around, I tried on a load of stuff. I worked the two assistants to death. Rode 'em ragged: "*Could you bring me that*", "*I'll try a size up*", "*Maybe try a size down*", "*Do you think this goes? Be a sweetheart and take the tag off, it's ruining the line.*" Then under a false name and number, I got them to put the two most expensive items on hold for me and I walked right out of the door with a $5,000 ermine jacket over my arm! How do you like that?'

'Not a lot, exactly. $5,000? Oh, Em . . .'

'All this time, I thought I wanted to do outrageous things on stage, but now I think it's much more of a rush to be daring and unique and outrageous in real life. I felt so hot walking down the sidewalk with that jacket in my arms, I even called Royston up. Remember him?'

'Em!'

'But unfortunately he was busy,' Em said. 'That jacket has changed my life,' she went on. Her eyes were shining with something which looked dangerously like conviction. 'I want to think big. Take big chances, live on the edge and be handsomely rewarded for it. Amber, these jewels might be our one and only chance. Daddy took his gamble, and now we have to take ours. Who dares, wins.'

Before Amber could laugh, yell, or protest at Em's craziness, her cell bleeped with a text.

'Wow . . . who's trying to get hold of you at one in the morning?' Em asked, snatching up the phone before Amber could get to it.

'Hv 2 seats for Dallas Cwboys v Giants tmrw. Oh today now. Wd ya like to? C'mon. Might be fun. Jack Desmoine,' Em read out. 'Who in the heck is Jack Desmoine?'

Amber felt the prickle of a blush . . . a slight churn in her stomach. The cop was asking her out. The cop maybe had a little crush too.

'He's the detective,' she said shyly.

'Why, butter my ears with jelly and lay me on an anthill!' Em shrieked. 'I decide to become a criminal just as you start dating a *detective*!'

Amber switched off the phone and shot Em a look which was supposed to mean: don't ask.

Em moved closer to her sister. 'What bit of the blog are you reading?'

Amber scrolled down and began to read out: *'There is no reward without risk. Every farmer knows this. Every year we put seeds into the ground, help calves to be born and there is no guarantee that anything will grow up tall and strong or fetch a good price. It is all risk. But the more you risk, the sweeter the reward. God knows I love my ranch. I would risk anything, except of course my family, for my ranch.'*

'Ha. How do you like that?' Em asked. 'The more you risk, the sweeter the reward. It's a sign, Amber. He's telling us to go for it. Amber, I can't do this without you.'

'Em, you can't do this, *period*. You'll go to jail. For years!'

'Look, will you at least do some research for me?' Em pleaded. 'You're the smart one. At least find out who the collectors are and what kind of people they are? And tell me something about moving big sums of money around. I guess I can't just walk into Chase Manhattan and ask to open a new account for $3 million in a fake name?'

Amber gave a little snort. 'Not unless you want to be arrested right away.'

'Just look into it, Amber, just have a little look for me. You're so clever, I know you'll figure out a way for us.'

'Em this is crazy talk,' Amber sighed. 'All of this is completely impossible.'

'What did Daddy always say? The only things that are impossible are the ones you never try. Just one victimless crime, Amber, and everything could work out fine, *for ever.*'

# Chapter Eighteen

*'Do you know just what job would be perfect for her husband?'*

*'Yes: millionaire!'*

It was 8 a.m. and Amber was already at her computer, showered, dressed, fresh cup of coffee by her side, sending résumés to potential employers, when Em stepped out of her bedroom.

'Oooh, aren't you kinda late?' Amber asked.

'It's my day off,' Em reminded her, 'I worked last Saturday.'

'Right . . . have you got plans?' Amber asked, hoping they didn't involve hanging round the apartment all day, bugging her.

'Oh yeah – very, very big plans,' Em replied, heading for the kitchenette to click on the coffee machine.

'Aside from the jewel theft of the century, obviously,' Amber said, heavy on the sarcasm.

'C'mon, Amber, just do a little research for me. Just show me the basics. Unlock the key to the door for me and then I'll go in all by myself.'

Amber shook her head.

'Fine, just go back to your stupid little job, selling bad financial advice to people who don't know any better. Didn't you describe it as stealing? Isn't stealing a little every day for ever just as bad as stealing something big once? Everywhere I look, people are stealing, including our own daddy! Maybe all that advice we got when we were kids about being honest was just to keep us in the dark. Everyone, everywhere is stealing. They're all looking after number one and taking everything they feel entitled to.'

Amber sighed and shook her head.

'There are other ways to make a living, Em,' she said gently, 'it doesn't have to be acting or stealing. Those aren't the only ways. And I quit my crappy job, remember.'

Em brought her mug of coffee over to Amber's desk.

'Just show me how to open a Swiss bank account, please?' she asked, in her best, little sister, wheedling voice.

Amber turned to her screen.

'Sure, I can definitely show you how to open a

Swiss bank account and why you can't hide stolen money in it,' she replied.

She typed the words 'Open Swiss bank account' and hit search. Screeds of information filled her screen.

'*How To Open a Swiss Bank Account*,' she read out aloud from a banking site. '*Opening a bank account in Switzerland is much the same as opening an account in any other country. You will require full documentation: passport, proof of address, tax returns and so on. In addition, to comply with international laws against money laundering, you will need to provide proof of where the money for the account comes from.*'

'What!' Em protested. 'But I thought you just showed up in Switzerland, gave them your money and they gave you a key!'

'Maybe in old movies,' Amber said, 'but nowadays, when someone can check you out with the click of a button, I don't think so.'

She read on down the page and summarized for Em: 'It says you can still hold a numbered account but the bank has to know who you are, again with full documentation.'

'Huh,' Em grumbled sulkily.

'Moving your stolen millions around the world isn't going to be quite as easy as you thought,' Amber teased her gently.

'Huh!' Em repeated, looking angry.

The apartment phone began to ring. 'Sapphire,' Amber said, seeing the number.

Em hit the speaker button, telling Amber, 'This should be fun.'

'Hi?' Sapphire's voice came into the room.

'Woo-hoo and how was your sleepover?' Em wanted to know.

'Hey, Sapphire, how are you?' Amber asked.

'Oh hi, are you both there? Are you both OK? How much more margarita did you all drink?'

'A lot,' Em confirmed. 'Did Fergus survive?'

'Oh yeah, as he puts it, he's *lived to fight another day.* Isn't that sweet?'

'Totally,' Amber told her.

'How did the rest of the night go with Mother?' Sapphire asked.

'Interesting . . . let's just say it was pretty interesting,' Em said.

'I'm hoping she didn't lead the bar in a singalong of "The Yellow Rose of Texas".'

'No. Thankfully,' Amber replied. 'Are you coming home after work?'

'Yeah. I need new clothes. I cannot believe I've showed up today in the same dress. People will talk. I'm wearing Fergus's underwear,' she confided in an agitated whisper. 'There was nothing else I could do. No way was I wearing yesterday's! Eeek!'

'Just flip 'em over, baby girl,' Amber said.

'Yeeee-ha!' Em cheered.

'Oh – he's here!' Sapphire said. 'I have to go.' There was a clunk, then Fergus's voice, a little muffled, said sweetly, 'Good morning, Sapphire, I've brought you a tea.'

'She hasn't turned off her cell,' Amber said to Em. She reached over to switch off the speaker phone, but Em held her hand back.

'Shhh! I want to hear what he's really like with her. Is he for real?'

'How perfect. Thank you!' Sapphire replied.

'Budge over,' Fergus said. 'I want to show you the photos.'

Amber and Em could hear the scrape of chairs as Fergus settled himself in beside Sapphire, then the click of the keyboard and a little giggle from Sapphire.

'Look at that!' Fergus said. 'Isn't that breathtaking? Isn't that the most wonderful brooch you've ever seen? The Duchess had superb taste. Every single thing she ever wore was supremely elegant.'

'Wow!' Sapphire agreed.

'It could be here next Wednesday.'

'*Next Wednesday?!*' Em repeated, voice full of surprise. 'Doesn't give me long . . .'

'Along with this,' Fergus added. 'Look at this necklace. Four-carat emeralds, surrounded by diamonds and set in platinum in one of the most striking art deco designs I've ever seen.'

'Amazing!' Sapphire gasped. 'That is going to sell for at least a million, isn't it?'

'We're hoping two and a half,' Fergus replied.

'No!'

'So next Wednesday, they'll obviously come up here to Mr Wilson's office first. The plan is to bring them in by armoured car at 10 a.m. . . . it's so exciting.'

'No!' Sapphire squeaked. 'I'm sure you're not supposed to tell me.'

'I'm not supposed to tell anyone, but I . . .'

Amber didn't hear the rest of his words but she had a suspicion they were romantic because Sapphire's voice also dropped to a whisper.

Then she asked: 'But they'll go on view before the sale, won't they?'

'Of course, it's wonderful publicity for Wilson's. They'll be on view over the holidays before the sale, but Mr Wilson is hiring armed security guards, metal detectors at the doors and bulletproof glass cases.'

'So no one will be able to try them on?' Sapphire asked.

'I don't think so. I don't think the people who are lining up to buy these pieces really care about finding the perfect fit. Have you seen the list of collectors?'

'No,' Sapphire said and then came more clicking noises. Fergus was obviously calling up the info on her computer.

'This guy – Montanari,' Fergus began, 'he's an industrialist based in Italy and Switzerland. He's already spent $7 million on the Duchess's jewels. He owns two necklaces, a ring and a brooch, but not a panther. He's desperate for a panther, apparently.

'These two are just as obsessed,' Fergus went on: 'Kaydo Tanaka and Mr Wei Kanebo.'

Amber looked over at Em and saw the rapt concentration on her face. She leaned over, pressed the button and ended the call.

'Amber!' Em hissed. 'It was just getting interesting!'

'Too interesting,' Amber said. 'Em, we weren't supposed to hear that. We were eavesdropping on our own sister! Please just forget about it. Apart from the part about the armed security guards and bulletproof glass – try and keep *that* right at the front of your overactive imagination.'

'How exactly did Mrs De La Hoz get you fired?' Em asked.

'I don't know if she did, they said they had to downsize anyway.'

'Yeah but, she complained about you. Why was that?'

'She had this charity which only paid out money to her relatives and I looked into it and told her that she couldn't do that. Well, not for long anyhow – the tax guys were going to come after her. Now she's selling off her jewels because the tax guys are after her.'

'Nothing to do with you?' Em asked, arching an eyebrow.

Amber laughed. 'No! I didn't tell. But maybe she's winding down the charity and making them a peace offering.'

'How do you set up a charity?'

'Ummm . . . I don't know much about it. But I guess you go to your local IRS office and start by filling in lots and lots of forms.'

'Can charities have bank accounts?'

'Of course.'

'In the name of the charity?'

'I guess.'

'Right . . . and what are those countries called where the US government can't get to you, no matter what you've done?'

Amber smiled. 'OK and now you're scaring me again.'

'What's it called?' Em persisted.

'Countries with no extradition treaty to the US.'

'Well, there's a mouthful. So which countries are those?'

'I don't know! But I'm guessing we can google.' She turned to her screen again.

'Really?' Em bounced off the sofa and stood beside Amber as she typed the words 'countries without extradition to the USA'. A whole list came up on Wikipedia.

'Algeria, Namibia, Montenegro . . .' Em said, reading out some of the names at random. 'I've never heard of them. Jeez, I was kinda planning on hanging round Manhattan and spending big at Tiffany's. When I get rich I don't want to have to move to Namibia!'

Amber clicked onto the link.

'It's in Africa,' she said. 'It has beaches.'

Then she tried Montenegro.

The photos were incredibly pretty. Snow-covered mountains, beaches, wooden chalets. 'It's in Europe,' she said, surprised.

'You've always wanted to go to Europe. The Eiffel Tower, the Roman ruins,' Em reminded her.

'Yeah, as a tourist. Not as America's Most Wanted.'

'It has the tallest men in Europe,' Em said, a paragraph catching her eye. 'This isn't sounding so bad. We could lie low there for a while, get ourselves some really tall boyfriends.'

Just as Amber began to laugh, her cell bleeped. Em snatched it up from the desk and read out loud: 'Ballgame tonight. Still no reply from you. Yes or no? Just say yes. Please? Jack'

'Give me that,' Amber ordered, but Em darted to the other side of the sofa.

'EM!' Amber yelled.

'And yes,' Em said, typing at speed, then very obviously hitting send.

Before Amber could get to Em, the cell bleeped with a new message.

'Good girl. G8, stand 5, see ya,' Em read out.

'Give me that!' Amber insisted. But her cheeks were burning and her heart thumping with the thrill. She wanted to go on a date with Jack, yes, she really wanted to. But she would never have dared to say yes without Em's interference.

'Too late, Amber's got a date. You've got to keep the cop sweet, Amber,' Em teased. 'If we become international criminals, we'll need a cop on our side. Take one for the team if you have to.'

'Shut up, Em, you crazy girl!'

# Chapter Nineteen

*'He proposed to her at the Knicks game, on the giant screen!'*

*'But she hates basketball.'*

*'Not any more, Betty. The rock was the size of a basketball.'*

Amber followed the crowds out of the train station and walked towards the stadium.

She was going out on a date. A proper date. One where she'd met the guy before and he'd asked her out: a 'come to the game' date. An old-fashioned date. One she could understand . . . one which was giving her stomach butterflies, in a way she remembered from high school.

She was no longer in Manhattan. There were no skinny blonde girls in high heels looking down their noses at her and making her feel like a cheaply dressed frump. And no corporate drones in suits and on cells making her feel like the least successful career girl in town.

She felt the warm grip of her beat-up old leather jacket round her shoulders. Underneath was the comfort of her favourite red and white plaid shirt. Her oldest, most worn-in jeans were finished off with a pair of deep-tan, burnished leather boots.

She'd had these boots for five years now. She could almost hear her daddy's voice: 'Bet they're just starting to get comfortable now, huh, Ambie?'

No one else in the world had ever or would ever get to call her Ambie. That was Daddy's name for her.

She fitted right in with this crowd she realized, feeling her shoulders drop away from her ears a little. She could hear lots of Texan accents – all the biggest fans had travelled north to spend a couple of days in the 'big ol Apple' and support the Cowboys.

'Heya, Roy . . . ya don't wanna trust any goddam Yankee chow . . . I got ma cool-box fulla beer and Leanne's burritos,' a hulk of a man in a thick black and red lumberjack shirt assured his friend, the massive yellow and white cool-box swaying between them.

Amber stopped and tried to get her bearings. He'd said he'd be at this entrance. She looked around and tried to spot him.

All at once she felt a heavy clap on her back.

'There y'are!'

She turned and saw Jack grinning at her.

'Look at you!' he added. 'I hardly recognize you. Last time I saw you, you were wearing ermine – now you're dressed like a cowgirl!'

'Hey, you look a little different yourself,' she was quick to point out, taking in his jeans and NY Giants jacket. 'Oh my. You're gonna sit in the Cowboys stand wearing that jacket?'

Jack shook his head slowly and his grin widened, revealing those cheek dimples she'd noticed before.

'No!' she shrieked. 'You're taking me to your stand?!'

'Hey, you're the girl. If I go to your side, those big Texans'll beat up on me.'

'Oh man. The Giants stand. This is a big deal . . . my poor ol' daddy will turn in his grave.'

She was teasing but Jack's face switched to sympathetic.

'Oh . . . when you were talking about him last time . . . I didn't realize you'd lost him.'

'Yeah . . .' She tailed off. This was a date, wasn't it? She didn't want to get into all this already. But . . .

'When did it happen?' Jack asked.

'Well . . . it was a year and a half ago. Very sudden. He wasn't sick or nothing. He just had a heart attack. Right out of the blue.'

'I'm sorry.'

They exchanged a look and Amber had the feeling that he understood. He understood that she was trying not to say too much about it, but there was a world of sadness even in her very few words.

'I lost my dad four years ago and I still miss him,' he said, slipping her hand into his and beginning to walk them towards the entrance. 'There's so many conversations I'd still like to have with him, you know.'

'Yeah, that's just it,' Amber agreed, vividly conscious of her hand, held tightly by his, 'I never took his advice much. But I still liked to talk things through with him.'

'It's just the worst thing that can come between people.'

She looked at him and suddenly felt like she wanted to smile. 'Death?' she asked.

'Yeah.' He grinned 'OK – the first few minutes of this have gone well. We've done death, now shall we go and find something to eat?'

'Sure.'

'I'm so gonna miss eating when I'm dead,' he added.

'If we're sitting in the Yankees stand, then we have to eat Texan,' she insisted, pointing in the direction of the Tex-Mex stall.

'Lead on, cowgirl.'

'I don't think you should call me that.'

'Didn't you grow up on a ranch?'

'Yes.'

'Can you ride?'

'Sure.'

'Did your daddy have cattle?'

'Uhuh.'

'Then you are so totally a cowgirl. I rest my case.'

'I'm an unemployed asset manager.'

Jack brought them to a halt in front of the Tex-Mex stall. 'OK, what do I order?'

As Amber went through the menu with him explaining the ins and outs of refried beans, a huge, bearded Texan, wearing (yee-ha) a Stetson, leaned across and interrupted her.

'Yeah, but this is just the pappy, fast-food stuff. Ya need to come to Texas to see how it's really done.' He jerked his head at Jack. 'Is this your Yankee boyfriend?' he asked Amber.

She blushed in reply.

'Cos I'm gonna suggest you ditch him right now and come watch the game with me.'

'Why, I am flattered, sir, but—'

'Hey!' interrupted Jack. 'This is our first date, you have to let her give me a chance.'

'Besides, he's police,' Amber told the Texan.

'Oh boy, now I'm messing with the sheriff's girl. No good's gonna come of that,' the Texan said with a good-natured smile. 'Enjoy the game y'all. But we're gonna TRASH ya'all. Is all.'

'Is all?' Jack turned to ask her, once the man-mountain had lumbered off.

'Is all . . . is all,' Amber said with a smile and a shrug. 'Better get used to it . . . is all! Oh my gosh, are you gonna eat all of that?' she asked, staring at Jack's order in horror.

'Hey, are you messing with the sheriff? Like I said, I'm so going to miss eating when I'm dead.'

'Is all,' Amber joked.

When they took their seats, Amber could see that they were good seats with a great view. Expensive seats.

'Uhuh,' Jack agreed, chewing and swallowing before he could say more. 'I did someone a favour and they gave me a very nice present in return.'

'Isn't that police corruption?' Amber teased.

'Ooooh, sharp. Don't you worry, I registered my gift. I'm as straight as a die,' Jack replied, through a mouthful of bean burrito. 'Mmmmm, I am loving this. Can you cook this stuff?'

Amber shook her head, then exaggerating her Texan accent, told him: 'No one cooks Tex-Mex. I'm telling ya, there's a sensational Tex-Mex restaurant on the corner of practically every street back home. Why make ya own when it's so good and so cheap to eat out?'

'Mmmm . . . can you cook at all?'

'Honey, I can make a peach pie to make you cry . . .'

'Don't tell me: it's someone's secret recipe passed down the family.'

'Great-Aunt May-Beth's.'

'Told you,' he said through his full mouth.

'Naw, just kidding. I got it from *Parker County Magazine*.'

Now Jack laughed properly.

'Hey, that's a big deal getting your recipe in *Parker County Magazine*. Em's been on the cover twice.'

'Em?'

'My baby sister.'

'Oh yeah, I remember. How's Sapphire?'

'She's good.'

'No post-traumatic stress? No odd out-of-character behaviour? She's recovering well?'

'Yeah,' Amber replied.

'What about you?'

'Oh . . . I'm like a different person. I don't know myself,' Amber joked, biting into a corn dog.

'How come?' Jack asked.

'First off, I've never had a fun date in New York until . . .'

'Now,' he grinned at her. 'Oh boy, so if I mess up you might never go on a date again.' He took a swig of beer. 'We got the guys, by the way.'

'The guys I dated before?' she joked. 'I hope you locked 'em up.'

'Ha ha. No. The ones who did Ori's.'

'Oh my gosh . . .' But as Amber tried to register this there was a massive roar of tannoy and crowd as the players walked onto the pitch.

Amber glanced at Jack urgently. He was clapping and pointing out a player, but all she could think was: they caught the guys! The cops got the robbers. The jewels had been found. The thieves had *not* got away with it. She had to let Em know asap before she even had another thought about her crazy scheme.

'Don't worry,' Jack said above the noise, 'I'll tell ya all about it as soon as it quiets down.'

Finally, everyone took their seats, play began and over corn dogs, refried beans, breaks for roars and cheers and watching the best shots, Jack told her as much as he was allowed to.

'You're gonna be called as a witness in due course, so when I tell you stuff, I'm sticking to the facts as I see them. But you're so smart, Amber, you know the difference.'

She nodded.

'It was very simple. Not like in those crime books where it's all so complicated and all kindsa clues have to be unravelled by a super-sleuth.'

'Agatha Christie style?'

'Exactly. I've read some of her books. Very clever.'

'Really?'

'Yeah, so someone matching the description turns up at one of the jewellers we have on our list. He tries to sell something big. He gets in an argument about the price and pulls a gun. Police are close enough to arrest him at the scene. Gun matches the one fired at the store, the jewels are Ori's, more were found at this guy's place, along with a few of Ori's little puppets they must have scooped up. You remember? Anyhow, you, Sapphire and Ori will probably have to do an ID.'

'Oh my gosh. Sapphire will be freaked.'

'But not you?'

'I don't think so.'

'We'll help her through it.'

'What about the other guy?'

'Well – did you see that pass?!' he exclaimed, pointing at the game. 'Unbelievable!'

For several minutes they focused on the game, standing up to take a better look, Jack roaring at the player to make it to the touchline, Amber cheering on the Texans to bring him down.

The ball went into touch.

'Nice play!' Jack shouted and bit into his burrito.

'Terrible!' Amber moaned, settling back into her seat. 'So what about the other guy?'

Jack shook his head. 'I don't think you're going to like this.'

'Did he get killed? Did you guys shoot him?' she asked anxiously.

'Whoa! No way! I think you'd have seen that on the news. No . . . ummm . . . we've . . . well, I've let him go. He's a kid. He's only sixteen. He was doing what his uncle forced him into.'

'You let him go?'

'You look a little relieved. I thought you'd be furious. His uncle held a gun to your sister's head!'

'Jeez,' Amber said, not trusting herself to make any comment.

'I met him. I met his mom and, unusually, I met his dad. Robbers don't usually have a dad knocking around,' Jack went on. 'The kid doesn't have a record. He just did a crazy thing which could have ruined the rest of his life.'

'But you let him off? How can you do that?'

'Not enough evidence to convict. That's how we left it. I scared the hell out of him and his folks, but sometimes it's good police to save someone from a wrong turn . . . save them from themselves.'

'Huh.'

'Cost me a promotion, though,' Jack said, turning his attention back to the match.

'Why?'

'My boss is an a-hole. Enough said.'

'All bosses are a-holes as far as I can tell.'

'Yeah, I get that you're a bit of a lone star. You'll

probably work for yourself one day, won't ya, cow-girl? I like that. Maybe I'll work for myself one day too.'

'How do you do that in the police?'

'I have no idea. Maybe I'll have to become the sheriff.'

Jack laughed and she laughed with him. Then he looked at her, his eyebrows raised a little and he moved his face questioningly towards hers.

In the split second she had to decide, she realized that she did want the detective with the dimples and the sense of humour to kiss her.

And then they were kissing and despite the burrito taste and the teasing catcalls from the guys in the seats behind them, she felt Jack's hands hold tight to the side of her face and she closed her eyes and felt this real person so close to her. This real, interesting person who wanted to be with her.

And it felt amazing.

# Chapter Twenty

*'I packed up my dinner to go and when I tried to give it to the hobo on the corner . . .'*

*'Don't tell me: lactose intolerant?'*

It was late Saturday afternoon when Amber got back to the apartment. She'd spent several hours at the community gardens, then she'd ridden the subway out to Williamsburg to check out three apartments for rent in their kind of budget.

Everything she'd seen had looked much worse than the place they were in and the landlords showing her round had made it clear that all three sisters would have to have jobs before they could be given a lease.

The thought of having to go back to Jed in Hoboken to beg for a second chance was making Amber depressed, despite the little flashbacks to kissing Jack goodbye at the subway station which kept jumping to mind and pushing the gloomy thoughts away.

Jack was one of life's truly great kissers. She had no doubt about that.

'Amber!' Em exclaimed. 'Where have you been all day? And we want a full scorecard on the game last night, please. Don't we, Sapph?'

'You bet,' Sapph agreed and sat down to listen, draped in a towel with wet hair dripping over her shoulders.

'It was good . . . he was good company,' Amber said, earning herself howls from Em.

'Good company!' Em repeated. 'You sound like Aunt Mamie. Was he hawt, girl? Did you guys click? I know you didn't stay over, because I saw your jacket on the couch when I got home last night, but did you want to?'

'He was real nice and that's all I'm saying. Are you going out with Fergus tonight?' Amber, wanting out of the line of questioning, turned to Sapphire.

'Yeah, I'm just getting washed and changed and then we're going to go eat in some English bar down on the waterfront.'

'English bar? I think maybe the word you need is pub,' Em told her.

'Yes, it's called The Old Pub. Have you guys got plans? Are you going out to eat or something?'

'We're not eating in,' Amber replied. 'If we don't eat in, maybe we'll starve the rats out.'

'Oh jeez. I don't want to live here any longer,' Sapphire complained and jumped to her feet. 'It gives me the creeps.'

'Don't worry, we won't be living here much longer,' Amber replied, 'just two more weeks before we have to go. I went to look at places in Williamsburg.'

'Williamsburg! Oh, please don't tell me we have to move out there.'

'Didn't see anything good – and I'll need a job before we can sign the lease.'

'Stop worrying, I'm coming up with a plan,' Em assured her from the sofa. Sapphire went back into the bathroom to apply lotions, potions and make-up, and Em headed for her room, taking, Amber noticed, Sapphire's cellphone with her.

Once Em had closed the door, Sapphire's cell rang. Amber could hear Em talking, then she came out of the bedroom just as Sapphire emerged from the bathroom.

'Oh, too bad and you look so pretty . . .' Em began.

'What?' Sapphire asked.

'I just answered your cell, I hope you don't mind but I thought it might be important.'

'That's OK. Was it Fergus?'

'Yeah. He says he's feeling really tired and if it's OK with you, he wants to skip meeting for dinner.

He sounded really apologetic. Really sweet,' Em added.

'Oh. Is he OK? Does he want me to call him? I'll call him,' Sapphire decided and reached for the phone.

'No. He said he was going for takeout, then planning to get to bed really early. He said could I pass on a goodnight kiss?!'

'Aw . . . sweet,' Sapphire said, but she looked really disappointed.

'And I'm going to have to get ready for work,' Em added.

'I thought you were getting a night off. You've worked five nights straight,' Amber reminded her.

'I know, but they've just called. Apparently some office birthday party has showed up and they're going crazy. Sapph? Would it be OK if I took your phone? My one's out of charge and I hate going home late at night without a phone.'

'Sure,' Sapphire said and Em slipped her sister's cell into her bag.

'Amber, I need to ask you a favour . . .' Em hung her head and looked unusually pleading.

'What?'

'Well, it's just . . . could you come to work with me?'

'What?' Amber asked, astonished. 'What in the heck for?'

'They're really short staffed. They're paying double

time, plus the tips on a Saturday night this close to Christmas . . .'

'You've volunteered me for a shift?!'

Amber couldn't believe it.

'Well, you could clear 300 bucks tonight and I thought you'd be grateful for that. Please?' Em wheedled, 'I said you'd do it.'

'I can't waitress! The last waiting job I had was at the school summer fair when I was twelve and I dropped a whole pitcher of iced lemonade into the mayor's lap.'

'You can be front of house, you just need to man the reservations desk and show people to their tables. You'll be fine. C'mon, change, dress up – honestly, it'll be more fun than sitting in waiting for your cop to call.'

'I'm not sitting waiting for the cop to call!'

'Has he called?' Sapphire asked.

'He's sent a message,' Amber said and immediately regretted it, because now both sisters were crowding in on her, desperate to know more.

'He'd like to meet up again – but I haven't replied. That is all I'm saying. OK?'

'Are you really going to leave me home alone with the rat?' Sapphire asked as Em and Amber headed for their rooms to change.

'Only for a few hours,' Amber promised. 'Keep the broom to hand then you can whack it if it appears!'

At the thought of this, Sapphire gave a little scream.

As soon as Amber and Em were in the street, Em took her big sister by the arm and began to steer her towards the subway. 'OK,' she began, 'what I said upstairs, forget about it. This is the real plan . . .'

# Chapter Twenty-One

*'Apparently they also serve wonderful craft beers in this place.'*

*'Too bad we only drink champagne.'*

Em and Amber walked along the unfamiliar riverside street quickly, their coats pulled tightly around them. This close to the water on a December night, it was bitterly cold.

'That must be it,' Em said, pointing ahead to a welcoming bar with long windows, brightly lit.

'The Old Pub,' Amber said, reading from the sign.

Amber was still trying to work out what Em really wanted from hijacking Sapphire's date. Em kept telling her they needed to get to know Fergus better before Sapphire made another terrible, heartbreaking mistake. And that was true, they did need to know Fergus better . . . but Amber didn't think it should be like this, behind Sapphire's back.

Really, she thought Em wanted to get Fergus on his own because she was going to ask him more about the jewels coming to the auction house. Ever since the day in the department store, all of Em's questions to Sapphire had been met with stony silence.

Amber hoped Em had let go of her crazy jewel theft plan, but she couldn't be sure.

'Don't you think Fergus is going to find it more than weird – us turning up instead of Sapphire?'

Em shrugged.

'We're here to tell him to take it easy. We're here to explain all about how Forde broke her heart and he is not allowed to. We're here to tell him that she can't move in with him yet. It's way too early.'

'But that is her choice,' Amber said. 'We can't interfere.'

'Yes we can, I wish we'd interfered before that low-life, lousy Forde named the day.'

As they entered the bar, Em straightened up and set a smile on her face. 'I feel great,' she said. 'Ever since I took this jacket – ' she ran her fingertips over the white ermine jacket '– I feel unstoppable. I feel like everything is going to work out just fine.'

Amber couldn't help smiling. 'Wish I felt the same.'

One quick sweep of the place and Amber saw

Fergus sitting at the bar, golden haired in a tweedy jacket. In front of him was a small glass of that weird black Irish beer.

He was reading a newspaper and Amber understood immediately why Sapphire was so crazy about him. He looked like a character from an old black and white movie. Sapphire had always wanted to be the heroine in her very own black and white movie and here was her hero.

'Hi, Fergus, do you remember us?'

Em was the first to speak. Fergus looked up and a surprised smile crossed his face.

'Em . . . Amber? How are you? Are you looking for Sapphire? I'm expecting her here any minute.'

'I know,' Em said, 'that's why we're here.'

Em slid off her fur jacket, revealing the tight vest top underneath, that she was wearing with her miniskirt and boots. 'May I?' she asked, pointing to the chair next to his.

'Of course. And, Amber, let me find you a chair . . . but she is OK? Nothing's happened to Sapphire, has it?'

'Oh you are too cute,' Em said, smiling. 'No. Nothing's happened to Sapphire. But she's tired and we've sent her to bed. Then we decided that we should come out and meet you instead.'

'Really?' Fergus looked slightly nervous.

'It's OK,' Amber assured him.

'Yeah, we just need to know a bit more about you, Fergus.'

'Really? Such as? Do you want to see my degree from Cambridge University?'

Amber couldn't tell if he was annoyed now or trying to be funny. 'Sapphire's had a terrible year,' she began. 'We need to look after her a little. You know that she fell in love before . . .'

'I do,' Fergus said solemnly. 'With a rat. A man who was not worthy.'

'Exactly. So we want to make sure that never, ever happens again.' Em sounded deadly serious.

'I quite understand.'

'What are ya drinking?' Em asked.

'Me? Oh, don't worry. Half a pint is fine. I'm not much of a drinker, but allow me to get you something. What's your poison?'

Em gestured to the barman.

'Two dirty martinis, a proper serving of that beer he's drinking, plus three shots of bourbon. Don't worry, I'm paying and then we can start to talk.'

Fergus raised an eyebrow as the drinks were lined up in front of them, but he didn't protest.

'Cheers,' Em said and tossed the shot down. 'If you want to start understanding Texas and understanding Texans, you've got to start drinking bourbon. Right, Amber?'

'I guess,' Amber replied, but she sipped hesitantly

at the drink. In all honesty, she could only really stand bourbon with a half can of Coke poured on top.

'Right . . .' Fergus sounded hesitant, but he drank his shot down, then pulled a face.

He coughed and said, 'We'll try something Scottish and a lot smoother next.'

'Bring it on,' Em challenged. Once Fergus had ordered, she asked, 'How old are you?'

'Twenty-eight,' Fergus replied, fidgeting in his seat.

'How many serious girlfriends have you had?'

'Three.'

'How did the last one end?' Amber asked.

'Posy wanted to get married and I didn't. So she broke up with me and moved to London. I was pretty upset . . . so I decided to look for a job in New York.'

'And why didn't you want to marry Posy?' Em asked, taking a sip of her cocktail.

'She wasn't the one for me.'

'The One . . . the One,' Amber sighed, 'what is it with everybody and the One?'

'Sapphire's the One,' Fergus said simply. 'When it happens to you, you'll just know.'

'Crapola,' Em told him. 'Maybe you're just ready to settle . . . for now.'

Fergus shook his head. 'The One,' he repeated.

The Scotch whisky shots had arrived now. Fergus

paid for these and he, Em and Amber clinked glasses.

Fergus wished them something which sounded like 'Slanjevarrrrrr' before they tossed the shots back.

'If you say so,' Amber teased. 'Now tell us all about yourself. Work – college – your Scottish family.'

Fergus did, sipping occasionally from his huge black pint of beer. As he talked about his mother, father and older sister, Em and Amber listened and saw that he was beginning to sweat.

'Are you telling us the truth?' Em asked suspiciously. 'You look kinda guilty.'

'Just hot,' he said, taking off his jacket, 'think I'll go to the bathroom and splash my face. I told you I wasn't much of a drinker.'

He got up and walked away unsteadily.

'He doesn't look good,' Amber told Em. 'He looks like he did the other night, when Sapphire had to take him home.'

'He's just a little drunk,' Em said, 'and that's good because we'll get the truth out of him like this. Come on, let's line up some more drinks. Ooooh, he left his cellphone on the bar. Interesting.'

'Em . . .' Amber warned.

But Em already had it in her hand. 'Better just check through his most recent calls. If there is another the One in his life, we need to know.'

'Em!' Amber hissed.

'You look for useful stuff in there,' Em said, picking

up Fergus's briefcase and putting it into Amber's lap.

'What?!' Amber protested, but still, she lowered her eyes to the bag and looked inside.

'Yves M? That sounds completely suspicious,' Em said. 'I'm copying me that cell number. It's foreign. Probably English. The girl he left back home, maybe.'

'Put it back,' Amber said, handing the briefcase to her sister then adding urgently, 'he'll be here any second!'

Em dropped the cell onto the bar then hurried to put the briefcase back against his chair, but she misjudged. The case fell over and several brochures and files tipped out onto the floor.

'Shiiiit!' Em hissed.

Amber glanced down and saw a thin white folder labelled 'Security Procedure' among the other spilled brochures and documents. Em picked it up and flipped through it, scanning the pages.

'Em! He's coming!' Amber warned. Em put the folder back in the case as Fergus appeared.

'Sorry, we're so sorry. I guess I must have kicked your bag over and it emptied out,' Amber tried to explain.

'Oh!' Fergus knelt down, looking concerned.

Both Amber and Em scrambled to gather up the other files that had escaped.

There was a draft sale brochure with 'Treasures of the Duchess' written across the front in elaborate script. 'You must be very busy planning for this sale,' Amber said, handing it over.

'Yes,' Fergus replied tersely.

'Oh the Duchess's jewels,' Em gushed with a big smile, 'I wanna hear every little wrinkle and winkle about them. Apparently you're hoping to get $2 million a piece.'

'At least,' Fergus replied. 'That's a very conservative estimate.'

Once the briefcase had been repacked, Fergus sat back in his seat, still looking sweaty and overheated.

'Maybe we should take a walk?' Em suggested.

Out on the street in the biting cold wind, Fergus seemed to revive.

'It's been very interesting to meet you both,' he told them, his perfect manners back in place. 'Your sister is lovely. I'm going to look after her. Treasure her,' he added.

'Please, just don't make her hope for things you're not prepared to give,' Amber said.

'I think we have to be a little more clear than that,' Em chipped in. 'This is all way too fast, way too soon. You need to cool it right down buddy, you need to leave Sapphire alone for a while,' she said and moved closer to him. 'How can you be talking about marriage – already? After what she's been through?'

'But she thinks she loves me,' Fergus insisted.

'Do you know why we're really here tonight?' Em continued. 'We're really here to tell you to back off from Sapphire. Cool down. Call it off. Leave her alone. However you want to hear it. She's not ready yet. She's still in love with Houghton. How could she not be? She was supposed to marry him in June. That's only a few months ago!'

Amber nudged her sister hard. 'Don't,' she hissed. 'You're going too far. It's not fair.'

Fergus looked stunned by Em's outburst.

'I can wait,' he said finally, 'I can wait for her. Whatever I have to do . . .'

'Well what you have to do right now is back off,' Em said firmly, 'back right off. Understand? Or maybe we'll try and find out more about Yves M . . .' Em narrowed her eyes and glared at Fergus.

'What?' he asked, looking genuinely surprised.

'Exactly,' said Em, 'there are things we know . . . you don't think we know. But we do know,' she added in a voice that sounded mysterious, but was really, Amber knew, the voice of Em after two dirty martinis, a bourbon and a Scotch.

'Do you want to take this cab?' Amber asked, as tyres rattled over the old cobbles of this part of town. 'We're walking to the subway.'

'OK – if you're sure?' Fergus asked, still looking a little dazed.

'Yeah,' Amber said. 'Taxi!' she called, thrusting her arm out. 'Over here!'

'Back off from Sapphire,' Em reminded him as he headed for the cab.

'Right, I hear you,' he said, his voice tense.

As soon as the taxi had set off, Amber rounded on her sister. 'I know you've had a lot to drink but what in the hell was all that about?'

'Maybe if Sapphire doesn't have her dreamboat to rely on at the auction house she'll be a little more helpful about my plans,' Em replied.

'Your plans? Your plans! You don't have a plan, Em,' Amber exclaimed. 'You just have a crazy, impossible, illegal fantasy!'

Cold, wet rain landed on Amber's face, except, now that she looked at it properly, it wasn't rain. It was cold, white and freezing wet.

'It's snow,' she told Em, not able to keep the amazement from her voice, 'it's snowing!'

Growing up in Texas, Amber had only experienced snow a handful of times in her life, always with complete excitement.

The anger fell from Em's face now. In its place was the mischievous smile, a sign of the slightly dangerous, impetuous mood that often made Amber feel wary.

Em spread her arms and twirled in the snow. 'I want to be rich and famous. Famous and rich. And

I'm gonna do it. Better believe it, baby. What do you want, Amber? Have you ever really thought about that? What do you really want?'

'I need to get a job, Em, otherwise we won't be able to rent a new apartment.'

Em took hold of her arm. 'Amber, you worry too much. Do you know that? Always worrying, always thinking, always planning. Can't you just *be*, Amber, can't you live for the moment, just once in a while?'

'I think that's the bourbon talking,' Amber smiled.

'Maybe you should have had a little more. It's snowing! Snow in Manhattan. Could anything be more wonderful?' Em asked excitedly. 'Think about what you really want. Then come with me and we'll go get it.'

Amber laughed, but still couldn't help thinking that it must be fun to be as carefree as Em. She floated through life as light and happy as a snowflake. Em wanted money, she wanted to be famous. Sapphire wanted to find Mr Wonderful and make a beautiful home and family with him.

What did Amber really want? She'd thought she wanted to come to New York. She'd thought she wanted to work hard for the bank and pay down that chunk of ranch mortgage.

Now that the job was gone and the apartment was going she felt like a compass without the North

Pole. She was spinning wildly, trying to find her bearings. Trying to work out what was the best way ahead.

'Stop worrying and start singing,' Em urged, arms wide, twirling and spinning in the falling snow: 'Just tell me what you really want, Amber, and I'll help to make it yours.'

# Chapter Twenty-Two

*'Oh my, what a wonderful view of the park they have.*
*You've seen it, haven't you?'*

*'Of course. Central Park always looks best from*
*the terrace of a $30 million apartment.'*

'Have you got a good set of wrenches in your apartment?'

'Excuse me?!'

Amber recognized Jack's voice, but wasn't prepared for this crazy request for a Sunday morning.

'*Wrenches?*'

'No. I'm only kidding. I have the wrenches. I'm in your street, outside your apartment and I have a flat tyre. That's what ya get for stalking, I guess.'

'Why are you in my street?' she asked, feeling a smile spread across her face.

'Look, I could lie and say I was dropping something

off at Ori's store . . . but really, I just thought you might like to go for a walk or something.'

'A walk? There's snow outside and it's like ten degrees. And anyway, shouldn't you have called?'

'Where's the fun in that? Isn't it much more fun to have someone just turn up and get a puncture and have to change their tyre on your doorstep in the snow and the freezing cold?'

She went to the window and looked down.

Jack was standing beside a big silver car, trunk open, tools already out on the sidewalk. 'Yeah, I see ya!' he said into the phone and waved at her. 'Are ya dressed? Warm enough to come and change tyres?'

'I'll come down,' Amber said, feeling a leap of excitement. Ever since the football date, she'd been thinking of him constantly. Because . . . Because? Because he was a surprise.

She was bowled over by how much she liked him. He wasn't her type, but then – who was? No boyfriend had ever worked out well for her. So maybe she was wrong about her type and she needed to branch out.

Jack could change a car wheel, crack a joke and kiss good. Maybe these were key qualities. All this time, she could have been looking at the wrong guys for the wrong things. Jack was different. He was a grown-up. He was thirty-something, she guessed. He was a detective. He was all kinds of things she didn't know much about. But she was very interested.

She felt almost caught out by how much he seemed to like her. He was doing all the running here and Amber was beginning to realize how good it made her feel.

She hurried into her bedroom, grateful that Sapphire had gone out to meet a friend and Em was still asleep, so no one could be curious or teasing.

Quickly she pulled on jeans, boots, sweater, scarf and thick jacket, then looked herself over in the mirror. She messed her hair a little, applied blush and lip balm. She felt that whole panic of wanting to look nice, but not wanting to have tried too hard.

Looking around, she located a pair of gloves, her little purse and her keys. Then, feeling her heart jump with nerves, she headed out of the apartment and down the stairs.

'Hi there,' she called to Jack, giving him a little wave as she came out of the main door.

'Hello, Amber,' he said, walking towards her, 'I thought we got past the hi-with-a-wave stage at the ball game. Didn't we?'

'Yeah, I guess we did,' she said and smiled.

'I hope we did. That *was* you I was kissing? Right?'

She began to laugh as he walked right up to her, placed his hands on her shoulders and pulled her in.

He kissed good.

When Jack kissed her, Amber felt in safe hands.

'Hello,' he said. 'I would have called you yesterday but I was working a long day. Did you go out last night?'

'Just with Em.'

'OK, back to the job at hand. I need to get this car to the precinct by lunchtime or I'll be in even more trouble than usual. Damn it's cold,' he added, stomping his feet and rubbing his bare hands. 'Snow in December is early. Have you even seen snow before, cowgirl?'

'Yes! Shall I go buy us coffees?'

'Good plan. Meanwhile, Jack better get busy with the jack. Groan. Terrible. Sorry. '

When Amber came back from the cafe on the corner with two steaming cups and a doughnut for Jack, he had raised up the back end of the car. She watched as he took a large wrench out of the toolbox and began to loosen the nuts that held the wheel in place.

He worked calmly and patiently, without any fuss. When one of the bolts wouldn't turn and he suspected it was frozen, he poured a little coffee on top to get it moving.

He was wearing black boots with thick rubber soles. Working boots. Nothing leather soled and fancy, like the preppy boys she'd worked with and dated. None of them would be able to change the wheel on the car. They'd all have a rescue service on speed dial.

Watching Jack work made her think of her daddy and the other ranchers back home; capable, practical men who figured stuff out and got the job done.

He took the spare tyre from the trunk, checked it over, put it in place and then began to bolt it back into position.

'Nearly there,' he told her. 'Looking good. The tyre. Not just you,' he joked. 'So do you trust me enough to take a ride in this thing? I still have a couple of hours till I'm due back in work.'

'Sure,' she told him, 'where will we go?'

'Have you been skating on the Wollman Rink in Central Park?'

'No!'

'Have you ever been skating?'

'In fact, no.'

'I think we have ourselves an idea then.'

'Can you skate?'

'Yeah,' he said, raising an eyebrow at her.

'You are surprising.'

'Now so are you. Very surprising.'

It took some time to get uptown, find a space to leave the car, make their way to the frozen pond in the park, then get to the head of the queue to hire skates. But the time passed quickly, because they were talking the whole time. Plus it was unusually pretty, the grass dusted with snow and the rink busy with New York skaters: gliding or posing, some pirouetting, just about everybody showing off their winter finery.

'So why did you leave Texas? What made you actually pack up your bags and head up here?' Jack asked as he laced up his boots.

'I wanted to work for a big city bank, I wanted the experience . . . and I needed a change,' she told him. 'I'd lived in the same house in Parker County for my whole life, had all the same friends since kindergarten. I needed something more. And, it was a year after my daddy died, so I guessed everyone would cope fine without me. I didn't expect both my sisters to move up and join me within months. It was like I let the genie out of the bottle. Amber goes to New York and suddenly everyone else wants to come to New York too. Oh my gosh, look at those amazing apartments!'

She pointed to the impressive blocks on the West Side, built to give every one of the residents a breathtaking ringside view of the park.

'Must be amazing to live in something like that. What a life! What a completely different life.'

Jack held a finger right in front of her face. 'Aha, now follow the line. OK, do you see where I'm pointing, to the floor four down from the top there?'

'Yeah.'

'That family got so upset fighting about the inheritance that little brother shot big sister in the head. The doorman on the apartment block, who'd been working there for twenty-eight years told me it was the third murder over money in that building. He also said: "The rich don't control their fortunes. Their fortunes control them." Interesting, huh? Now are you ready?'

'Kinda.'

'I'm gonna pull you up and then you just tuck your arm in here and I'll pull you along.'

Amber took his hand and wobbled up to her feet. She felt too tall in the skates and way too unsteady.

'Whoa,' Jack instructed her. 'I'm trying to teach Bambi to walk. Soften your knees, lean forward a little, now just trust me here. The more slowly you go, the more you'll wobble – you've got to move forward, throw yourself at it.'

'Whoooaaaa!' Amber couldn't help exclaiming as they took off, but she held on tight and Jack steered her smoothly along.

'OK and now I have you like this and you can't get away from me, I want to know all about your record.'

'What?!'

'All your past dates, boyfriends, lovers. Is there someone pining for you back home in Texas?'

'No. There is no one pining. Do I get to hear about yours?' she asked.

'Oh, my. How long have you got? Let's skate first then we'll pull up, get something to eat and I'll confess. A little.'

'Ex-wives?'Amber blurted the question out, feeling a little scared of the reply.

'No. No ex-wives,' he assured her, 'but some pretty mean and twisted exes.'

'Oh. That doesn't sound so good.'

'No . . . I don't mean anything serious by it. Maybe there's something about being a cop. I think we attract strange girls.'

'Oh . . .'

'Hell. Sorry, that didn't sound so good either! Forget I said it. Maybe you're making me nervous.'

'Nervous? Why would I make you nervous? Hey, I'm the one wearing skates for the very first time.'

'Maybe I'm nervous because I like you. I like you a lot.'

They carried on skating, picked up a little speed even, but it wasn't the rush of whizzing over the ice that was making Amber fizzle with happiness.

He liked her a lot!

She wanted to shout it out loud. The detective, the great kisser, the guy who could skate and change car wheels and let baby criminals go if he liked their dads, this interesting, grown-up guy Liked Her A Lot!

'Never mind me,' he said, 'I want to hear about you. Much, much more about you. What do you like? What are you into? Tell me all about it.'

And all of a sudden, she felt as if she had too much to say, as if there couldn't possibly be enough time to talk to him before he had to go back to the precinct.

It was almost two hours later when Amber got back to the apartment. As she came in, she could see immediately that something was wrong. Sapphire was sitting on the couch in a tearful huddle surrounded by crumpled tissues, Em was at her side, rubbing Sapphire's back.

'What's up?' Amber asked, hurrying over to Sapphire.

'Fergus cancelled our date for today – just like he cancelled last night. And worse than that . . .' Sapphire's voice gave way and with a tiny sob she pushed a tissue against her face.

'What?' Amber asked urgently. 'What is it?'

'He said he doesn't think we should see so much of each other right now. He says we need to slow down. Take it easy. He's worried we're taking things too fast.'

For a moment, no one said anything.

Sapphire just sobbed into fresh tissues and Amber and Em glared at each other across her back.

Em was shaking her head, as if to say: Don't even think about telling her.

Amber was also shaking her head, which was supposed to mean: Do you see what you've done?

'It's all my fault,' Sapphire sobbed, 'it's completely my fault.'

'No. No, it's really not,' Amber assured her.

'But it is. I was the one moving too fast. I was the one talking about moving in. He's the best man I've ever met – could *ever* meet – and I've scared him off.

'It's Forde Houghton all over again,' Sapphire exclaimed, looking up. 'Why can't I just take things slowly? Why am I always in such a rush?'

'Shhh . . .' Amber soothed. 'Fergus is not like Forde. He's nice and he's so into you. I'm sure it's not you. But slowing it up a little . . . maybe that's a good thing.'

'We've only been going out for a couple of weeks . . . and I've already talked about rings and venues and – ' big sob – 'dinnerware!' Sapphire blurted out. 'This is all my fault. I've scared him off. I've totally terrified him. He's probably going to run like a jackrabbit right home to Scotland.'

'Sapphire, please don't! You're going to see him at work tomorrow. Everything might work out just fine. Please don't panic.'

'I hardly see him at work,' Sapphire said. 'He is obsessed with the Duchess of Windsor's jewels. He's an expert on everything about them and everyone who wants them. He's already rewritten the sales brochure like fifty times! Oh, I have to go and wash my face . . .'

With that, she darted off to the tiny bathroom.

As soon as the door was shut, Amber turned on Em: 'Look what you've done,' she hissed, 'you should not have interfered.'

'OK,' Em said. 'Fine, let her fall head over heels with some guy from England we know next to nothing about. Cos she picked such a great guy to fall in love with the last time.'

'Jeeez. I don't know,' Amber admitted, 'I just don't know . . . Em?'

'Yeah?'

Amber lowered her voice. 'When he was talking to Mother, he told her he went to Edinburgh University, then in the bar, remember, he asked . . .'

'Would we like to see his degree from Cambridge!'

'That's a biggie,' Amber said. 'There's no way anyone would forget where they went to college. So why would Fergus lie about it?'

# Chapter Twenty-Three

*'So she gets the heel of her $500 Prada shoes caught in the escalator and it snaps right off.'*

*'Lauren, that'll happen when you wear cheap shoes.'*

Late on Monday afternoon, Amber's cell rang. It was Em.

'Look I have an idea,' Em began.

'Uh-oh.'

'You have to come and work with me in the club tonight.'

'What?!'

'Yes you do, because when I'm gone you can have my job. I'll speak to Dino, he's a very reasonable man. He'll maybe even sign your lease to say you're working for him so you and Sapphire can get a new place. If you start coming in from tonight then I'll have time to show you the ropes.'

'What do you mean I can have your job when you're *gone*? Where are you going?'

Em's voice dropped to a whisper: 'Once I've stolen the jewels I'll either have to lie low over here or someplace abroad.'

'What? Once you've stolen – Em, please, you are not going to steal those jewels,' Amber hissed. 'We've already heard they're coming by armoured car. Plus Wilson's are hiring *armed* security guards and *bulletproof* glass cases. You are not going to steal them. You are not going to try either. Totally forget about it! Sapphire and I have no intention of spending every Sunday afternoon from now until for ever visiting you in jail.'

'Amber, go to your wardrobe and dress up,' Em instructed. 'Put on a cool club outfit, do your hair, add make-up, just try lightening up and looking like a young person for once and then get over here by 7 p.m. When we are not serving drinks, showing people to their tables or cleaning up spills from the dance floor, I will tell you just exactly how I am going to do it.'

Bill's Place – NoHo's hippest – was much bigger, louder and swankier than Amber had imagined. As soon as she'd entered the bar area, all sleek mirrors, groovy lampshades and velvet, she'd known she was in the heart of cool and happening New York City central . . . and in an outfit which was so not working.

But it had been such a long, long time since she'd been anywhere cool. In fact, had she ever gone clubbing since college? She couldn't remember.

But never mind. Em swooped down on her, wrinkled her face and sighed just briefly at Amber's boring black pants and green top with sparkles. Then, after introducing her to Dino, she began to show her all the tasks of a Bill's Place hostess.

Over the throbbing, thumping music as they watched New York's beautiful people sip at cocktails and slink, hipbone first, across the dance floor, Amber told Em: 'I can never work here. I'm a fish outta water. A guppy in a glass of beer.'

'Shut up!' Em said. 'I'm clearing $300 a night with tips. They have openings five nights a week, you could rent in Manhattan with that kind of money. And it's easy . . .'

'Sir, good evening, let me find you one of our very best tables.' Em directed her most charming smile at a tall, shaven-headed black guy with diamond earrings and a grey fur coat.

When she hurried back to Amber, Em told her: 'Now he is cool, uber-cool. I'm going to bring him drinks all night long. He's the biggest gangster on the Lower East Side and his tips are legendary. He's rich, rich, rich. When I have my millions, I am going to buy furs and diamonds first. Even if I have nowhere to sleep at night, I'm going to be wearing fur and diamonds.'

'Em, you have to stop with this stuff. Seriously,' Amber said, and she put what she hoped was a calming hand on Em's shoulder, 'the fantasy is over. Sapphire called and she was all het up because those jewels are arriving a whole day early. They're coming in tomorrow not Wednesday. They'll be on display under lock, key and armed guard from tomorrow. You are not going to steal them, or sell them – or be shopping for fur and diamonds. I don't know what kind of dream you've been in lately – but you have to Get Real.'

'Tomorrow morning . . . *tomorrow*? Are you sure?'

'That's what she said.'

'Is *she* sure? I have to call her.'

'Fine, call her,' Amber said, 'but first of all, you know what? I would really like to hear your plan.'

'Really?'

'Yeah, really. I would really like to hear just exactly how you're planning to make $4 million worth of jewellery disappear.'

'Fine. We'll both take trays, we'll fill 'em up with empty glasses, then we'll walk slowly to the kitchen. That way we can look busy and I can tell you.'

As they went between tables, loading up with

empties and promising to come right back for new orders, Em began to explain.

'I've seen the security plans . . .'

'I know,' Amber said.

'They fell outta Fergus's briefcase—'

'And you looked at them.'

'The jewels arrive at 10 a.m. by car,' Em went on, 'and go straight up to Mr Wilson's office. Mr Wilson, Sapphire and Fergus are going to examine and photograph them, then at 10.45 approximately they'll be taken down to the special cases in the viewing room and from then on they'll be under armed guard.'

'Right – so you haven't got a chance.'

'No. Wrong. My chance is when they're in the cataloguing room. They won't be in the cases, they won't be under armed guard, they'll just be out there on the table with three people I know.'

'Yeah, three people who won't let them out of sight for a moment – and won't there be guards at the door?'

'Two. It says in the plans.'

'So?' Amber turned to her sister.

'I'll let myself in the staff entrance' – Em's voice had dropped to a whisper although they were in the corridor now and no one was about – 'I'm going to go up to Sapphire's room and there's a connecting door—'

'Which will be locked.'

Em reached for a chain around her neck. On it was a key, which she dangled at her sister.

'Ta-dah!' Em said triumphantly. 'Borrowed, copied and replaced.'

'The guards will be right beside Sapphire's office because Mr Wilson is just next door. They're not going to let you in.'

'I will cause a diversion.'

'A diversion?!' Amber snorted. 'That only works in the movies and even if you do get in, how are you going to get the jewels from Sapphire, Mr Wilson and Fergus?'

'I can't tell you.'

'Why not?'

'You won't like it.'

Amber turned to her sister, horrified. 'Em, you don't have a gun, do you? Em, if you have a gun, I'm going to call the cops.'

'Ooooh, got Jackie boy on speed dial, have we? Going to get him to round up your naughty little sister, are you?'

'Em, seriously. Please tell me you do not have a gun.'

'Amber, seriously, I do not have a gun,' Em teased. 'Because this is not a crime. There will be no victims because even Mrs De La Hoz is insured. This is an elegant, clever jewel theft.'

'Were you planning on a disguise?' Amber wanted to know.

'Of course, a fantastic disguise, a truly irresistible Lady Who Doesn't Work disguise. Sunglasses, blonde wig, fake tan and camel-coloured cashmere.'

'Except you don't have any cashmere.'

'No, so I might have to improvise there. But the ermine is coming with me. It's my lucky charm.'

'I always thought criminals should dress up as cleaners,' Amber said. 'No one ever notices cleaners or pays any attention to them and Wilson's is full of them. The whole place sparkles; there must be cleaners going around there all day long and you never even see them.'

'Good idea!'

Amber now wished she hadn't mentioned it. But Em could not be serious. She really could not be serious about this.

'What about all the cameras, Em? There must be a camera in every corridor and on every exit.'

'I don't think there's a camera in the boss's office.'

'Why is he taking the jewels there, then?' Amber wondered out loud. 'To the one place where there's no camera? That is a crazy move.'

'That, girlfriend, is an opportunity.'

'And what about the rest of it?'

Amber could hardly hide her exasperation. 'I mean, let's just say by some amazing stroke of luck you manage to *distract* the guards, *avoid* all the cameras, *steal* the jewels from *three* people who just happen not to be *looking* . . . how do you get out of the building when the *alarm* is ringing?'

'Climb out the restroom window,' Em replied. 'I'm a high school gymnast. Piece of cake.'

Infuriated, Amber went on: 'So how do you hide $4 million worth of treasure? How do you smuggle it out of the country? How do you find a collector then sell it to him? And just where do you plan to hide the stolen money?'

'I've set up a charity account,' Em said.

'You've set up a charity account? For real? You've set up a bogus charity account?

They were at the end of the corridor. Both girls set their drinks trays down in the hatch to the kitchens. Amber turned to Em and gripped her tightly by the shoulders, desperate to talk some sense into her.

'Please stop now,' she insisted. 'Just stop right now, while it's still just an idea. This is not going to happen. I'm really sorry things are not working out for you. But this doesn't even come close to being an answer . . .'

Em shrugged her shoulders free from Amber's hold. But Amber continued: 'I mean jeeez, Em! I have lost my job, I am about to lose my apartment, I can't help Mother with the mortgage and my lovely daddy turns out to have been a cheat! But I am *still* a completely honest person, I am still figuring out how to make a living without stealing one single cent from anyone,' she glared at her sister angrily. 'Those two guys who did the jewellery store in our street, they got caught, Em! One of them is going to jail, the other is on a youth probation programme. Yeah, you may have shoplifted a few times, but now you've got to grow up and stop. Maybe there's no happy ever after for us. Maybe there's no Plan A, or B or C! Maybe we don't get to make it big, Em. Maybe we just have to work hard and struggle on like almost everybody else on the face of the earth. Maybe we don't get to join the special club.'

'No way!' Em exclaimed. 'No way. I'm going to do it or go down trying. Don't you even think about trying to stop me!' With that she turned on her heel and began to walk away.

'Em, I will do every single thing I can to stop you,' Amber called after her. 'I'll tell Sapphire. When she goes into work tomorrow, security will be double – triple – what it was supposed to be. You're not even going to get into the building. If I have to, I'll even lock you into your bedroom tomorrow.'

For the next four hours, Amber and Em were the hardest-working hostesses in the club. They went back and forward to the kitchens, bars and the tables tirelessly; they wiped, they mopped, they smiled, they charmed, but they didn't say another single word to each other.

Then at four in the morning, when the long, exhausting shift was over, Em approached Amber with a tall glass of Coke, crammed with ice.

'It's Cherry, your favourite,' Em said and her smile looked apologetic.

'Thanks,' Amber replied and took several thirsty gulps.

'That tastes really weird,' was the last thing she remembered saying to Em.

# Chapter Twenty-Four

*'I'll tell you what's the matter with her: she's vegetarian.'*

*'She's vegetarian?! I thought she was an alcoholic.'*

Amber knew she was awake. She could hear herself breathing . . . she could hear a car engine revving up in the street below, but she couldn't open her eyes.

Plus her mouth was so dry, her tongue felt as if it had been glued into place.

What in the heck was going on?!

She strained at her eyelids and gradually a crack of light began to appear, then at last she was able to look around properly. She was in her room, lying on top of her bed, fully dressed in the silky trousers and top she'd worn to the nightclub. Her eyes were swollen and crunchy with the make-up she'd put on last night.

She unstuck her tongue from the roof of her mouth and felt a heavy throb at the back of her head.

What exactly had happened to her?

She looked at her bedside clock. It was 9.16 a.m. She stood up, wobbled unsteadily and opened the bedroom door.

The apartment was silent. Somehow, she'd slept through the noise of Sapphire and Em both getting up and leaving for work.

Amber could remember being at the nightclub at the end of the shift – but then what? She tried hard to remember how she'd got home. But found she couldn't.

Something bright yellow, on her door just below eye level caught her attention. It was a Post-it note in Em's handwriting.

Amber took it down and read aloud: '*Sorry, Amber, but I can't let you stop me. I have to do it or go down trying. Em xx*'

'Oh my,' Amber whispered, as the pieces fell together and she realized what Em had done.

'My sister roofied me.' She sat down heavily on the sofa. 'My kid sister roofied me. My kid sister put drugs into my Cherry Coke.'

Then she leapt up, rushed back into the bedroom and checked her alarm clock again: 9.19 a.m. The jewels were arriving at Wilson's in forty-one minutes

– which meant Amber had to get to the Upper East Side in under forty-one minutes and stop Em from going to jail.

She pulled on a sweater, a jacket, then boots and a hat. There was no time to fix the panda eyes or even to take a drink of water. As she ran out of the door and down the stairs, she punched Sapphire's number into her cell.

Voicemail.

'Sapph, call me. Call me just as soon as you get this message. It's URGENT!'

Em's cell went straight to message too. 'Don't do this!' she yelled and hung up.

Out on 17th, Amber ran to the subway station at the end of the road. As she rounded the corner, about to rush down the staircase, a guy coming up told her: 'Don't even bother. Lines are out to 34th again.'

'What? Are you serious?' she panted, but now she could see the crowd of commuters coming up towards the exit.

'Yup. Welcome to another day of hell and start walking.'

Amber looked at her watch: 9.27. She couldn't walk to the Upper East Side and be there in time. If the trains were out, every cab would be taken, she had no time to wait for a bus – she would have to race back to the apartment and get her bike.

She'd have to pedal to Wilson & Sons. Somehow, she had to get there in time to stop Em making the biggest mistake of her entire life.

# Chapter Twenty-Five

*'Now, Betty, that diamond has so many carats . . . you could just about feed it to a horse!'*

At 9.44 a.m. this Wednesday the doorman standing outside Aubrey Wilson & Sons in a long, braided coat, peaked cap and white gloves, is joined by a second doorman and the in-house security guard. Together they chat nervously, fidget, straighten and re-straighten their ties and wait.

One of the doormen takes a call.

When it ends, he tucks away the phone and fires instructions to the other two. The security guard disappears inside for several moments, then comes back out onto the street again; all three look alert and primed for action.

A long, black car pulls into the street and parks in the specially cleared space outside the building.

Certainly no press has been alerted and only a handful of key personnel inside the building know the exact arrival time.

A sign in the windows informs passers-by that the viewing rooms will not open until 11 a.m. today: 'due to special circumstances'.

As a uniformed man carrying a large black brief-case steps out of the car and strides quickly into the auctioneer's, Em, in a thick layer of fake tan and a long black wig, is sitting watching from a window seat at Ernie's cafe, right across the road. She drains the last of her coffee, then stands and hurries over to pay her bill.

She knows that the doors to Aubrey Wilson & Sons will be shut but, thanks to Sapphire, she also knows the punch-in code for the back door, so that doesn't worry her. In fact Em feels calm, prepared and exhilarated, like the star performer standing in the wings, waiting for curtain up.

She is waiting to give the performance of a lifetime. No more Em . . . it's time for Emerald to step forward.

With a small backpack on her shoulder, Emerald crosses the street to the left of the auctioneers and hurries down a small side alley. She darts to the right into a narrow street and approaches the back entrance. No one else is about; she pulls the white headscarf from her backpack and wraps it over her hair and down under her chin.

Then she punches in the code, pushes open the back door and steps in. She does not know yet how this will all work out, exactly, but there is no denying the exhilarating surge of adrenalin in her veins.

Emerald races into a small side corridor, whips off her raincoat and stuffs it into the backpack. She is now dressed just like a cleaner in jeans, sneakers, and a pink and white overall with a home-made staff pass dangling from her neck.

She heads for the staff restroom which she knows is on the ground floor. Keeping her eyes low, she doesn't look up at anyone who walks past her. In her headscarf and cleaner's overalls, she feels strangely invisible, just like Amber said. No one stops her, no one asks any questions. She sees the restroom and hurries into the cubicle with the window.

It is a tiny window, six feet off the floor. But Emerald reminds herself that she did gymnastics for twelve years. She can hold herself on the gym rings for more than ten minutes, so this should be a cinch. Plus, it's on the ground floor. It's not like she has to drop from a height on the other side.

She rifles through her backpack, taking out an aerosol can and cleaning cloths. She pulls her white scarf right up over her chin and secures it with a pin. Then she stuffs everything back in the backpack and listens to make sure she's the only person in the room.

She unlocks the cubicle door and steps out. Just

up there is the supplies cupboard where she figures she can keep her backpack for a few minutes. She reaches up and pushes it in. Then she decides to get going, before she can change her mind.

Out in the corridor, Emerald whispers under her breath: 'Turn right to the staircase, up one floor; then left down the corridor, right turn and second door along on the left.'

She follows her own instructions as quickly as she can. She passes a smartly dressed woman in the corridor, but keeps her eyes down.

Now she is in the corridor with both Sapphire and Mr Wilson's offices. There is only one security guard standing outside Mr Wilson's door. Emerald had expected two. She'd given up on her idea of causing a diversion: she'd decided just to walk calmly into Sapphire's office as if cleaning that office right now was the most normal thing.

But as she walks towards the guard, holding her cloths and her aerosol can, she wonders how that will work out.

Why would he let her go in this close to the room with the jewels? And wouldn't he get a dangerously close look at her face?

Just as she begins to slow up, not knowing if she really has the nerve to walk straight into Sapphire's office, the guard turns abruptly and runs off in the other direction.

Emerald's face lights up. She knows she has only moments, he might be right back, but right now she has opportunity. Golden opportunity!

She tries the handle of Sapphire's office . . . open. She steps into the room. It is neat, tidy and smells of Sapphire's rose-scented perfume.

As Emerald tiptoes towards the adjoining door, feeling for the key at her neck, she catches sight of the family photo Sapphire has in a silver frame on her desk. It's years old, a faded snapshot of the five of them. All of a sudden Emerald can remember the day more vividly than yesterday.

A rare day off for her parents, they'd all piled into the pickup truck with a huge picnic and gone fishing. Of course all the usual adventures and disasters had occurred. Amber had slipped, fallen in and picked up a leech, Mother had been stung on the nose, they'd only caught one tiny fish and everyone got sunburned. But looking at the picture now, Emerald realizes with tears in her eyes that days like this are a slice of heaven and you only know just how precious they are, once they're gone.

She looks down at the key in her right hand and the can of mace in her left and wonders if she has lost her mind.

Really? Really!!

Is she really thinking she can unlock that door,

burst in and mace her very own sweet sister, Sapphire, in the face?

She can't do this.

She is standing right here with the tools in her hands . . . but she's never, ever felt as uncertain as this about a shop-lift. She doesn't believe she can do it. Where there is doubt, there's sure to be failure.

'AAAARGH!!!!'

A cry, a scream and a crash come from Mr Wilson's office, followed by the sounds of a struggle.

Another scream.

'No! No!' a man's voice calls.

Again a scream.

'Sapphire!' Em cries out. 'Are you OK?'

A door slams, Em can hear shouts and sobs. Her hands shaking, she fumbles to get her copied key into the lock.

She opens the door and sees the chaos in Mr Wilson's office.

Sapphire is sitting on a chair with her hands clutched in front of her eyes. Mr Wilson is on the floor, also with his hands in front of his face.

On the table and the desk are a briefcase and two jewel boxes, both opened, upended and empty.

'I think it's mace!' Sapphire cries out. 'I think we've been maced!'

'The alarm!' Mr Wilson shouts. 'Someone get to the alarm.'

Em is standing in the doorway in a heavy disguise with a can of mace in her hands . . . Even though she is innocent, even though Sapphire is hurt, Emerald tells herself she has to turn and make a run for it. Right now.

'What's going on? What's happened?'

Emerald recognizes Fergus's voice in the distance. He must be in the corridor, running towards the door.

She pulls the connecting door shut and rushes back out into the corridor. She turns a corner blindly, then the great shrieking, terrifying wail of the alarm starts up.

Emerald, panicked, ducks in through a door and finds she is in another office. She can't stay here. She can't stay anywhere! She has to carry on pretending to be an innocent cleaner and she has to get the hell out of here.

She snatches up a wastepaper basket from underneath the desk and heads back out into the corridor.

Left, right, down the stairs . . . finally, Emerald makes it to the restroom. But, despite the alarm shrilling through the building, someone else is in the cubicle with the window. Heart pounding, she pulls her backpack from the supplies cupboard and locks herself into the second cubicle. All at once she feels both terrified and furious. She is trying to stop herself from weeping with confusion and fear and rage. She has been thwarted! By another thief!

Someone else has carried out the crime she was supposed to do. Someone else has the treasures. Right now this very moment . . . someone else is getting away with it.

Emerald didn't have the nerve. Right at the last moment, she couldn't do it. She feels broken. As if she will never recover from this.

Emerald pulls off the headscarf, the cleaning overall and the long dark wig. Now she bundles her hair into a short, red, curly wig.

She packs everything into her bag, not forgetting the fake ID. She zips up and she waits, listening. A flush sounds. She hears the bolt of the other cubicle being shot. She hears the tap running. Then despite the alarm, she hears the dryer. Finally the door opens and shuts. Emerald crouches, listening intently: as soon as it's clear, she's going to spring from her cubicle, lock herself in the other one and escape from the window.

As she waits, the sun breaks from a cloud and a beam of light travels through the window, over the gap at the top of the partition wall, and straight into the wastepaper basket which Emerald has brought with her into the cubicle, just because she's not thought to put it down yet.

Emerald sees the glint.

She crouches down.

She parts the coffee cups, scrunched envelopes and pieces of paper, and with a gasp of amazement sees the glint of diamonds and emeralds, part of a necklace more fabulous than any she could ever have imagined.

She reaches for it, pulls it out and stares at it in disbelief. The necklace? How can the necklace be here? How has it ended up in a trash can . . . in an office . . . down the corridor from the theft? Em frantically pulls papers and an old chips packet out and now she can see . . . the panther! The Duchess of Windsor's panther brooch is also here. How can this be possible?

She picks it out of the trash and holds it up. The panther is breathtaking. His ruby eyes glitter as if he is truly alive.

Emerald makes one final sweep of the trash can, right down to the bottom, scrabbling amongst the torn papers.

The restroom door opens: 'Anyone in here?' calls a deep, male voice over the screaming alarm.

Em feels her heart stop.

She is going to be caught. How will anyone ever believe that even though she planned to steal, she did nothing? She's in disguise, she's holding the jewels . . . she looks completely guilty. She will never escape from this.

'Hey, you in there,' the voice calls.

Em stays silent.

'You – in the stall.'

He rattles on the door.

'Yes?' Em squeaks.

'You'll need to come out. It's a lockdown. Everyone to the reception hall.'

'OK,' she squeaks back.

With trembling fingers she stuffs the cleaning cloths, the mace and the treasures she has found into her backpack, then pushes the flush on the toilet and opens the stall door.

Instead of coming face to face with the security guard, she finds that he has stepped out of the restroom, maybe to give her a moment of privacy. This is her one and only chance of escape. She runs to the cubicle next to the window, throws her bag out, then lifts herself up, scrambles through and drops down to the ground.

Snatching up the bag, she allows herself to sprint the length of the back alleyway.

As soon as she turns a corner, she slows to a walk.

She runs shaking hands over her short red wig to make sure it's still on and everything is in place. Her heart has never in her life pumped so hard. She feels weak with fright. No performance was ever so difficult. So impossible. So terrifying! She will never, ever do anything like this again.

Emerald wants to shriek and scream to release the terror. She also wants to curl up in a ball and cry. But she hurries on, walking as briskly as she dares; round the next corner . . . She has no idea, not the slightest idea what to do next.

Already she can hear sirens.

The police are on their way. A major crime has been committed, a major investigation is about to begin.

Em is walking in a daze with a backpack full of treasure.

She turns another corner and almost crashes straight into Amber on her bicycle.

## Chapter Twenty-Six

*'They met on the Brooklyn Bridge.'*

*'How romantic.'*

*'Not really. He knocked her off her bicycle with his Porsche Cayenne.'*

'Amber!' Em says, voice low, barely above a whisper.

'Em? Is that you? Is that really you?'

Amber stares. Her sister is dark with fake tan and her hair has been bundled up under the red wig. Although Amber is right next to her, she barely recognizes her.

'Oh, thank goodness I found you, thank goodness. I was so worried I wasn't going to make it in time!' Amber pants. Her face is bright red and sweaty, she's never pedalled so hard ever before.

Em just looks at her, saying nothing.

'Em?' Amber asks.

Still Em makes no reply.

That's when Amber hears the sirens for the first time and the distant peal of the alarm. 'Em?' she asks again. 'You didn't . . . you haven't . . .' Her voice is rising with panic.

Em turns pleading eyes on Amber: 'It's a mistake,' she whispers, 'it's all a mistake. You have to believe me. Help me, Amber! Help me . . . no one else will believe me. Help, help! Or I'm going to jail.'

Amber looks at her little sister in astonishment.

'Jail? What do you mean?'

'They'll think I did it. But it wasn't me. I've got them – but it wasn't me!'

She has never seen Em look more frightened or more vulnerable. Every maternal, protective and sisterly instinct in Amber immediately wakes up and prepares to fight. Whatever mistake has been made, Amber is not going to let Em go to jail.

She will do whatever she has to do.

'Have you got the jewels?' Amber asks, trying to keep her voice calm, trying to keep herself calm.

Em nods and goes on in a terrified whisper: 'I didn't do the robbery. There was someone else. But I have them . . . I have them, by *mistake*,' Em repeats, looking desperate.

'Where are they?' Amber asks.

Em points to her backpack.

Amber looks around the empty alleyway. Someone could appear at any moment. Hell, the police could appear at any moment.

She reaches for Em's rucksack and unzips the front pocket.

'No shit!' she exclaims under her breath as she looks inside and sees a dazzling bundle of gold, diamond, emerald and platinum sparkling back at her.

Quickly she takes a plastic bag from her bicycle basket, scoops up the jewels and transfers the plastic bag now filled with Royal treasure into her messenger bag.

'Go to Daffy's,' Amber instructs Em, who is standing still, looking dazed. 'You know, Daffy's the department store, it's just a block away. Go in there, to the restrooms and change. Then go to work. Tell Marlese you slept in. But just go to work and have a regular day.'

Em nods.

'Sapphire is OK, isn't she?' Amber asks, suddenly remembering that their other sister might be involved.

Em nods: 'I think so . . .'

'Does she know you were there?'

Now Em shakes her head: 'I don't think so.'

'Go to Daffy's,' Amber repeats, worried that Em's so dazed she might forget.

'Where are you going?' Em asks.

'Me? I have to get these out of here. I have to try and come up with an idea.'

## Chapter Twenty-Seven

*'Oh there's no more gold-digging going on.*
*Gold's in a bubble.'*

*'I hear girls today are only after diamonds*
*or Chinese yen.'*

The loud, whooping alarm was still raging through Aubrey Wilson & Sons. It was roaring in Sapphire's ears, mingling with all the other sounds of panic: doors crashing, feet running up and down corridors, anguished shouts and yells. She could hear more sirens out in the street.

On the other side of the room Mr Wilson was shouting:

'Stop! Help! Someone help! The jewels!'

Then, his voice dropping, he asked incredulously: 'Have they gone? Have they really gone?'

'Just tell me, exactly what has happened in here?'

'Fergus!' Sapphire called out at the sound of his voice. 'Fergus – help!'

She felt his arm around her shoulder. 'Are you OK?' he asked urgently.

'My eyes . . .'

'Oh good grief! Let me go and get water for your eyes, for both of you.'

'No!' Mr Wilson protested. 'You have to do something. You have to stop the thief. You have to get the jewels back!'

'The doors are locked, the police are on their way,' Fergus assured him.

His arm slipped from Sapphire's shoulder.

'No wait,' she protested, wanting to keep him right there beside her.

'You need water,' he insisted. 'I'll be right back, I promise.' She could hear him hurrying out of the room, just as someone else rushed in.

'Mr Wilson? What's happened?'

More footsteps followed . . . she could hear a rush of people entering the room, crowding round her, laying helping hands on her shoulders.

'Sapphire!'

'Mr Wilson!'

'Are you OK?'

'What's happened?'

'We heard the alarm . . .'

'We've been robbed!' Mr Wilson yelled. 'We've

been blinded! The jewels have gone! Why the hell do you think I sounded the alarm? Have you found him? Did the doormen see him? Has no one stopped him?!'

Mr Wilson sounded frantic, desperate and angry.

'Oh my God. Have they gone? Have the jewels gone?' someone demanded.

'The jewels!'

'Has someone taken them?'

Panic began to build up in the room.

'Could everyone calm down? As soon as the alarm is sounded, every door in the building is locked and the police are called. They'll be here any minute. For all we know, the thief might still be in the building.'

Sapphire recognized the voice. It was Mark Holgate, one of Mr Wilson's favourite auctioneers.

'The police? Any minute? It's all too late!' Mr Wilson shouted. 'He'll be gone. It's New York City out there. We need to stop him now!'

'Sapphire, here, I've got some wet towels. You poor thing, you poor darling.'

Sapphire heard Fergus once again at her shoulder. Then felt cool wetness soothing her aching eyes.

The next time she opened her eyelids, she could make out a blurry scene.

Fergus, Mark, Mr Wilson and a few others were crowded into the room.

'Just what exactly happened?' Mark asked, urgency in his voice.

'There was a knock on the door and I opened it,' Mr Wilson began. 'A man in overalls with a black stocking pulled down over his face came in. He sprayed stuff at our faces. We were blind. Then . . .'

Mr Wilson's voice shook as he added, 'He took the jewels.'

'All of them?' Mark asked, shocked.

'I don't know. Look on the table. Look through the cases. I can't see. I can't check. I can't see anything!'

'I can't find them,' Sapphire said tearfully, 'I've been feeling with my hands. I can't find them.'

More clean, cold towels were handed to Mr Wilson.

After a moment or so, Mark confirmed: 'There's nothing here and the cases are empty.'

Footsteps and more voices sounded in the corridor; they were growing louder, approaching.

'OK . . . Mike and three others are going all round the building, checking and sealing off all the exits. Christine, get a team together to do a quick routine search of everyone, plus names, addresses, contact details. All staff in the building and everyone's areas. We want desks, briefcases, filing cabinets, all furniture checked over. Lewis, you're on the cameras. Check all the footage for the last twenty minutes as fast as possible. We need every clue. And quickly! Call in help. There are some very impatient, rich folks involved here and we all know they can never stand to wait.'

'Yessir.'

'Matt, you're in here with me. This is the crime scene. These are our number one witnesses. Hey guys! This is a crime scene,' the voice repeated. 'Can everyone who wasn't in here when the jewellery was stolen please take their DNA out of the room now. Go to the lobby where you will be searched, ID-ed and . . .'

The detective glanced at the sign above the adjoining door and inspiration struck: '*Catalogued.*'

He came into the room properly now.

In a voice full of surprise, he asked, 'Sapphire Jewel? Is that you?'

Sapphire moved the towel from her eyes. Cold water and hot tears were rapidly clearing the blur.

Standing before her, raincoat over his shoulders and with a half-astonished, half-friendly expression on his face, was Jack Desmoine.

He came over and knelt down beside her.

'How are ya doing? You didn't get hurt, did ya?'

'Just my eyes.'

He leaned towards her face and took a look.

'Ouch. A strong dose of mace at close range. Looks like your boss got the same.'

Sapphire couldn't help herself; she suddenly burst into violent sobs.

Jack's arm went around her shoulders.

'It's OK. You're going to be OK.'

'I'm not,' she cried, 'I'm not ever going to be OK ever again. This is a disaster.'

The violence of her sobs startled everyone in the room.

'You are going to be OK,' Jack insisted. 'Everyone needs to calm right down. The quicker we can get the information out there, the better. Mr Wilson, you may or may not know that Sapphire was the witness in another robbery I dealt with recently. She was made to lie on the ground and the robber held a gun to her head.'

At the memory of that night, Sapphire began to cry harder.

'So I'll keep the questions for Miss Jewel as brief as I can, then I'll call her sister to come get her.'

In a blur of tears, Sapphire answered Jack's questions. Only vaguely was she aware of the forensic team going round the room: searching, dusting, scrutinizing.

'Tell me any details you remember about the person who came into the room. Did you have time to see anything at all? Eye colour? Height? Anything about the hands. Anything unusual or recognizable at all?'

'Blue eyes,' Mr Wilson put in.

'You sound sure of that.'

'I am sure of it. Distinctive, bright-blue eyes.'

'Did you notice that, Sapphire?'

'No,' Sapphire shook her head and wiped at her face with the towel.

'Tall,' Mr Wilson added, 'and muscular. It was a big guy under that overall.'

'Yes,' Sapphire agreed. 'Brown shoes. Brown leather shoes,' she added.

'Did he say anything?' Jack asked. 'Was there any kind of accent you could place?'

Both Sapphire and Mr Wilson shook their heads.

'He didn't say a word,' Sapphire replied, 'he just came in and it was obvious from the stocking over his face why he was there and then he sprayed Mr Wilson and then me. I tried to get away, but he held me down.'

'Was he wearing gloves?'

Sapphire nodded.

'There was a voice . . .' Mr Wilson remembered. 'Now that I think about it, there was a voice. I'm certain I heard a girl's voice call out Sapphire's name.'

'Oh my gosh!' Sapphire exclaimed. 'I thought I imagined it. I thought I was hearing things.'

'It was right after it happened,' Mr Wilson continued: 'The adjoining door opened and a girl asked if she was OK.'

'Did you recognize the voice?' Jack asked.

Sapphire looked up at him; through the blur she could make out his face, very serious, very concerned.

This was an important question. She knew just how important it was and how many clues her answer could give. But she couldn't tell them. She couldn't say that she was sure her sister Em had asked the question.

'No,' she said simply.

'Detective, please tell me your team is not just in here, please tell me they're combing the building, combing the streets,' Mr Wilson said, beginning to sound desperate. 'I mean this is $4 million worth. These are world-famous jewels. And nothing – nothing – has ever, *ever* been stolen from Aubrey Wilson & Sons before, in our 150 year history! This is a disaster. An outrage. A tragedy.'

'Nothing's ever been stolen from you guys before? I don't believe it.' Jack sounded a little testy.

'Well . . . nothing that wasn't an inside job that couldn't be put quietly right,' Mr Wilson confided.

'Huh . . . and we'll need to know all about the possibilities of an inside job here. How many people knew exactly when the armoured car was arriving? And you think a passer-by would find their way to the right room just by chance? And where was your security? Your staff are going to be my main suspects unless something happens to suggest otherwise.'

'My staff!' Mr Wilson gasped.

Footsteps were hurrying down the corridor towards the room.

'Detective!'

One of the cops on the team stuck his head around the door.

'We've found something,' he said. 'We have footage of a short-haired girl jumping out of a restroom window with a backpack!'

## Chapter Twenty-Eight

*'I don't know who has the time to garden any more.'*

*'Oh I know. All that hiring and firing of gardeners. It's exhausting.'*

This was ridiculous. Crazy!

How had it happened?

How had Amber gone from last night's: 'Em, please stop, you can't do this' to right now, this morning . . . cycling though Manhattan traffic with millions of dollars' worth of stolen treasure in a bicycle basket?

She, Amber Jewel, asset manager, girl with the glowing résumé, was on a bicycle, wobbling, weaving, barely able to get up enough speed to go in a straight line with $4 million . . . $4 MILLION WORTH of stolen jewellery in her basket. She was so scared, it was beyond panic. Her breath was rasping in and out of her chest as if she'd just run a marathon.

*Royal* jewels!!

*Stolen Royal jewels* – for freak's sake!!

Emeralds and diamonds, which had once hung around the pampered neck of the most famous Duchess in the world, were wrapped up in a plastic bag from Bed, Bath & Beyond in her messenger bag as she pedalled them in a blind panic around New York.

'Watchit, lady!!' a pedestrian barked at her as she nearly smashed into his ankles.

Amber wanted to scream.

She didn't want to do this. She wanted out. Now! She'd never even wanted in.

But it was too late: she was in.

Amber thought of other crazy things she'd done in the past to stop her little sister getting in trouble. There really had never been anything to compare with this. It may have started with: 'No, Em would never have thrown a rock at that window' – even though her hands were dirty from holding the rock – but now it was hiding stolen jewels so Em didn't go to jail!

Amber hit a bump in the road and clung to the handlebars. She couldn't help yelling out and heads turned in her direction.

She was wanted! Maybe the police were already radioing a description of her all around the city. This was a living, waking, breathing nightmare. But she had to stay calm.

If she could just stay calm and think straight she might figure out a way for them to get out of this mess.

First of all she had to hide the jewels. Then she could go someplace quiet and calm, listen to Em's whole story and figure out a way forward.

'Oh my gosh, ohmigosh, ohmigosh . . .' Amber repeated to herself like a mantra as she pedalled, 'stay calm, stay calm.'

She took a deep breath and let it out slowly, thinking back to her favourite self-help books. 'I'm moving towards my goals,' she said out loud. 'I am achieving,' she whispered. 'I can achieve everything I wish to achieve. I am calm. I am feeling quite, quite calm . . .'

Somehow, her jello legs and shaking hands moved the bicycle forward. In fact, her bicycle was moving towards the place it knew best. It was taking Amber and the Duchess of Windsor's jewels towards the 6B Community Gardens.

'Hey, Amber! Hi!'

Fitch, the full-time park keeper, waved at her as she came in through the park gates. He was a fit, skinny guy, with a ponytail and year-round tan. No matter what the weather, he always wore trail boots and shorts.

'We missed ya Sunday!' he called over. 'But you're here now, so – great.'

'Hi!' she called back, realizing immediately how weird and high-pitched her voice sounded.

She parked up the bicycle and went towards him wondering how she was managing to walk on her shaking legs.

She even thought she could hear the chink-chink of the diamonds and emeralds jiggling in her bag.

'Hi . . . I've got a bit of time today and I thought I'd spend it in the garden. Help you plant more trees.'

'It's cold work right now. But we're trying to do a little line of maples.'

'How come you're planting trees in December, anyhow?'

'I know, it might not work. But we got gifted them and they arrived and so . . .' He shrugged. 'We're gonna give it a go.'

'OK.' He was still planting trees. Today! Somehow, she'd known this was the best place to come because where better to hide the treasures than a hole in the ground?

She followed Fitch with his relaxed stride and long hippie ponytail to the store where the tools and new plants were kept.

'Load up a wheelbarrow and get yourself started. I need to finish my bulb planting before I can come over and help ya.'

'Sure,' Amber said.

She breathed in and out, trying to calm herself.

She liked the smell in the tool store. It was oily and earthy; it reminded her of the ranch.

She loaded the wheelbarrow with two spades of different sizes, a bag of compost and three of the spindly little maples, then she pushed it over to the spot Fitch had shown her.

Only when she had the pointed spade in her hands and had begun digging did she feel the terror slacken just slightly in her chest.

For long, concentrated minutes, Amber dug hard until she'd made a deep hole about two foot square. Then she looked around to see if there was anyone about. Fitch was talking to the one other volunteer here today. Then together, they began to walk towards the store.

As soon as they were in the store, she would do this, she told herself. But no . . . now, a mom with a stroller was coming in through the park gate – heading in her direction.

She had to do this. She couldn't wait here all day for the perfect moment. Amber turned her back on the store and the stroller mom, then began to feel about in her bag.

Her trembling fingers got hold of the plastic bag. For a moment, she held it in her lap and opened it so she could look inside. The dazzle of diamond, gold, jewels and platinum was shocking.

This was real.

It had really happened.

The stolen jewels which most of New York was looking for by now were here. In her lap. In a plastic bag.

She scrunched the bag shut, rushed it into the hole and threw earth on top as fast as she could.

'Amber?'

The voice was so close by and she was so wound up that she actually shrieked.

'Take it easy there,' Fitch said and put a hand on her shoulder.

'Oh . . . hi . . . you scared me.'

'I can see that. I hate to say this, but you dug your hole in the wrong place. You're gonna have to shift it over.'

'Huh?' she looked from Fitch to the hole and back again.

'Yeah, I want them to start just two feet to the left of that. Will that be OK?'

'No! No it won't be OK,' Amber exclaimed. 'What the . . . ? You've just watched me dig this hole and now you come over here and ask me to move it. Tough luck, partner. I'm putting the goddam tree in this here goddam hole.'

Her outburst startled them both.

Fitch held up his hands. 'Hey, man . . . I know it's kinda rough out there in the corporate jungle right now but don't take it out on me.'

'I'm sorry, Fitch. I'm sorry.'

She looked at him, knowing she couldn't give in to his request. How the *freak* would she ever find that bag again if she didn't plant a great big tree on top of it?

For a flash of a moment, Amber imagined herself creeping into the park at night to dig the whole place up, searching endlessly like some desperate pirate for the buried treasure.

'C'mon . . .' she began sweetly, 'I'll put this tree in here, then just space the other ones out some more. It'll be good. Maples need a lot of room. They grow up and out real quick.'

For a moment Fitch paused. He tilted his head to the side, closed his eyes a little as if trying to imagine the trees.

'OK. Cool,' he said. 'And Amber?'

'Yeah?'

'Chill.'

'Right . . .'

She turned and, hands still shaking, reached for the tree and shook the earth gently from its roots before she placed it into the hole.

'Are you OK?' Fitch asked.

'I'm fine.'

'Your hands.' He pointed to her trembling fingers.

'I came by bike and I nearly got hit by a cab,' she said, first lie she could think of.

'Man . . . biking in Manhattan is rough,' Fitch said. 'Even I'm scared to do that.'

'Fitch?' Amber was still digging, holding the tree with one hand and moving earth onto its roots with the other. 'Do you have a cigarette?'

'Do you smoke?' he asked, sounding surprised.

'No, not usually, but I think it might help.'

'Here, let me finish that.'

With the spade, he moved the remaining earth quickly onto the tree, then stamped it down with his thick boots.

'Sit down,' he suggested.

Amber looked at the grass. It was a dry day and Sunday's snow had already melted, but a cold wind was blowing. Not perfect sitting out in the park weather.

But she lowered her butt to the grass and accepted the Camel Light which Fitch offered.

'Oh thank the Lord, I thought you were going to give me a roll-up.'

'Do I look like a roll-up kinda guy?'

'Hell yeah.'

He lit the cigarette.

Amber inhaled. It was the first time she'd smoked since college exactly two years ago. But hey, this was a big day. It was the first time she'd taken $4 million worth of stolen Royal jewels around New York on a bicycle, then buried them under a tree.

What was going to happen next?

She had no idea.

She blew the smoke out gently. Her pulse was still jumping like a frog in her neck.

'You look freaked,' Fitch offered.

'Tell me about it.'

# Chapter Twenty-Nine

*'He said he came to New York to meet*
*his own, beautiful princess.'*

*'What a shame the city turned him into a frog.'*

Amber was back in the apartment. She couldn't sit down, she couldn't stand still she was so jumpy.

She wasn't sure if she could believe what had happened this morning. Em had run out of Wilson's with $4 million worth of jewels, which she claimed she hadn't stolen.

Amber had buried the treasure in the gardens, to save her sister from jail.

Now what?

The robbery was already on the news. There was talk of full-scale searches, staff under surveillance and a reward. At least she knew that Sapphire was OK.

Amber couldn't think straight. She'd switched her computer on, but she hadn't been able to look at the screen for more than a few seconds. Now she was standing in the kitchenette making herb tea instead of coffee – because herb tea was supposed to be soothing, wasn't it?

Amber wondered if Em had any of those tranquillizers around. The ones that had found their way into her Cherry Coke last night. But then she heard the sound of voices approaching and footsteps on the stairs outside.

'It's fine. Really, I'll be fine.'

That was Sapphire's voice.

'You can go now, I'll get in by myself,' Sapphire said and Amber heard the jangle as her sister brought out her keys.

'No. I'm escorting you in. I'm going to see you to your couch and I'll even pour a small brandy down your throat if I have to. If your sister isn't home, I'll sit with you until you've called a friend over or found someone to take care of you.'

That was Jack's voice!

Amber breathed sharply in and out. What was Jack doing here? Why was Jack at her door? If there had been time, she'd have fled to her bedroom and hidden. But already the door was opening.

As soon as she saw Sapphire, pale with fright, eyes swollen and angry red, Amber rushed over to hug her.

'Are you OK?' Are you sure you're OK?' she asked, holding her tightly.

'I'm surviving,' Sapphire said lightly. 'In better shape than Mr Wilson, I think. He's really upset.'

Amber looked over her sister's shoulder and met Jack's eyes.

She felt that whole heart-stomach-flip-churn thing once again: the physical symptoms of liking him so much.

'What are you doing here?' she asked. 'Did you meet her in the street? Are you checking up on Ori? Sapph, come in . . . sit down. You look really, really pale.'

'You know about the robbery, right?' Jack asked.

Amber nodded.

'Plus Sapphire and Mr Wilson got maced right in the face,' he added.

'You got maced? Oh my goodness! What does that mean? Are you going to be OK? Sapphire?'

But already Sapphire had gone into the bathroom to wash every last trace of the poison from her skin.

'Her eyes are fine, just inflamed. They'll take a few days to recover. But she's had a terrible shock. She's been involved in two robberies in two weeks.'

'Involved? She's not involved!' Amber protested.

'No, I know she's not *involved*. What I mean is, she

was there. She was right there when it happened, she's a key witness. Once again. That's a whole load of stress.'

'So did you see her in the street?' Amber asked. 'I hope they at least sent her home in a cab after everything she's been through.'

Jack smiled. 'I met her at Wilson's, at the auction house. Then I brought her home.'

'What do you mean?'

'I'm a detective, remember?'

Amber looked at him blankly.

'On the case, Amber . . . I'm one of the detectives investigating the robbery at the auctioneer's. It's a huge case, obviously everybody is going to be pulled in one way or another.'

The astonishment registering on Amber's face made Jack laugh.

'You look very worried. I'm not that bad you know, in fact I'm quite good at my job.'

'*You're* investigating the robbery?'

The blood began to pound in Amber's ears and for a moment she thought she might faint.

'Yeah!' Jack was leaning against the door frame, smiling. 'Why's that so hard to understand? Because I did Ori's case and caught the guy, the chief has me figured as the jewel thief expert.'

Amber stood frozen to the spot.

'So I guess I'm not going to get invited in then?'

Amber tried to think it through. Was there anything incriminating in here? 'Erm . . . umm . . .' she hesitated, 'maybe just for a couple of minutes. Sapphire looks exhausted.'

She held open the door and let Jack step into the tiny living area. But she backed away from him, because kissing him hello didn't feel like the right thing just now.

He looked around at the small, cluttered space.

'A little cosy for three, isn't it?'

'We're moving next week.'

'Oh. Where to?'

'We don't know yet.'

'Were you going to tell me?'

'Umm . . . yeah, sure. Of course.'

'Sunday, with the skating, I thought it went really well. But you haven't called. I've tried to call you, but no answer.'

Amber could feel a blush creeping up her neck towards her ears.

He'd tried to call.

'I've been busy,' she said. 'I helped Em out at her nightclub last night and . . . I was going to call you back.'

'Well, that sounds good. What were you going to say?'

He raised his eyebrows and waited.

She wanted to kiss him. She wanted to go right up

to him, kiss him, be folded up against him and say: 'Jack we're in trouble. Please help!' But it was impossible. He was here with Sapphire, investigating the stolen jewels.

'I . . . umm . . . you know,' she began vaguely, 'I don't know if this is . . . a great time to . . .'

Jack was now wandering freely about the apartment. He was heading for the little table with her computer. Suddenly Amber remembered Em's pile of photocopied news stories lying right beside it. She had to stop him.

'You've been looking into those jewels, ha?' he asked, picking up one of the stories about the Duchess of Windsor's collection.

Amber felt her face redden with panic.

'Well . . . Sapphire was so excited about the sale . . . I guess we all wanted to know more.'

'*The Rough Guide to Montenegro*, huh?'

He picked the book up and flipped through the pictures. Amber felt her heart stop. 'Planning a vacation?' he asked

'No,' she gasped. 'No. I've no idea . . . it's Em's, some guy she's seeing is from . . . hey, what about tomorrow night? Are you doing anything?'

It was the best Amber could come up with under the circumstances. It certainly got Jack to put the book down and turn his attention to her.

'You mean, another date?' he asked.

'Yeah, if you want to. Is all,' Amber gave a little shrug.

'Do *you* want to?' he asked.

She nodded enthusiastically.

Jack's face brightened. 'Today and pretty much all day tomorrow, I'm going to be very, very busy. But got a pen and paper? Write down this address. OK?'

'Queens?' she asked, once she'd repeated the address back to him. 'You want me to go all the way to Queens?'

'It's a great place, you'll like it. We'll try to meet there for dinner at 8 p.m. But it's gonna depend a lot on how Sapphire is doing and how busy I am with the investigation. The chief usually lets me go grab a bite to eat, though.'

'J's Place, 164 Alexander Gardens, Queens.' She looked at the piece of paper: 'So what kinda place is it?'

'You'll love it. Fantastic food,' he promised.

His cell began to ring and he made straight for the door. 'Gotta get back. Shouldn't have left. But I wanted to see her safely home . . . plus, well, I was hoping I'd run into you again, cowgirl.'

He kissed her right on the lips, then the door was shut and he was gone before she even had the chance to react.

Jack.

Despite the whirlwind of fear, panic and

everything else racing about her system, she couldn't help smiling at Jack and feeling a thrill at the thought of their date.

But she knew all at once that it was impossible. Just like everything else right now.

Amber went to the bathroom door and tapped gently.

'Sapphire, are you OK?' she asked.

Sapphire came to the door, her face scrubbed clean, her eyes still an angry, watery red.

'I don't understand what happened,' she said in a whisper. 'A man came in. He maced us and he took the jewels. It wasn't Em.'

Amber shook her head. 'No.'

'But then I heard Em's voice,' Sapphire went on. 'Em asked me if I was OK, then she disappeared.'

'I don't know what happened yet. I haven't had time to talk to her, but . . .' Amber hesitated, knowing this would be very hard to believe. 'Em said she stole the jewels by mistake. And I think we have to believe her.'

'What?!'

'In fact, I do believe her,' Amber said. 'But once she had them, it looked as if she was guilty. So she had to hide them. Well, in fact, I hid them.'

'WHAT!' Sapphire repeated. She seemed to have faded to an even paler shade.

'What have you done?' she asked in a whisper. 'Em

took the jewels? Em stole them? And you *hid* them?'

For a moment the two sisters stared at each other.

Under Sapphire's horrified gaze, Amber suddenly felt truly ashamed.

'How *could* you?' Sapphire asked. 'You have ruined my life.'

'No . . . you didn't . . . you weren't . . .' Amber began.

'We'll get caught. I'll never be able to work in this business again. We'll all go to *jail*. No one will believe she stole them by mistake! And no one will believe that I didn't help you. I mean, I work there, Amber. So the police – they're looking for us. For US!' Sapphire exclaimed, her voice panicked.

'No. There was a man . . .'

Sapphire shook her head. 'Yes, but there was also a girl. A short-haired girl jumping from the window of the restroom. They've got it on camera, Amber. They'll show it now on all the new bulletins, they'll digitally enhance it and Em will get caught. We'll all get caught!'

She began to pace around the tiny sitting room, running her fingers frantically through her hair.

'It's going to be OK,' Amber said, but she didn't really believe it. 'We need to keep calm and think straight. Em needs our help, Sapphire. We can get out of this.'

'No, it is not going to be OK!' Sapphire insisted. 'It is *never, ever* going to be OK *ever* again.'

'But you didn't know about it,' Amber said urgently. 'Em never told you anything. You can't be a thief if you didn't know.'

'But I'm the one who spilled the information. She wouldn't have known about the car, or the time, or Mr Wilson's office or even the code to the door lock if I hadn't told. I might as well have taken the jewels and put them into her hands myself!'

'Calm down,' Amber instructed her. 'We all need to calm down and think straight.'

'Calm down? So we can just think our way out of this, can we? And life is going to carry on like normal? You suppose you can just go out on dates with the detective, like normal? That it doesn't matter that you've got stolen treasure somewhere . . . somewhere in this apartment!'

She waved her arms about desperately.

'It's not in the apartment. I wouldn't do anything that could bring you into it, Sapphire.'

'Right.'

You heard that,' Amber had to ask, 'about the date?'

'Yeah. Think it through, Amber. It's not rocket science – he's the detective in charge of *our* crime.'

'I thought if I didn't go, it would be more suspicious,' Amber said. 'Plus, he was looking through stuff on my desk and I had to stop him somehow.'

'Amber, there are inappropriate guys and then

there's *dating* the *detective* who's investigating your *crime*. Believe me, that is inappropriate. That's like . . .'

'The whole enchilada?' Amber suggested.

A glimmer of a smile flitted across Sapphire's cheeks then she looked sadly at Amber.

'So just what is going to happen now?'

# Chapter Thirty

*'I hate it when people say New York makes you tough.'*

*'I know, New York makes you realize you're nowhere near as rich as you thought you were.'*

It was past 7 p.m. when Em arrived back at the apartment with a bag of food.

'I bought it,' she announced as soon as she came in the door. 'I called in sick, I'm not going to Bill's tonight. So I had to buy dinner. There's enough for three.' Her voice sounded flat with not a trace of the usual Em enthusiasm.

Amber and Sapphire turned from the TV news channel to look at her.

'They've got footage,' Amber began, 'on TV, of someone leaving the restroom window. I guess it must be you?'

'Aw jeeeeez, Sapphire, look at you,' Em exclaimed

at the sight of pale, red-eyed Sapphire and she went over to give her sister a hug.

For a moment, it looked as if Sapphire was resisting, but then she seemed to change her mind and reached up over the sofa to hug Em back.

Em sagged against her. 'I'm sorry,' she whispered, 'I'm really, really sorry. I knew just as soon as I was in your office that I couldn't do it. I couldn't mace you. I couldn't take things from you. And then somebody else did. I'm really sorry.'

Em pulled away and wiped her eyes quickly with her hands. She looked exhausted.

'How did it happen?' Sapphire asked.

Amber's eyes fixed on her youngest sister. She too wanted to know the full story.

'I was in your office . . .' Em began, leaning against the kitchen countertop for support, 'realizing I wasn't going to do it when I heard someone else come into Mr Wilson's room. I heard the struggle, I heard you both yelling. I opened the connecting door and made sure you were OK—'

'It *was* you!' Sapphire exclaimed. 'I knew it was you.'

'But then I saw what had happened, and I was standing right there in disguise with a can of mace in my hands and then I heard Fergus coming down the corridor and I ran for it. I hope you'll forgive me for not helping, but I looked so guilty.'

'I guess so . . .' Sapphire said slowly.

'And then?' Amber wanted to know.

'I ran. I ducked into an office . . . I was dressed as a cleaner, so I thought if I carried a wastepaper basket, no one would look at me. So I picked it up and I found my way back to the restroom . . .'

She paused. Her brow furrowed as if she was still puzzled by what had happened next.

'In the cubicle, I saw the jewels were in the trash can. They were right there and then this security guard comes in and tells me to get out and get into the hall . . . so I put the jewels in my bag. I don't know – maybe I should have flushed them down the pan . . .'

Sapphire gasped at the thought.

'But I knew as soon as I went to the hall I'd be busted anyway, so I might as well take the evidence and try . . . somehow to get out. Then the guard leaves the restroom and I take my one and only chance.'

'You go out of the restroom window, run down a couple of streets and bump into me,' Amber finished the story.

'Oh my gosh . . . oh my, oh my gosh . . .' Sapphire squeaked. 'Where did you hide them?' she asked, turning to Amber.

'I can't tell you, you know that. You're not involved in any way and we don't want you to be,' Amber replied.

'What are you going to do?' Sapphire asked.

Amber realized that both of her sisters were looking at her with the same expectant expression. She was supposed to come up with the plan here; she was supposed to solve this and save them all.

'Couldn't we just hand them in?' Sapphire suggested. 'They've even posted a reward. Wilson's and Mrs De La Hoz have put together a $100,000 reward.'

'For $4 million worth of jewels?!' Amber asked, 'I guess Mrs De La Hoz was always mean when it came to sharing her money with other people.' She shook her head. 'None of us can hand them in, Sapphire, because it would look really, really bad for you. You'd be investigated to death. Even if no one could prove we planned it to get the reward money, people would talk about it for ever.'

'They have me on tape,' Em said, sounding scared. 'What if they find some DNA? What if they digitally enhance my face and post it all over New York? Someone will tell. Someone will say that it's me. Unless you both help me, I'll get caught. I'm going to go to jail for something I didn't even mean to do.'

'There's only one thing we can do,' Amber said finally. She'd been thinking about it all afternoon. And now she'd made up her mind.

'What's that?' Em asked.

'We have to leave the country. We have to go to a place where we can be safe.'

'And just how are we going to do that?' Em exclaimed. 'We have hardly any money and hardly any credit. There's no point asking Mother to help because she can't. And what will we live on when we get there? The only language I can speak is American.'

Amber shook her head.

'No, the only way to get the money we'll need,' she said, her voice steady and deeply serious, 'is to sell the jewels.'

# Chapter Thirty-One

*'Europe? I ask you, Lauren, who wants to go back there?'*

*'I know, it's so old it's not even last century.'*

One hour later, Em's dinner offerings had been finished off, along with most of a bottle of wine and the sisters were still debating the why, how and what to do next.

'I still think you could hand them in!' Sapphire would put in every ten minutes or so. She kept coming up with new and elaborate ways to organize an anonymous handover.

'But that doesn't prove me innocent,' Em kept reminding her. 'It could still leave everyone thinking we organized this whole thing for the reward money. And you could end up looking guilty! That's the worst thing.'

'We need to find out who the world's biggest

collectors of the Duchess's jewels are, then try and guess which one might be the most likely to want to do an "under the counter" deal. Then we need to try and contact him . . .' Amber repeated.

'That's all going to be so easy. Let me just look up the billionaire phone directory, shall I?' Em said sarcastically. 'Is there a website: phone numbers of the rich and famous?'

'Do you know who brought Sapphire home from the auctioneer's?' Amber asked Em, because she suddenly realized Em didn't even know about this yet.

'Who?'

'Jack Desmoine. The same detective who covered Ori's robbery. He's on the Wilson's case. The same guy, Em, that I've been *dating*.'

'Oh no . . . Jack? Didn't he catch those guys already? He's good at his job,' Em said, growing visibly pale.

'We'll just have to be clever,' Amber told her. 'Super-smart. We have to get away with this. I've hidden the jewels to protect you. I'm already in up to my neck. If we don't get away with this, *Jack* will be the one sending us to jail.'

It was a horrible thought.

'I'm not going to leave the country,' Sapphire declared from her end of the couch, 'you can't make me. I haven't done anything. I'm not going to leave Mother, or Fergus. You should have seen how upset

Fergus was. He was storming all over the place, fetching me water, demanding to know where the jewels were and why the police weren't moving heaven and earth to find them.'

'You're going to stay for Fergus? But I thought you and Fergus were taking things easy,' Em recalled.

'I don't think so.' Sapphire shook her head. 'I'm just going to stay at Wilson's and say you got a job abroad,' she added. 'If no one knows it was you, then why can't I stay here?'

Em and Amber looked at each other.

'A job abroad . . . you know, that's a good idea,' Amber said. 'I could get an interview . . . I could get an interview for a banking job . . . in Geneva. Geneva would be a fantastic place, we could sell them there. We could—'

Then she remembered all the problems with opening Swiss bank accounts with money you couldn't account for.

'What about the charity I set up, could we open an account for it in Geneva?' Em asked. 'Then say we got a huge, anonymous donation?'

Amber was silent for a moment. It was all crooked and wrong. It was built on so many ifs and maybes. But they had to do *something*! Em was already on camera. In a few days' time, a single strand of her hair might be found, or a witness might come forward . . .

They were all already at risk. If Em was caught,

no one would believe Sapphire wasn't involved and then Fitch would remember about Amber digging a frantic hole right after ten on a Monday morning.

They were already at risk.

Now they had to risk more to get away. There was no alternative.

'I'll get an interview in Geneva,' Amber said again. 'Em will come over with me . . . we'll contact a collector and try and sell the jewels over there. If we manage, then I guess we'll have to hide abroad . . . for a while.'

The thought of leaving Mother and New York and all her plans for the future behind was terrible. But Em had taken away their choices. They had to escape.

Even as Amber told them her plan, it sounded impossible. She had no idea if it could be done.

'Montenegro,' Em said. 'It's not far from Switzerland, plus it has the tallest men.'

No one laughed.

It was all too frightening, too risky, and they knew it.

'Switzerland is a good place to do the sale,' Amber said, trying to sound calm and reasonable. 'Whichever collector we get in touch with, we should get paid in Switzerland because there you can move big sums of money about without looking like a one-legged man dancing the Cotton-Eyed Joe.'

'Yeah but, Missy Amber,' Em began, 'just how are we going to get through airport security to Switzerland carrying the most famous stolen jewels in the whole world without looking like a no-legged man dancing the Cotton-Eyed Joe?'

Sapphire looked at Amber, wide eyed with fright. 'It can't be done,' she said. 'This is a nightmare. You can't do this!'

'What did Daddy always say?' Amber said, trying to smile: 'The only things that are impossible are the ones you don't try.'

'How long will you have to live over there for?' Sapphire asked.

'I don't know,' Amber replied. 'Until everyone's forgotten about it. Or until the real criminal gets caught and maybe we can explain ourselves . . .'

'You'll never be able to explain why you didn't hand the jewels in right away,' Sapphire pointed out.

'Especially once we've sold them,' Em added.

'Well . . . I guess we'll be away for a while then,' Amber said. 'Till everyone forgets about it.'

Sapphire began to cry.

'Please don't,' Em said, putting her arms around her sister, 'I really feel so very bad already. Please don't cry.' Em turned to Amber. 'What did Jack say to you?'

She shrugged: 'We talked about Sapphire, we talked about the robbery . . .'

'But he didn't seem suspicious in any way?'

'No. Not at all. He was totally sympathetic . . . he asked me out again. Tomorrow night. If he's not working late . . . on our robbery.'

'Jeez, Amber, I hope you said no. You can't date our detective!'

'I said yes. I thought it was much better to say yes. Isn't it way less suspicious if I say yes?'

'Less suspicious?! Are you crazy?! What do you think you two will be talking about? A coupla glasses of wine and some tongue action and you'll probably tell him everything. No. Totally no. You have to cancel. Just say you're sick. Call him tomorrow, tell him Sapphire's sick and you have to stay home and look after her.'

'Please stop it, Em. I can handle him. If I go out for dinner with him and talk about Sapphire, I can put him right off our trail.' Amber decided it was best not to mention to Em just how much she wanted to go out for dinner with Jack – even if he was the detective on their case.

'*If* we get away with this . . .' Amber paused and tried to let the consequences of this settle down on her: '*If* we get away with this, we *might* have enough money . . .'

It was too huge, she couldn't think about it. She had to think about one problem and one solution at a time.

But if they got away with it – not one of them would ever have to work again. They would be free. All three of them – if they could get Sapphire to join them.

They'd be able to do just as they pleased.

Plus, they could pay off the entire mortgage on the ranch and never have to worry about that again either.

'Jack caught the guys who robbed Ori's store,' Em reminded her, then tossed the last of the contents of her wine glass down her throat. 'Isn't there any more of this? I'll have to go out and get some more.'

'Those guys were probably so dumb they couldn't pour piss out of a boot if you wrote instructions on the heel,' Amber said, using a Daddy expression which always made Mother pull a face.

Em couldn't even smile at this she was so tense.

'Geneva,' Amber whispered, 'we'll get ourselves to Geneva and see if we can make things happen.'

'Geneva? Can we live there when we're multi-millionaires?'

'Em, get real,' Amber shook her head. 'We'll have to lie low for years.'

Em looked sulky. 'I don't wanna lie low. If we're really gonna do this, I wanna buy diamonds and furs and show off!'

'If you show off, we'll all get caught,' Amber warned. She leaned over the makeshift table they'd set up for dinner, took hold of Em's hands and squeezed them. 'Em, are we really going to do this?'

Em nodded.

'Just how far are you willing to go?' Amber asked.

For a long moment, Em looked into her big sister's eyes. Then she said, 'All the way, baby. I'm willing to go all the way.'

'Yves Montanari,' Sapphire blurted out. 'He's the collector you need. He will go anywhere and pay any price to get his hands on jewels that once belonged to the Duchess.'

# Chapter Thirty-Two

*'What do you need to have to get the waiter's attention in this place?'*

*'A gun.'*

Amber's stomach was roiling with nervousness. 'Is this it?' she asked the cab driver, who'd slowed to a standstill.

'This is Alexander Gardens, number 164.'

'But where is J's Place? It's supposed to be a restaurant.'

The driver shrugged.

Amber looked out of the window. It was just an ordinary residential street with apartment blocks and a convenience store. Corona, Queens, wasn't a district of New York she'd ever visited before.

'I don't know what to do.'

'Better decide, lady, I ain't got all night.'

'Can you just wait for me for two minutes? I'll go take a look-see.'

'Sure. But the meter is running.'

Amber stepped out of the cab and went to the door of number 164. It was the glass-fronted lobby of an apartment block. Glancing at the rows of labelled bells, Amber suddenly understood.

She scanned the labels and found 'Desmoine'. He was going to cook her dinner. It was so unexpected, so un-New-York, so downright weird that for a moment she considered jumping back in the cab and asking to be taken to the station.

Then a voice boomed out at her from the intercom: 'It's OK, you can send your cab away and c'mon in, Missy Amber. I'm not going to eat ya.'

'Right . . . OK, fine . . . I was just checking I had the right address.'

She paid her cab, then took the elevator up to the sixth floor as instructed.

Thud . . . thud . . . thud . . . heart still racing on overdrive – and *ping.*

'Hello, cowgirl.'

Jack stood in the plushly carpeted corridor, holding his apartment door open for her. His hair was still wet. A smart blue and white checked shirt had come partly untucked from his waistband and he had a kitchen towel, slightly stained with what looked like tomato sauce, over his shoulder.

'You should have told me you were inviting me to your place,' Amber protested.

'It's OK. You're with the police. Nothing dangerous is going to happen – unless you want it to,' he added with a grin.

This made her smile. A little.

She still felt tense and on edge. And Jack leaning in to kiss her at the doorway didn't make it any better.

'OK,' he said, pulling back, 'maybe you need to come in, relax, have some dinner, then I'll make my best moves on you.'

'I was just planning on dinner,' Amber told him.

'I getcha.'

She was suddenly feeling overdressed for eating in, that was for sure. Under her blue silk jacket was a dress with a tight bodice, a flared knee-length skirt and delicate shoulder straps. It was also silk, the thick sheeny kind, with a bold pattern of blue and white horizontal stripes.

Sapphire had convinced her to wear it. 'So perfect for dinner out, sooooo adorably cute!' she had insisted from Amber's bed, where she'd taken up residence and was planning to stay, in denial of everything that had happened. All day long she had read and reread *A Touch of Grace* while watching *High Society* on a loop.

Amber felt so sorry for Sapphire that she'd agreed

to wear the dress, even though she'd last worn it on a disastrous preppy New Yorker date.

'Do you want me to take your jacket?' Jack asked as she stepped in and he closed the door behind her.

'No . . . I'm good, thanks.'

'Please, don't be nervous.' He put his hands on her shoulders in a soothing, grounding kind of way and tilted his head a little to the side as they made eye contact. 'I will not poison you, I'm in fact quite a good cook.'

This made her smile a little more.

'Apparently girls think guys who can cook are more sexy,' he added.

'Where'd you read that? *Cosmopolitan*?'

'C'mon in.'

As she walked in, they passed an open door which led to a tiny kitchenette.

'Smells good.'

'After the day I've had, I need a good dinner. Don't suppose you know where any missing Royal jewels are, do you?' he joked.

Amber laughed nervously and gulped for air.

They were now in a small sitting room with a big, long window and a view right over the city.

'On a good day I can see all the way to the Empire State,' Jack told her.

'Nice,' she said, and glanced around the room.

'Looking for clues?' he asked.

'Huh?' she said, startled.

'Clues. As to my real personality. That's what I was doing when I came round to your place. I didn't find much. I think you must have lots of secrets and I'm desperate to know what they are.'

'Ha ha.' Amber smiled it off and tried for just a few moments to put the jewels out of her mind. She took in the comfortable brown leather sofa. The big bookcase, packed to overflowing, the traditional rugs on the dark wooden floor. This was a casual, tasteful apartment. He was a guy who liked to read too, plus he cooked, and she guessed he hung out a lot here with the large stereo, TV and stack of DVDs in the corner.

She was drawn to the collection of framed photographs on one of the walls.

'Oh, the family history section,' Jack said, when he saw her looking. 'Feel free to browse.'

She went over to the wall and found black and white photos of cops. They went way back. Back to when the NYPD wore long black coats with brass buttons and flat peaked caps.

'Are these your relatives?' Amber asked.

'Yeah. That's my great-grandfather Liam McIlvaney from County Tyrone in the old country.' Jack tried to deliver this with an Irish accent.

'Oh my gosh – McIlvaney?'

'Yes, but his granddaughter, my mom, married

into another fine upstanding NYPD family, the Desmoines from Queens.'

'So you're police . . . by birth? I didn't know that happened.'

'My great-grandfather, his brothers, his sons, their sons, my uncles, my mom's dad, her brothers and sister – everyone's police. My brother's a chief right here in Queens. I'm kind of a rebel by being in the city like my great-grandaddy.'

'So they came over from Ireland to become police?'

'No. Not exactly . . . Look, I need to get you a drink. What would you like? Beer? Soda? I have some wine too, but I have no idea if it's any good. The guy in the store convinced me . . .'

Amber shook her head. 'Beer is good. But in a glass. Right? I mean, you're fixing dinner 'n' all.'

'Beer in a glass,' Jack laughed. 'You are way too refined for me.'

'I don't think so. Your couch is 1950s vintage. That's pretty refined.'

'Inherited.'

'Oh.'

When he returned from the fridge with the beer, Amber was still looking at the photos.

'So your great-grandfather and his brothers left Ireland to come to New York to join the police?' She took a sip of beer and felt her shoulders relax a little. It wasn't the mouthful of alcohol, it was him. Even though he was police and she was now, technically, a criminal, she felt happy to be with him.

In fact, she felt warm, she felt safe in his company. She even felt much prettier when he looked at her and much cleverer when he spoke to her. Jack had a big effect on her and she liked it.

'Not exactly,' Jack said. 'They were country boys, farmhands, who couldn't get work. So they did that usual crazy thing of cashing in their life savings for a ticket to New York. Two of them never left the city. The story is: one of them meets a beautiful County Tyrone girl who turns out to have a brother on the force. He gets two of the brothers a job. But the youngest, he misses the countryside so much that he finds a way to get out of town.'

'So where did he go?' Amber asked. She took another sip of beer and felt calmer, although she knew perfectly well she couldn't get too relaxed with Jack. She had too much too hide.

'Well . . . interesting story. This younger brother carries on travelling upstate. It's September, so he gets a job picking apples in Vermont. The widow who owns the farm and the orchard falls in love with him. Marries him. McIlvaneys been running the farm ever since. Now that picture there,' Jack leaned down and pointed, 'that's me, aged eight, with a whole basket of apples I picked by myself.'

'You look very proud.'

'Darn right. I spent every summer vacation at the farm, helping my aunt and uncle out. They have two lovely, hard-working daughters. But I think they would've liked a boy, just like me.'

'Ah.'

Amber took another sip from her glass.

'You're from a family of three girls on the land, of course.'

'Uhuh.'

'Do you think your daddy was disappointed?'

'I think the only thing that disappointed him was that none of us wanted to farm.'

'Why's that?' Jack asked and pointed at the little table and two chairs he'd set out in front of the window. 'Hold that thought, I'm just going to bring in our dinner.'

Amber watched as he fetched a steaming oven dish covered with mashed potato, broiled brown, from the kitchen. Then he came back into the room with a bowl of green salad.

'You made salad?' Amber asked.

'Oh, I know girls like salad.'

Amber looked at his face, caught the glance from his eyes and suddenly felt jealous of any other girl Jack might ever have served salad to.

'Fish and tomato pie. Family recipe . . . you're not allergic to fish?'

'No. I love fish.'

Jack sat down and together they began to eat. And talk.

All about summers in Vermont and living on a ranch in Texas.

Then Amber found herself talking about everything that had happened since Daddy had died.

'There's still a big mortgage on the ranch. The land barely seems to make enough to cover the costs, but none of us has the heart to sell Daddy's ranch . . . so I went into the best-paid profession I'd heard of. I had a banking job in Texas, but it didn't pay near as good as the jobs in New York, so I moved up here.'

Jack sensed her hesitation: 'So you're planning to go home to Texas?'

'I don't know . . . and if I do . . . I don't know when,' Amber replied, thinking with a lurch about Switzerland, Montenegro and a stolen fortune. If she really did want to go back to Texas, she hadn't exactly made it easy for herself.

'Did you have a plan to come home a wealthy city girl and buy the ranch?' Jack asked.

'Maybe.'

'I'm sorry you lost your job. It's hard when your plans don't work out. People do all kinds of crazy stuff when their plans don't work out.'

'Ha . . .' she said softly. He didn't know how true that was.

'You should run your own show,' he said. 'A little brokers, down in – where is it? Parker County.'

'What d'you mean?'

'Weren't you an asset manager? So open up your own asset management office, do small-scale pensions, loans, savings accounts. I bet people down there would like that. Everyone's fed up with big city banks, big city thinking, aren't they? Especially in the wilds of Texas I guess.'

'We're so not in the wilds,' she said a little defensively. But it was an interesting idea and she kind of liked it.

'I'd need money to start up,' she told him.

'Maybe not as much as you think.'

And then there was the fact that she was now a criminal. She couldn't imagine many people wanting to trust their money to an international jewel thief.

'You'd make a nice living with your own investment company,' Jack went on. 'It would probably keep you in fur jackets.'

'Oh, I'm not really a fur jacket kinda girl. That was kind of a dare.'

'White ermine . . . those jackets cost a lot. We had a report in from some uptown store that had one stolen round about the time I saw you in yours: $5,000.'

*'Really?'*

Amber was horrified. For a moment, she wondered

if he was about to arrest her. 'Where did your sister get hers?'

'Mother bought it.' This was a lot of questions suddenly. 'What about you? Do you think you'll ever leave NYC?' she asked, desperate to change the subject. 'Become a detective in Vermont?'

Jack smiled and let his eyebrows slide up.

'Aha . . . well, when I have kids. Yeah, I'm that kind of old-fashioned guy. Over thirty, bakes fish pies, plans on having kids . . . yeah, so I have a fantasy of raising them out of doors: chopping wood, feeding the farm animals, your regular picture postcard kind of stuff.'

'Really?' Amber grinned. She couldn't think when she'd ever gone on a date and there had been talk of a raising kids fantasy. The kind of fantasies New York date guys usually brought up was the stuff that curled your hair and had you running for the door. 'I bet you see a lot of the ugly side of the city.'

'Oh yeah. Beautiful, expensively raised Upper West Side teenagers dead at fifteen from a heroin overdose and all that kind of thing. I've seen enough to make a person head for the hills. But police rarely leave town. We're too caught up in the system. Waiting for the next promotion, the next little pay rise. Too much a part of the precinct and all that bullshit.'

When he said that, he suddenly seemed much older than her. She'd only been working for a few years and already Jack sounded like someone who'd grown weary of his career.

'Sorry if I sound a little cynical,' he said. 'Did you enjoy that?' He was looking at her plate, scraped clean.

'You make a damn fine pie, Mr Desmoine,' she told him.

'D'you want to have some more?'

She shook her head.

'Salad?'

'Maybe.'

'What did I say about girls and salad?'

She let him load up her plate with a second helping of leaves and then she slipped off her jacket, because it was warm in the apartment now.

'Nice dress,' he said. 'Even nicer shoulders.'

'Thanks.' She suddenly felt shy again.

'When did your father . . . ?'

'Pass?'

'*Pass?*' he repeated, trying not to smile.

'Sorry, Texans pass. They are afraid to die.'

'Aren't we all?'

'About eighteen months ago. In the summer. Not a good time. But there's never a good time.'

'My mom died in the fall of 2002, my dad three years later and I'm still sorry about it too. Worst thing that can come between people – death.'

'I'm sorry,' Amber told him. 'Your mom and then

your dad. That's real tough.' For a moment she was thoughtful, then she added, 'I always liked just hanging out with my daddy. He was a big guy – strong and quiet, a cattle man. Just real peaceful to be with. I didn't always agree with him. In fact, I almost never agreed with him. But I respected his point of view. He'd always considered it carefully.'

'Suppose that's what you do on a ranch. Take your time, make your mind up slowly,' Jack said.

'Yeah. Did you get along with your dad?'

'Kinda. He was hard to like. Very, very hard to impress. Suppose that's what we're all trying to do, get our daddies to be impressed by us. OK, let me clear up those plates.' He reached for hers. 'Cute bracelet. Antique?'

Jack stood up and skilfully stacked plates, cutlery, the salad bowl and the pie dish into his hands.

'My daddy gave it me. Em has the matching ring, Sapphire has the earrings. Something to do with Sapphire being the face of the family, Em being the hands and me the arms, holding us together. We're a matching set.' She watched him head for the kitchen. 'You could wait tables,' Amber teased.

'I used to,' he called back. 'Another vacation job, when I wasn't apple picking, obviously. Sit on the couch. I'm going to bring you a dessert so good you're probably going to want to marry me or something.'

Amber gave an outraged laugh. But still, she felt

her heart jump. To even joke about this. To even mention the 'm' word. It was kind of daring, and refreshing.

He really did like her.

And she already knew just how much she liked him.

She sat on the couch and looked out of the window at the night sky. City lights twinkled as far away into the distance as the eye could see. New York City. She hadn't expected to come to Queens and find a view of Manhattan like this. She'd always thought of Queens as grimy, suburban and uninteresting. But, just like Detective Desmoine, it was full of surprises.

'Close your eyes,' Jack instructed, coming out of the kitchen. 'No, it's nothing weird. I just think you should try the first spoonful with your eyes shut. Because it is so damn good.'

Amber closed her eyes. She heard Jack walk round the couch, and felt him sit down beside her. Her pulse began to race. The hairs on her bare arms and shoulders stood up at the touch of his shirtsleeve.

She heard the sound of a spoon clink against glass, then his fingertip brushed a strand of fallen hair away from her cheek and tucked it behind her ear.

At that the tip of her ear began to tingle and all the hairs on the back of her neck began to rise.

'Open wide,' Jack instructed and his voice sounded just a little husky.

Amber parted her lips, then closed them over a small, cool teaspoon.

An extraordinary burst of something chocolatey, coffee-flavoured and something else she couldn't place . . . sweet, nutty . . . delicious, spread across her tongue.

Then Jack's lips were on hers.

Her whole body seemed to leap to attention. She kissed him back urgently.

He set the glass of dessert down on the table in front of them and turned to concentrate on her fully.

'Hello,' he whispered.

'I love your dessert,' she whispered back, kissing his face: the cheek, the forehead . . . holding his face in her hands and wondering at the newness of this . . . the strangeness. The totally fizzy delight.

'I'm loving my dessert too,' he said, finding her mouth with his, running his hands over her shoulders, down her back, pulling her in tightly against him.

'I'm not dessert,' she whispered.

'Oh yes you are. You are definitely good enough to eat.'

Amber put her finger into the groove on his chin and felt the slight hint of stubble. Again she thought, it must be hard to shave. She ran her hand over the back of his neck and felt his dark hair as soft as fur and the smooth skin.

Her other hand moved under his shirt and she explored the firm, hairless skin of his chest.

Then his fingers were at the top of the zipper at the side of her dress. 'Would this be OK?' he whispered against her ear.

Amber's body hummed with the answer – *yes, yes, please.*

But in her head, she wasn't sure yet if she wanted to be half naked on Jack's couch. It was too exposed. Too vulnerable.

'I don't know,' she whispered back.

'Let's keep kissing and find out.'

During the next kiss, they slid down across the couch. Lying side by side, pressed together, Amber felt more turned on than she could remember in a very long time.

But . . .

Still the but.

She wasn't prepared for this. She'd expected dinner in a restaurant, kissing on the pavement and a cab home. Her toes curled at the thought of sex, and the afterwards. But, oh no . . . the awkwardness . . . the when to leave. Tonight? Tomorrow morning?

No – there had been too many unbearable mornings-after in the past that she wasn't willing to go there yet. Not even for him.

He slid the strap of her dress from her shoulder

and ran his fingertip over her skin. She kissed him and felt him press right against her, stirring up their bodies. Fierce longing in every kiss.

She slid her leg between his.

Then felt the brush of his fingertips tingle against her skin.

'It's OK . . .' he said. 'This is fantastic. We can keep it right here.'

He kissed her on the cheek. It felt kind and loving. She liked him even more for this than any other kiss.

Then the loud shrill of a cellphone made them both jump.

'*Shiiit,*' Jack said, and rolled from the couch to his feet, revealing one heck of an impressive trouser tent.

He found the cell and snapped it open. 'Desmoine.'

He listened intently as Amber sat up, blinked, breathed, felt the blood rush ease off all over her body.

'OK. So just how long does it take to get a piece of world-famous jewellery up on the Interpol wanted list?'

Amber's heart began to race again. For several, wonderful, blissed-out moments, she had somehow managed to forget that she was part of a $4 million theft and Jack was one of the detectives looking for her.

She had to go. She had to collect her bag, her jacket, call a cab and get out of here. This was impossible.

'Twenty-four hours!' he barked into the phone. 'Are you kidding me? Are you bullshitting me? How, when I can send an email to Hong Kong, to Russia, to wherever I goddam please in two seconds, can it take twenty-four hours to post missing jewellery on Interpol? Procedures? I don't give a damn about the proper procedures!'

When Jack hung up, he was surprised to see Amber putting on her jacket. 'Hey, you don't have to go,' he said, coming over and taking hold of her hands. 'I'm not expecting any other work calls. No other interruptions.'

'No. It's late. I need to get back. Em's working, Sapphire's home alone tonight and I promised I wouldn't be too late.'

'Please tell me you had a good time.'

She let her eyes wander over his face. The thick eyebrows, the brown eyes, the lips and the intriguing cleft on his chin. 'I had a really good time. Thank you for dinner.'

'Amber?' He ran his thumbs tenderly across the back of her hands.

'Yeah?'

If he was about to ask her when they were going to see each other again she didn't know how she'd be able to tell him that they couldn't.

'There's something I just have to ask . . .'

'Right,' she said evenly, and looked up into his eyes.

'Where were you on the morning of the robbery at Wilson's auction house?'

# Chapter Thirty-Three

*'Now her granddaughter, she's smart as a whip, that girl.'*

*'That's no good, Lauren, smart is for grandsons. Granddaughters need to be charming and cute as a button.'*

'How did it go?'

When Amber let herself into the apartment that evening, she found only Em awake, sitting in dim silence with a very serious look on her face.

'It went OK. Nothing to report.'

'Did you have sex with him?'

'No!'

'You shudda.'

'Why?'

'Men are just much more damn persuadable when you have sex with them.'

'He asked what I was doing the morning of the robbery.'

Em looked alarmed. 'Do you think he's guessing at something?'

'No. I nearly died, but turned out he was just kidding around.'

'But you gave him your alibi?'

'Yeah. I was at the gardens. Em, we have twenty-four hours to leave the country.'

'I thought we could keep the apartment till the end of next week.'

'It turns out it'll take another twenty-four hours for Interpol to post the jewellery all over the world. So for the next twenty-four hours, we can go through airports and no one will have photos yet of the jewels.'

'Are you kidding me?' Em held up a copy of the *New York Post,* then the *New York Times,* then the *Washington Post*. Each had two huge front-page photographs of the panther and the necklace.

'Then there's all the TV coverage. Amber, believe me, this has already gone all the way round the world and back. At the club tonight, it was all everyone was talking about.'

'Oh . . . my . . . is that the Duchess, wearing it?'

Em handed her the paper.

Amber looked at the elegant woman, half turned towards the camera. The poise, the glamour expressed in that slim, pale neck with millions of dollars' worth of jewels clasped around it.

'She looks amazing,' Amber said, feeling a terrible stab of guilt.

'We're going to take photographs of ourselves wearing that necklace before we sell it. We have to,' Em said.

'But how in the hell are we going to get the jewels out of the country?'

'Maybe we don't need to. Maybe our collector will fly in and pick them up himself. Maybe he'll come by private plane.'

At the word 'collector', Amber felt nauseous. She was in now. She was right in deep.

'How are we going to find the collector?' she asked. 'I've looked for him on the internet, I've managed to get numbers for some of his companies, but no one I've spoken to there will put me through to him direct. Some guy even told me to write him a letter!'

'Turns out I can help you there,' Em began with something of the old mischievous glitter in her eyes. She reached down into her handbag, brought out her cellphone and waved it at Amber.

'Huh?' Amber asked.

'Turns out I've had his personal cell number all this time.'

'What? How?'

'Yeah – Yves Montanari. What do you want to bet

that he's the "Yves M" with the long foreign number I took off Fergus's phone in the bar that night.'

'Fergus? Why would Fergus have his number?'

'Fergus is one of Mr Wilson's right-hand guys. He probably spoke to Mr Montanari personally about the jewels coming up for auction, inviting him to bid.'

'You have got Yves Montanari's cellphone number right there in your hand?'

'I think so. We'll need to call it to find out.'

'Well, call it then.'

Em shook her head.

'I don't think so. Not from this number or we could end up with the police at our door. Tomorrow morning.'

'We get up early,' Amber said, jumping straight into Em's train of thought, 'and we go to Grand Central Station and call him from a call box.'

'Exactly. You see, we're *smart*. We're going to do this!'

# Chapter Thirty-Four

*'It used to be bad manners to take a phone call at dinner . . .'*

*'Now, if everyone around you isn't trading stocks on their iPhone at the table, you worry they can't afford the bill.'*

'Sapphire is still a mess,' Em declared. 'I have no freaking idea why she decided she was OK to go into work today.'

'Maybe she'll be OK at work,' Amber replied. 'Maybe it's just when she's in the apartment with nothing to do that she freaks out the most.'

They both felt very bad about Sapphire. She had not asked for any of this trouble and at every stage she wanted her sisters to at least try and get themselves out.

Side by side, Amber and Em were hurrying towards Grand Central Station to make the telephone call. There were rows and rows of call boxes in the station and thousands of commuters, so Em figured two more girls at a call box would go unnoticed.

Amber's hands felt damp with fear and her mouth was dry. She had no idea how she was going to do this.

'This one looks fine,' Em said, then took out her purse and began counting out dollar coins, as if they were schoolkids about to call Mom.

'When did you last use a payphone?' Amber asked. 'It's been so long, I've forgotten how to do it.'

'We'll load it up with $30 worth. We're calling a cellphone in Switzerland. It will cost a fortune.'

'How much have you got? It might cost like $100 or something.'

'I've got $50 in coins. I'm organized.'

'Jeez. Maybe we should get a card,' Amber suggested. Anything to put off the moment of making the call a bit longer.

'Look, let's just try and if it doesn't work, we can call again.'

'Call again? The stress of calling once might kill me! I'm already sweating like a gigged frog.'

'OK, just get it together, Amber. You're the money person, you're the best one to make this call,' Em reminded her. 'So just take a deep breath and pretend you're playing a part. Pretend like you're back at the bank and you're putting together a tough deal for a very ball-breaking customer. Hang tough. OK?'

With her hand visibly shaking, Amber picked up the receiver as Em slotted coin after coin into the box. Amber unfolded the corner of paper on which Em had scribbled down the Swiss number, and dialled.

She and Em had gone through what she was going to say so many times, she knew the speech off by heart, but it didn't make her feel any less like puking on her shoes.

After a long pause, she heard an unfamiliar dial tone. And before she could even think of hanging up, a male voice answered in French.

'Do you speak English?' she asked, trying to sound as un-Texan, and unrecognizable, as she possibly could.

'But of course. How may I be of assistance?'

'I'd like to speak to Mr Montanari.'

'Yes, Mademoiselle, if you could tell me what it is regarding, I may be able to assist you.'

This man spoke English better than she did.

'I'm afraid I can only speak with Mr Montanari.'

'Monsieur Montanari is a very busy man. You are speaking to Pierre, his personal assistant, and I need to have some idea of the reason for the urgency.'

'It's very urgent, I know he will want to speak to me . . . I know about his jewellery collection and his . . .' she paused and took a breath, 'special interest.' Amber was concentrating hard, to keep her voice from squeaking with terror.

'Could you perhaps explain a little further?'

'I may be able to assist him with a purchase,' Amber said. So far she was managing to stick to the script.

'What is your name, Mademoiselle?'

'I'd prefer not to say.'

'You wish me to connect you with Mr Montanari but you won't even tell me your name. This is not possible.'

'I know he will want to speak to me,' Amber insisted, feeling sweat running down her sides. She looked at Em for help.

'Tell him you'll call Mr Kaydo Tanaka instead,' Em hissed.

Amber obeyed. 'If I can't speak with Mr Montanari then I will pass my information on to Kaydo Tanaka.' Her voice no longer sounded cool and controlled; panic was breaking through.

What if the police were watching them? What if Mr Montanari's assistant was recording this call? What if the call box number was somehow displaying on his phone and they were calling the police right now while they kept her on the line?

'I will ask Mr Montanari,' came the clipped reply.

Then the line went silent.

'What's happening?' Em asked, hardly able to contain herself.

'The guy who answered the phone is speaking to Mr Montanari.'

'Mr Montanari will come on the line, trust me,' Em grinned. She was enjoying this every bit as much as Amber was hating it.

'Good afternoon. This is Monsieur Montanari.'

Amber nearly dropped the receiver in fright.

'Hi there . . . hello . . . Mr Montanari.'

Amber closed her eyes. She tried to block out the panic and imagine that she was at the bank, speaking to one of her clients on a routine call.

'Thank you for talking with me, Mr Montanari. I have the Duchess of Windsor's emerald and diamond necklace and her Cartier panther brooch. They are available for purchase.'

Mr Montanari made no reply. Amber was only aware of a tense transatlantic silence. And then the line went dead.

Amber looked at Em in astonishment. 'Did we run out of money?' she asked.

'No!' Em said. 'Still $9.50. What happened?'

'He hung up.'

'He hung up? Why would he hang up? We have what he wants. Shit! How are we going to get numbers for the Japanese guy? Sapphire won't get them from work.'

'She can't,' Amber reminded her. 'She can't access that information. It was Fergus . . .'

'Shut up. Shut up about Fergus. SHIT!'

Em put her hands up against her ears, as if trying to find some peace and quiet to think.

The call box phone began to ring.

Amber looked at Em in horror. 'Don't answer it,' Amber hissed. 'They know where we are! It could be the police!'

'Are you girls going to finish soon?'

A man peered into the call box, angry and impatient.

'Find another phone!' Em snapped, then picked up the receiver and handed it to Amber.

'Hi,' Amber squeaked, eyes wide. She scanned the station, panicking, sure that the police were about to swoop.

'Why am I speaking to someone new?' a heavily accented voice asked. 'This is not what was arranged. Where is Mr B?'

For a moment, Amber's mind went blank. Mr B??

Then she realized in a rush that this must have something to do with the other thief – the man who was in Mr Wilson's office, who'd taken the jewels. Mr Montanari must have had dealings with him or maybe with a whole criminal gang. Mr Montanari obviously didn't know yet that Mr B didn't have the jewels.

'Mr B has asked me to speak to you. I am Miss . . . C,' she managed.

Em's eyebrows shot up with surprise.

'Here's the deal,' Amber said. 'We have them. And we're offering them to you first. Four million dollars. Take it or leave it. You can meet us in New York or Geneva.' She waited, too nervous to breathe.

'Geneva, as arranged,' the voice told her. 'Are you still prepared to use the Bank of Obersaxen?'

'I think so. I will confirm,' Amber said, her mind racing.

'Very well. When you arrive in Geneva, call this number and we will make the transfer arrangements . . . Miss C.'

'Very well.'

With that Amber hung up.

'OK,' she turned to face Em with a tense, scared smile in place: 'Geneva here we come.'

'Oh my gosh . . . really. We're really going to Geneva? Oh my . . . well, I guess you only get lard if you boil the hog.'

'I never knew what in the hell that was supposed to mean.'

'I guess we'll have to wait and see.'

'So now what?'

'Now you go dig us up some jewels, baby. I'll squeeze some room onto my plastic and book the tickets.'

# Chapter Thirty-Five

*'She's always wanting him to be romantic.'*

*'How many times do we have to spell it out for her? Only poor men have the time to be romantic.'*

It was almost 2.30 p.m. when Amber got to the gardens. She wondered what Fitch would make of her pitching up to volunteer on a work day for the second time this week.

As soon as she got into the park, she headed straight for the trees she'd planted and saw to her astonishment that there was now a much longer row. She tried to get her bearings, to work out which maple sapling was harbouring $4 million of jewels.

'Hey, Amber, you again?' Suddenly Fitch was slapping her on the shoulder, startling her so much that she jumped. 'I'm going to really miss you when you get yourself another job. I've got a whole new flower bed needs planted up today, so the more the merrier.'

'You've put in a lot more trees over here.' Amber pointed to the row.

'Yeah . . . the suppliers made a mistake and sent us another eight, so we chucked 'em in too. Looks nice, ha?'

'Yeah,' she swallowed. Her throat felt completely dry. 'Fitch, I think I might have forgotten to put in the compost . . . you know . . . for those trees I planted . . .' Her voice trailed away. She was so lame at lying that she knew she should say as little as possible.

'Huh?' Fitch looked at her in surprise.

'The compost for the trees I planted. I forgot it,' she waded on, 'and they'll need it come spring. I thought I'd just get a little bag of it, dig down and sprinkle it over. It won't take long.'

'Really? Nah. Don't bother with that. Come and see the new flower planting plans. We're gonna do a Star-Spangled Banner and other cheese.'

'But it won't take any time,' Amber protested, 'and you don't want three stunted trees in the middle of your row!'

Fitch shrugged. 'OK, whatever.'

So Amber rushed off to the work shed and armed herself with a small spade and a bag of compost. Then she walked towards the row of trees slowly, trying to figure it out. She *had* to figure it out.

She crouched down at the foot of her guesstimate tree and tried to get her bearings. Is this the angle she'd been able to see Fitch's shed from? And was this how she'd seen the park gate when she'd been waiting for a quiet moment to make her drop?

She looked up at the tree and saw the fork in its branch and the strange-looking knot. Her heart gave a little start of hope. Now she remembered. She was sure this was the tree.

She began to dig, with purpose.

Amber had made a reasonable size of hole, about a foot square and a foot deep, when she put her hand in and began to feel around. This should be the place. Surely . . . the bag should be around about here.

She dug deeper, then felt to the left. Then to the right.

She stuck her fingers deep into the earth and scrabbled about.

Nothing.

She told herself not to panic. 'I'm experiencing a setback,' she whispered, 'but I'm going to achieve my goals calmly and successfully.'

'You talking to yourself? You can be weird.' Fitch was at her shoulder again. How did he manage to keep sneaking up on her? 'You should probably know, in case you think you're going crazy, that I did have to move a couple of the trees along just a touch.

Not because I wanted to win that argument we had, but to make some more room.'

Three large holes later and Amber was trying not to meltdown. She told herself that she could come back tonight; with a metal detector, even. She could leave now, go find out where you buy a metal detector then, when it was dark, she could climb over the fence and hunt.

In the dark? With a flashlight? How would she find anything?

No panicking!

She looked closely at the bank where the trees had been planted. Was there any kind of indentation to show where a tree might have been before it was moved?

Amber tilted her head and brought it down low to look across the ground. She remembered crouching down looking for cougar tracks with Daddy at the ranch and an overwhelming pang of sorrow reared over her like an unexpected wave.

She let the pain out with a gasp and tried to concentrate on the ground again.

There was a slight dip. Just there, she could see it now, possibly where she'd dug much deeper than she'd needed to for the jewels, and Fitch had maybe not filled the hole all the way back in again.

She began to dig slowly, trying to push back the dread that if this didn't work, she wasn't sure what could be done. Moving the earth carefully out of the way, she put her fingers into the hole to feel for any hint of a plastic bag. She pushed her fingers in deep. There! Her fingertip had just brushed over something . . .

Using the spade, she began to dig again, trying to keep the rush of adrenalin under control.

When she felt the plastic and saw the words: 'Bed Bath, & Beyond', she almost wanted to cry with relief. She ran her fingers over the bag, feeling the hard surfaces of the brooch and the necklace inside.

She slid the bag out of the ground and leaned over it for a surreptitious peek.

'Whatcha got there? Buried treasure?'

Amber let out a shriek of fright.

She couldn't help it. She was so tense and terrified that she probably would have screamed if a fly had landed on her shoulder.

Scrunching the bag closed, she looked round.

She found herself facing Jack Desmoine – in a raincoat, with a slightly amused, slightly puzzled look on his face.

'Sorry,' he said, 'I didn't mean to give you such a fright. Whoa. You're kinda jumpy, arencha?'

'Sorry, sorry . . . Hi. What are you doing here?'

She tried to replace the blank panic on her face with a smile, but it was an effort. She was kneeling in the park, in front of a large hole, with two majorly important items of stolen jewellery in her lap and a detective by her side.

'What are *you* doing here?' he asked.

'I'm adding compost!' she said, trying to sound cheerful and relaxed. She even put her spade into the rooting treatment bag and sprinkled a little into the hole.

'And the plastic bag? Is that a time capsule thing you're planting in with the tree?' he joked.

'No, no, it's just . . . ummm . . . nothing . . . nothing. Private,' she forced out a giggle.

'It's your lunch and you're trying to hide it from me, right? Cos you know I'm always hungry.'

'No, it's really nothing.' She clutched the top of the bag shut and shook her head which was supposed to mean: it's girlie, embarrassing, don't ask any more.

She could feel the sweat of fear in her armpits.

'Right . . . OK. Look, I'm here because I need to speak to you. And for some reason you're not answering my calls, which makes it kind of hard. So I called Sapphire and she thought you might be here.'

'OK, you found me.' Amber decided she would just casually push the plastic bag into her messenger bag and stand up.

It would be normal.

It would not be normal to carry on sitting down

here in the earth, trying to squeeze a plastic bag full of emeralds, diamonds, platinum and gold between her knees.

She coughed to cover any strange diamond-rattling sounds, moved the bag of jewellery into her messenger bag, then stood up as planned.

She was aware that her heart was pumping so hard, she might actually die before there was any chance of selling the Duchess's jewels to anyone.

'So do you like it here? Working in the garden?' Jack asked.

Amber brushed her earthy hands off on her jeans. 'Sure. Reminds me of home.'

'You look at home,' he told her, 'in your jeans. So, I need to ask you a coupla things. This is business. My guy's in the squad car over there, so there will be no kissing.'

'OK . . .'

She found herself looking deep, deep into his eyes.

'Sapphire and Fergus. Were they an item?'

Amber hesitated. She didn't want to do anything that might make Sapphire's life more difficult than she and Em had already made it.

'Is this like a proper question? Is it to do with the robbery?'

'Yes it is.'

'Sapphire is absolutely 110 per cent innocent.

Look, I know Sapphire and she is the sweetest, kindest, most honest person you will ever meet. Please leave her right out of this.'

'That's not what I asked, Amber.'

There was more than a trace of irritation in Jack's voice and Amber felt the gap between them again. He was a grown-up, with a proper career and a serious job to do. Jack was obviously just checking out all the staff.

She rubbed at an imaginary itch on her nose and gave a half-shrug. 'Sapphire really likes Fergus . . . and maybe they could be an item . . . but I don't know much about it.' She risked looking directly into the eyes again. 'Why?'

'I'm checking everyone out, Amber. It's routine. I'm checking and re-checking, looking for the clue that's going to unlock the story. Sapphire . . . well, she was such an amazing witness at Ori's robbery and now she can't recall one single significant detail clearly. It's a little unusual.'

'Not really. She's been in two robberies in two weeks. She's freaked out! Sapphire is as straight as a die,' Amber insisted. 'I can tell you that for free. She would never be involved with stealing anything. Ask Ori. She had a tiny stud earring stuck in the sole of her sneaker after that robbery and she took it right back to him.'

'Yeah, he told me about that.' Jack gave her one

of his head slightly tilted, killer smiles. Like he was amused by her.

Amber felt herself smile back. Despite the lunacy of this situation, Jack Desmoine, detective on the case, was the only person who could make her feel calm.

'You now have dirt on your nose, by the way.'

'Oh.'

She tried to rub it off, but judging by his expression . . .

'I've just gone and made it a whole lot worse, right?'

'Is all,' he said, and grinned. He reached into his pocket and took out a paper napkin.

'You carry napkins?'

She took one and rubbed it over her nose.

'I have to eat on the go a lot.'

'You need to watch that. Eating on the go, drinking too much coffee, you could get stomach ulcers.'

'Every second police officer has ulcers.'

'That's not good.'

'It's sweet of you to care. And it's kind of hard not to kiss you. Do you know that?'

Amber giggled.

'I'm pretty sure I cannot date you right now because you and your sister are about to be asked to testify in the Ori Kogon case – and your sister's now a key witness in another major robbery.'

'Yeah. I know,' she said, feeling a rush of disappointment, 'it's kinda complicated.'

'But maybe when this is all over? I don't know how long it might take. But can you wait a little while?'

She scanned his face. His eyes were fixed on hers and he looked as if he really meant it. This man – this grown-up, career policeman – was *seriously* interested in her. It felt big. Overwhelming. Important.

She reached out and slipped her hand into his. He gave it a warm and comforting squeeze. 'What do you think?' he asked.

'I don't know . . . when this is all over,' she repeated, wondering when it would ever be. Then she added, 'I have a job interview.'

She hadn't meant to tell him, because telling him would probably be the end of it and although she knew it had to end, she didn't want to be the one to do it. But now, here with him, she couldn't just leave without letting him know.

'I think I'm going to be offered a great new opportunity. But it's . . . it's kind of out of town.'

'Well that's fantastic for you,' he said, squeezing her hand and sounding less than enthusiastic. 'Where is it?'

For a moment, Amber hesitated. She didn't know if she was supposed to tell him. But if he was watching Sapphire, he'd find out anyway. Besides, the job interview was their cover story and it made perfect sense.

'It's in Geneva.'

'Geneva? Geneva, where?'

'Geneva, Switzerland.'

Jack looked stunned. 'Geneva, Switzerland?' he repeated. 'Yes, that is definitely kinda out of town. Amber, you're about to move to Switzerland and you weren't even gonna mention it?'

Amber looked down, feeling her face redden. 'I didn't know if you'd mind . . .'

'Yes – of course I mind. I definitely mind. When do you go?'

This she was definitely not supposed to tell him.

'On Sunday,' she lied.

'What?! Are you kidding me? You mean if I hadn't come over to the park and found you here today that might have been it? By next week, you'll be in Geneva and I'll never see you again.'

'I might not get the job.'

'But they're flying you out there – that's promising, isn't it?'

'No. I'm flying out myself. Em's coming with me because . . . I didn't want to go on my own and she's . . . she's always wanted to go to Switzerland.'

Amber coloured up. She was going to have to get much better at lying.

'What about the testifying?'

'Well, I guess I can come back if I'm needed. Jack, I need a new job. My mother is counting on me.'

'Is there nothing else? Is there no other way? I mean, do you really want to leave New York? Leave the country?'

A car horn blasted across the park. Jack looked at his watch: 'That's my guy. I have to get back.'

'Right.'

They looked at each other again: a long, searching look.

She wished she could explain some of it to him, or find something to say to make it easier.

'OK, well . . . I guess it's been nice to meet you, Miss Amber.' Jack was suddenly shaking her hand. He looked flushed and a little angry. 'Have fun in Geneva and maybe we'll meet again some day.'

He turned on his heel and marched out of the garden, tossing his coffee cup into the trash as he went.

Amber stared after him and fought hard against the urge to cry.

# Chapter Thirty-Six

*'I love your earrings. You have absolutely got to tell me where you got those earrings.'*

*'Now, Lauren, I think they look better on me.'*

The door buzzer made all three sisters jump.

'Who's that?' Sapphire blurted out, freezing in the act of sticking the last pieces of tape onto her boxes.

'It's probably the FedEx pick-up,' Em hissed. 'Please, try and stay calm.'

'It's early. I thought they were going to be here at seven?' Amber said forcing the flaps on her last cardboard box shut.

Tomorrow the flat would no longer be theirs.

Tomorrow Em and Amber would fly to Geneva and Sapphire would take two suitcases round to Fergus's apartment. All their other possessions were going to be FedEx-ed home to the ranch.

'Fergus needs me,' Sapphire had assured them. 'He's been devastated by the robbery, totally upset. He can't sleep properly, he can't eat properly. He looks exhausted. I know you think it's way too soon to move in together, but he needs me. He keeps saying he can't forgive himself for not being outside the door, protecting us. Unlike those security guards. I mean, they both went to the bathroom – at the same time! It's just unbelievable. They say they both had some kind of stomach upset and they had to go. But still . . .'

Now, as Em went to answer the door, Amber took the tape from Sapphire and looked anxiously between her red suitcase and the cardboard boxes. Had she put enough of the important things into the suitcase? She had no idea when she might be back in the States or when she might be able to collect her other belongings again.

When would she see Jack again?

She'd tried to put Jack into a cardboard box in her mind and tape him shut. But he kept climbing back out again.

'C'mon up,' Emerald told the guy at the door.

As Amber watched her boxes being carried out, her anxiety kicked up to a new level.

'What are we going to do here tonight?' Sapphire asked, looking around the empty apartment.

'All the packing's done,' Em said. 'We're all ready

to go tomorrow. Maybe we should just go out and get something to eat. Last night in New York . . . last night together till . . . who knows when?'

'I can't go out, what about the jewels?' Amber said, pointing to the plastic bag sitting beside her computer.

'Just bring them,' Em said with a shrug. 'Put 'em in your messenger bag and, trust me here, no one is going to steal that sorry sack of a bag.'

In a cramped, noisy restaurant, the sisters went over their plans carefully as the waiter brought them beers, salads and bean burritos.

Texan food. Comforting food which reminded them of home.

'So, Sapphire, you know what you have to do. You just go to and from work. You stay calm and quiet. And as soon as we're all sorted out with the sale . . .' Amber paused to let the significance of this fall on both sisters, 'then please, you need to catch a plane and come join us. Because even if anyone is starting to get the tiniest bit suspicious, where we're going, they cannot follow.'

'Where are you going again?' Sapphire asked. She couldn't help whispering, even though Em kept telling her not to.

'Montenegro,' Em replied.

'It's very small,' Amber added. 'It used to be part

of Yugoslavia, it's right on the coast, opposite Italy. It looks beautiful: sea and mountains.'

Sapphire screwed up her nose. Geography wasn't one of her strong points. 'And why do we all have to go there?'

'Because no one can make us come back to the States from Montenegro,' Amber answered. 'You know – if anyone finds out.'

'Which they won't,' Em added.

'Don't you think it's going to look suspicious if all three of us move out of the country?' Sapphire asked.

Em shrugged. 'I think that nice-looking Jackie boy will just think Amber got the job in Geneva and her sisters went out there, fell in love with the place and stayed. He won't trouble himself about it because he'll probably meet another girl who won't mind being a police wife.'

'Huh?' Amber asked sharply. 'What's a police wife? How is that different to any other kind of wife?'

'Ooooh, have you thought about it?' Em asked, eyes wide.

'Have I thought about what?' Amber asked, annoyed.

'Being Jackie's police wife?'

'Oh shut up, Em. You are such a pain,' Amber declared, knowing she was being unreasonably angry. But Em had touched a very sore spot here.

'Please stop it,' Sapphire intervened, 'please, both of you. Nothing ever got solved by you two saying mean things to each other. You'll feel much better once you're out of New York. This is just stress. You're panicking.'

'No wonder,' Amber said, darkly.

'If you want out now, Amber, you just say the word,' Em said. She looked over at her sister: 'Sorry,' she said, 'I know you liked the cop.'

'Yeah,' Amber agreed, 'I did like the cop. But I guess it's too bad. Things have gone in a different direction.'

'How true is that!' Sapphire smiled weakly at her sisters.

The waiter came over to ask if everything was OK and when Em replied, she turned and squeezed her cleavage at him. For her last night in New York, she'd picked a low-cut black vest, a high-cut black skirt, long studded black boots and a simple green pendant on a chain.

Sometimes, Amber couldn't help thinking people must cast a glance at the three of them and wonder how they knew each other. Sapphire wore her shift dress with pearls and an immaculately groomed bob, Amber was in jeans and T-shirt, her long hair hanging loose; Em was dressed to thrill.

'You know you can never go back to Jack,' Em warned, 'because if you fall in love with him, then one of these days, you're gonna want to tell him the truth so bad that you'll just give in.'

'I'm not going back to Jack and I'm not about to split with you,' Amber insisted. 'We've started this. We'll see it through. But it scares me, is all. I still don't know how we get the jewels through the airports or how it's going to work when we meet . . .' her voice dropped low, 'the collector.'

'We're smart, Amber,' Em said, 'we'll figure it out.'

As they walked up the stairs to their apartment later that evening, Amber told her sisters, with more than a shade of regret, 'This could be the last time we ever share an apartment.'

'Yeah, when I'm rich,' Em added, 'I'm so getting my own place. But you guys can live next door if you want.'

When they reached the door, Em was the first to see the piece of paper taped to it.

'What the freak is that? Amber, it's got your name on it.'

Amber reached up, feeling a jolt of fear. A message on the door? From someone who knew where they lived? What could it mean?

She took the paper down, unfolded it and read aloud, Em and Sapphire reading over her shoulders: *I'm looking for you. Jack.*

'Oh *freak*!' Emerald was the first to react.

'We do not want some detective wandering about looking for us. Why is he looking for us? Did anything happen at work, Sapph? Did you notice anything? What about in the park, Amber? Did he say anything that sounded suspicious?'

'He's not looking for *us*,' Amber pointed out. 'He's looking for *me*.'

'But why is he looking for you?'

'Well, I don't know exactly. But I guess maybe he wants to tell me something . . . or ask me something. He knows that I'm leaving town,' she added quietly, knowing just how pissed this would make Em.

'What? Are you outta your mind? You told him you were leaving town? Please just do not tell me that you said Geneva and gave him the flight time and number too.'

'I did say Geneva,' Amber admitted, 'but I told him we were going on Sunday.'

'Amber, Amber! Then that's why he's knocking at our door! Do you think he doesn't have a list of all the jewel collectors? What do you think was the first thought that crossed his mind when you said you were going to Geneva? Oh hell, Amber. Did you say I was going?'

Amber nodded, but began to protest: 'Honestly, please, don't panic, I told him it was for a job interview. And he has no reason not to believe that. Anyway, if the police are watching Sapphire, they would find out we're going anyway. It's better he hears it from me with a proper reason. That's what I figured.'

'Yeah, but it would have been better for him not to hear a word till after we'd gone. Then they wouldn't be able to stop us!'

There was no denying that Em had a point there.

'Jeez! We have to get out of here. Right now!' Em declared. 'We have to get our bags, and leave. He could be downstairs at the front door. He could have seen us come in. There might be a gang of them. If we get searched . . .'

Obviously the jewels, still in a plastic bag inside Amber's messenger bag, slung over her shoulder, would be found.

'How do we get out?' Sapphire asked, sounding scared.

'We get our stuff and we go down the fire escape,' Em replied. 'Then it's through the back lane and out into 16th Street.

'And where do we go?' Amber asked.

'An all-night cafe, if we can't think of anywhere else.'

'But my bags are heavy,' Sapphire complained, 'I have all the things I'll be using for the next few weeks. Plus my books.'

'C'mon, just take what you can carry. Jeez,' Em said urgently, 'we need to get away. No one wants to wind up in jail, do they?'

# Chapter Thirty-Seven

*'I can just bet I know what you say when you sweep past the line at the airport and make for the VIP check-in.'*

*'Oh yes, in a loud voice, I tell them: "Maybe if your husbands had worked a little harder, you'd be flying first class too."'*

'Hello and how are you this morning?'

'Good. We're good,' Em replied with a smile as bright and cheerful as the airline check-in girl's.

'You're very early for your flight. Check in for the Geneva flight doesn't officially open for another forty-five minutes.'

'Can't you just let us in? We have like a ton of duty-free shopping to do,' Em said with another big, friendly smile.

'Well . . . since it's quiet right now. I guess no harm done.'

She took their tickets and scanned their passports. Amber's passport was run twice through the machine. It seemed to take an age.

All three sisters had been awake the whole night. Now, at six in the morning, Amber felt so wired and freaked out that she wondered how she was managing to stand up, smile and look normal.

She and Sapphire had cried when the time had come to say goodbye. It had suddenly occurred to Amber that if anything went wrong – if she and Em got arrested – then for years to come they might only see Sapphire at visiting times. As she hugged Sapphire and felt tears stream down her face, she wondered if Sapphire really would follow them. Even if they were truly safe with the money tucked away, would Sapphire leave Mother and Fergus and get on a plane all by herself and fly to the other side of the world to find them in exile? Put herself into exile too?

Amber just couldn't be sure.

'Please come. You will come, won't you?' she'd whispered urgently into Sapphire's ear.

'Of course I'll come, eventually,' Sapphire had told both her sisters. 'I'll be too lonely without you. I'll miss you. I'll miss you so much.'

But Amber had felt something wildly urgent and sad in Sapphire's hug. As if she was saying goodbye for a very long time.

'Here are your boarding passes,' the check-in girl interrupted her thoughts. 'And here's the checklist of items you can't take on board.'

Somehow Amber didn't think the list would include $4 million worth of stolen jewels.

She had the panther brooch in her small holdall and Em was in charge of the necklace. Em had come up with the plan to get the jewels through security, but Amber wasn't convinced it would work. The thought of it was making her palms sweat.

'Have a great flight,' the check-in girl said brightly, her cherry-lipsticked mouth beaming one last smile. 'Love your necklace,' she added, pointing to the large green pendant dangling from Em's neck.

'Oh thanks, I got it in Daffy's for $35,' Em told her.

'No!' the girl responded. 'But it looks so classy.'

'Straight up,' Em said.

Then as they turned from the check-in desk, she whispered to Amber, 'OK, let's make for the restrooms.'

In the bathroom, Em opened the door on the disabled stall and pulled them both inside. She unzipped her case and felt around in the tumble of clothes for the wash-bag where she'd stored her jewellery.

First of all, she brought out a rope of brightly coloured green and turquoise beads and wrapped it round her neck. Then she added several silver chains, and a punky, black leather and silver number. Now she was ready to bring out the Duchess's jewels.

Even in the dim, fluorescent light of an airport bathroom at six o'clock in the morning, the emeralds and diamonds sparkled so impressively that Amber and Em had to pause for a moment and stand in awe.

'They are so beautiful,' Amber said, running her fingers over the glittering green surface.

'Aha. Let's just hope the guy we're meeting in Geneva thinks so too.'

Em clipped the necklace into place over all the other things she'd placed round her neck. The idea was that in a forest of bling the emerald and diamond necklace would look just like a big, fat fake too.

But somehow, it ruled over the other jewellery. It sat, regal and proud, and glittered impressively.

'I don't know,' Amber told her sister, 'I don't know if this will work.'

Em went to the stall's small mirror and checked herself out. She adjusted some of the necklaces, repositioning the punky one so that it passed over the emeralds and diamonds. She messed with her hair and pulled it over her shoulders.

Then she took a lipstick from her handbag and painted her lips a trashy pink.

All of a sudden, the glamour of the necklace began to tone down. Yes, it did finally look a little bit fake . . .

'OK, now you.' Em turned to her sister.

Amber opened her case and brought out her jewellery roll. Inside was the glittering panther and a whole collection of other brooches: some Amber's, some belonging to Sapphire and Em; two had even belonged to their grandmother.

Em helped and together, they pinned everything on the lapels of Amber's dark jacket.

The panther stood out. The deep, burnished gold and the gleaming gems drew the eye towards it.

'Try and relax,' Em told her sister. 'You've got to believe. If you *believe* we can do this, if you *believe* those jewels look fake . . . if you *believe* we're going to sail through security and no one's gonna stop us, then it will happen. That's what acting is all about, honey. You gotta *believe.*'

Amber examined herself in the mirror. She looked weird. She would never, ever wear this amount of jewellery. It didn't feel right.

'Lipstick?' Em offered.

'Not that pink stuff,' Amber warned.

'Berry cherry?' Em suggested and applied a smudge. 'Amber, if we pull this off,' she whispered, 'we are never going to have to work again. Never. We will have enough money in the bank to live just as we please. For the rest of our lives. Have you forgotten about that? This is what people dream of. This is a once-in-a-lifetime opportunity. Now straighten up, sister. Take a breath and big it up because we're on.'

With these words, Em opened the stall door and together the sisters walked out of the bathroom and towards the departure gates.

Em handed over the boarding passes and they walked through the gates to security.

'Hi and how are you?' She directed a smile at the guard who took the bags and set them on the conveyor belt.

'Walk this way.' He gestured for Em to pass through one of the metal detector frames. 'And over here, Miss.' Amber was to use the other one.

Em's machine bleeped immediately.

'Sorry, it's all my bling, probably,' she apologized with a charming smile.

Amber's machine bleeped too.

'We're from Texas,' Em added, 'we like to add a piece of flash 'n' dash and then some.'

The woman now waving her over with a metal detector barely raised a smile.

'OK . . .' she cleared Em, 'and now you, Miss,' she said, and waved Amber forward.

As she ran the hand-held detector over Amber, her eyes fell on the panther brooch. Amber felt prickling beads of sweat break out on her forehead and upper lip.

Her chest began to tighten with panic.

'Now that is a lovely brooch,' the woman murmured. 'A real beauty. Stunning.'

Amber saw her eyes fasten onto the piece; maybe she was wondering where she'd seen it before. Any moment now and the news bulletins, the pictures in the newspapers, the wanted posters would enter this woman's head and she'd know exactly what she was looking at.

'Oh, the panther, I know, doncha just love it?' Amber heard herself gush in full-on Fort Worth drawl. 'Claire's Accessories. They're doing all these tribute pieces. Copies of famous pieces of jewellery. You can even get a Princess Diana tiara, but I thought that was a little tacky. I mean, there's tacky. And then there's tacky tacky.'

The security guard laughed, then looked past Amber. 'I'll get myself down there. Oh, we're holding up the line. You have a good flight now.'

Once they were out of earshot, Em took hold of her arm. 'That was genius,' she hissed. 'Brilliant. Oscar-worthy. Now let's just get to a stall and get these things back into our hand luggage before anyone else asks us about them.'

As they were walking towards the bathroom, Amber saw a cafe counter piled high with chocolate chip muffins and found herself thinking of Jack and their first little 'date' in the Muffin Bakery.

She walked on, trying hard to push him out of her mind.

But in the stall, unpinning her brooches and packing them into her hand luggage, her head was filled with thoughts of Jack. More than anything, she wanted to know why he'd been looking for her last night. Was it to do with the theft? Or . . . surely more likely, was it to do with him and her? Maybe he'd come round to persuade her not to go to Geneva . . .

She'd have liked to have heard what he was going to say.

She tied the bow on the jewellery roll and considered. This was her very last chance. She could still give Em the panther and ask the security guards to let her out of the airport. There would be a fuss and she'd have to go through all sorts of checks and reclaim her luggage. But she could still leave now.

She could still go back to Jack.

She couldn't help feeling that Jack was something real, a brand new opportunity that she was turning her back on. The jewels . . . selling the jewels . . . living somewhere off the radar with millions in the bank. That did not feel like any kind of real. That felt like a dream she was sleepwalking towards.

This was her very last chance to pull herself out. To walk away from a life of crime.

But Em needed her. Amber pulled the zipper case

shut. Who knew how it might all turn out? She tried not to let herself think that far ahead. She would play each step on the journey as well as she could. Amber would do what she had to do.

# Chapter Thirty-Eight

*'She said she just wanted to meet an ordinary, loving guy to share her life with!'*

*'Ha! In New York? Honey, she has got to be kidding. Ordinary, loving guys died out here in like 1912.'*

It was 9.02 a.m. and Sapphire had already been in her office at Wilson's for four hours.

She'd fallen asleep in the all-night cafe not long after her sisters had left, only to be shaken awake by an angry waiter. 'This ain't a hotel, lady!' he'd told her. 'Order another coffee or get outta here.'

She didn't think it would be polite to turn up at Fergus's unexpectedly at five in the morning and her sisters had told her not to go back to the apartment until their flight had left for Geneva, so she'd climbed into a cab with her bags and headed to work.

Now her exhausted eyes were burning in her head.

She looked in her desk drawer and found the bottle of eye drops she'd kept in there ever since the robbery. What with the macing and all the worried, sleepless nights, plus the crying she'd been doing lately, she'd come to rely on this soothing little bottle.

As no one else was about yet, she leaned right back in her chair, tipped up her face and began to squeeze the liquid onto her eyeballs.

Then she brushed her hair and applied a smudge of lipstick. Princess Grace would approve of this behaviour, Sapphire couldn't help thinking.

She was being calm in the storm.

She was showing grace under pressure.

Now totally composed, she switched on her computer and tried to think about what work she might be able to force herself to do today, although things were still very far from normal at Wilson & Sons.

'Chinese watches of the Eighteenth Century,' she said to herself, clicking on the file and trying to concentrate. This sale was slated for January and there were still many missing pieces of information. Maybe she could try and lose herself in here for the next few hours.

She glanced at her watch. No word had come from Amber or Em. Their plane should have taken off by now. Sapphire hoped, more than anything, that they were on it, not sitting in a police interview room somewhere, under arrest. She gave a little shudder at the thought and turned to her computer screen, determined to concentrate. There was a firm tap-tap at the door.

'C'mon in,' she said and set a smile upon her face.

Her smile froze when the door opened and two uniformed police officers were standing in front of her.

'Miss Sapphire Jewel?' one of them asked.

'Yes,' Sapphire whispered.

There could be only one reason why police officers were marching into her office: the game was up. They were going to arrest her.

'You're Sapphire Jewel of 6P 566 17th Street?'

'Yes . . . oh my gosh!' she breathed, the colour draining from her face.

This was the moment. The cops knew. They knew all about how Em had come in to steal the jewels, even though she'd changed her mind and she'd only picked up the wastepaper basket by mistake!

Like Em had said, who would believe that? Or believe that Sapphire was innocent? That she'd told Em not to do it, that she'd given Em the important information entirely by accident.

'Have we got the right person?' the second officer asked.

'Yes, I'm Sapphire,' she whispered. 'What do you want me to do?'

She thought of Princess Grace and set her shoulders

back. She wouldn't make any kind of fuss. She would explain it all from the beginning, telling them how Amber had lost her job and couldn't find another one and Mother needed money for the mortgage and poor Em was in that terrible play – opposite that lovely Angelina who was so beautiful and talented that she was going straight to Hollywood – and then news of the jewels had come. And Em had thought it wouldn't be so bad, because it was the dreadful Mrs De La Hoz – who by the way had got Amber sacked from the bank. And she'd be insured and Wilson's would be insured . . . and then Amber had gone on her bicycle to try to stop her, but it was all too late because the car was early . . .

'The car was early,' she said out loud and began to cry, 'oh, oh, the car was early! If only the traffic had been bad on Lexington that morning, or if they'd got held up on a cross-street . . . then none of this would have happened. None of it!'

'Miss? Don't get upset. Don't get upset now,' the first cop said. He looked a little upset himself for making her cry.

'We need to take your computer, Miss.'

'Oh! But what about the Chinese watches?' Sapphire protested. 'I haven't saved anything. I always forget to copy onto memory sticks. Do you remember to do that? I mean, everyone's so busy, there's so much to do, does anyone remember to back stuff up onto memory sticks, really?'

'Miss . . . just relax. We're taking in a few computers – it's part of the investigation, it doesn't mean . . .'

'You'll probably get it back.' The second cop tried to sound reassuring: 'And all your files will probably be fine.'

'OK, take the computer,' she said, moving her chair back from the desk.

'And if it's OK, you're to come with us too. Just some questions. Just routine,' the cop tried to make it sound fine.

But Sapphire knew it was not fine. It was not fine at all.

She was too wobbly to stand up, so the first officer came over, put his arm under hers and helped her up from her chair.

'But it was a man,' Sapphire said, 'it was a big, tall man with brown leather shoes and there was a smell, just before the mace . . . you know, I recognized the smell, but I just can't remember what it is. If I could just remember, we might know . . . and then Em. Oh Em!' She broke into fresh sobs and began to search in her handbag for a paper tissue.

Why weren't they putting her in handcuffs? Surely they must be worried that she'd try and make a run for it?

She wondered whether they already had Em and Amber?

She wasn't supposed to say anything about Em and Amber, she knew that. Not one word. Maybe there was still a chance they'd got away. She couldn't spoil that for them. She wasn't supposed to breathe a word about Geneva, but obviously she'd told Fergus.

But then hadn't Amber told Jack they were going to Geneva?

Oh, this was *so* complicated. Sapphire didn't think she would ever get the hang of it.

'Where are we going?' she asked the policemen.

'We're going to take you and your computer to Detective Desmoine. He wants to talk to you again.'

'Here?' Sapphire asked hopefully. Somehow, if Detective Desmoine wanted to talk to her here at Aubrey Wilson & Sons, that wouldn't be so bad.

'No, this time it's at the station. But don't worry about it.'

'OK . . .' Sapphire tried not to tremble with fear, then remembering her manners, she corrected herself: 'OK, *officer*.'

As one of the policemen took hold, gently, of her trembling arm, he turned to give her a reassuring smile. In the top of his pocket a small green packet of gum was just visible.

'Lime green . . .' Sapphire whispered to herself, then with a jolt of shock she realized what it was and what it meant: 'Lime green *soap*!'

# Chapter Thirty-Nine

*'She wanted to know how I kept so skinny.'*

*'If you've spent as much money on French labels as we have, you're never ever going to let yourself slip up a dress size . . .'*

*'Exactly.'*

'The plane is now cruising at 22,000 feet and we're passing over the coast of Newfoundland. We expect to touch down in Geneva in eight hours and forty minutes approximately. Please enjoy your flight.'

Amber was in the window seat, watching as the last glimpse of land disappeared beneath them. A few dark, dotted islands flashed by and then there was just sea stretching out below as far as the eye could see.

Amber had never left the States before. She

considered herself well travelled. She'd been to many different states and cities and she'd spent one vacation in Mexico. But journeying across the Atlantic to Europe – this was an adventure.

And to be travelling with a small holdall containing the world's most famous stolen jewels – well, that was breathtakingly adventurous.

'I think we should order champagne!' Em suggested with an excited smile.

'It's only 9.20 a.m.,' Amber said, glancing at her wristwatch.

'But we've been up the whole night. We've been through some unbelievable stress. Honey, I think we should drink some champagne, then put on our eye masks and wake up in Switzerland.'

Just the word Switzerland had the effect of a jump-start on Amber's heart.

As the stewardess approached, Em made her request. 'It's her birthday,' she explained, pointing at Amber.

Two small glasses of straw-coloured fizz were poured out for them.

'Happy birthday,' the stewardess said, with a smile.

Amber picked up her glass and took a sip, then closed her eyes.

She thought of what still lay ahead . . . and how impossible it seemed.

The jewels still had to clear customs at Geneva airport. Then she and Em had to open their not-for-profit bank account at the Bank of Obersaxen, meet the collector, and hope that he would give them a good price.

If he did, then Amber, with all her knowledge of the banking system, had to make their money flow quickly through the NPO's account and into as many innocent-looking accounts as she possibly could. Before anyone could catch up with them.

She drained the rest of the glass, hoping that Em was right, that she would be able to sleep all the way to Switzerland.

'It's going to be OK,' Em whispered, 'I can tell you that it's all going to be OK, because I can just feel it.'

# Chapter Forty

*'They're planning a move out of Manhattan. Can you imagine?'*

*'I find the suburbs extremely frightening. I mean, I know they have air conditioning and all, but still . . .'*

'It's time to relax and smile,' Em whispered to her big sister. 'We made it out of New York with these babies on full display, we'll make it through Geneva airport. OK?'

As Amber stepped out of the plane door and into the long walkway that led to the exit, she felt her breathing shallow in her chest. But just like Em, she tried to walk with a jaunty stride, her head up and something close to a smile on her face.

The airport was gleamingly clean and bright with wintry sunlight streaming in through the large windows. A couple walked past talking rapidly in

French. It was so excitingly foreign, so different to the US. Maybe Amber could be someone else over here. Maybe she could play this part.

'I think we'll take a taxi to our hotel. We'll dump our bags,' she said, going through the plan, 'then we'll go open our account.'

'Sure . . .' Em agreed.

Amber had found a scarf in her hand luggage, so when the time came to put on all the jewellery again, she'd knotted the scarf around her neck so that it trailed loosely over the brooches, hiding them a little.

The passport queue moved slowly.

It occurred to Amber that if there was any sort of alert out on them, this was where they might get pulled up.

But then . . . hadn't Jack been cursing about how long it took to get information on to an international database?

Jack. Oh no.

There he was again, popping up in her mind when she was trying so hard not to think about him.

'Merci, mademoiselle.'

The guy in the booth opened her passport, scanned it and then scrutinized her face for several long, breath-holding seconds.

'*Bonne visite,*' he said finally, and handed her passport back.

With Em's arm tucked comfortingly through hers,

they went to the luggage carousel, loaded their bags onto trolleys and sailed without the slightest delay straight through the green, Nothing to Declare channel.

'Like a charm,' Emerald said, and let her fingers wander over the Duchess's necklace she was wearing so brazenly.

'I thought green was an unlucky colour,' Amber said.

'Not for us, I guess. There's the taxi rank.'

A driver loaded their bags into the trunk and then opened the door for them to climb into his silver car.

'Welcome to Genève. Where can I take you?' he asked in perfect English.

'We have reservations at the Hotel du Conte,' Amber replied.

'Ah. This is a very nice hotel with a view of the lake. Beautiful.'

The driver was right. When he pulled up in front of their hotel, it looked just as antique and charming as it had done on the internet. They paid the fare, took their bags and went inside.

'Are we booked in under our real names?' Amber hissed at Em as she pulled her red suitcase and hold-all into an ornate lobby decorated with gilt-edged mirrors and antiques, plus a Christmas tree tastefully trimmed in white and gold.

'Yeah,' Em shrugged, 'no reason why not. I've put everything on your credit card . . . never to be repaid once you and I vamoose,' she whispered back.

'Jeeez. This looks like a five star place. You put it all on my card?'

Em nodded. 'The flights are on mine,' she added, as if this made it OK. 'Now we've both got bills so big that we really do need to leave the country.'

'Good afternoon, Mesdemoiselles, you have a reservation?' the receptionist wanted to know.

'Yup. One twin room for Jewel,' Em said with a smile. 'Just two nights, unfortunately. This is a beautiful hotel.'

'Thank you. You are wearing a beautiful necklace.'

The comment took Amber by surprise and she looked over at Em. She'd packed her panther back into her case in the taxi and Em had put away the fabulous emerald and diamond piece, but the man was looking at Em's green pendant.

'Oh thank you. Fake, obviously,' she told the man behind the desk. 'If I could afford the real thing, well . . .' she glanced at his name badge, 'I guess I'd be living here, Maurizio.'

Upstairs in their room, gazing open-mouthed at the vast, still lake and snow-capped mountains in the distance, Amber felt the thrilling beat of adventure.

'Oh my gosh! It is so beautiful, I just can't believe we landed somewhere so beautiful.'

'Think of all the places we can travel to now,' Em exclaimed. 'We're going to be free, Amber. We're really going to do it!'

Em threw her arms up in the air and gave a theatrical pirouette.

'We're not free yet,' Amber had to remind her. 'We've still got some really, really difficult things to do.'

'We have what that man wants, and we're going to give it to him for a bargain price. Why shouldn't this go to plan?'

'Just don't jinx it,' Amber warned. She looked at her watch: 'We have to call Mr Montanari from a call box. Then we have to get to the bank. If it's anything like in the States, they might shut by 5 p.m.'

'OK.'

'We'll carry the jewels with us, though. It just wouldn't feel right leaving them here in the hotel room.'

'Do you think it will be safe? Carrying them in our handbags?'

'Jeez, Em, we left them buried in a park just a few days ago and we've carried them all round New York City. We're walking around in Geneva, I bet no one ever got mugged in Geneva, it looks like the safest place on earth.'

'Yeah. OK.'

The jewellery, Mr Montanari's cellphone number, their passports and the other documents they needed, some real, some carefully designed, were transferred from cases to handbags.

'Mr Montanari doesn't know where we're staying, does he?' Em asked.

'No. Why?'

'Well . . . I don't know. It would give me a creepy feeling. What if he knew we were here, then he could try and steal the jewels from us before we meet him tomorrow?'

'Oh my! I never thought of that,' Amber admitted, 'I thought he was supposed to be . . . an OK guy.'

'He's a billionaire who wants to buy stolen jewels,' Em pointed out. 'Not many billionaires are "OK" guys. I think ruthless money-making machine might be nearer the mark.'

'If he's a billionaire, then I guess he could find out just exactly where we were staying if he wanted to.'

'Good point. We have to be careful,' Em said.

Just before they left the room, Amber asked, 'Em, did you see a guy in a big overcoat with a hat at Geneva airport?'

'I dunno. There must have been lots of guys in hats and big coats at the airport.'

'Yeah, but . . .'

Amber wasn't sure, maybe she'd imagined it.

'When we got out of the cab, I thought I saw the same guy again . . .'

'Really? Like he was following us?' Now it was Em's turn to look anxious.

'Maybe it was nothing. Maybe I just imagined it, you know. We're so wired. Like you said, I guess we need to be careful.'

# Chapter Forty-One

*'There's bad news there: I'm afraid Nathan had to go into banking.'*

*'Oh dear, would nobody else have him?'*

After the brief conversation with Mr Montanari, in which he instructed 'Miss C' to meet him with the jewels outside the Bank of Obersaxen at 10 a.m. the next day, Amber and Em went to open the bank account in the name of Em's bogus charity.

'Stop calling it bogus,' Em hissed at her sister. 'Maybe we'll give lots of money away. And then, just like that, we'll be a real charity.'

'Now that is a comforting thought,' Amber told her. 'Maybe I won't feel so bad about stealing millions if I give lots of money away.'

'OK, but can we concentrate on getting the millions into our bank accounts before we start deciding what to do with them?' Em asked.

The Bank of Obersaxen was in a small but beautifully appointed street. The kind of street that had boutique watch and jewellery shops and a chocolatier with a Christmas window display which slowed even Amber and Emerald down, despite the urgency of their mission.

'Oh my gosh, Cinderella's pumpkin coach, in chocolate?' Em pointed.

'Look there's her slipper in pink sugar.'

'The chocolate clock has just struck twelve . . .'

'Her chocolate prince is about to melt . . . well, don't they always?'

'Why did you pick this bank?' Em asked, as they came to the ornate oak door and the discreet brass plaque fixed into the wall.

'It was Montanari's suggestion,' Amber whispered. 'He'd arranged it with the real thief. Maybe it's a bank that doesn't ask many questions. Maybe he has some personal connection with it.'

'The real thief was going to use this bank?' Em repeated. 'That's kinda scary, Amber. I can't help feeling the real thief must be really, really pissed with us right now.'

'Like we keep saying: we've gotta be real careful.'

Walking in through the double doors, both sisters felt awed. They had to press a buzzer to get past internal locked glass doors. Then they were shown through to a marble-floored room with a huge golden and glass chandelier. There were red leather armchairs and mahogany side tables for waiting clients. Obersaxen was obviously one uber-rich bank.

'Oh my gosh,' Amber whispered. She swallowed nervously, but felt her throat go dry.

A man in a severely tailored suit hurried over to greet them at the door. He asked a question in French which Amber only half understood.

'Do you speak any English?' she asked, feeling like a shy and awkward tourist.

'But of course,' the man replied, and smiled graciously. 'How may I be of assistance?'

'We would like to open an account.'

'Do you have an appointment?'

'No. Are we supposed to have an appointment?'

'Well, this is usual. It is not entirely straightforward to open an account at the Obersaxen Bank.'

'This bank was recommended to us by Monsieur Montanari,' Amber said, bending the truth, but hopeful that this might ease their way into an appointment.

'Oh, Monsieur Montanari!' the man in the suit recognized the name at once. 'Please, take a seat, Mesdemoiselles. I will go and speak to the new accounts manager. Can I offer you a glass of water, or perhaps a cup of coffee?'

'I'm fine, thanks,' Amber said, just as Em answered, 'Coffee please, milk and two sugars.'

This was just how Amber's bank had treated its five star clients. No queuing in the lobby like the rest of the world. No, for five star clients it was comfortable armchairs, brand new finance magazines and a steady supply of light refreshments. It felt strange to be on the receiving end for the very first time.

The man in the suit was back almost as soon as they'd sat down.

'I would like to direct you into the office of Monsieur Colmar. Your coffee will be brought to you there, mademoiselle.'

Amber and Em exchanged a glance. They were on.

Just as Amber began to tingle with nerves, Em switched up a gear. Her back straightened, her face became fully alert. She seemed to relish these performances.

They were shown into a stylish office with lashings of mahogany, leather and here and there a modern art moment framed on the walls.

Monsieur Colmar shook their hands, told them to be seated and asked how he could be of assistance.

'My sister and I would like to open an account,' Amber began. 'We are the trustees of an American charity. We're bringing the charity to Europe because of a substantial European donation. We're planning to open a parent account at this bank and then, as trustees, we want to be able to move the money into subsidiary accounts as and when required.

'This is how we operate the accounts in the States,' she added.

A charity account was inspired. It would be registered with the bank under its fictitious name, so it would hopefully take the police a very long time to find this account and by then, if all went well, it would be empty. The money would have moved several times and Amber would have closed down all the linked accounts. The drawbridge would have been pulled up behind them.

'I think we may be able to help in this instance, if you are friends of Mr Montanari.'

'Yes, he recommended this bank.'

'Indeed. We will require all the official documents both on the charity and your status as trustees . . .'

'No problem, I have everything right here,' Amber said, and brought out a file from her handbag.

'The documents which record the inaugural meetings of the charity and its registration number in the States, and obviously we will be registering over here just as soon as the funds begin to come in. Here are our passports too.'

Monsieur Colmar took a careful look through all of the paperwork.

Amber knew that there was enough here. Some of it was a little faked, it made the charity look older than it really was. But it was good fake. Unless he actually phoned up the US passport office or the charities register, there was no reason for him to suspect that anything was amiss.

Why should he make those phone calls? He wanted money sitting in his bank. No one was asking for a loan here. This would be easy.

But still she ran the tip of her dry tongue over lips which felt parched.

'How big a donation are you expecting to raise?'

'It could be as much as $4 million,' Em said, breaking her silence and flashing him a charming smile.

'Really. How wonderful. What does your charity do?'

'It's all about supporting and encouraging women who want to set up their own business,' Em replied.

Amber bit her lip. Somehow this didn't sound quite right the way Em said it. It didn't exactly sound like a good cause. It sounded like they were helping themselves.

Which they were.

'A charity for female entrepreneurs?' Mr Colmar asked. 'How remarkable. Has it been successful in the States?'

'Oh yes,' Amber jumped in, 'especially in some of the poorest neighbourhoods. That's where we've been focusing our efforts.'

'So, *les Mesdemoiselles Jewel*, you have chosen the

Obersaxen Bank on the recommendation of our friend Monsieur Montanari. May I ask: does he intend to donate to the charity?'

'We couldn't possibly answer that question, Monsieur. Donations are as public or as confidential as the donor wishes them to be.'

'Normally, I would require a charity to be registered somewhere in Europe before I could open an account in its name. But in your case, as friends of our friend, I will be honoured to make this exception.'

'Does the account open straight away?' Amber wondered.

'I need a little time to complete the paperwork and enter the data onto the computer, but this is a small bank. You will be able to use the account tomorrow.'

'How do we transfer money once the account is open?'

'You can come into the bank and make a withdrawal. For this, we require twenty-four hours' notice for amounts over 500,000 Swiss francs. To move the money into another bank account, you make simple electronic transfers.

'You go onto the bank's website, you log on, you use your account number, which I will give you today, and you create passwords. Then you can move money into other accounts. *Tout simple.* If you have a smartphone, you can do this,' he clicked his fingers, '*comme ça.*'

'Now you must fill in these forms and sign, sign,

sign in all the relevant boxes. I'm sorry, even with a private bank it must be tedious. Maybe in the future when we bring in fingerprint ID, it will all be much more straightforward. Then the fraudsters will have to go to great lengths to fool us. No more fake passports, they will have to remove the fingertips of the people they wish to imitate.'

'Eeek!' Amber couldn't help squeaking.

Amber pushed the card into the key slot and opened the hotel room door.

'Oh!' she exclaimed.

'What?'

Em pushed in through the doorway.

They stared in shock. 'We've been burgled!' Amber gasped, looking at the chaos. Their bags had been emptied onto the floor, their beds had been searched, every drawer in the room had been opened and left hanging.

Quickly Amber shut the door behind them. 'Em,' she began, 'what if the real thief has come looking for the jewels?'

The real thief, Amber reminded herself, was a tall, muscular man who'd held Sapphire down and sprayed mace into her eyes. What else would he be prepared to do to get what he wanted? Amber felt a shudder of fear. Now she knew they were being followed.

'Shiiiiit!' Em exclaimed. 'What are we going to do?'

For several minutes the sisters searched through their belongings, only to realize nothing had been taken.

'We have to move out of this hotel. Right away,' Amber said.

'No, no,' Em replied, 'he'd expect us to do that – he's probably watching the street. So he can follow us wherever we go. We need to ask Maurizio to give us a new room, under a different name, and every time we come and go we'll use the back door.'

'I don't know if that will be enough, Em.'

'We can't go out there. He'll follow us wherever we go. We'll change rooms in this hotel, hide under another name and stay in tonight. Maybe he'll think he missed us leaving.'

'Are you sure?' Amber asked, not feeling sure of anything herself.

'We'll bolt the door and order room service. Besides, I want to sit in my jammies, watching movies and wearing the Duchess's necklace for the very last time,' Em said, desperate to lighten the mood a little.

'A different room . . . under another name,' Amber wondered. 'How are we going to get Maurizio to agree to that?'

'Oh easy, we just tell him we're in a whole load of boyfriend trouble. He'll totally understand.'

## Chapter Forty-Two

*'Oh he doesn't know anybody!'*

*'He's the kind of man who has to stay in a hotel when he travels abroad.'*

When Amber woke early the next morning, for a few moments she had no idea where she was. Then she turned, saw Em asleep beside her and understood.

The heavy weight of fear returned immediately and settled on her chest. She pushed the covers back, got out of bed and went to shower and then dress.

Amber had decided days ago what she would wear for the meeting with Mr Montanari: her smartest and most sober business suit. Her interview suit. The navy-blue pinstripe which said 'serious, ambitious, professional banker'.

As she put on her white blouse and then the trousers, the jacket and finally the black patent Mary

Janes, she felt the panic ease a little. Putting on her work armour was soothing. She had fought all kind of battles in this suit and suddenly she felt she could fight this battle too.

This was business. This was negotiation. This was her field.

She knew how to do this.

By the time Em had raised her mussed-up head from the pillow, Amber was sitting cool and calm in the room's desk chair, ready to do business.

'You look great,' Em told her, propping herself up. 'You look like a million dollars . . . even four.'

'So I'm going to go to the bank and wait for the money to come in,' Em said. 'When it's there, I'll walk out, down the street, past the car where you'll be with Mr M and you'll know everything's fine, so you can give him the jewels.'

'It sounds too simple.'

'We have what he wants and he has the money to pay us. Please try not to worry.'

'Try not to worry?' Amber gave a weak smile. 'I'll try,' she added.

'I just have a feeling that he'll keep to his side of the deal,' Em said.

Amber looked at her sister. Em's green pendant was still round her neck. It was a beautiful green stone in a simple setting.

'Do you sleep with that on?'

Em's hand went up to her chest. 'Oh yeah. Haven't taken it off since the day . . . it's my lucky charm. I'm kinda scared now that if I take it off, something bad will happen.'

'From Daffy's?' Amber asked. 'You bought it the day you took the jewels?'

'Yup. $34.99.'

'Huh . . . it looks nice. Suits you.'

'How the hell are we gonna pass the time . . .' Em groped on the bedside table for her watch: 'three hours until we need to be there.'

'Guess we're gonna have us some mighty fine eeeeeeggs for breakfast.'

This was such a good imitation of one of their daddy's most over-used phrases that it made them both burst into nerve-releasing giggles.

At exactly 9.56 a.m., Amber watched as a vast silver BMW slid into a parking space four doors up from the bank, right opposite the chocolatier's. The licence plate was just as she'd been told to expect so, swallowing down her acute anxiety, she began to walk towards the car. Over her shoulder was her simple leather messenger bag which contained the two most wanted items of jewellery in the world.

As a rule, Amber didn't like to swear, but right now, she couldn't help muttering: 'Shiiiit, shiiiit, shiiiit,' under her breath.

This was the most scary thing she'd ever, ever done.

No. In fact, it wasn't. All of a sudden she realized what the most frightening moment of her life had been. It was when she'd walked in through the front door of the ranch-house that day, knowing that for the first time ever, Daddy wasn't going to be there. And there was not one single thing she could do about it.

At the memory, Amber felt a cold shudder pass down her backbone.

Here, there was plenty she could do. She could run. She could hide the jewels somewhere else. Throw them away. Leave them to be found. There were still *choices*.

But walking into her family home that day, she'd had to bow to her fate. That day she was a 23-year-old girl who'd lost the most important man in her life way, way too soon.

As she walked along the pavement, she wondered if Mr Montanari had a daughter. He was certainly old enough to be her father. She wondered why she hadn't googled him some more, found out more about him. Did he have kids? It was suddenly important to know.

She was at the car now. Leaning down, she tried to look through the tinted window. It immediately slid down halfway.

Inside were two men. She recognized the one sitting closest to the window straight away – it was him, looking much more deeply tanned and sophisticated than he had done in the photos she'd found on the internet.

'Mademoiselle de Clavel?' he asked in a rich, accented voice. 'Good morning, please come and join us.'

The door opened and Amber stepped into the large back seat area of the car. Mr Montanari gestured to the plush leather seat which faced his own.

'Hello, I am Yves Montanari.' He held out his hand and shook hers.

'Hi, I'm Philippa de Clavel.'

'Is that your real name?'

When she replied, 'Not exactly,' he smiled.

She guessed he was late sixties. Steely grey hair swept back, a pair of slightly tinted aviator glasses on his still handsome face. Amber took in the luxurious cashmere rollneck and the expensive drape of the suede pilot's jacket he was wearing.

Maybe he had his own plane . . .

'You don't look like a jewel thief . . . but then, I've never had dealings with one before. Usually I buy everything I want at auction or from a very well-trusted dealer. Luigi, this is Mademoiselle de Clavel – ' he turned to the slight man in an old-fashioned three-piece suit sitting beside him.

'Mademoiselle de Clavel,' he went on, giving the French name the pronunciation it deserved, 'this is Luigi, no last name, please – my dealer.'

When Amber shook Luigi's hand she registered that it was as cool, damp and nervous as her own.

'Luigi and I don't deal with thieves. But in this very, very rare situation . . . I was prepared to make an exception. Luigi is still not so sure he wishes to be involved.'

Luigi turned to Mr Montanari and asked a question in rapid French.

'A busy street is perfect,' Mr Montanari replied, in English. 'No one expects you to do such secret business in a busy street. I read many crime novels and this I learn.'

He turned to Amber and gave her a smile.

'So, you are not what I expected at all. You look like a nice, well-educated, young American girl. How have you come to be selling stolen jewellery?'

Amber felt as if every one of her nerve endings was alight. Her eyes kept darting nervously to the windows to watch people in the street. She was frightened that this was a trap. There was absolutely no guarantee that Mr Montanari hadn't informed the police of this meeting and the car was about to be surrounded.

'I lost my job. I can't find a new one. Times are tough.'

'Where did you work?'

'I worked for a big bank. They lost a lot of money and I was one of the casualties.'

'Ah. Credit crunch, no? This is very sad for you. But now, maybe you have the skill to make a lot of money. More than you would have made working all your life for the bank. Have you thought about how to move this money around once I place it into your account? If you've worked for a bank, you must know that it is very difficult to move big sums of money around the world without people asking lots of questions.'

'Yes. I've thought about it,' Amber said.

Mr Montanari nodded.

'Where are you from in the States? You don't sound like a New Yorker.'

'I'm from Texas.'

'Ahhh!' Mr Montanari's smile expanded. '*Les cowboys*. Maybe this explains why you become a thief.'

Thief.

*Thief*.

The word rang in Amber's ears and she hated it.

Em was the thief. She was making the deal. That's how she'd justified it in her mind.

'Well, I would love to see the jewels you have brought for us, Mademoiselle.'

Amber scrutinized the men carefully. Did she

trust them enough to do this? Could she be sure they weren't going to try to snatch them and make off without paying her?

She glanced out of the window. Was anything suspicious going on outside?

'This is a difficult moment,' Mr Montanari said, 'I understand that you do not trust us and we do not trust you. Well . . . it is the price we must pay for not choosing to go through Sotheby's, no?' He chuckled as he reached for a black briefcase on the floor which she hadn't noticed before. As he moved for it, Amber gasped. She was thinking: guns! Nerve gas! Something that would make her pass out while they put on gas masks . . .

'No, no, my apologies, I do not wish to alarm you. There is nothing bad inside.'

'Are the doors unlocked?' Amber asked anxiously.

With a click, the electric lights changed to green. She put her fingers nervously on the handle.

'Please, don't worry and just open the case.' Mr Montanari smiled affably and handed it to her: 'It is a goodwill gesture. A down payment. I want you to feel that you can trust us to do good business.'

With one hand on the door, Amber used the other to pop open the two catches on the case.

She lifted the lid and saw stacks of euro notes inside. Wads and wads of them. Just like in the movies.

'This is 30,000 euros. You can take this now. Keep

it on your side of the car. This is what we are paying to look at the jewels. If we like the jewels we will buy them. As arranged.'

Amber opened the flap of her messenger bag. Carefully, she pulled out the jewellery roll and put it in her lap. As she untied the bow and unfolded the velvet, she sensed both Mr Montanari and Luigi leaning forward to look.

Now the emerald and diamond necklace and the panther brooch were uncovered and, despite the low light from the tinted windows, they glittered against the velvet.

'Mon Dieu!' Mr Montanari gasped.

He held out his hand and asked her politely, 'May I take a closer look, Miss de Clavel?'

Although she knew this was the most dangerous moment, Amber picked up the brooch and handed it over to him.

Mr Montanari let the brooch sit in his palm for a moment. He looked at it carefully and felt its weight.

'This is so beautiful. I have no doubt that it is the original. The Duchess of Windsor's *panthère*.' He brought it towards his face.

Amber kept one hand on the handle of the brief-case, the other over the emerald necklace.

'May I show this to Luigi?' Mr Montanari asked, understanding Amber's anxiety.

She nodded.

Luigi brought out a jeweller's eyeglass from a pocket. He took the brooch and studied it through the magnifying lens.

'Highest-quality gold, studded with rubies and diamonds. This is the original,' Luigi declared solemnly. 'It has an antique quality it would be almost impossible to reproduce, and there is the Cartier signature,' he showed Mr Montanari.

'Absolutely beautiful. Unmistakable,' Mr Montanari said quietly. 'The Duchess was a woman of the highest, most exquisite taste.'

He handed the panther back to Amber. 'And the necklace?' he asked.

Amber put the panther back on top of her roll.

A velveteen jewellery roll she remembered buying in a Fort Worth drugstore years ago, when she was going to college. How could she possibly have guessed what she would one day store inside it?

She picked up the necklace and placed it in Mr Montanari's hand.

'*Incroyable*,' Mr Montanari exclaimed in a whisper as he looked at the necklace. 'The emeralds are the finest I've ever seen. Look at the diamonds surrounding them. And the workmanship. This is a treasure.'

Luigi worked the necklace over with his eyeglass and seemed equally impressed.

'Colombian emeralds. Each one about 4 carats.

It must have been a very special piece. For a very special occasion.'

'The poor Duke of Windsor. He had nothing to do,' Mr Montanari declared. 'No country to rule, no business empire. I think he spent all his time adoring and adorning his beautiful wife.' He held the necklace up in both hands. 'Well, Miss de Clavel . . . these are just as you promised. I would love to be their legitimate owner, so *my* beautiful wife could wear them and I could exhibit them along with the other pieces in my collection. But . . . that is not possible any more . . .'

He sighed.

'Generally, I am an honest man. I find I sleep better at night that way.'

Amber had no reply to this. Generally, she was an honest person too. Yet here she was in the back of a billionaire's BMW trying to convince him to part with a few million for the jewels she'd somehow got involved with stealing.

'I cannot pay you the full value of the jewels,' Mr Montanari went on, 'because now that they are stolen, they are in many ways worthless. They can never be displayed, they can never be publicly acknowledged, they can never be resold. I will always feel somewhat ashamed of owning these jewels.'

Amber's heart was sinking like a stone. But,

keeping her voice just as calm and collected as if she was making an ordinary banking transaction, she said: 'Then I will have to take them away, there are many other collectors even more interested in these jewels than you.'

'Then why did you come to me first?' he asked.

'You happened to be on the top of our list.'

She had already folded the velvet flaps over the panther and the emeralds.

A small movement outside the window caught her eye. She saw a man with his back to them, admiring the window of the chocolatier's. He was broad-shouldered and for a moment she thought it was the man from the airport. But he was wearing a light-coloured raincoat, and he didn't have a hat, he had neat dark hair . . .

She gave a start of fright.

Could it be Jack?!

Impossible!

She made herself look away. Of course Jack wasn't wandering up and down this street in Switzerland, looking in windows and wondering how to find her. Her freaked-out imagination was running away with her.

'I would like to offer you one million euros for these jewels,' Mr Montanari said.

Now he had her attention.

'Impossible,' she said, almost annoyed with him.

'You know that's completely impossible. My sis—other people are involved in this theft. We committed it for a reason. To achieve a certain amount of money.'

'What figure did you have in mind?'

'Three and a half million dollars,' she said and drew her lips together firmly to make it clear that she was unwilling to negotiate.

Mr Montanari tilted his head a little to the side and looked at her.

'Now you are the one being impossible.'

Amber turned back to the velvet roll. She folded it carefully over the jewels then began to tie the bow back in place.

Of course there were other collectors, all over the world. But she did not want to do this any more: smuggle stolen jewels through airports . . . arrange clandestine rendezvous with unknown rich men. It was too dangerous. She would either get caught or have a heart attack – whichever came first.

'Two million,' Mr Montanari said.

She raced through the math: $2 million was about $660,000 each. If they invested and made 20 per cent, they would have about $132,000 a year . . . for the rest of their lives, without spending one cent of the original sum. They wouldn't be rich. But they wouldn't have to work again.

Was it enough?

Could she get more?

Would Em be happy?

She and Em hadn't talked about how low they might go for the jewels. They should have. Because now she had to make the decision on her own, and she could destroy Em's dream.

Em would hold out for more. Em would want to head to Tokyo to find the avid Duchess-obsessive over there.

'Two point three,' Amber said in the steeliest voice she could manage, 'that really is going to have to be my final offer, Mr Montanari.'

'Why point three?'

'Three is my lucky number.'

'Are three of you involved?'

She turned her face away from him and looked out of the window.

'Two point three million dollars . . .' he sighed. 'It is a lot of money for jewels I am never going to be able to say I own. What are you going to do with the money?'

'We're . . . I'm just going to try and be free.'

'Will you be free?'

'There's no reason for anyone to come looking for me, so yes. I think I will be free.'

'No one at all? No one will miss you? That seems very sad.' There was a long silence. Then Mr Montanari took his cellphone from his pocket and pressed a button. A voice answered almost immediately.

*'Bertrand? Oui c'est moi, Yves Montanari. Je voudrais faire une transaction.'*

Amber listened intently. She understood just enough to make out that Mr Montanari had called his bank. He was poised to place $2.3 million in their bank account.

*'Le numéro, Mademoiselle?'* He looked at her questioningly.

Amber gave him the nine-digit account code she had memorized, plus the bank code. Then the transaction was made and after some small talk had been exchanged with Bertrand, the call was over.

*'C'est fini!'* Mr Montanari exclaimed. 'But you are a clever girl, you have a way of checking the transaction I've made is genuine, do you not?'

Amber nodded, her eyes already on the street. Just as soon as she saw Em walk past the car, she would give Mr Montanari the jewels and she would leave. 'Just give me a little moment.'

She watched as a man, his back to her, walked down the street about twenty yards away. Once again she found herself believing it was Jack and her heart began to race. Was this a plot? A trap? Was Mr Montanari in on it? Suddenly, the fact that they hadn't been able to speak to Sapphire last night, either on her cell or at Fergus's number, seemed very sinister.

But then to Amber's huge relief, the man disappeared around a corner, and she saw Emerald walk briskly out of the bank and straight past the car.

Quickly, Amber passed Mr Montanari the jewellery roll. 'Thank you,' she said, and reached for the door handle.

'Don't forget your briefcase,' he told her, holding out his hand for her to shake. '*Au revoir,* my Texan, friend, *et bonne chance.*'

Amber hurried along the pavement to catch up with Em. As soon as she was within reach, she put her hand on her sister's shoulder.

'Keep walking,' she told her, 'keep walking fast. Turn down the first street you see.'

Em understood the urgency in her sister's voice. 'Is something wrong?' she asked.

'I don't know. But I don't feel good.'

'You never feel good,' Em complained, but kept walking quickly all the same. 'Even when $2.3 million lands in our account.'

'Was that enough?'

'I figure if that's what you got us, that's as much as we could get.' Em couldn't help grinning: 'We did it, Amber! We've got it. We've got the money!'

Together they made the left into the next street.

'Let's just keep turning. Take the weirdest possible way back to the hotel.'

'Do you think we're being followed?'
'I don't know!'
'Why are you carrying a briefcase?'
'Oh! Oh, Em, I nearly forgot. He gave me 30,000 euros in cash. It was . . . I dunno . . . it was a goodwill payment . . . just to look at the jewels.'
'You have 30,000 euros in that bag?' Em turned, eyes wide. 'You have got to be kidding me.'
'No . . . I'd show it to you but we're in the middle of—'
They both took a moment to look at the street they'd hurried into. It was old, narrow and beautiful. Strings of delicate Christmas lights criss-crossed above their heads and every window twinkled with luxuries.
Gold watches, diamond rings, fur coats, designer dresses. Each snow and Christmas tree decked window they passed was more alluring than the last.
'So what spooked you?' Em asked, now that she was facing her sister. 'Did you see the man in the hat again?'
Amber thought carefully. She'd seen the back of a tall, dark-haired man without a hat. Her imagination had supplied the rest.
'Nothing,' she replied, 'I don't think it was anything.'
'Amber,' Em's voice was hushed but her face was bright with excitement, 'we've *sold* the jewels! We

have *$2.3 million* in an untraceable account and a bonus 30,000 euros in your briefcase – and we happen to be in the most beautiful shopping street I've ever seen in my entire life. Amber!! Guess what we're going to do right after we get ourselves a little nerve-calming cocktail . . .'

# Chapter Forty-Three

*'Have you seen the new Gucci collection for babies?'*

*'That is beyond vulgar. I mean, what next? An alligator sleepsuit?'*

'Look at this place. Look at it! They have everything I've ever wanted! *Chanel shoes!'* Em rushed over to the display and took down a perfect black and nude pump.

'Ow may I 'elp you, Mademoiselle?'

'Do you have these in my size?'

Em's enthusiasm for the shoes, for the ornate gilded, fantasy bags, for the jewel-coloured dresses, for the fur-trimmed everything was so infectious that Amber found herself heading straight for a chocolate-coloured sheepskin coat with a glorious Russian princess collar.

As soon as Amber slipped it on, Em squealed, 'You

have to have that! You look wonderful. Isn't it going to be very cold where we're headed?'

'I have no idea! There's skiing, so I guess it could be real cold.'

Tomorrow morning they were going to move to Montenegro.

Tomorrow morning!

Amber had looked through the guidebook, but that was all. She had no idea what it would be like. She didn't even know what language people spoke there!

How long would they have to stay in Montenegro before it would once again be safe to come home? Years, maybe? She was about to spend years in a country she'd never even heard of until a few weeks ago.

'Take the coat,' Em was whispering into her ear, 'you know you want to . . . and you have a whole briefcase full of cash beside you.'

A glance at the price tag told Amber the coat was 4,000 euros. More than she'd ever paid for an item of clothing before. More than she'd ever paid for *anything* before.

'I'm going to buy fur,' Em purred. 'Real slinky mink, or even sable. But I know you're more a sheepskin kind of girl.'

'Didn't you bring your white ermine jacket?' Amber asked.

'Yeah, but if it's going to be cold, best to have more than one.'

Amber raised her eyebrows.

'Very millionairess,' Em added.

'We're not going to be super-rich,' Amber warned her, still whispering because the shop assistant was probably still on the other side of the fitting room curtain. 'We're going to have a private income. If we burn through the money, there won't be enough to invest—'

'Amber . . .' Em pulled a fabulous green fox fur coat over her shoulders, and turned to her sister. 'It must be such hard work being you! Doing all the worrying for everyone. Chill out! Please! We did this, we pulled it off! If we run out of money, maybe we can do something just like it again.'

'Again?!' Amber hissed, horrified. 'No way!'

Em gazed at herself in the mirror. She looked extraordinary in the green fur.

'I could sooooo get used to this,' she declared. 'Maybe I can find a hunky, single billionaire who will drape me in fox and sables for the rest of my life.'

Amber rolled her eyes. The sooner they divided up the money and ran their own affairs, the better as far as she could see. She might be Em's big sister, but she didn't want to be Em's banker or Em's surrogate parent for the rest of her life.

'When we've finished in here,' Em turned back to her sister, eyes wide with delight, 'I think we should go buy jewellery.'

Amber didn't buy the sheepskin coat. Instead, she opened up her briefcase at the counter and watched the assistant's astonished face as she took out 7,000 euros in cash to settle Emerald's bill for the Chanel shoes and the fantastic green fox.

'I guess you must have a safe?' Amber asked.

'But of course. Usually, we use it only when the Russians are shopping.'

'We're not drug dealers,' Em added with a smile, 'we've just inherited a lot of money.'

'How very exciting,' the assistant said, but her face was a little pained.

Amber wondered if she could get used to people being jealous of her, or if it would always make her feel this uncomfortable.

When they stepped into the tiny, gilded jeweller's shop further along the street, Amber thought of Ori. With a flash of guilt she wondered when the court case was coming up and if the robber would be convicted without her or Sapphire there to testify.

Sapphire!

She glanced at her watch. They should try to call Sapphire, just as soon as they were done in here. But that could take some time, Amber realized, as she watched Em admire herself in a diamond-studded chain.

'Amber, please have a look around the store,' Em insisted, 'there are so many beautiful things.'

Towards the back of the jeweller's, glass and gilt cases with velvet-lined shelves displayed a collection of antique jewellery. Sapphire had taught Amber to love old jewellery. But ever since she'd seen the Duchess's emeralds and her panther brooch, Amber felt that she'd held the best quality jewellery in her hands and nothing else would ever look as good to her. It was probably like couture clothing: if you wore it once, you'd never go back to buying an off-the-peg dress. You'd be spoiled for life.

She walked over to the antique treasures in the glass cases. The dulled gold and non-bling jewels obviously didn't look as astonishing as the Duchess's million-dollar treasures. But they still looked beautiful.

There on a lower shelf, not stealing the show, was a little pin brooch. Amber looked at it more closely. Amazingly, it held just three stones: an emerald, a sapphire and, between the two, a slightly larger diamond.

Her mother had wanted to call her Diamond, but Daddy had overruled it. Way too showy. So she'd been named Amber. Their mother had got her way with naming Sapphire and Emerald. Sapphire was so called because of her beautiful blue eyes and

Emerald, well, since she was a teenager, Em had used contact lenses to turn her blue eyes green.

So this little pin, this was about the three of them, and it suddenly felt very important to her to have some symbol of them all together.

'Could I take a look at this?' she asked the jeweller.

'Made in the 1850s,' he told her as he took the pin out of the case. 'The diamonds are cut the old-fashioned way. Not so shiny as today.'

'I like that.'

'This has beautiful quality stones at a wonderful price for you,' he added as he pinned it onto her sober jacket. 'So. *Très chic*.'

She looked in the mirror.

Suddenly, having a briefcase full of cash at her disposal didn't seem so bad.

'These jewels in a modern piece would cost at least 1,000 euros,' the jeweller told her. 'But in an antique pin, much less: 600. There is not so much demand for old jewellery, which makes me sad. It is usually much better quality.'

Em came over to glance at the display cabinet, but quickly turned back to the shinier, brighter things at the front of the shop.

'I'm going to take this necklace,' she said of the sparkling, diamond-studded chain she was holding in her hand, 'and I'd like to see if you have that ring there in my size – ' she pointed into the case at a fat golden band, set with a blizzard of sparkling diamond chips.

'The necklace you are wearing is very special,' the jeweller said, turning his attention from Amber back to Emerald.

'Oh, this? she pointed to her chest. 'It looks good, but it's a big, fat fake from a department store.'

'Really?' the man sounded surprised. 'But the jewel looks so . . .'

Em let her hand drop back to her side. 'Amazing what they can do with plastic nowadays, I guess.'

The diamond-studded ring, the diamond chain and Amber's pin came to an astonishing 6,300 euros.

'We're paying in cash, does that get us any kind of discount?' Em wondered.

'I can make it 6,000 for cash,' the jeweller told them.

'Oh my Lord. I am buying diamonds and paying for them in cash.' Em turned to her sister with a wide-eyed grin. 'I haven't had so much fun since a pig ate my brother!'

The jeweller looked on bemused as Amber snapped open her briefcase and brought out a bundle of notes.

'We're on our way to the bank,' Em told him. 'I just hope it's not too far from here or our briefcase will be empty!'

Amber dug her sister hard in the ribs. Em was always too much. She spent too much, she said too much. Any moment now and she'd be naming their bank and telling some elaborate inheritance tale sure to make the jeweller suspicious.

'Thank you,' Amber said as their purchases were handed over to them in small golden shopping bags.

'Enjoy your jewels and your good fortune,' the jeweller said.

'Cocktails! We must have more cocktails!' Em demanded, as soon as they were back in the street.

It was growing dark. Amber looked again at her watch and couldn't believe how much time had passed.

'We should go to the hotel,' she insisted. 'It's getting late, we don't want to be out here in the dark when someone might still be looking for us . . .'

'The man in the hat? He's too late!' Em exclaimed. 'What's he going to do? Rob our bank? Even if he tracked us down now, he couldn't take our money away.'

'Don't,' Amber warned. 'I don't like the thought of anyone tracking us down. We'll go back to the hotel and we'll call Sapphire, she'll be so worried about us. Hell, I'm worried about her. Why do you think we couldn't speak to her last night?'

'Cocktails,' Em replied. 'Maybe she needed cocktails too.'

As they walked through the hotel lobby, Em whispered to her sister, 'Look in there, at the bar!'

Amber glanced through the doors and saw a handsome guy in a suit sitting up by the bar in the dark, lavishly furnished room. The handsome guy must have felt their gaze because he turned and smiled at them.

'I may have to go in there straight away, before someone else gets him.'

'Em! He's probably sitting there waiting for his beautiful wife.'

'Well I'll never know unless I go, will I?'

With that, she handed her shopping bags to Amber and sashayed right into the room.

# Chapter Forty-Four

*'He was wearing a fur coat, Lauren, there is no excuse for that!'*

*'Well, not unless your name ends in "otzky" and you have your own gas field.'*

Amber, weighed down with the briefcase and bags full of diamonds, Chanel shoes and green fox fur – for goodness sake – headed for the elevator.

At the door to their room, she set down the bags and the briefcase and fumbled with the key card and the handle just as her cell began to ring.

'Jeez!' she complained, trying to find the phone.

Once she had it in her hands, she wasn't sure whether she should answer it or not. But the thought that it might be news from her sister made her press the green button.

'Hi?'

'Amber! It's me, it's Sapphire!'

'Sapphire! How are you? You're not in any kind of trouble, are you? We've been trying to call.'

'Oh, Amber, I haven't got long. I'm using a call box and it's so fussy about the kind of quarters it needs . . . some of them work but some of them don't.'

Sapphire's voice sounded strained and on the verge of tears.

'Are you OK?'

'Yes,' Sapphire replied, 'but I'm . . . I'm . . .'

'WHAT?' Amber couldn't bear the suspense. Did someone know? Had someone asked Sapphire questions which she'd had to answer? Still standing in the corridor outside the hotel room, Amber glanced anxiously around. She couldn't shake off the feeling that someone was watching them. Someone was on their trail.

'Oh, Amber, the police have me . . .'

'Are you under arrest?' Amber asked, horrified at the thought. They'd just been shopping for diamonds when their sister – the one who hadn't done anything – was under arrest?

'No . . . I'm, I'm a protected witness,' Sapphire said and began to sob.

'What do you mean?'

'I don't know exactly,' Sapphire said. 'They keep explaining it, but I'm so freaked out nothing makes sense. They think someone involved with the

Wilson's robbery might want to get to me, so I'm in a safe place. Someone's listening to this call,' she added, quickly.

The real thieves. Had they worked out that Sapphire had a connection to the jewels?

How long would the police protect her? And would the thieves keep looking for the three of them until they found them? Would she, Sapphire and Em be in danger for the rest of their lives?

'Sapphire,' Amber whispered down the line, 'I am so sorry. How long have you been with the police?'

'Since yesterday morning. I'm not allowed to contact anyone from Wilson's. I have no idea what's going on there or what's going to happen to Fergus—'

'Sapphire, what's going on? What have they told you?' Amber interrupted.

'I just don't know, Amber. Yesterday Jack asked me a whole load of questions. Today I've been left alone.'

Jack's name startled Amber. It was too strange to think that she was trying to get her head around never seeing him ever again, while her sister had been right there with him just yesterday.

'Did Jack ask about us?'

'Yes, and he seemed to know . . .' Sapphire began, her voice breaking up tearfully once again.

'Oh my gosh, Sapphire, know what? But you didn't . . .'

'No . . . I don't think I . . . but there were so many questions. I don't know if . . .'

'Oh my gosh . . . ohmigosh . . .'

'Amber, there's something real important. I can't believe it, but I think it could be important . . .'

The dial tone sounded in Amber's ear. 'Sapphire?' she said, uselessly into the cell, 'Sapphire!'

Of course, there was no reply. Amber pushed the key card into the door and dragged the bags into their hotel room. This time, it didn't look as if anything had been disturbed. She hoped Em's idea of moving to a different floor under a different name – they were now Monsieur et Madame Dupont – had worked. Whoever was out there looking for them had not been able to find them yet. But was it safe to stay here?

Amber sat down on the edge of her bed and tried to work out what Sapphire had wanted to tell her. Something important . . . Something she couldn't believe, but could be important . . .

She looked at her cellphone, hoping it would burst back into life and Sapphire would be able to finish her sentence. But silence. Sapphire had said she didn't have long. Amber should just have let her speak.

Had Sapphire let the police know what had happened? Were the police now after them as well as the real thieves?

Amber looked at her watch. It was after 7 p.m. Their flight to Montenegro would leave at 10.30 tomorrow morning from Geneva airport.

They only had to get through the next fifteen and a half hours. If they could hide from everyone for just that long, then maybe they would get away. The police couldn't follow them to Montenegro . . . but the real thieves could.

Amber felt a cold shiver pass down her neck at the thought. Maybe when they arrived in the strange new country, the man in the hat would be there, waiting for them.

Or – she tried to remind herself – maybe he wouldn't. Maybe they would get away with the money, just like they'd planned. They'd got this far. They'd already got this close.

If they got safely to Montenegro with the money, then Sapphire could come out of police protection and join them there. Surely she'd be allowed to go home to Texas for Christmas? Once she was in Texas, Amber would book her flights out to Amsterdam and on to Montenegro. She'd already looked them up back in New York.

Then they would all be together . . . and they'd have the money . . . and they'd be free.

This whole train of thought was making her feel uneasy because there were still so many problems ahead.

Did the NYPD know?

Would the real thieves follow them?

Would Sapphire honestly leave Mother and Fergus and get on a transatlantic flight all by herself to join her sisters in a life of crime? It just didn't sound like the kind of thing Sapphire would do. Hell, a life of crime? It didn't even sound like the kind of thing Amber would do.

She felt a painful lump in the back of her throat. She couldn't quite believe in any of it. Here she was sitting in a hotel room in Switzerland with a briefcase full of money, bags full of diamonds and furs, and a bank account containing millions of dollars. But all she could feel was panicked. She could lose her sister. She might not see Sapphire or Mother again for years. Plus, the NYPD and the real thieves could still catch up with them.

Amber wanted to throw herself across her bed and sob. But she knew she had to head back downstairs.

She had to get back to the bar before Em got too drunk or too amorous. Already she could imagine her sister telling the perfect, handsome stranger all about how clever they'd been . . . all about the Swiss bank account they'd set up and the fabulously famous jewels they'd stolen and sold.

* * *

A phone was ringing.

Loudly. Right beside her head. Shocking her out of her sleep.

Amber opened eyes which felt dry and prickly. She remembered being upset, crying and drinking too much wine . . .

The unfamiliar ceiling and curtains startled her. Where was she?

She sat bolt upright.

The hotel room. Yesterday and then last night returned in a jumbled rush of memories and nerves. Em!

Amber turned to see that Em's bed was empty. Hand poised over the ringing phone, she tried to remember their evening.

They had eaten dinner with Em's Swiss hotel-bar date. Em had hardly been able to eat much, she'd been so busy devouring the handsome man at the table. But she'd swallowed so much wine and become so loud and showy that Amber had begun to fear for their secrets. Several times she'd dragged Em off to the bathroom and told her to tone it down. But Em had just laughed her off.

The phone . . .

Em must be calling. Maybe she wanted back into the room after her night with the handsome hotel guest. Maybe she'd lost her key card.

'Hello,' Amber said into the heavy, old-fashioned telephone receiver.

'Amber?'

Immediately Amber was wide, screaming awake. She felt as if she had been thrown into a pond of ice water.

The voice was Jack's.

And Detective Jack Desmoine of the NYPD calling her hotel room in Geneva was not in any way good.

'Amber, is that you?' Jack asked.

Amber said nothing. But she was aware of how laboured her breathing sounded. She was panting with fear.

'Amber, why are you in Switzerland? Did you steal the jewels?'

# Chapter Forty-Five

*'I've never seen anybody get so worked up, Betty.'*

*'Then you've obviously not lived very long.'*

*'Not as long as you, honey!'*

Amber hung up.

She dropped the receiver straight down into its cradle and leapt out of bed, scrambling for her clothes, pulling on jeans and a top, then flinging her suitcase onto the bed. She began to throw everything in the room into it. A glance at her watch told her it was 5.31 a.m.

She had to find Em. Then she and Em had to get out of this hotel in like ten seconds. He could already be in the lobby . . . in the elevator . . . on his way up. Within moments she and Em could be under arrest.

They would be dragged back to the US to face a

truly shocking trial and – oh no, oh freaking no, no, NO!

She picked up the phone and dialled reception. What was the guy's name? *C'mon, c'mon,* she could remember.

Benjamin, Benjamin . . . Benjamin what?!

'Hi there, hello, I need to speak with Benjamin . . .' aaargh! 'Müller, please.'

'Certainly, I will try his room.'

A moment later a thick, sleepy voice answered. *'Ja, was ist?'*

'Em. Is Em there? I have to speak with her. This is an emergency.'

There was a pause. Amber thought she could hear footsteps in the corridor outside. This was unbearable. She flung the last items into her suitcase with her free hand, cradling the phone with the other.

'Hello . . .'

Em's voice sounded rough and cracked. She'd obviously had very little sleep.

'Jack knows! He knows, Em! He just called my room. We have to get out of here now. Head out the fire escape right now. I'll meet you with the bags.'

'Shit,' Em said, and hung up.

Shutting her suitcase, Amber knew it was hopeless. They couldn't possibly make a run for it with two suitcases. She could maybe take the briefcase and the overnight bag with all the documents, but that was all.

Shit. Shit. *Shit!*

They would have to leave her red suitcase and Em's blue one here, along with all their treasures, all the sentimental things they'd brought from New York because they couldn't bear to part with them.

She opened up the case and rifled through it very quickly for her folder of family photographs. Daddy and Sapph, she had to have their pictures with her. She didn't know where she would find the strength to run away without them. Her hands were shaking so hard it was almost impossible to search for the folder.

Amber pushed the folder of photos into her small holdall and glanced around the room. She spotted the shopping bags and stuffed the jewellery they'd bought into the holdall. Then she slipped Em's shaggy green fox coat over her shoulders and ran with the holdall and the briefcase out of the room.

The door locked shut behind her.

She looked frantically up and down the corridor for the fire escape, raced to the door, flung it open and began to run down the stairs.

'Amber!' She heard the hiss from several flights below.

'Em!'

She sped on, until she'd caught up with her younger sister.

'Shit!' Em exclaimed as soon as she saw her. '*Shit!* What are we going to do?'

'We'll go straight to the airport and fly somewhere,' Amber said, running down the concrete stairs. 'If we can't fly direct to Montenegro, we'll fly somewhere else first. We'll use cash and try to stay ahead of them. We just have to get to the airport.'

'But what if the police are there?'

'Have you got any better ideas?'

They carried on racing down the stairs . . . only one more floor to go.

'Where are the suitcases?' Em asked, still hurrying on.

'In the room. We couldn't run with them. Don't say anything, I know!' Amber exclaimed. 'I know it's terrible. But I took the photos and the jewellery and your jacket. That's the best I could do.'

'Thank you,' Em said.

It sounded genuine and Amber felt grateful for her sister's thanks. She'd expected a volley of complaints.

They reached the bottom. The fire exit door was straight ahead, but already the sisters could see the large notices on it, in three languages, informing them that this door was alarmed.

'We can't get out here!' Amber shrieked. 'We'll set every bell in the entire hotel ringing.'

Em looked at the signs, then over at a second door which led to the hotel's ground floor. 'Set a smile on your face, and follow me. We'll go out the back door.'

But as they approached the small back door they'd used once before, Amber pulled Em back.

'Look!' she cried urgently.

The tall, vertical window beside the back door revealed a shadowy figure waiting outside.

'Jack?' Em asked.

Amber shook her head: 'A hat,' she whispered, 'that man's wearing a hat.'

'This way,' Em said and pulled Amber towards the hotel's dining room. Although it was early, a handful of guests were already seated at the tables, coffee cups in hand, a waiter scribbling down the breakfast orders.

As Amber walked through the room in the ludicrous green fur jacket, carrying her briefcase and holdall, she felt completely exposed. She really expected Jack and the man in the hat to appear right in front of them at any moment.

Em threw Amber a confident smile, then proceeded to follow the waiter straight out of the dining room and into the hotel kitchen.

When he looked round to see the two sisters behind him, Em beamed and said, in her winning way, 'Hi there, we need to get out of the back door.

There's this guy I met at the bar last night and . . . I don't want to bump into him again.'

The waiter laughed and shrugged his shoulders. 'This way,' he directed them.

Amber followed Em past rows of shelves, then through the kitchens, where several startled chefs glanced up at them. They finally made it to the big double doors open against the fierce heat.

'Where there's a kitchen, there's always a back door,' Em told Amber, 'I've been a waitress long enough to have that figured.'

'We need a cab,' Amber said as they hurried out into the street.

'Down this street,' Em said, 'it looks promising.'

Even when the cab had begun to move smoothly through the early morning streets, Amber did not feel the slightest sense of relief.

Jack *knew.*

And they might not get away from him in time.

'Sapphire must have told them,' Em declared, 'there's no other way.'

'Sapphire didn't have time to tell me what she'd had to tell them . . . I just hope she's left completely out of this. None of this is her fault.'

Em kept her face towards the car window and folded her arms. 'Do you really think Jack knows?' she asked.

'Yeah,' Amber replied, 'he asked me on the phone if we'd stolen them. If he doesn't know everything then he's guessing and he's really close to knowing.'

'I warned you, Amber. Didn't I keep warning you to not see the guy? To cut him loose. '

'I was trying to play along. I didn't want him to get suspicious,' Amber protested, but she coloured up a little. This was not entirely the truth, she knew she'd carried on seeing Jack because she'd wanted to, so very much.

Hey,' Em turned to her big sister. 'You and Jack aren't working on this together, are you? You're not about to turn me in and keep the reward money?'

'Em! Are you out of your mind?'

'Sorry,' Em apologized quickly, 'I guess I'm kinda scared now, Amber. None of us was supposed to go to jail. That was never the plan.'

'If we can get to Montenegro then we're safe. We don't have the . . . items on us,' she whispered, mindful of the taxi driver, although he had the morning news on loud in the front of the car. 'The money is being moved in small amounts from a charity account. There's nothing to prove we—'

'The collector could identify you,' Em pointed out. 'Maybe they've got to him . . .'

'Please, let's not talk about it any more,' Amber snapped. 'I'm so scared I can't even think straight.'

# Chapter Forty-Six

*'So I'm trying on this fabulous jacket and she's telling me to buy it . . .'*

*'But $15,000? That's kind of steep for a jacket.'*

*'I know and at our age, it's not like we can sell an ovary.'*

'Hi, we're booked onto a flight to Montenegro at 10.30 a.m. today. But is there any way of getting there sooner? Could we fly somewhere else and connect?'

Em did the talking as Amber tried to hold herself together. She kept looking over her shoulder, scanning the airport frantically for any sign of Jack, or the man in the hat.

If only they didn't look so unusual, maybe they could blend in more, but right now she and Em looked like fugitives from a swanky party. Their faces were unwashed, Em's was still smudged with traces of lipstick and last night's mascara, their hair was wild and Em was still wearing the black satin dress, high heels and ermine jacket she'd changed into for dinner with Benjamin.

Amber may have been wearing jeans but from her shoulders hung the kind of vibrant green fox fur jacket you didn't see round an airport much, not even in Geneva.

The woman at the airline desk tapped at her computer for several minutes.

Amber felt the weight of the briefcase in her hand. *The cash* – she remembered! They couldn't take 17,000-plus euros through customs in cash . . . could they?

She glanced around looking for a bureau de change. Could they make a deposit? Pay the money onto a charge card? She had no idea.

'There is a flight to Amsterdam in forty-five minutes,' the woman informed them. 'From Amsterdam, you can connect to Montenegro, but you will only arrive half an hour earlier than if you wait for the 10.30 flight.'

'That's great, we'll take it. Two tickets please,' Em said and handed over their passports.

Amber's grip on the briefcase tightened and she bit her lower lip. If there was an alert out on their passports, then they were about to be arrested – right now.

'That will be 2,300 euros,' the woman said with a cheerful smile, and handed the passports back.

Amber felt small gush of relief, and hell, at those kind of prices, they wouldn't be carrying around a briefcase full of cash for long. She put the case on the counter, clicked it open and tried to bring out the bundle of notes without drawing attention to the thousands more stacked up inside .

'How much cash can we take through customs?' she asked, trying to sound casual.

'As much as you like, provided there is documentation to show where the money has come from,' the woman informed her.

Right.

No problems there, then . . .

Amber and Em exchanged a glance. Somehow they had to lose a huge amount of money in less than half an hour.

The woman handed over their tickets and boarding cards: 'Any luggage to check in?'

'No we're fine, thanks.'

'Enjoy your flight.'

Amber glanced anxiously through the window and there on the airport concourse she saw the man in the heavy overcoat, hat pulled down low, paying his cab fare. He was definitely the man she'd seen before.

She gripped Em's arm and pulled her away from the counter. 'Run!' she hissed.

Together they sprinted, Amber scanning for the nearest restrooms.

'In here!' she urged her sister.

Just like at JFK airport, they found themselves together locked into the disabled stall of an airport toilet.

'Was it Jack?' Em asked, her cheeks pale against her panda eyes.

Amber shook her head: 'The other one.'

'Shiiiit,' Em whispered, 'we have to get away from him. If he doesn't see us, he can't find out we're going to Amsterdam. He'll have no way of knowing where we've gone if we can just get onto that plane without being seen.'

'And how do we do that?' Amber asked.

'I don't know, I have no disguises . . . how *stupid*! I should always travel with spare wigs. We'll just have to go very, very carefully.'

'Oh, Em . . . what do we do with all the money? We can't risk being pulled up by security for all this cash. We'll have to dump it.'

Em looked deeply unhappy at this thought.

'How much can we take without risking questions?'

'I dunno,' Amber shrugged, 'maybe a few thousand each.'

'A few thousand!'

Em took the briefcase from Amber and flipped open the catches. She took out two bundles of cash, stuffed one into her handbag and handed the other to Amber.

'What about the rest?' Em asked looking down at the rows and rows of purple and yellow notes in front of them.

Amber looked around the stall. There was a flip-top wastepaper bin underneath the hand towel dispenser.

Em saw her eyes fix on it and immediately protested: 'Oh no! No, Amber, we can't! This is 15,000 euros. I mean, isn't that like nearly $15,000?'

'We have to,' Amber said. 'We can't be pulled up for this. We have more money than we'll ever need in our bank account.'

'But, Amber!'

Em grabbed one more bundle from the pile and put it down the front of her dress before Amber emptied the briefcase into the bin.

'OK,' Amber flashed a look at her watch. 'We have to go. We have to get to the Amsterdam gate without being stopped by anyone.'

As soon as they stepped out of the restroom it was obvious something was wrong. They could hear loud shouting and the sound of whistles being blown. Shocked passengers were turning towards the noise.

Three policemen began running down the corridor towards them.

*'Ohmigosh!!'* Em exclaimed and, despite her tight satin dress and high heels, she took off at a sprint.

Amber followed but instinctively veered left for the spiral staircase. She began to run up the stairs, astonished to see that the policemen were right behind Em but not following her.

Her heart was racing, her breath was rasping in and out. She was so frightened she thought she was going to collapse.

But she was getting away – they weren't behind her. She could see the huge illuminated sign for Departures right ahead of her.

Maybe Em would make it . . . maybe Em would get here any moment too.

Amber rounded the top of the stairs, then smacked straight into a tall man in a raincoat holding a cell to his ear.

It was Detective Jack Desmoine.

# Chapter Forty-Seven

*'They sent him to jail?'*

*'Yes, but it was the good one, with the organic garden and the Shaker wood-working classes. There was even a laundry service which didn't spoil a single one of his Brooks Brothers shirts.'*

Amber stepped backwards with fright.

No! It couldn't be!

She couldn't meet up with Jack like this. He couldn't be here in Geneva to arrest her? Please . . . that just couldn't be how this was going to end.

At the sight of her, his eyebrows shot up and he told the caller: 'Great work. Gotta go.'

She spun on her heel – maybe he wasn't fast, maybe she could still make it down the staircase and get away from him.

'Hold it right there,' he ordered.

Amber stood rooted to the spot, feeling her knees buckle with fear. They were going to be caught! They weren't going to get away . . . the police must already have Em.

Jack's hands were on her shoulders now, holding her tight. He moved to stand in front of her.

'W-w-what are you doing in Geneva?' she asked, her voice husky with fright.

'I was about to ask you the same question.'

'Are you here to arrest me?' she asked, feeling a tear squeeze from the corner of her eye because it was terrible to be in this situation with him. Seeing him right here in front of her, looking tired and unshaven, she realized how much she'd missed him. How much she'd longed to be with him again.

But he was the detective on *her* case! He was here to take her to jail.

'Am I here to arrest *you*?' he repeated. 'Not exactly.'

He fixed his intelligent eyes on hers and frowned.

'Is there any way you could let us go?' she whispered urgently, knowing how crazy her words sounded.

'Did you steal the jewels?' he asked, his eyes looking deep into hers, as if he might be able to read the answer there.

'Not . . . exactly.' She dropped her gaze to the floor.

'You sold them, didn't you? Well, in fact, I know it was a Miss Philippa de Clavel . . . but she sounds as if she could have been your double.'

So he knew.

He knew!

In just a few minutes it would all be over. In fact, she could hear sirens in the distance; more police on their way to the airport.

He took hold of her hands and pulled her closer towards him.

'Nice jacket,' he said, taking her by surprise. 'I didn't realize how much you liked fur.'

'No. No, this isn't really . . . it's not mine—'

He stepped in closer and suddenly they couldn't stop moving towards each other until they were kissing.

Wildly.

Her mouth on his, she felt his arms clasp round her back and she pressed in tightly against him, tasted coffee in his mouth and felt incredibly, completely inappropriately happy.

It was definitely not supposed to feel this good to have the detective appear at your getaway . . . but it did. It felt so good to have him here.

Finally, she pulled away.

'You have to let us go,' she whispered, her face just inches from his.

'I can't.'

'You can. Just let us walk through the gate. Say you didn't catch us in time.'

'I can't,' he repeated. 'If I let you go, I'll never see you again. I think I know what happened and there's a way out of this if you trust me.'

Beyond Jack's shoulder, through the window, Amber could see a policeman opening the back doors of a van. More policemen were leading someone towards it. Was it Em? Did they have Em?!

She stood on tiptoes to get a better view.

Jack turned to see what she was looking at.

They were leading a man to the van, a man in a heavy overcoat, his hat was in his hand now, but still Amber was sure it was the man who'd been following them ever since they'd arrived in Geneva.

Just as he reached the van, he turned and Amber saw his face properly. She gasped with surprise. 'No!' she said out loud. 'It's *Fergus*!'

Open-mouthed, she looked up at Jack.

'Why do you have Fergus?' she asked. 'Why is *Fergus* here? What's Fergus *done*?'

'You don't know?'

It was a short question, but the way he was looking at her made her realize just how important it was.

'No,' she said and shook her head.

'Fergus is the thief. He dosed the guards with laxative, maced your sister and Mr Wilson, then he took the jewels. He's the first criminal I've caught because of the smell of his soap.'

'Fergus? *Fergus?* Sapphire's boyfriend?'

It wouldn't sink in, but still Amber wanted to make one thing clear. 'Sapphire is completely innocent. She would never . . . never *ever* . . .'

'It's OK. We know. But what about you and I'm guessing that's Em over there?'

Amber looked over her shoulder. There under the Departures sign was Em, in satin dress, heels and ermine, tickets in her hand, looking frantically around for her sister.

'Boy, you girls sure dress up,' Jack said. 'C'mon.'

Amber began to jog towards her sister in total confusion. Were they caught? Or was Jack going to let them go? She didn't know.

Em caught sight of Amber, but then she saw Jack and her expression changed to horrified.

'RUN!' she mouthed. 'RUN!'

Amber caught up with Em just as Jack caught up with her.

'C'mon,' Em urged, taking hold of Amber's arm, 'the plane leaves in twelve minutes. He won't stop us because he likes you too much. C'mon, we can get away! We're not going to jail!'

'Maybe you don't have to go to jail,' Jack insisted, catching hold of Amber's other arm. 'Maybe you were helping to trap the real thief.'

'They've got him!' Amber exclaimed wildly. 'It was Fergus!'

Em's eyes widened. 'Jeeez!' she gasped. 'Our sister sure can pick 'em.'

'Amber, is this what you want to do?' Jack asked urgently. 'Run away and live on stolen money? Is this what you want for your life?'

Before she could answer, he asked another question: 'Did you just pretend to like me, the cop on the case?'

'No,' she replied immediately, shaking her head, 'I wasn't pretending.'

'Good. Now tell me, how did you two get your hands on the jewels?'

'C'mon,' Em urged, pulling at her arm, 'we'll miss the plane.'

But Amber couldn't take her eyes from Jack's.

'They were in a trash can in an office. It must have been Fergus's office. He must have hidden them there . . . Em picked them up by mistake. No one would believe her, so she ran away. I had to help her hide them.'

'She's the girl with the red wig jumping from the restroom window?' Jack asked.

'Amber, shut up,' Em insisted, 'don't say anything. We have to go!'

'This is the final boarding call for passengers to Amsterdam. All passengers for Amsterdam make your way now to Gate 17,' the tannoy announced.

'I can't stay,' Amber said, her voice cracking with the effort. 'We sold the jewels, we'll go to jail. I can't walk out on my kid sister. You have to let me go.'

'I could get you both out, if you trust me,' Jack insisted, still not letting go of her arm. 'Montanari is on my side. He's handed the jewellery in.'

Amber almost dropped her bag in fright. Just wait a minute . . . if Montanari was on his side, then this was a set-up! Jack knew everything. It was a trap! Any moment now, more police would swoop down on her and Em. They would be dragged out of here in handcuffs, taken to separate cells . . .

'He can't give you the jewels, he's paid us the money,' she whispered, feeling her knees shake. She had to get away. Escape while she still could. 'He's paid us $2.3 million,' she added. 'It's in a secret bank account.'

'Amber, shut up!' Em begged.

Amber suddenly felt as if she was in a waking dream. Was she really going to leave? Run away to Montenegro?

'Have you checked the Women of Enterprise bank account lately?' Jack asked. His voice sounded too warm. He sounded almost amused. It wasn't the right tone for a detective cornering his suspects.

'Montanari *owns* the Bank of Obersaxen, Miss

Clavel. I figured out what you were doing after I met you in the garden. I tried to stop you leaving New York and digging yourself in deeper. You're not a criminal, Amber, you joined in to protect your sister, did the wrong thing, for the right reasons. Just like your daddy.'

'Huh?!'

Em and Amber looked at him in astonishment.

'I checked it out. He won a ranch so deep in debt it was about to foreclose. He took it on and saved everyone's livelihood.'

'Time to go!' Em tugged her. 'Once we're through, we'll be safe.'

'But we don't have the money!'

At that moment, Amber's eyes fell on the green pendant round Em's neck. The one she'd worn day and night since the robbery . . . and suddenly she understood. There had been a third piece in the trash can.

Em's 'lucky charm' was real. It was a real antique emerald. Enormous, probably worth hundreds of thousands. Maybe the police hadn't released details about it to help them catch the thief.

Jack's hand slid down her arm and caught hold of her hand. He held it tight. 'Please trust me.'

Now it was her turn to look deep into his eyes to see if she could read an answer there.

'Amber, are you nuts? You'll go to jail! So will

Sapphire! There is no back door to this Alamo. You have to come walk on the wild side with me.'

'Montanari gave us a briefcase full of cash,' Amber told Jack.

'Ah yeah, now that's an advance on the reward money. If you play it my way, you, Em and Montanari are the people who caught the thief and saved the jewels. Anonymously, by the way. No publicity. Too many awkward questions.'

'It's bullshit,' Em declared. 'Come with me. We'll be fine.'

Amber looked at Em. She saw the fierce spirit, the adventuress, the actress in those green-tinted eyes.

'I don't want to come,' Amber told her.

'Aw, man!' her face fell. 'Are you going to split on me? Damn it! I thought we were in this together.' She tossed her head: 'Fine! Split! But I'm going to Montenegro and I'm taking my jacket and the money in the restroom trash! If it's still there.'

As Amber slipped the fox fur from her shoulders and handed it to her sister, Jack held out his hand and told Em, 'I'm going to need that necklace, Miss Jewel.'

'You can't have the necklace!' Em hissed at him. 'I keep the necklace!'

'If you run away with that, then Sapphire and Amber go to jail and Mr Montanari needs his reward money back.'

'Oh. Goddam it!!' Em spat out, stamping her foot, 'I hate you!'

She unclipped the pendant and threw it at Jack.

'That's OK,' he said, catching it. 'No one likes their sister's boyfriend. It's only natural.'

'Passengers Jewel travelling to Amsterdam. This is a final call for boarding,' the tannoy blared.

'Last chance, Amber! Stay with the cop, or escape with me!' Em urged.

Amber closed her eyes. Despite the drama of the last few hours, despite the noise of the airport, she tried to find a quiet place.

She tied to work out just what it was that she really wanted.

She gripped Jack's hand tightly.

'Ever thought about leaving town?' she asked him, voice low, eyes still shut.

'Haven't I already left the country for ya?'

After that, the decision was easy.

# Chapter Forty-Eight

*'Can we still buy at Wilson's after what happened to poor Eugenie De La Hoz?'*

*'She got her jewels back, didn't she? She's just bitter she had to pay out the reward money then couldn't claim it on insurance. Imagine! Not even tax-deductible, she said.'*

*'Ouch! And you know what a penny-pincher she is.'*

**One month later**

Em looked down at her real Chanel pumps. They were so breathtakingly beautiful. The perfect wear-with-anything nude with shiny, classy black toecaps. The heel was high but ladylike and she'd never worn anything so perfect or so appropriate in her life.

She pulled the fabulous green fur around her a little tighter. She was wearing this jacket every single day because it was so amazing. She loved it. It was completely and perfectly her. In fact, she was beginning to worry about summer. Maybe she would have to move to Alaska so she could wear the fur all year round.

But could summer in Alaska ever be as much fun as summer in New York?

And as for Montenegro . . . well, it had been a blast. A fantastic vacation. She'd blown through a whole heap of money paying for skiing lessons and all-night cocktail extravaganzas with some very, very tall men.

But in the end, she'd missed her family and her friends too much and she'd just wanted to come home.

So thank goodness she could.

Thank goodness she wasn't one of America's Most Wanted.

Putting the remains of the reward money into the bank, she and Sapphire had rented a cute little two-bed owned by a friend of Ori's, in their old neighbourhood, just two streets away from the jeweller's store.

After Sapphire had helped to put Ori's robber in jail, there wasn't enough that the jeweller could do for her.

Em was back hostessing at Bill's place five nights a week, but she'd given Marlese's chic boutique the elbow, because her days now were focused on her real career. The one she'd always dreamed of and the one her sisters had once again convinced her she could do.

Sitting, waiting here for this audition, she wanted to puke with fear because this role sounded so unbelievably perfect. She had to get it. She just knew she could get it.

If she could just hold it together and dazzle them.

'Emerald Jewel?'

A paunchy guy with a sparse goatee beard appeared in the doorway.

'Hi, I'm Walt, the director. We are *so* excited to meet you!'

Em stood up and walked daintily towards him in the Chanel shoes. 'Hey, Walt,' she said, flashing him a smile of red-lipsticked perfection, 'it's fantastic to meet you. This sounds like an amazing show.'

'So you're called Emerald Jewel and you really are a real-life actress and shoplifter?'

'Hell, yeah.'

Opening the door for her, Walt asked: 'So what's the biggest thing you've ever stolen?'

'Well, that would be telling, but can I just say these shoes and this wonderful fox fur jacket . . . I got them in Geneva. I didn't steal them, but wipe that look of disappointment off your face, because I bought them with a briefcase full of stolen cash.'

'No!'

'Hell, yeah! Doncha find life just too boring if you can't walk on the wild side now and then?'

Two beautifully turned out, elderly New York ladies walked along one of the loveliest streets in the Upper East Side with a rather dashing and elegantly dressed much younger man between them.

Mrs Henry St Claire-Trevellian, wearing Yves Saint Laurent *circa* 1987 with sensible alligator shoes, was holding onto one of the gentleman's arms. Mrs Emery Hewitt III, in Diane von Furstenberg's 1995 collection accessorized with a Hermès clutch, was supported by the other.

As they approached the window of Aubrey Wilson & Sons Auctioneers, the trio slowed down to look at the treasures on display.

'Chinese watches of the Eighteenth Century,' Betty St Claire-Trevellian declared, once she'd put the glasses hanging on a gold chain round her neck up to her eyes. 'Now I won't be going along to that. I think watches are dreadfully dull. But it's maybe one for you, Bobo.'

'Maybe,' the gentleman replied with an agreeable smile. He looked around the thirty-something mark; young enough to be a grandson, or maybe a young nephew.

'I rather like the painting at the back there.'

Lauren Hewitt pointed with a hand which was

nearly seventy-two years old, but nevertheless had been lovingly manicured in an up-to-the-moment Mac nude.

'But have you got the space for it?' Betty wondered. 'I've had to stop going to the painting sales, because I just don't know where to hang anything any more. The apartment is full. The beach house is packed. I can't even give paintings away because none of the grandchildren are interested in old things. They want modern art with *unjustifiable* price tags.'

'Now you know you have wonderful taste,' the man assured her, patting her arm soothingly. 'I'm sure your grandchildren would be delighted to receive some of your paintings.'

'I do have good taste, you are so right there, Bobo. We both have good taste, don't we, Lauren? Our eyes may be dim, but we can still pick out a jolly fine thing.'

'Which is why we're here; the girl, remember,' Lauren said and began to walk again, so the others followed her in the direction of the door.

'All the good girls that we know have been snapped up now,' Betty told Bobo sadly. 'You missed a few good chances, my darling. I kept telling you not to hang around. But you didn't listen.'

Bobo laughed gently at this.

'Yes, but it won't be so funny when you're a lonely

old forty-something bachelor with only divorcees with all their children and all their problems to choose from,' Lauren added. 'Trust me. I've seen my youngest son go through all that and it's not pretty.'

'So we've had to venture out on your behalf,' Betty said, as Bobo escorted her towards the revolving door then moved it at a slow and steady pace for her.

Once his two elderly friends were through the door and back safely on his arm, Betty went on: 'We've had to find a new girl for you. One we don't know yet. But one who looks utterly gorgeous and totally promising.'

'Now obviously, we might be wrong,' Lauren pointed out. 'We haven't had a chance to meet her family. But there's land in the background and I think land is always a good thing. You can't go wrong with a girl who's been brought up on the land.'

'So much more wholesome,' Betty agreed. 'Some of these young New York girls. They are faster than a hurricane and much more trouble.'

Bobo pressed his lips together and tried to suppress a smile. He looked as if he was used to hearing a lot of advice from his two adopted 'aunties'.

An assistant approached the trio.

'Can I be of any help? Have you come to tour our viewing rooms today?'

'No,' Betty replied, holding her glasses up in front of her eyes, 'we have an appointment. We're here to meet your charming jewellery assessor, the very appropriately named Miss Sapphire Jewel.'

'Miss Sapphire Jewel?' Bobo repeated, a smile twitching at the corner of his lips. 'Now that is a little unusual.'

'It's a Southern name,' Lauren explained. 'She's a beautiful Southern belle.'

'Please come in,' Sapphire called out when she heard the tap on her office door. She smoothed over her hair and smiled in anticipation.

She couldn't wait to meet with Mrs St Claire-Trevellian and her friend Mrs Hewitt again. Last week they'd brought some wonderful old jewels to the auction house and they'd been full of eye-opening stories and gossip about 'the old days' on the Upper East Side.

She stood up politely as the two old ladies were escorted in by a younger man in a beautiful dark-grey suit.

'Good afternoon, how lovely to see you again Mrs St Claire-Trevellian and Mrs Hewitt!' Sapphire greeted the pair, going around her desk to shake them both by the hand.

'Wonderful to see you too, my dear,' Betty replied, taking hold of Sapphire's soft, white hand. 'Now I hope you don't mind, but we've brought our young friend Bobo along. He is a regular at the sales, a collector of paintings, watches and jewellery. We thought you'd love to meet him.'

'Of course!' Sapphire said, turning her eyes to the man.

He had kind brown eyes, she noticed straight away, and he wore the kind of navy-blue tie with white spots, which was a favourite of Cary Grant's. In fact, with his smooth dark hair, parted sharply on the side, he bore a passing resemblance to her monochrome hero.

'This is Prince Roberto Zanzotto di Lampedusa. But that's so grand that we all call him Bobo.'

Sapphire extended her hand and made a little curtsy, 'How lovely to meet you . . . Your Royal Highness.'

Bobo smiled. 'Oh my, I'm sorry, you don't have to do anything like that. My pocket-sized principality was swallowed up by invading armies a long, long time ago. Just the title remains and I don't use it much. What an absolutely stunning necklace you're wearing . . .'

Sapphire's hand went up to the pendant at the base of her throat. 'Oh thank you!' she said and blushed shyly.

Bobo took a little step closer to admire the antique heart fashioned from a large sapphire and surrounded with old-cut diamonds for Amber and emeralds for Em.

'What a beautiful treasure. Very special,' he said, his brown eyes meeting hers once again.

'Yes . . . well . . . I came into a little money and I wanted to buy something I could maybe hand on to my own little girl one day.'

She immediately blushed, because it was such a private hope and now she'd gone and blurted it out to this complete stranger.

'My goodness,' Bobo said, full of admiration. 'Miss Jewel, you're like a cool breeze of fresh air.'

Sapphire locked her shimmering blue eyes onto his and suddenly felt the hairs stand up on the back of her neck. Could he know? she wondered. Could he possibly know that this was exactly how Bob Hope had once described Grace Kelly?

# Chapter Forty-Nine

*'You never did tell me what happened to her ex-husband.'*

*'He moved to Minnesota, Lauren, and no one ever heard of him again.'*

**Four Months Later**

'Hey, you goin' out for lunch already?'

'Uhuh. That's my prerogative. I am the boss.'

'OK, baw-ss.' Chuck's voice was so deep and drawlingly Texan that Amber had to bite back her smile as she walked, oh-so-proudly, through the sunshine-flooded front room of her brand new office. There was still a smell of fresh white paint and the lettering on the window cast shadows against the back wall.

Her receptionist, Darlene, looked up as she headed out towards the front door. 'Have you seen this?'

Darlene held out this month's copy of *Parker County Magazine*.

Amber took it and was astonished to see a gorgeous head shot of Sapphire on the cover.

*'Fairytale Royal engagement for Bluff Dale's beautiful bride-to-be,'* ran the strapline.

'Oh my gaaaawsh,' Amber exclaimed, noting with satisfaction how yee-haw her accent had become ever since she'd come home.

'There isn't any chance of anything going wrong *this* time?' Darlene wondered.

'Do they bring all that up inside?'

'I'm sorry to say that they do: pages 4, 5 and 6. Well, Forde is one of the Annetta North Houghtons.'

'Oh boy, and one day I'll tell you all about the *rat* of a Scottish boyfriend she had in New York. But no, I don't think anything like that will happen with Bobo. Em and I checked him out good. Real good. Bobo is the genuine item, a total gem. Can I read this over lunch?' she asked. 'Obviously Mother and I will be out later buying up every copy in the whole of the county.'

'Sure.'

Amber smiled at the cover. She wondered if Sapphire knew about it yet. Hopefully, she would love it, in her quietly shy way.

As she stepped out of the front door into the blazing midday sunshine, Amber turned round, unable to resist another look at her front of house.

*Amber Jewel – a broker you can trust* was stencilled, the old-fashioned way, on the big glass window.

She'd only been open for a couple of weeks, but business was already surprisingly good. Just like her, folks down here had had enough of big banks, of faceless institutions taking their money and doing who-knew-what with it.

She'd always suspected that in Parker County, people wanted to trust their savings to an ordinary down-to-earth kind of person who could offer them honest advice, even if she did wear jeans and sometimes even a cowgirl shirt. And now she thought she might be right. Word of her service was growing.

'I hope you're mighty proud of yourself,' called a deep voice from the driver's seat of the dusty red pickup truck parked on the other side of the street.

'Oh I am, is all.'

'Are you gonna git over here and ride shotgun with me, Missy Amber? Cos I'm fixin' to be hungry. Is all.'

Amber laughed and ran across the road to the pickup.

The passenger's door swung open and she climbed in.

'Howdy, sheriff. How was court?' she asked and leaned over to kiss Jack hello. He was in a short-sleeved khaki shirt with epaulettes. He might nickname it his 'boy scout uniform', but she thought he looked pretty good in it.

'Court was terrible, but I'm feeling better at the sight of you. Did you see this?' He reached over the dash and handed her another copy of the magazine with Sapphire on the cover.

'Oh, I already have one in my bag.'

'She's very pretty. Your mother is going to cry with joy.' He reached into the pocket of his truck door and brought out a newspaper. 'Betcha wanna see this too.'

He'd circled an item on the TV news page.

'Coming soon: *It's A Steal!* an exciting new reality show which pits real-life shoplifters against some of the toughest security in the mall. Sure to be a ratings winner and starring actress Emerald Jewel of Parker County.'

'She made the newspaper!' Amber exclaimed. 'The Fort Worth *Star-Telegram*! She's going to be *famous*, just like she always wanted to be. And lovely Sapphire's getting her white wedding to her handsome prince.'

Jack couldn't help laughing at that.

'He is a prince,' Amber protested.

'Without a princedom,' Jack reminded her.

'Probably just as well. Who wants subjects? I bet they're a whole lot more trouble than you could believe.'

'And you, Missy Amber?' Jack pushed back the brim of his Stetson.

When he'd first moved to Texas, he'd had no intention of wearing a Stetson, but it was so goddam hot and bright. The sun burned your eyeballs wherever you looked . . . so after just three weeks, Amber had bought him his first hat and he'd buckled.

'Did *you* get everything you wanted?'

There he was looking at her with his irresistible smile, knowing her answer almost before she did. He was beginning to know her very well and she was doing the same, getting right under his tough ol' cop skin and figuring out the real Jack Desmoine. Amber and Jack had fallen in love first, and were now getting to know each other.

'I think it's all working out just fine,' she said and leaned across the passenger's seat to kiss him fiercely.

Whenever Amber thought of the months she'd spent in New York trying to make her dreams come true or the crazy week of the jewellery theft, it was like a dream. A dream in another lifetime.

But she was all wide awake now. And even when she'd been right in the middle of that dream, she'd recognized Jack as someone she could take right back to real life in Texas with her.

He put the truck into gear and drove off.

He knew nothing yet about the bumper sticker Amber had slapped on the back of his pride and joy that morning. The one which read, *I wasn't born in Texas, but I got here as quick as I could.*

'So, you Jewel girls all got just what you wanted,' Jack said with a grin.

'Oh heck yeah, I figure we all got just what we deserve. Is all.'

THE END

## *Acknowledgements*

Four very special girls – my daughter Claudie and her friends Shivani, Eva and Caitie – wrote a script when they were in Primary 2 and I loved it. It was sweet and very funny, with a beach, ponies, a plane crash (everyone survived!), delicious ice-cream-based meals and the line: 'Three beautiful girls decided to rob a jewellery shop.'

That line set my mind racing.

What about three sisters? Maybe living in New York . . . and one of them works at an auction house. What would drive them to steal? What kind of jewels . . . what about the Duchess of Windsor's jewels? I pitched the idea to my husband, who pulled a surprised face and said: 'Really?!' So I suspected I was on to something . . .

I worked up a synopsis. Romantic comedy meets crime. Rom com crime. I plotted and planned. A devastatingly sexy cop, then a posh Scottish bloke came to life.

Every time a friend asked: 'What are you working on?' I'd say: three sisters, in New York, planning on stealing some very famous jewels.

'Oooooh, I like the sound of that!'

This is when writing gets exciting – when everyone loves the idea and can't wait to see what you come up with.

This is also when writing gets difficult because you've promised this fantastic story and then as you write it, it gets harder and *harder* to get it bright, shiny and perfectly right.

But my characters grew. I love the Jewel sisters, so sparky, so very different but so deeply alike, the way sisters really are. As usual, I'm a little in love with my man-interest.

So here I am, about to hand in the final version and there are many people to thank: my agent Darley Anderson, for telling me I'd 'hit the jackpot with this one' when it was just a synopsis. (Bless you for always knowing just how to encourage a writer!) Thank you also to Darley's brilliant team, always so helpful and enthusiastic.

To my editor Sarah Adams and assistant editor, Jess Thomas, thank you both so much for reading and rereading and for so many *inspired* editing ideas. Editors are like coaches. They holler from the sidelines, review the tactics, supply the cool analysis, then send you back out there to do your best work ever. Many thanks also to the lovely people at Transworld who work very hard to make the covers and the copy just right and to get the books out there into the hands of the readers.

Please step forward and take a bow, Ronda Carman, my Texan *girlfrien'*. Oh I love the way you talk, I can't blame you for all the phrases in the book but you sure inspired one whole heck of 'em. Is all.

Blame childhood exposure to *Dallas*, Helen Bryant's funny book *Fixing to be Texan* and www.overheardinnewyork.com for the quirky language of this story. I also used a beautiful edition of *A Touch of Grace* by Cindy De La Hoz for many Grace Kelly details. (Hopefully Cindy will forgive me for borrowing her surname for Mrs De La Hoz!)

Some details about the Duchess of Windsor's jewels are based on fact, some are embellished fiction. I'm hoping no one will mind too much.

Now, I am blessed with two lovely sisters and while that did inspire my sisterly threesome, I hope you'll realize that although Amber is a little bit me, Sapphire and Em are almost 99 per cent fiction!

At home, I'm incredibly lucky to have Team Reid. Thomas: thank you for ever for reading, rereading, encouraging me endlessly, plus cooking dinners and picking up a whole heap of domestic slack. Sam: loads of love – keep writing! And Claudie: one more thank-you kiss for letting me read your story, which gave me this gem (!) of an idea.

a diamond worth £1000

*Fancy a bit more sparkle in your life?*

Amber, Sapphire and Em were prepared to go to crazy lengths to steal their dream, but you don't have to! You could win a glamorous diamond worth £1,000, without risking arrest, just by visiting carmenreid.com and telling us why you deserve a gorgeous, glittering jewel.

**www.carmenreid.com**

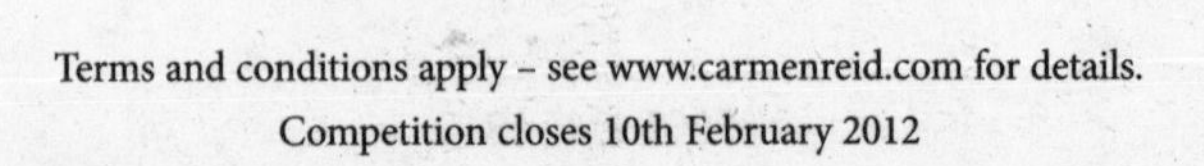